Critical ac

'McBain is so good that

Publishers Weekly

'A virtuoso'   *Guardian*

'Ed McBain effectively invented the police procedural ...
McBain delivers his complex story with panache and real zest
... *Money Money Money* may be the fifty-first of the series
but it's as fresh and vivid as the first. Great'   *Observer*

'Sick, taut, inventive, modern and (as always) funny'
Glasgow Herald

'This much-loved and seminal writer is a national treasure. If
you're a mystery reader, you've undoubtedly read Ed
McBain. If you haven't read one for a while, try this one. It's
so good it will immediately send you scurrying back for the
ones you missed'   Otto Penzler

'A master ... as always in his novels, sharp, clear sentences
trot briskly one after another ... As always, the funny stuff is
funny and the scary parts scary. McBain gets it right, of
course ... as he has done for dozens of books and years'
Time

'One of the masters of crime fiction'   *Sunday Telegraph*

'McBain steadily unrolls a tapestry of adultery, jealousy, and
revenge. Amazingly, all the mind-boggling complexities are
kept perfectly clear, thanks to McBain's unsurpassed mastery
of exposition, the story's still gaining in force when the
curtain finally thunders down'   *Kirkus Reviews*

'McBain has a great approach, great attitude, terrific style,
strong plots, excellent dialogue, sense of place, and sense of
reality'   Elmore Leonard

'A master storyteller'   *Washington Times*

Ed McBain is one of the most illustrious names in crime fiction. In 1998, he was the first non-British author to be awarded the Crime Writers' Association/Cartier Diamond Dagger Award and he was also holder of the Mystery Writers of America coveted Grand Master Award. He died in 2005. His latest novel available in Orion paperback is Fiddlers. Visit his website at www.edmcbain.com.

By Ed McBain

THE 87TH PRECINCT NOVELS

Cop Hater • The Mugger • The Pusher • The Con Man
Killer's Choice • Killer's Payoff • Killer's Wedge • Lady Killer
'Til Death • King's Ransom • Give the Boys a Great Big Hand
The Heckler • See Them Die • Lady, Lady, I Did It!
The Empty Hours • Like Love • Ten Plus One • Ax
He Who Hesitates • Doll • Eighty Million Eyes • Fuzz • Shotgun
Jigsaw • Hail, Hail, the Gang's All Here • Sadie When She Died
Let's Hear It for the Deaf Man • Hail to the Chief • Bread
Blood Relatives • So Long As You Both Shall Live
Long Time, No See • Calypso • Ghosts • Heat • Ice • Lightning
Eight Black Horses • Poison • Tricks • Lullaby • Vespers • Widows
Kiss • Mischief • And All Through the House • Romance
Nocturne • The Big Bad City • The Last Dance
Money Money Money • Fat Ollie's Book • The Frumious
Bandersnatch • Hark! • Fiddlers

THE MATTHEW HOPE NOVELS

Goldilocks • Rumpelstiltskin • Beauty & the Beast
Jack & the Beanstalk • Snow White and Rose Red
Cinderella • Puss in Boots • The House That Jack Built
Three Blind Mice • Mary, Mary • There Was a Little Girl
Gladly the Cross-Eyed Bear • The Last Best Hope

OTHER NOVELS

The Sentries • Where There's Smoke • Doors • Guns
Another Part of the City • Downtown • Driving Lessons
Candyland • The Moment She Was Gone • Alice in Jeopardy

COP HATER

THE MUGGER

Ed McBAIN

Cop Hater
First published in Great Britain
by T. V. Boardman in 1958

The Mugger
First published in Great Britain
by Penguin Books in 1963

This omnibus edition published in 2007
by Orion Books Ltd
Orion House, 5 Upper St Martin's Lane
London WC2H 9EA

A CIP catalogue record for this book is available
from the British Library.

ISBN 978-1-4072-1105-3

Printed in Great Britain by
Clays Ltd, St Ives plc

The Orion Publishing Group's policy is to use papers that
are natural, renewable and recyclable products and
made from wood grown in sustainable forests. The logging
and manufacturing processes are expected to conform to
the environmental regulations of the country of origin.

COP HATER

Ed McBAIN

This is for Dodie and Ray

INTRODUCTION

Cop Hater, the first of the 87th Precinct novels, was originally published in paperback early in 1956. My records indicate that I received payment for the book on January 4, 1956, which would further seem to indicate that it was delivered sometime in December of 1955. I don't remember how long it took to write. The early McBains usually took a month. Nowadays, perhaps because the novels are longer, they take *two* months. *Cop Hater* took a much a longer time because there was a lot of research to do for the first book in the series. I still do research, of course, but not as much as I had to do when I was initially figuring out police procedures and routines. In any case, the actual writing time is vague in my memory. I didn't keep work calendars then, as I do now.

What is *not* vague is the genesis of the series.

I had written a great many mystery short stories and a few mystery novels before *The Blackboard Jungle* was published in October of 1954. Some of these stories were published under my own name (Evan Hunter), others under various pseudonyms. I would often have two or three stories in the same issue of a magazine like *Manhunt*, for example, all under different pseudonyms. One mystery novel written under the pseudonym had not yet sold by the time *The Blackboard Jungle* was published, and my agent was still shopping it around in 1955. Pocket Books was, at the time, publishing a handful of paperback originals in its Permabooks line, so my agent sent this novel (I believe it was *Runaway Black* as by Richard Marsten, but I'm not sure) to Herbert Alexander, then editor-in-chief of Pocket Books, and a man who was instrumental in purchasing reprint rights to *The Blackboard Jungle*.

He is possibly the smartest man who ever lived.

He is also a good detective.

He finished reading the pseudonymous mystery novel, called my agent immediately, and asked, 'Is this our friend Hunter?' When he learned that the true author was *indeed* Hunter, he said he would like to have a meeting with me (the Hollywood term, 'take a meeting' had not yet been invented, and anyway this was New York.)

Over lunch, Herb told me that the mainstay of Pocket Books was Erle Stanley Gardner, whose books they reissued on a regular rotating schedule, with new covers on them each time out. He told me that Gardner was getting old (I don't know how old he was in 1955) and that they were looking for a mystery writer who would eventually replace him. Herb hadn't much liked the pseudonymous novel (he didn't *buy* it, did he?) but he recognized from it that I was familiar with the form, and if I had an idea for a mystery series with a fresh and original lead character, then I was the man for them. I said I didn't have an idea in my head, but that I would like some time to think about it. We promised we'd stay in touch.

The mystery stories I'd written up to that point were a mixed bag. Private Eye, Woman in Jeopardy, Innocent Bystander, Man on the Run, Biter Bit, *and* several police stories. The novels, if I recall, were either Innocent Bystander or Man on the Run. I had most enjoyed writing the police stories – which were frankly influenced by the old *Dragnet* series on *radio* – and it seemed to me that a good series character would be a cop, even though I knew next to nothing about cops at the time. I knew for certain, though, that any *other* character dealing with murder was unconvincing. If you came home late at night and found your wife murdered in the bed you shared, you didn't call a private eye, and you didn't call a little old lady with knitting needles, and if you called your lawyer it was to ask what you should say when you called the police. In fiction, there is always a quantum jump to be made when anyone but a police detective is investigating a murder. I come up against it in my

Matthew Hope series. Hope is a lawyer who has no right investigating murders. Disbelief must be overcome, first by the author himself, then by the reader. This isn't the case with a police detective. He is *supposed* to investigate murders.

So, yes, a cop.

But then, thinking it through further, it seemed to me that a single cop did not a series make, and it further seemed to me that something new in the annals of police procedurals (I don't even know if they were called that back then) would be a squadroom *full* of cops, each with different traits, who – when put together – would form a *conglomerate* hero. There had been police novels before I began the 87th Precinct series. There had not, to my knowledge, been any to utilize such a concept. I felt, at the time, that it was unique. So, then, a squadroom of police detectives as my conglomerate hero. And, of course, New York City as the setting.

I called Herb Alexander. I told him that I wanted to use a *lot* of cops as my hero, one cop stepping forward in one novel, another in the next novel, cops getting killed and disappearing from the series, other cops coming in, all of them visible to varying extents in each of the books. He said he liked the idea, and would give me a contract for three novels – 'to see how it goes'.

I began my research.

I found that the New York City Police Department was somewhat reluctant to let the author of *The Blackboard Jungle* into its precincts or its cars. Perhaps they felt I was about to do a number on them. A contact told me I could gain access by paying off a judge, a captain, and God knew how many sergeants. I told him that wasn't the kind of access I wanted. Finally, and after much perseverance, I was allowed to visit and take notes, except when prisoners were being interrogated. I rode with cops, I talked with cops, I spent hours in squadrooms and labs and at line-ups (now defunct except for identification purposes), and in court, and in holding cells – until I felt I knew what being a cop was all about. And then – promising every cop I met that I would undoubtedly be calling him for further information once I got into the first book – I sat down to write.

And discovered that I was calling the NYPD almost daily. As gracious as they were, I soon learned that cops had *real* crimes to solve, lab technicians were often too busy to discuss my problems at length, forensics specialists had open corpses on the table at the moment and could not be bothered with fictitious ones. I learned, in short, that I was becoming a pain in the neck. And I realized early on that if I had to count on the NYPD to verify every detail of the procedure in the books I was writing, I would have to spend more time on the phone than I was spending at the typewriter.

So I asked myself why I had to use a *real* city. What if I premised my geography only loosely on the real city, stuck with routine that was realistic for any police department in America ('clinical verity,' Herb later called it), and then winged it from there? Wouldn't this free me from the telephone and get me back to the typewriter? And wouldn't it provide me with creative freedom?

Thus was the mythical city born.

Out of desperation, I guess.

I've never regretted the choice. If a conglomerate detective hero was something new in detective fiction, then the mythical city as a backdrop was similarly new. At least, I knew of no other writer who had used it before. Anyway, I thought it would be more fun to *create* a city than to write about an existing one. It has turned out to be a *lot* of fun. I can't describe how much joy I experience each time I write about another section of a city that doesn't exist, inventing historical background, naming places as suits my fancy, and then fitting it all together in a jigsaw pattern that sometimes even *I* don't fully understand. It is next to impossible to overlay a map of my city on a map of New York. It's not simply a matter of north being east and south being west or Isola representing Manhattan and Calm's Point representing

Brooklyn. The geography won't jibe exactly, the city remains a mystery.

The city, then, became a character.

So did the weather, which figures prominently in *Cop Hater* and in each subsequent book in the series.

But there is one other character worth mentioning: the author. I know that in these books I frequently commit the unpardonable sin of author intrusion. Somebody will suddenly start talking or thinking or commenting and it won't be any of the cops or crooks, it'll just be this faceless anonymous 'someone' sticking his nose into the proceedings like an unwanted guest. Sorry. That's me. Or rather, it's Ed McBain.

Where did the name come from?

Out of the blue.

I did not want to use Evan Hunter on the series; I felt at the time that Evan Hunter was supposed to write so-called 'serious' novels and maybe crime novels weren't serious enough. I now know they are very serious indeed, and many years ago I voluntarily blew the McBain cover (which really *was* a secret for a good long while.) But neither did I want to use Marsten or Collins if this was to be a *new* series by a supposedly *new* writer.

I had just pulled the last page of *Cop Hater* out of the typewriter. I read the final lines, and sat there thinking for several moments. I used to work in the back bedroom of a development house on Long Island. I walked out of the bedroom, and into the kitchen, where my former wife was spoon-feeding our infant twins.

I said, 'How's Ed McBain?'

She said, 'Good,' and went back to feeding the twins.

So here's *Cop Hater*. By Ed McBain.

The first of them.

Ed McBain

CHAPTER ONE

From the river bounding the city on the north, you saw only the magnificent skyline. You stared up at it in something like awe, and sometimes you caught your breath because the view was one of majestic splendour. The clear silhouettes of the buildings slashed at the sky, devouring the blue; flat planes and long planes, rough rectangles and needle-sharp spires, minarets and peaks, pattern upon pattern laid in geometric unity against the wash of blue and white which was the sky.

And at night, coming down the River Highway, you were caught in a dazzling galaxy of brilliant suns, a web of lights strung out from the river and then south to capture the city in a brilliant display of electrical wizardry. The highway lights glistened close and glistened farther as they skirted the city and reflected in the dark waters of the river. The windows of the buildings climbed in brilliant rectangular luminosity, climbed to the stars, and joined the wash of red and green and yellow and orange neon which tinted the sky. The traffic lights blinked their gaudy eyes and along the Stem, the incandescent display tangled in a riot of colour and eye-aching splash.

The city lay like a sparkling nest of rare gems, shimmering in layer upon layer of pulsating intensity.

The buildings were a stage-set.

They faced the river, and they glowed with man-made brilliance, and you stared up at them in awe, and you caught your breath.

Behind the buildings, behind the lights, were the streets.

There was garbage in the streets.

The alarm sounded at 11 p.m.

He reached out for it, groping in the darkness, finding the

1

lever and pressing it against the back of the clock. The buzzing stopped. The room was very silent. Beside him, he could hear May's even breathing. The windows were wide open, but the room was hot and damp, and he thought again about the air-conditioning unit he'd wanted to buy since the summer began. Reluctantly, he sat up and rubbed hamlike fists into his eyes.

He was a big man, his head topped with straight blond hair that was unruly now. His eyes were normally grey, but they were virtually colourless in the darkness of the room, puffed with sleep. He stood up and stretched. He slept only in pyjama pants, and when he raised his arms over his head, the pants slipped down over the flatness of his hard belly. He let out a grunt, pulled up the pants, and then glanced at May again.

The sheet was wadded at the foot of the bed, a soggy lifeless mass. May lay curled into a sprawling C, her gown twisted up over her thigh. He went to the bed and put his hand on her thigh for an instant. She murmured and rolled over. He grinned in the darkness and then went into the bathroom to shave.

He had timed every step of the operation, and so he knew just how long it took to shave, just how long it took to dress, just how long it took to gulp a quick cup of coffee. He took off his wrist watch before he began shaving, leaving it on the wash-basin where he could glance at it occasionally. At eleven ten, he began dressing. He put on an Aloha shirt his brother had sent him from Hawaii. He put on a pair of tan gaberdine slacks, and a light poplin windbreaker. He put a handkerchief in his left hip pocket, and then scooped his wallet and change off the dresser.

He opened the top drawer of the dresser and took the ·38 from where it lay next to May's jewellery box. His thumb passed over the hard leather of the holster, and then he shoved the holster and gun into his right hip pocket, beneath the poplin jacket. He lit a cigarette, went into the kitchen to put up the coffee water, and then went to check on the kids.

Mickey was asleep, his thumb in his mouth as usual. He passed his hand over the boy's head. Christ, he was sweating like a pig. He'd have to talk to May about the air conditioning again. It wasn't fair to the kids, cooped up like this in a sweat box. He walked to Cathy's bed and went through the same ritual. She wasn't as perspired as her brother. Well, she was a girl, girls didn't sweat as much. He heard the kettle in the kitchen, whistling loudly. He glanced at his watch, and then grinned.

He went into the kitchen, spooned two teaspoonsful of instant coffee into a large cup, and then poured the boiling water over the powder. He drank the coffee black, without sugar. He felt himself coming awake at last, and he vowed for the hundredth time that he wouldn't try to catch any sleep before this tour, it was plain stupid. He should sleep when he got home, hell, what did he average this way? A couple of hours? And then it was time to go in. No, it was foolish. He'd have to talk to May about it. He gulped the coffee down, and then went into his bedroom again.

He liked to look at her asleep. He always felt a little sneaky and a little horny when he took advantage of her that way. Sleep was a kind of private thing, and it wasn't right to pry when somebody was completely unaware. But, God, she was beautiful when she was asleep, so what the hell, it wasn't fair. He watched her for several moments, the dark hair spread out over the pillow, the rich sweep of her hip and thigh, the femaleness of the raised gown and the exposed white flesh. He went to the side of the bed, and brushed the hair back from her temple. He kissed her very gently, but she stirred and said, 'Mike?'

'Go back to sleep, honey.'

'Are you leaving?' she murmured hoarsely.

'Yes.'

'Be careful, Mike.'

3

'I will.' He grinned. 'And you be good.'

'Uhm,' she said, and then she rolled over into the pillow. He sneaked a last look at her from the doorway, and then went through the living-room and out of the house. He glanced at his watch. It was eleven-thirty. Right on schedule, and damn if it wasn't a lot cooler in the street.

At eleven forty-one, when Mike Reardon was three blocks away from his place of business, two bullets entered the back of his skull and ripped away half his face when they left his body. He felt only impact and sudden unbearable pain, and then vaguely heard the shots, and then everything inside him went dark, and he crumpled to the pavement.

He was dead before he struck the ground.

He had been a citizen of the city, and now his blood poured from his broken face and spread around him in a sticky red smear.

Another citizen found him at eleven fifty-six, and went to call the police. There was very little difference between the citizen who rushed down the street to a phone booth, and the citizen named Mike Reardon who lay crumpled and lifeless against the concrete.

Except one.

Mike Reardon was a cop.

CHAPTER TWO

The two Homicide cops looked down at the body on the sidewalk. It was a hot night, and the flies swarmed around the sticky blood on the pavement. The assistant medical examiner was kneeling alongside the body, gravely studying it. A photographer from the Bureau of Identification was busily popping flash-bulbs. Cars 23 and 24 were parked across the street, and the patrolmen from those cars were unhappily engaged in keeping back spectators.

The call had gone to one of the two switchboards at Headquarters where a sleepy patrolman had listlessly taken down the information and then shot it via pneumatic tube to the Radio Room. The dispatcher in the Radio Room, after consulting the huge precinct map on the wall behind him, had sent Car 23 to investigate and report on the allegedly bleeding man in the street. When Car 23 had reported back with a homicide, the dispatcher had contacted Car 24 and sent it to the scene. At the same time, the patrolman on the switchboard had called Homicide North and also the 87th Precinct, in which territory the body had been found.

The body lay outside an abandoned, boarded-up theatre. The theatre had started as a first-run movie house, many years back when the neighbourhood had still been fashionable. As the neighbourhood began rotting, the theatre began showing second-run films, and then old movies, and finally foreign-language films. There was a door to the left of the movie house, and the door had once been boarded too, but the planks had been ripped loose and the staircase inside was littered with cigarette butts, empty pint whisky bottles, and contraceptives. The marquee above the theatre stretched to the sidewalk, punched with jagged holes, the victim of thrown rocks, tin cans, hunks of pipe and general debris.

Across the street from the theatre was an empty lot. The lot had once owned an apartment house, and the house had been a good one with high rents. It had not been unusual, in the old days, to see an occasional mink coat drifting from the marbled doorway of that apartment house. But the crawling tendrils of the slum had reached out for the brick, clutching it with tenacious fingers, pulling it into the ever-widening circle it called its own. The old building had succumbed, becoming a part of the slum, so that people rarely remembered it had once been a proud and elegant dwelling. And then it had been condemned, and the building had been razed to the ground, and now the lot was clear and open, except for the scattered brick rubble that still clung to the ground in some places. A City housing project, it was rumoured, was going up in the lot. In the meantime, the kids used the lot for various purposes. Most of the purposes were concerned with bodily functions, and so a stench hung on the air over the lot, and the stench was particularly strong on a hot summer night, and it drifted over towards the theatre, captured beneath the canopy of the overhanging marquee, smothering the sidewalk with its smell of life, mingling with the smell of death on the pavement.

One of the Homicide cops moved away from the body and began scouring the sidewalk. The second cop stood with his hands in his back pockets. The assistant m.e. went through the ritual of ascertaining the death of a man who was certainly dead. The first cop came back.

'You see these?' he asked.

'What've you got?'

'Couple of ejected cartridge cases.'

'Mm?'

'Remington slugs. ·45 calibre.'

'Put 'em in an envelope and tag 'em. You about finished, Doc?'

'In a minute.'

The flash-bulbs kept popping. The photographer worked

6

like the Press agent for a hit musical. He circled the star of the show, and he snapped his pictures from different angles, and all the while his face showed no expression, and the sweat streamed down his back, sticking his shirt to his flesh. The assistant m.e. ran his hand across his forehead.

'What the hell's keeping the boys from the 87th?' the first cop asked.

'Big poker game going, probably. We're better off without them.' He turned to the assistant m.e. 'What do you say, Doc?'

'I'm through.' He rose wearily.

'What've you got?'

'Just what it looks like. He was shot twice in the back of the head. Death was probably instantaneous.'

'Want to give us a time?'

'On a gunshot wound? Don't kid me.'

'I thought you guys worked miracles.'

'We do. But not during the summer.'

'Can't you even guess?'

'Sure, guessing's free. No rigor mortis yet, so I'd say he was killed maybe a half-hour ago. With this heat, though . . . hell, he might maintain normal body warmth for hours. You won't get us to go out on a limb with this one. Not even after the autopsy is—'

'All right, all right. Mind if we find out who he is?'

'Just don't mess it up for the Lab boys. I'm taking off.' The assistant m.e. glanced at his watch. 'For the benefit of the timekeeper, it's twelve-nineteen.'

'Short day today,' the first Homicide cop said. He jotted the time down on the time-table he'd kept since his arrival at the scene.

The second cop was kneeling near the body. He looked up suddenly. 'He's heeled,' he said.

'Yeah?'

The assistant m.e. walked away, mopping his brow.

'Looks like a ·38,' the second cop said. He examined the

holstered gun more closely. 'Yeah. Detective's Special. Want to tag this?'

'Sure.' The first cop heard a car brake to a stop across the street. The front doors opened, and two men stepped out and headed for the knot around the body. 'Here's the 87th now.'

'Just in time for tea,' the second cop said dryly. 'Who'd they send?'

'Looks like Carella and Bush.' The first cop took a packet of rubber-banded tags from his right-hand jacket pocket. He slipped one of the tags free from the rubber band, and then returned the rest to his pocket. The tag was a three-by-five rectangle of an oatmeal colour. The hole was punched in one end of the tag, and a thin wire was threaded through the hole and twisted to form two loose ends. The tag read POLICE DEPARTMENT, and beneath that in bolder type: EVIDENCE.

Carella and Bush, from the 87th Precinct, walked over leisurely. The Homicide cop glanced at them cursorily, turned to the *Where found* space on the tag, and began filling it out. Carella wore a blue suit, his grey tie neatly clasped to his white shirt. Bush was wearing an orange sports shirt and khaki trousers.

'If it ain't Speedy Gonzales and Whirlaway,' the second Homicide cop said. 'You guys certainly move fast, all right. What do you do on a bomb scare?'

'We leave it to the Bomb Squad,' Carella said dryly. 'What do you do?'

'You're very comical,' the Homicide cop said.

'We got hung up.'

'I can see that.'

'I was catching alone when the squeal came in,' Carella said. 'Bush was out with Foster on a bar knifing. Reardon didn't show.' Carella paused. 'Ain't that right, Bush?' Bush nodded.

'If you're catching, what the hell are you doing here?' the first Homicide cop said.

8

Carella grinned. He was a big man, but not a heavy one. He gave an impression of great power, but the power was not a meaty one. It was, instead, a fine-honed muscular power. He wore his brown hair short. His eyes were brown, with a peculiar downward slant that gave him a clean-shaved Oriental appearance. He had wide shoulders and narrow hips, and he managed to look well-dressed and elegant even when he was dressed in a leather jacket for a waterfront plant. He had thick wrists and big hands, and he spread the hands wide now and said, 'Me answer the phone when there's a homicide in progress?' His grin widened. 'I left Foster to catch. Hell, he's practically a rookie.'

'How's the graft these days?' the second Homicide cop asked.

'Up yours,' Carella answered dryly.

'Some guys get all the luck. You sure as hell don't get anything from a stiff.'

'Except *tsores*,' the first cop said.

'Talk English,' Bush said genially. He was a soft-spoken man, and his quiet voice came as a surprise because he was all of six feet four inches and weighed at least two-twenty, bone dry. His hair was wild and unkempt, as if a wise Providence had fashioned his unruly thatch after his surname. His hair was also red, and it clashed violently against the orange sports shirt he wore. His arms hung from the sleeves of the shirt, muscular and thick. A jagged knife scar ran the length of his right arm.

The photographer walked over to where the detectives were chatting.

'What the hell are you doing?' he asked angrily.

'We're trying to find out who he is,' the second cop said. 'Why? What's the matter?'

'I didn't say I was finished with him yet.'

'Well, ain't you?'

'Yeah, but you should've asked.'

'For Christ's sake, who are you working for? Conover?'

9

'You Homicide dicks give me a pain in the—'

'Go home and emulsify some negatives or something, will you?'

The photographer glanced at his watch. He grunted and withheld the time purposely, so that the first cop had to glance at his own watch before jotting down the time on his time-table. He subtracted a few minutes, and indicated a t.o.a. for Carella and Bush, too.

Carella looked down at the back of the dead man's head. His face remained expressionless, except for a faint, passing film of pain which covered his eyes for a moment, and then darted away as fleetingly as a jack-rabbit.

'What'd they use?' he asked. 'A cannon?'

'A ·45,' the first cop said. 'We've got the cartridge cases.'

'How many?'

'Two.'

'Figures,' Carella said. 'Why don't we flip him over?'

'Ambulance coming?' Bush said quietly.

'Yeah,' the first cop said. 'Everybody's late tonight.'

'Everybody's drowning in sweat tonight,' Bush said. 'I can use a beer.'

'Come on,' Carella said, 'give me a hand here.'

The second cop bent down to help Carella. Together, they rolled the body over. The flies swarmed up angrily, and then descended to the sidewalk again, and to the bloody, broken flesh that had once been a face. In the darkness, Carella saw a gaping hole where the left eye should have been. There was another hole beneath the right eye, and the cheek bone was splintered outward, the jagged shards piercing the skin.

'Poor bastard,' Carella said. He would never get used to staring death in the face. He had been a cop for twelve years now, and he had learned to stomach the sheer, overwhelming, physical impact of death – but he would never get used to the other thing about death, the invasion of privacy that came with death, the reduction of pulsating life to a pile of bloody, fleshy rubbish.

'Anybody got a flash?' Bush asked.

The first cop reached into his left hip pocket. He thumbed a button, and a circle of light splashed on to the sidewalk.

'On his face,' Bush said.

The light swung up on to the dead man's face.

Bush swallowed. 'That's Reardon,' he said, his voice very quiet. And then, almost in a whisper, 'Jesus, that's Mike Reardon.'

CHAPTER THREE

There were sixteen detectives assigned to the 87th Precinct, and David Foster was one of them. The precinct, in all truth, could have used a hundred and sixteen detectives and even then been understaffed. The precinct area spread south from the River Highway and the tall buildings which still boasted doormen and elevator operators to the Stem with its delicatessens and movie houses, on south to Culver Avenue and the Irish section, still south to the Puerto Rican section and then into Grover's Park, where muggers and rapists ran rife. Running east and west, the precinct covered a long total of some thirty-five city streets. And packed into this rectangle – north and south from the river to the park, east and west for thirty-five blocks – was a population of 90,000 people.

David Foster was one of those people.

David Foster was a Negro.

He had been born in the precinct territory, and he had grown up there, and when he'd turned 21, being of sound mind and body, being four inches over the minimum requirement of five feet eight inches, having 20/20 vision without glasses, and not having any criminal record, he had taken the competitive Civil Service examination and had been appointed a patrolman.

The starting salary at the time had been $3,725 per annum, and Foster had earned his salary well. He had earned it so well that in the space of five years he had been appointed to the Detective Division. He was now a 3rd Grade Detective, and his salary was now $5,230 per annum, and he still earned it.

At 1 a.m., on the morning of 24 July, while a colleague named Mike Reardon lay spilling his blood into the gutter,

David Foster was earning his salary by interrogating the man he and Bush had picked up in the bar knifing.

The interrogation was being conducted on the second floor of the precinct house. To the right of the desk on the first floor, there was an inconspicuous and dirty white sign with black letters which announced DETECTIVE DIVISION, and a pointing hand advised any visitor that the bulls hung out upstairs.

The stairs were metal and narrow, but scrupulously clean. They went up for a total of sixteen risers, then turned back on themselves and continued on up for another sixteen risers, and there you were.

Where you were was a narrow, dimly-lighted corridor. There were two doors on the right of the open stairway, and a sign labelled them LOCKERS. If you turned left and walked down the corridor, you passed a wooden slatted bench on your left, a bench without a back on your right (set into a narrow alcove before the sealed doors of what had once been an elevator shaft), a door on your right marked MEN'S LAVATORY, and a door on your left over which a small sign hung, and the sign simply read CLERICAL.

At the end of the corridor was the Detective Squad Room.

You saw first a slatted rail divider. Beyond that, you saw desks and telephones, and a bulletin board with various photographs and notices on it, and a hanging light globe, and beyond that more desks and the grilled windows that opened on the front of the building. You couldn't see very much that went on beyond the railing on your right because two huge metal filing cabinets blocked the desks on that side of the room. It was on that side of the room that Foster was interrogating the man he'd picked up in the bar earlier that night.

'What's your name?' he asked the man.

'*No hablo inglés*,' the man said.

'Oh, hell,' Foster said. He was a burly man with a deep chocolate colouring and warm brown eyes. He wore a white

13

dress shirt, open at the throat. His sleeves were rolled up over muscular forearms.

'*Cuál es su nombre?*' he asked in hesitant Spanish.

'Tomas Perillo.'

'Your address?' He paused, thinking. '*Dirección?*'

'*Tres-tres-cuatro Mei-son.*'

'Age? *Edad?*'

Perillo shrugged.

'All right,' Foster said, 'where's the knife? Oh, crap, we'll never get anywhere tonight. Look, *dónde está el cuchillo? Puede usted decirme?*'

'*Creo que no.*'

'Why not? For Christ's sake, you had a knife, didn't you?'

'*No sé.*'

'Look, you son of a bitch, you know damn well you had a knife. A dozen people saw you with it. Now how about it?'

Perillo was silent.

'*Tiene usted un cuchillo?*' Foster asked.

'*No.*'

'You're a liar!' Foster said. 'You *do* have a knife. What'd you do with it after you slashed that guy in the bar?'

'*Dónde está el servicio?*' Perillo asked.

'Never mind where the hell the man's room is,' Foster snapped. 'Stand up straight, for Christ's sake. What the hell do you think this is, the pool room? Take your hands out of your pockets.'

Perillo took his hands from his pockets.

'Now where's the knife?'

'*No sé.*'

'You don't know, you don't know,' Foster mimicked. 'All right, get the hell out of here. Sit down on the bench outside. I'm gonna get a cop in here who really speaks your language, pal. Now go sit down. Go ahead.'

'*Bien,*' Perillo said. '*Dónde está el servicio?*'

'Down the hall on your left. And don't take all night in there.'

Perillo went out. Foster grimaced. The man he'd cut hadn't been cut bad at all. If they knocked themselves out over every goddamn knifing they got, they'd be busy running down nothing but knifings. He wondered what it would be like to be stationed in a precinct where carving was something you did to a turkey. He grinned at his own humour, wheeled a typewriter over, and began typing up a report on the burglary they'd had several days back.

When Carella and Bush came in, they seemed in a big hurry. Carella walked directly to the phone, consulted a list of phone numbers beside it, and began dialling.

'What's up?' Foster said.

'That homicide,' Carella answered.

'Yeah?

'It was Mike.'

'What do you mean? Huh?'

'Mike Reardon.'

'What?' Foster said. 'What?'

'Two slugs at the back of his head. I'm calling the lieutenant. He's gonna want to move fast on this one.'

'Hey, is he kidding?' Foster said to Bush, and then he saw the look on Bush's face, and he knew this was not a joke.

Lieutenant Byrnes was the man in charge of the 87th Detective Squad. He had a small, compact body and a head like a rivet. His eyes were blue and tiny, but those eyes had seen a hell of a lot, and they didn't miss very much that went on around the lieutenant. The lieutenant knew his precinct was a trouble spot, and that was the way he liked it. It was the bad neighbourhoods that needed policemen, he was fond of saying, and he was proud to be a part of a squad that really earned its keep. There had once been sixteen men in his squad, and now there were fifteen.

Ten of those fifteen were gathered around him in the squad room, the remaining five being out on plants from which they could not be yanked. The men sat in their chairs,

15

or on the edges of desks, or they stood near the grilled windows, or they leaned against filing cabinets. The squad room looked the way it might look at any of the times when the new shift was coming in to relieve the old one, except that there were no dirty jokes now. The men all knew that Mike Reardon was dead.

Acting Lieutenant Lynch stood alongside Byrnes while Byrnes filled his pipe. Byrnes had thick capable fingers, and he wadded the tobacco with his thumb, not looking up at the men.

Carella watched him. Carella admired and respected the lieutenant, even though many of the other men called him 'an old turd'. Carella knew cops who worked in precincts where the old man wielded a whip instead of a cerebellum. It wasn't good to work for a tyrant. Byrnes was all right, and Byrnes was also a good cop and a smart cop, and so Carella gave him his undivided attention, even though the lieutenant had not yet begun speaking.

Byrnes struck a wooden match and lit his pipe. He gave the appearance of an unhurried man about to take his port after a heavy meal, but the wheels were grinding furiously inside his compact skull, and every fibre in his body was outraged at the death of one of his best men.

'No pep talk,' he said suddenly. 'Just go out and find the bastard.' He blew out a cloud of smoke and then waved it away with one of his short, wide hands. 'If you read the newspapers, and if you start believing them, you'll know that cops hate cop killers. That's the law of the jungle. That's the law of survival. The newspapers are full of crap if they think any revenge motive is attached. We can't let a cop be killed because a cop is a symbol of law and order. If you take away the symbol, you get animals in the streets. We've got enough animals in the streets now.

'So I want you to find Reardon's killer, but not because Reardon was a cop assigned to this precinct, and not even because Reardon was a good cop. I want you to find that bastard because Reardon was a *man* – and a damned fine man.

'Handle it however you want to, you know your jobs. Give me progress reports on whatever you get from the files, and whatever you get in the streets. But find him. That's all.'

The lieutenant went back into his office with Lynch, and some of the cops went to the *modus operandi* file and began digging for information on thugs who used ·45s. Some of the cops went to the Lousy file, the file of known criminals in the precinct, and they began searching for any cheap thieves who may have crossed Mike Reardon's path at one time or another. Some of the cops went to the Convictions file and began a methodical search of cards listing every conviction for which the precinct had been responsible, with a special eye out for cases on which Mike Reardon had worked. Foster went out into the corridor and told the suspect he'd questioned to get the hell home and to keep his nose clean. The rest of the cops took to the streets, and Carella and Bush were among them.

'He gripes my ass,' Bush said. 'He thinks he's Napoleon.'

'He's a good man,' Carella said.

'Well, *he* seems to think so, anyway.'

'Everything gripes you,' Carella said. 'You're maladjusted.'

'I'll tell you one thing,' Bush said. 'I'm getting an ulcer in this goddamn precinct. I never had trouble before, but since I got assigned to this precinct, I'm getting an ulcer. Now how do you account for that?'

There were a good many possible ways to account for Bush's ulcer and none of them had anything whatever to do with the precinct. But Carella didn't feel like arguing at the moment, and so he kept his peace. Bush simply nodded sourly.

'I want to call my wife,' he said.

'At two in the morning?' Carella asked incredulously.'

'What's the matter with that?' Bush wanted to know. He was suddenly antagonistic.

'Nothing. Go ahead, call her.'

'I just want to check,' Bush said, and then he said, 'Check in.'

'Sure.'

'Hell, we may be going for days on this one.'

'Sure.'

'Anything wrong with calling her to let her know what's up?'

'Listen, are you looking for an argument?' Carella asked, smiling.

'No.'

'Then go call your wife, and get the hell off my back.'

Bush nodded emphatically. They stopped outside an open candy store on Culver, and Bush went in to make his call. Carella stood outside, his back to the open counter at the store's front.

The city was very quiet. The tenements stretched grimy fingers towards the soft muzzle of the sky. Occasionally, a bathroom light winked like an opening eye in an otherwise blinded face. Two young Irish girls walked past the candy store, their high heels clattering on the pavement. He glanced momentarily at their legs and the thin summer frocks they wore. One of the girls winked unashamedly at him, and then both girls began giggling, and for no good reason he remembered something about lifting the skirts of an Irish lass, and the thought came to him full-blown so that he knew it was stored somewhere in his memory, and it seemed to him he had read it. Irish lasses, *Ulysses*? Christ, that had been one hell of a book to get through, pretty little lasses and all. I wonder what Bush reads? Bush is too busy to read. Bush is too busy worrying about his wife. Jesus, does that man worry.

He glanced over his shoulder. Bush was still in the booth, talking rapidly. The man behind the counter leaned over a racing form, a toothpick angling up out of his mouth. A young kid sat at the end of the counter drinking an egg cream. Carella sucked in a breath of fetid air. The door to the phone booth opened, and Bush stepped out, mopping his brow. He nodded at the counterman, and then went out to join Carella.

'Hot as hell in that booth,' he said.

'Everything okay?' Carella asked.

'Sure,' Bush said. He looked at Carella suspiciously. 'Why shouldn't it be?'

'No reason. Any ideas where we should start?'

'This isn't going to be such a cinch,' Bush said. 'Any stupid son of a bitch with a grudge could've done it.'

'Or anybody in the middle of committing a crime.'

'We ought to leave it to Homicide. We're in over our heads.'

'We haven't even started yet, and you say we're in over our heads. What the hell's wrong with you, Hank?'

'Nothing,' Bush said, 'only I don't happen to think of cops as master minds, that's all.'

'That's a nice thing for a cop to say.'

'It's the truth. Look, this detective tag is a bunch of crap, and you know it as well as I do. All you need to be a detective is a strong pair of legs, and a stubborn streak. The legs take you around to all the various dumps you have to go to, and the stubborn streak keeps you from quitting. You follow each separate trail mechanically, and if you're lucky, one of the trails pays off. If you're not lucky, it doesn't. Period.'

'And brains don't enter into it at all, huh?'

'Only a little. It doesn't take much brains to be a cop.'

'Okay.'

'Okay what?'

'Okay, I don't want to argue. If Reardon got it trying to stop somebody in the commission of a crime . . .'

'That's another thing that burns me up about cops,' Bush said.

'You're a regular cop hater, aren't you?' Carella asked.

'This whole goddamn city is full of cop haters. You think anybody respects a cop? Symbol of law and order, crap! The old man ought to get out there and face life. Anybody who ever got a parking tag is automatically a cop hater. That's the way it is.'

'Well, it sure as hell shouldn't be that way,' Carella said, somewhat angrily.

Bush shrugged. 'What burns me up about cops is they don't speak English.'

'What?'

'In the commission of a crime!' Bush mocked. 'Cop talk. Did you ever hear a cop say "We caught him"? No. He says, "We apprehended him."'

'I never heard a cop say "We apprehended him",' Carella said.

'I'm talking about for official publication,' Bush said.

'Well, that's different. Everybody talks fancy when it's for official publication.'

'Cops especially.'

'Why don't you turn in your shield? Become a hackie or something?'

'I'm toying with the idea.' Bush smiled suddenly. His entire tirade had been delivered in his normally hushed voice, and now that he was smiling, it was difficult to remember that he'd been angry at all.

'Anyway, I thought the bars,' Carella said. 'I mean, if this *is* a grudge kind of thing, it might've been somebody from the neighbourhood. And we may be able to pick up something in the bars. Who the hell knows?'

'I can use a beer, anyway,' Bush said. 'I've been wanting a beer ever since I come on tonight.'

The Shamrock was one of a million bars all over the world with the same name. It squatted on Culver Avenue between a pawn shop and a Chinese laundry. It was an all-night joint, and it catered to the Irish clientele that lined Culver. Occasionally, a Puerto Rican wandered into the Shamrock, but such off-trail excursions were discouraged by those among the Shamrock's customers who owned quick tempers and powerful fists. The cops stopped at the bar often, not to wet their whistles – because drinking on duty was strictly forbidden by the rules and regulations – but to make sure that too many quick tempers did not mix with too much whisky or too many fists. The flare-ups within the gaily decorated walls of the bar were now few and far between, or – to be poetic – less frequent than they had been in the good old days when the neighbourhood had first succumbed to the Puerto Rican assault wave. In those days, not speaking English too well, not reading signs too well, the Puerto Ricans stumbled into the Shamrock with remarkably ignorant rapidity. The staunch defenders of America for the Americans, casually ignoring the fact that Puerto Ricans were and are Americans, spent many a pugilistic evening proving their point. The bar was often brilliantly decorated with spilled blood. But that was in the good old days. In the bad new days, you could go into the Shamrock for a week running, and not see more than one or two broken heads.

There was a Ladies Invited sign in the window of the bar, but not many ladies accepted the invitation. The drinkers were, instead, neighbourhood men who tired of the four walls of their dreary tenement flats, who sought the carefree camaraderie of other men who had similarly grown weary of their own homes. Their wives were out playing Bingo on Tuesdays, or at the movies collecting a piece of china on Wednesdays, or across the street with the Sewing Club ('We so and so and so and so') on Thursdays, and so it went. So what was wrong with a friendly brew in a neighbourhood tavern? Nothing.

Except when the cops showed.

Now there was something very disgusting about policemen in general, and bulls in particular. Sure, you could go through the motions of saying, 'How are yuh, this evenin', Officer Dugan?' and all that sort of rot, and you could really and truly maybe hold a fond spot in the old ticker for the new rookie, but you still couldn't deny that a cop sitting next to you when you were half-way towards getting a snootful was a somewhat disconcerting thing and would likely bring on the goblins in the morning. Not that anyone had anything against cops. It was just that cops should not loiter around bars and spoil a man's earnest drinking. Nor should cops hang around book joints and spoil a man's earnest gambling. Nor should they hang around brothels and spoil a man's earnest endeavours, cops simply shouldn't hang around, that was all.

And bulls, bulls were cops in disguise, only worse.

So what did those two big jerks at the end of the bar want?

'A beer, Harry,' Bush said.

'Comin' up,' Harry the bartender answered. He drew the beer and brought it over to where Bush and Carella were seated. 'Good night for a beer, ain't it?' Harry said.

'I never knew a bartender who didn't give you a commercial when you ordered a beer on a hot night,' Bush said quietly.

Harry laughed, but only because his customer was a cop. Two men at the shuffleboard table were arguing about an Irish free state. The late movie on television was about a Russian empress.

'You fellows here on business?' Harry asked.

'Why?' Bush said. 'You got any for us?'

'No, I was just wonderin'. I mean, it ain't often we get the bu— it ain't often a detective drops by,' Harry said.

'That's because you run such a clean establishment,' Bush said.

'Ain't none cleaner on Culver.'

'Not since they ripped your phone booth out,' Bush said.

'Yeah, well, we were gettin' too many phone calls.'

'You were taking too many bets,' Bush said, his voice even. He picked up the glass of beer, dipped his upper lip into the foam, and then downed it.

'No, no kiddin',' Harry said. He did not like to think of the close call he'd had with that damn phone booth and the State Attorney's Commission. 'You fellows lookin' for somebody?'

'Kind of quiet tonight,' Carella said.

Harry smiled, and a gold tooth flashed at the front of his mouth. 'Oh, always quiet in here, fellows, you know that.'

'Sure,' Carella said, nodding. 'Danny Gimp drop in?'

'No, haven't seen him tonight. Why? What's up?'

'That's good beer,' Bush said.

'Like another?'

'No, thanks.'

'Say, are you sure nothing's wrong?' Harry asked.

'What's with you, Harry? Somebody do something wrong here?' Carella asked.

'What? No, hey no, I hope I didn't give you that impression. It's just kind of strange, you fellows dropping in. I mean, we haven't had any trouble here or anything.'

'Well, that's good,' Carella said. 'See anybody with a gun lately?'

'A gun?'

'Yeah.'

'What kind of a gun?'

'What kind did you see?

'I didn't see any kind.' Harry was sweating. He drew a beer for himself and drank it hastily.

'None of the young punks in with zip guns or anything?' Bush asked quietly.

'Oh, well zip guns,' Harry said, wiping the foam from his lip, 'I mean, you see them all the time.'

'And nothing bigger?'

'Bigger like what? Like you mean a ·32 or a ·38?'

'Like we mean a ·45,' Carella said.

'The last ·45 I seen in here,' Harry said, thinking, 'was away back in . . .' He shook his head. 'No, that wouldn't help you. What happened? Somebody get shot?'

'Away back *when*?' Bush asked.

'Fifty, fifty-one, it must've been. Kid discharged from the

Army. Come in here wavin' a ·45 around. He was lookin' for trouble, all right, that kid. Dooley busted it up. You remember Dooley? He used to have this beat before he got transferred out to another precinct. Nice kid. Always used to stop by and—'

'He still live in the neighbourhood?' Bush asked.

'Huh? Who?'

'The guy who was in here waving the ·45 around.'

'Oh, him.' Harry's brows swooped down over his eyes. 'Why?'

'I'm asking you,' Bush said. 'Does he or doesn't he?'

'Yeah. I guess. Why?'

'Where?'

'Listen,' Harry said, 'I don't want to get nobody in trouble.'

'You're not getting anybody in trouble,' Bush said. 'Does this guy still own the ·45?'

'I don't know.'

'What happened that night? When Dooley busted it up.'

'Nothing. The kid had a load on. You know, just out of the Army, like that.'

'Like what?'

'Like he was wavin' the gun around. I don't even think it was loaded. I think the barrel was leaded.'

'Are you sure it was?'

'Well, no.'

'Did Dooley take the gun away from him?'

'Well . . .' Harry paused and mopped his brow. 'Well, I don't think Dooley even saw the gun.'

'If he busted it up—'

'Well,' Harry said, 'one of the fellows saw Dooley comin' down the street, and they kind of calmed the kid down and got him out of here.'

'*Before* Dooley came in?'

'Well, yeah. Yeah.'

'And the kid took the gun with him when he left?'

'Yeah,' Harry said. 'Look, I didn't want no trouble in my place, you follow?'

'I follow,' Bush said. 'Where does he live?'

Harry blinked his eyes. He looked down at the bar top.

'Where?' Bush repeated.

'On Culver.'

'Where on Culver?'

'The house on the corner of Culver and Mason. Look, fellows . . .'

'This guy mention anything about not liking cops?' Carella asked.

'No, no,' Harry said. 'He's a fine boy. He just had a couple of sheets to the wind that night, that's all.'

'You know Mike Reardon?'

'Oh, sure,' Harry said.

'This kid know Mike?'

'Well, I can't say as I know. Look, the kid was just squiffed that night, that's all.'

'What's his name?'

'Look, he was only tanked up, that's all. Hell, it was away back in 1950.'

'What's his name?'

'Frank. Frank Clarke. With an "e".'

'What do you think, Steve?' Bush asked Carella.

Carella shrugged. 'It came too easy. It's never good when it comes that easy.'

'Let's check it, anyway,' Bush said.

CHAPTER FOUR

There are smells inside a tenement, and they are not only the smell of cabbage. The smell of cabbage, to many, is and always will be a good wholesome smell and there are many who resent the steady propaganda which links cabbage with poverty.

The smell inside a tenement is the smell of life.

It is the smell of every function of life, the sweating, the cooking, the elimination, the breeding. It is all these smells, and they are wedded into one gigantic smell which hits the nostrils the moment you enter the downstairs doorway. For the smell has been inside the building for decades. It has seeped through the floorboards and permeated the walls. It clings to the banister and the linoleum-covered steps. It crouches in corners and it hovers about the naked light bulbs on each landing. The smell is always there, day and night. It is the stench of living, and it never sees the light of day, and it never sees the crisp brittleness of starlight.

It was there on the morning of 24 July at 3 a.m. It was there in full force because the heat of the day had baked it into the walls. It hit Carella as he and Bush entered the building. He snorted through his nostrils and then struck a match and held it to the mailboxes.

'There it is,' Bush said. 'Clarke. 3B.'

Carella shook out the match and they walked towards the steps. The garbage cans were in for the night, stacked on the ground-floor landing behind the steps. Their aroma joined the other smells to clash in a medley of putridity. The building slept, but the smells were awake. On the second floor, a man – or a woman – snored loudly. On each door, close to the floor, the circular trap for a milk-bottle lock hung despondently awaiting the milkman's arrival. On one of the doors hung a plaque, and the plaque read IN GOD WE TRUST. And behind that door, there was undoubtedly the unbending steel bar of a police lock, embedded in the floor and tilted to lean against the door.

Carella and Bush laboured up to the third floor. The light bulb on the third-floor landing was out. Bush struck a match.

'Down the hall there.'

'You want to do this up big?' Carella asked.

'He's got a ·45 in there, hasn't he?'

'Still.'

'What the hell, my wife doesn't need my insurance money,' Bush said.

They walked to the door and flanked it. They drew their service revolvers with nonchalance. Carella didn't for a moment believe he'd need his gun, but caution never hurt. He drew back his left hand and knocked on the door.

'Probably asleep,' Bush said.

'Betokens a clear conscience,' Carella answered. He knocked again.

'Who is it?' a voice answered.

'Police. Want to open up?'

'Oh, for Christ's sake,' the voice mumbled. 'Just a minute.'

'We won't need these,' Bush said. He holstered his gun, and Carella followed suit. From within the apartment, they could hear bed springs creaking, and then a woman's voice asking, 'What is it?' They heard footsteps approaching the door, and then someone fumbled with the police lock on the inside, and the heavy steel bar clattered when it was dropped to the floor. The door opened a crack.

'What do you want?' the voice said.

'Police. We'd like to ask you a few questions.'

'At this time of the morning? Jesus Christ, can't it wait?'

'Afraid it can't.'

'Well, what's the matter? There a burglar in the building?'

'No. We'd just like to ask you some questions. You're Frank Clarke, aren't you?'

'Yeah.' Clark paused. 'Let me see your badge.'

Carella reached into his pocket for the leather case to which his shield was pinned. He held it up to the crack in the door.

'I can't see nothing,' Clarke said. 'Just a minute.'

'Who is it?' the woman asked.

'The cops,' Clarke mumbled. He stepped away from the door, and then a light flashed inside the apartment. He came back to the door. Carella held up the badge again.

'Yeah, okay,' Clarke said. 'What do you want?'

'You own a ·45, Clarke?'

'What?'

'A ·45. Do you own one?'

'Jesus, is that what you want to know? Is that what you come banging on the door for in the middle of the night? Ain't you guys got any sense at all? I got to go to work in the morning.'

'Do you have a ·45, or don't you?'

'Who said I had one?'

'Never mind who. How about it?'

'Why do you want to know? I been here all night.'

'Anybody to swear for that?'

Clarke's voice lowered. 'Hey, look, fellows, I got somebody with me, you know what I mean? Look, give me a break, will you?'

'What about the gun?'

'Yeah, I got one.'

'A ·45?'

'Yeah. Yeah, it's a ·45.'

'Mind if we take a look at it?'

'What for? I've got a permit for it.'

'We'd like to look at it anyway.'

'Hey, look, what the hell kind of a routine is this, anyway? I told you I got a permit for the gun. What did I do wrong? Whattya want from me, anyway?'

'We want to see the ·45,' Bush said. 'Get it.'

'You got a search warrant?' Clarke asked.

'Never mind the crap,' Bush said. 'Get the gun.'

'You can't come in here without a search warrant. And you can't bulldoze me into gettin' the gun, either. I don't want to get that gun, then you can whistle.'

'How old's the girl in there?' Bush asked.

'What?'

'You heard me. Wake up, Clarke!'

'She's 21, and you're barkin' up the wrong tree,' Clarke said. 'We're engaged.'

From down the hall, someone shouted, 'Hey, shut up, willya? For Christ's sake! Go down to the pool-room, you want to talk!'

'How about letting us in, Clarke?' Carella asked gently. 'We're waking your neighbours.'

'I don't have to let you in no place. Go get a search warrant.'

'I know you don't, Clarke. But a cop's been killed, and he was killed with a ·45, and if I were you I wouldn't play this so goddamn cosy. Now how about opening that door and showing us you're clean? How about it, Clarke?'

'A cop? Jesus, a cop! Jesus, why didn't you say so? Just a . . . just a minute, willya? Just a minute.' He moved away from the door. Carella could hear him talking to the woman, and he could hear the woman's whispered answer. Clarke came back to the door and took off the night chain. 'Come on in,' he said.

There were dishes stacked in the kitchen sink. The kitchen was a six-by-eight rectangle, and adjoining that was the bedroom. The girl stood in the bedroom doorway. She was a short blonde, somewhat dumpy. She wore a man's bathrobe. Her eyes were puffed with sleep, and she wore no make-up. She blinked her eyes and stared at Carella and Bush as they moved into the kitchen.

Clarke was a short man with bushy black brows and brown eyes. His nose was long, broken sharply in the middle. His lips were thick, and he needed a shave badly. He was wearing pyjama pants and nothing else. He stood bare-chested and bare-footed in the glare of the kitchen light. The water tap dripped its tattoo on to the dirty dishes in the sink.

'Let's see the gun,' Bush said.

'I got a permit for it,' Clarke answered. 'Okay if I smoke?'

'It's your apartment.'

'Gladys,' Clarke said, 'there's a pack on the dresser. Bring some matches, too, willya?' The girl moved into the darkness of the bedroom, and Clarke whispered, 'You guys sure picked a hell of a time to come calling, all right.' He tried a smile, but neither Carella nor Bush seemed amused, and so he dropped it instantly. The girl came back with the package of cigarettes. She hung one on her lip, and then handed the pack to Clarke. He lit his own cigarette and then handed the matches to the blonde.

'What kind of a permit?' Carella asked. 'Carry or premises?'

'Carry,' Clarke said.

'How come?'

'Well, it used to be premises. I registered the gun when I got out of the Army. It was a gift,' he said quickly. 'From my captain.'

'Go ahead.'

'So I got a premises permit when I was discharged. That's the law, ain't it?'

'You're telling the story,' Bush said.

'Well, that's the way I understood it. Either that, or I had to get the barrel leaded up. I don't remember. Anyway, I got the permit.'

'*Is* the barrel leaded?'

'Hell, no. What do I need a permit for a dead gun for? I had this premises permit, and then I got a job with a jeweller, you know? Like I had to make a lot of valuable deliveries, things like that. So I had it changed to a carry permit.'

'When was this?'

'Couple of months back.'

'Which jeweller do you work for?'

'I quit that job,' Clarke said.

'All right, get the gun. And get the permit, too, while you're at it.'

'Sure,' Clarke said. He went to the sink, held his cigarette under the dripping tap, and then dropped the soggy butt in with the dishes. He walked past the girl and into the bedroom.

'This is some time of night to be asking questions,' the girl said angrily.

'We're sorry, Miss,' Carella said.

'Yeah, I'll bet you are.'

'We didn't mean to disturb your beauty sleep,' Bush said nastily.

The girl raised one eyebrow. 'Then why did you?' She blew out a cloud of smoke, the way she had seen movie sirens do. Clarke came back into the room holding the ·45. Bush's hand moved imperceptibly towards his right hip and the holster there.

'Put it on the table,' Carella said.

Clark put the gun on the table.

'Is it loaded?' Carella asked.

'I think so.'

'Don't you know?'

'I ain't even looked at the thing since I quit that job.'

Carella draped a handkerchief over his spread fingers and picked up the gun. He slid the magazine out. 'It's loaded, all right,' he said. Quickly, he sniffed the barrel.

'You don't have to smell,' Clarke said. 'It ain't been fired since I got out of the Army.'

'It came close once, though, didn't it?'

'Huh?'

'That night in the Shamrock.'

'Oh, that,' Clarke said. 'Is that why you're here? Hell, I was looped that night. I didn't mean no harm.'

31

Carella slammed the magazine back into place. 'Where's the permit, Clarke?'

'Oh, yeah. I looked around in there. I couldn't find it.'

'You're sure you've got one?'

'Yeah, I'm sure. I just can't find it.'

'You'd better take another look. A good one, this time.'

'I did take a good look. I can't find it. Look, I got a permit. You can check on it. I wouldn't kid you. Who was the cop got killed?'

'Want to take another look for that permit?'

'I already told you, I can't find it. Look, I got one.'

'You *had* one, pal,' Carella said. 'You just lost it.'

'Huh? What? What'd you say?'

'When a cop asks you for your permit, you produce it or you lose it.'

'Well, Jesus, I just misplaced it temporarily. Look, you can check all this. I mean ... look, what's the matter with you guys, anyway? I didn't do nothing. I been here all night. You can ask Gladys. Ain't that right, Gladys?'

'He's been here all night,' Gladys said.

'We're taking the gun,' Carella said. 'Give him a receipt for it, Hank.'

'That ain't been fired in years,' Clarke said. 'You'll see. And you check on that permit. I got one. You check on it.'

'We'll let you know,' Carella said. 'You weren't planning on leaving the city, were you?'

'What?'

'You weren't plann—'

'Hell, no. Where would I go?'

'Back to sleep is as good a place as any,' the blonde said.

CHAPTER FIVE

The pistol permit was on Steve Carella's desk when he reported for work at 4 p.m. on the afternoon of 24 July. He had worked until eight in the morning, gone home for six hours' sleep, and was back at his desk now, looking a little bleary-eyed but otherwise none the worse for wear.

The heat had persisted all day long, a heavy yellow blanket that smothered the city in its woolly grip. Carella did not like the heat. He had never liked summer, even as a kid, and now that he was an adult and a cop, the only memorable characteristic summer seemed to have was that it made dead bodies stink quicker.

He loosened his collar the instant he entered the Squad Room, and when he got to his desk, he rolled up his sleeves, and then picked up the pistol permit.

Quickly, he scanned the printed form:

License No.	Date	Police Department	Year	

PISTOL LICENSE APPLICATION

(APPLICATION MUST BE MADE IN DUPLICATE)

I Hereby Apply for License to

Carry a Revolver or Pistol upon my person or Possession on premises _____

_____37–12 Culver Avenue_____

For the following reasons: __Make deliveries for__
__jewelry firm.__

Clarke_____Francis____D.__37–12 Culver Ave.
(PRINT) Surname Given Name Initials   Number   Street

There was more, a lot more, but it didn't interest Carella. Clarke had indeed owned a pistol permit – but that didn't mean he hadn't used the pistol on a cop named Mike Reardon.

Carella shoved the permit to one side of his desk, glanced at his watch, and then reached for the phone automatically. Quickly, he dialled Bush's home number and then waited, his hand sweating on the receiver. The phone rang six times, and then a woman's voice said, 'Hello?'

'Alice?'

'Who's this?'

'Steve Carella.'

'Oh. Hello, Steve.'

'Did I wake you?'

'Yes.'

'Hank's not here yet. He's all right, isn't he?'

'He left a little while ago,' Alice said. The sleep was beginning to leave her voice already. Alice Bush was a cop's wife who generally slept when her husband did, adjusting her schedule to fit his. Carella had spoken to her on a good many mornings and afternoons, and he always marvelled at the way she could come almost instantly awake within the space of three or four sentences. Her voice invariably sounded like the first faint rattle of impending death when she picked up the receiver. As the conversation progressed, it modulated into the dulcet whine of a middle-aged Airedale, and then into the disconcertingly sexy voice which was the normal speaking voice of Hank's wife. Carella had met her on one occasion, when he and Hank had shared a late snack with her, and he knew that she was a dynamic blonde with a magnificent figure and the brownest eyes he'd ever seen. From what Bush had expansively delivered about personal aspects of his home life, Carella knew that Alice slept in clinging black, sheer night-gowns. The knowledge was unnerving, for whenever Carella roused her out of bed, he automatically formed a mental picture of the well-rounded blonde he'd met, and the picture was always dressed as Hank had described it.

He generally, therefore, cut his conversations with Alice short, feeling somewhat guilty about the artistic inclinations of his mind. This morning, though, Alice seemed to be in a talkative mood.

'I understand one of your colleagues got knocked off,' she said.

Carella smiled, in spite of the topic's grimness. Alice sometimes had a peculiar way of mixing the King's English with choice bits of underworld and police vernacular.

'Yes,' he said.

'I'm awfully sorry,' she answered, her mood and her voice changing. 'Please be careful, you and Hank. If a cheap hood is shooting up the streets . . .'

'We'll be careful,' he said. 'I've got to go now, Alice.'

'I leave Hank in capable hands,' Alice said, and she hung up without saying good-bye.

Carella grinned and shrugged, and then put the receiver back into the cradle. David Foster, his brown face looking scrubbed and shining, ambled over to the desk. 'Afternoon, Steve,' he said.

'Hi, Dave. What've you got?'

'Ballistics report on that ·45 you brought in last night.'

'Any luck?'

'Hasn't been fired since Old King Cole ordered the bowl.'

'Well, that narrows it down,' Carella said. 'Now we've only got the nine million, nine hundred and ninety-nine thousand other people in this fair city to contend with.'

'I don't like it when cops get killed,' Foster said. His brow lowered menacingly, giving him the appearance of a bull ducking his head to charge at the *muleta*. 'Mike was my partner. He was a good guy.'

'I know.'

'I been trying to think who,' Foster said. 'I got my personal

I.B. right up here, and I been leafing through them mug shots one by one.' He tapped his temple. 'I been turning them over and studying them, and so far I haven't got anything, but give me time. Somebody musta had it in for Mike, and when that face falls into place, that guy's gonna wish he was in Alaska.'

'Tell you the truth,' Carella said, 'I wish I was there right now.'

'Hot, ain't it?' Foster said, classically understating the temperature and humidity.

'Yeah.' From the corner of his eye, Carella saw Bush walk down the corridor, push through the railing, and sign in. He walked to Carella's desk, pulled over a swivel chair and plopped into it disconsolately.

'Rough night?' Foster asked, grinning.

'The roughest,' Bush said in his quiet voice.

'Clarke was a blank,' Carella told him.

'I figured as much. Where do we go from here?'

'That's a good question.'

'Coroner's report in yet?'

'No.'

'The boys picked up some hoods for questioning,' Foster said. 'We might give them the once over.'

'Where are they? Downstairs?' Carella asked.

'In the Waldorf Suite,' Foster said, referring to the detention cells on the first floor of the building.

'Why don't you call down for them?'

'Sure,' Foster said.

'Where's the Skipper?'

'He's over at Homicide North. He's trying to goose them into some real action on this one.'

'You see the paper this morning?' Bush asked.

'No,' Carella said.

'Mike made the front page. Have a look.' He put the paper on Carella's desk. Carella held it up so that Foster could see it while he spoke on the phone.

'Shot him in the back,' Foster mumbled. 'That lousy bastard.' He spoke into the phone and then hung up. The men lit cigarettes, and Bush phoned out for coffee, and then they sat around gassing. The prisoners arrived before the coffee did.

There were two men, both unshaven, both tall, both wearing short-sleeved sports shirts. The physical resemblance ended there. One of the men owned a handsome face, with regular features and white, even teeth. The other man looked as if his face had challenged a concrete mixer and lost. Carella recognized both of them at once. Mentally, he flipped over their cards in the Lousy file.

'Were they picked up together?' he asked the uniformed cop who brought them into the squad room.

'Yeah,' the cop said.

'Where?'

'13th and Shippe. They were sitting in a parked car.'

'Any law against that?' the handsome one asked.

'At three in the morning,' the uniformed cop added.

'Okay,' Carella said. 'Thanks.'

'What's your name?' Bush asked the handsome one.

'You know my name, cop.'

'Say it again. I like the sound.'

'I'm tired.'

'You're gonna be a lot more tired before this is finished. Now cut the comedy, and answer the questions. Your name?'

'Terry.'

'Terry what?'

'Terry McCarthy. What the hell is this, a joke? You know my name.'

'How about your buddy?'

'You know him, too. He's Clarence Kelly.'

'What were you doing in that car?' Carella asked.

'Lookin' at dirty pictures,' McCarthy said.

'Possession of pornography,' Carella said dully. 'Take that down, Hank.'

'Hey, wait a minute,' McCarthy said. 'I was only wise-crackin'.'

'DON'T WISECRACK ON MY TIME!!' Carella shouted.

'Okay, okay, don't get sore.'

'What were you doing in that car?'

'Sitting.'

'You always sit in parked cars at three in the a.m.?' Foster asked.

'Sometimes,' McCarthy said.

'What else were you doing?'

'Talking.'

'What about?'

'Everything.'

'Philosophy?' Bush asked.

'Yeah,' McCarthy said.

'What'd you decide?'

'We decided it ain't wise to sit in parked cars at three in the morning. There's always some cop who's got to fill his pinch book.'

Carella tapped a pencil on the desk. 'Don't get me mad, McCarthy,' he said. 'I just come from six hours' sleep, and I don't feel like listening to a vaudeville routine. Did you know Mike Reardon?'

'Who?'

'Mike Reardon. A detective attached to this precinct.'

McCarthy shrugged. He turned to Kelly. 'We know him, Clarence?'

'Yeah,' Clarence said. 'Reardon. That rings a bell.'

'How big a bell?' Foster asked.

'Just a tiny tinkle so far,' Kelly said, and he began laughing. The laugh died when he saw the bulls weren't quite appreciating his humour.

'Did you see him last night?'

'No.'

'How do you know?'

'We didn't run across any bulls last night,' Kelly said.

'Do you usually?'

'Well, sometimes.'

'Were you heeled when they pulled you in?'

'What?'

'Come on,' Foster said.

'No.'

'We'll check that.'

'Yeah, go ahead,' McCarthy said. 'We didn't even have a water pistol between us.'

'What were you doing in the car?'

'I just told you,' McCarthy said.

'The story stinks. Try again,' Carella answered.

Kelly sighed. McCarthy looked at him.

'Well?' Carella said.

'I was checkin' up on my dame,' Kelly said.

'Yeah?' Bush said.

'Truth,' Kelly said. 'So help me Jesus, may I be struck dead right this goddamn minute.'

'What's there to check up on?' Bush asked

'Well, you know.'

'No, I don't know. Tell me.'

'I figured she was maybe slippin' around.'

'Slipping around with who?' Bush asked.

'Well, that's what I wanted to find out.'

'And what were you doing with him, McCarthy?'

'I was helping him check,' McCarthy said, smiling.

'Was she?' Bush asked, a bored expression on his face.

'No, I don't think so,' Kelly said.

'Don't check again,' Bush said. 'Next time we're liable to find you with the burglar's tools.'

'Burglar's tools!' McCarthy said, shocked.

'Gee, Detective Bush,' Kelly said, 'you know us better than that.'

'Get the hell out of here,' Bush said.

'We can go home?'

'You can go to hell, for my part,' Bush informed them.

'Here's the coffee,' Foster said.

The released prisoners sauntered out of the Squad Room. The three detectives paid the delivery boy for the coffee and then pulled chairs up to one of the desks.

'I heard a good one last night, Foster said.

'Let's hear it,' Carella prompted.

'This guy is a construction worker, you see?'

'Yeah.'

'Working up on a girder about sixty floors above the street.'

'Yeah?'

'The lunch whistle blows. He knocks off, goes to the end of the girder, sits down, and puts his lunch box on his lap. He opens the box, takes out a sandwich and very carefully unwraps the waxed paper. Then he bites into it. "Goddamn!" he says. "Peanut butter!" and he throws the sandwich down the sixty floors to the street.'

'I don't get it,' Bush said, sipping at his coffee.

'I'm not finished yet,' Foster said, grinning, hardly able to contain his glee.

'Go ahead,' Carella said.

'He reaches into the box,' Foster said, 'for the next sandwich. He very carefully unwraps the waxed paper. He bites into the sandwich. "Goddamn!" he says again. "Peanut butter!" and he flings that second sandwich down the sixty floors to the street.'

'Yeah,' Carella said.

'He opens the third sandwich,' Foster said. 'This time it's ham. This time he likes it. He eats the sandwich all up.'

'This is gonna go on all night,' Bush said. 'You shoulda stood in bed, Dave.'

'No, wait a minute, wait a minute,' Foster said. 'He opens the fourth sandwich. He bites into it. "Goddamn!" he says again. "Peanut butter!" and he flings that sandwich too down the sixty floors to the street. Well, there's another construction worker sitting on a girder just a little bit above this fellow. He looks down and says, "Say, fellow, I've been watching you with them sandwiches."

'"So what?" the first guy says.

'"You married?" the second guy asks.

'"Yes, I'm married."

'The second guy shakes his head. "How long you been married?"

'"Ten years," the first guy says.

'"And your wife still doesn't know what kind of sandwiches you like?"

'The first guy points his finger up at the guy above him and yells, "Listen, you son of a bitch, leave my wife out of this. I made those goddamn sandwiches myself!"'

Carella burst out laughing, almost choking on his coffee. Bush stared at Foster dead-panned.

'I still don't get it,' Bush said. 'What's so funny about a guy married ten years whose wife doesn't know what kind of sandwiches he likes? That's not funny. That's a tragedy.'

'He made the sandwiches *himself*,' Foster said.

'So then it's a psycho joke. Psycho jokes don't appeal to me. You got to be nuts to appreciate a psycho joke.'

'I appreciate it,' Carella said.

'So? That proves my point,' Bush answered.

'Hank didn't get enough sleep,' Carella said to Foster. Foster winked.

'I got plenty of sleep,' Bush said.

'Ah-ha,' Carella said. 'Then that explains it.'

'What the hell do you mean by that?' Bush said, annoyed.

'Oh, forget it. Drink your coffee.'

'A man doesn't get a joke, right away his sex life gets dragged in. Do I ask you how much sleep you get or don't get?'

'No,' Carella said.

'Okay. Okay.'

One of the patrolmen walked into the Squad Room. 'Desk sergeant asked me to give you this,' he said. 'Just came up from Downtown.'

'Probably that Coroner's report,' Carella said, taking the manila envelope. 'Thanks.'

The patrolman nodded and went out. Carella opened the envelope.

'Is it?' Foster asked.

'Yeah. Something else, too.' He pulled a card from the envelope. 'Oh, report on the slugs they dug out of the theatre booth.'

'Let's see it,' Hank said.

Carella handed him the card.

BULLET

Calibre	Weight	Twist	No. of Grooves
.45	230 grms.	16 L	6

Width of land marks		Width of groove marks	
.071			.158

Metal Case	Half Metal	Soft Point	
Brass		No	

Deceased		Date	
Michael Reardon		July 24th	

Remarks:	
Remington bullet taken from wooden booth behind body of Michael Reardon.	

'Argh, so what does it tell us?' Bush said, still smarting from the earlier badinage.

'Nothing,' Carella answered, 'until we get the gun that fired it.'

'What about the Coroner's report?' Foster asked.

Carella slipped it out of the envelope.

Male, apparent age 42; chronological age 38. Approximate weight 210 pounds; height 28.9 cm.

Gross Inspection

HEAD: 1·0 × 1·25 cm circular perforation visible 3·1 centimetres laterally to the left of external occipital protuberance (inion). Wound edges slightly inverted. Flame zone and second zone reveal heavy embedding of powder grains. A number 22 catheter inserted through the wound in the occipital region of the skull transverses ventrally and emerges through the right orbit. Point of emergence has left a gaping rough-edged wound measuring 3·7 centimetres in diameter.

There is a second perforation located 6·2 centimetres laterally to the left of the tip of the right mastoid process of the temporal bone, measuring 1·0 × 1·33 centimetres. A number 22 catheter inserted through this second wound passes anteriorly and ventrally and emerges through a perforation measuring approximately 3·5 centimetres in diameter through the right maxilla. The edges of the remaining portion of the right maxilla are splintered.

BODY: Gross inspection of remaining portion of body is negative for demonstrable pathology.

REMARKS: On craniotomy with brain examination, there is evidence of petechiae along course of projectile; small splinters of cranial bone are embedded within the brain substance.

MICROSCOPIC: Examination of brain reveals minute petechiae as well as bone substance within brain matter. Microscopic examination of brain tissue is essentially negative for pathology.

'He did a good job, the bastard,' Foster said.

'Yeah,' Bush answered.

Carella sighed and looked at his watch. 'It's going to be a long night, fellers,' he said.

CHAPTER SIX

He had not seen Teddy Franklin since Mike took the slugs.

Generally, in the course of running down something, he would drop in to see her, spending a few minutes with her before rushing off again. And, of course, he spent all his free time with her because he was in love with the girl.

He had met her less than six months ago, when she'd been working addressing envelopes for a small firm on the fringe of the precinct territory. The firm reported a burglary, and Carella had been assigned to it. He had been taken instantly with her buoyant beauty, asked her out, and that had been the beginning. He had also, in the course of investigation, cracked the burglary – but that didn't seem important now. The important thing now was Teddy. Even the firm had gone the way of most small firms, fading into the abyss of a corporate dissolution, leaving her without a job but with enough saved money to maintain herself for a while. He honestly hoped it would only be for a while, a short while at that. This was the girl he wanted to marry. This was the girl he wanted for his own.

Thinking of her, thinking of the progression of slow traffic lights which kept him from racing to her side, he cursed Ballistics reports and Coroner's reports, and people who shot cops in the back of the head, and he cursed the devilish instrument known as the telephone and the fact that the instrument was worthless with a girl like Teddy. He glanced at his watch. It was close to midnight, and she didn't know he was coming, but he'd take the chance, anyway. He wanted to see her.

When he reached her apartment building in Riverhead, he parked the car and locked it. The street was very quiet. The building was old and sedate, covered with lush ivy. A few windows blinked wide-eyed at the stifling heat of the night, but most of the tenants were asleep or trying to sleep. He glanced up at her window, pleased when he saw the light was still burning. Quickly, he mounted the steps, stopping outside her door.

He did not knock.

Knocking was no good with Teddy.

He took the knob in his hand and twisted it back and forth, back and forth. In a few moments, he heard her footsteps, and then the door opened a crack, and then the door opened wide.

She was wearing prisoner pyjamas, white-and-black striped cotton top and pants she'd picked up as a gag. Her hair was raven black, and the light in the foyer put a high sheen on to it. He closed the door behind him, and she went instantly into his arms, and then she moved back from him, and he marvelled at the expressiveness of her eyes and her mouth. There was joy in her eyes, pure soaring joy. Her lips parted, edging back over small white teeth, and then she lifted her face to his, and he took her kiss, and he felt the warmth of her body beneath the cotton pyjamas.

'Hello,' he said, and she kissed the words on his mouth, and then broke away, holding only his hand, pulling him into the warmly lighted living-room.

She held her right index finger alongside her face, calling for his attention.

'Yes?' he said, and then she shook her head, changing her mind, wanting him to sit first. She fluffed a pillow for him, and he sat in the easy chair, and she perched herself on the arm of the chair and cocked her head to one side, repeating the extended index finger gesture.

'Go ahead,' he said, 'I'm listening.'

She watched his lips carefully, and then she smiled. Her index finger dropped. There was a white tag sewed on to the prisoner pyjama top close to the mound of her left breast.

She ran the extended finger across the tag. He looked at it closely.

'I'm not examining your feminine attributes,' he said, smiling, and she shook her head, understanding. She had inked numbers on to the tag, carrying out the prison garb motif. He studied the numbers closely.

'My shield numbers,' he said, and the smile flowered on her mouth. 'You deserve a kiss for that,' he told her.

She shook her head.

'No kiss?'

She shook her head again.

'Why not?'

She opened and closed the fingers on her right hand.

'You want to talk?' he asked.

She nodded.

'What about?'

She left the arm of the chair suddenly. He watched her walking across the room, his eyes inadvertently following the swing of her small, rounded backside. She went to an end-table and picked up a newspaper. She carried it back to him and then pointed to the picture of Mike Reardon on page one, his brains spilling out on to the sidewalk.

'Yeah,' he said dully.

There was sadness on her face now, an exaggerated sadness because Teddy could not give tongue to words, Teddy could neither hear words, and so her face was her speaking tool, and she spoke in exaggerated syllables, even to Carella, who understood the slightest nuance of expression in her eyes or on her mouth. But the exaggeration did not lie, for there was genuineness to the grief she felt. She had never met Mike Reardon, but Carella had talked of him often, and she felt that she knew him well.

She raised her eyebrows and spread her hands simultaneously, asking Carella 'Who?' and Carella, understanding instantly, said, 'We don't know yet. That's why I haven't been around. We've been working on it.' He saw puzzlement in her eyes. 'Am I going too fast for you?' he asked.

She shook her head.

'What then? What's the matter?'

She threw herself into his arms and she was weeping suddenly and fiercely, and he said, 'Hey, hey, come on, now,' and then realized she could not read his lips because her head was buried in his shoulder. He lifted her chin.

'You're getting my shirt wet,' he said.

She nodded, trying to hold back the tears.

'What's the matter?'

She lifted her hand slowly, and she touched his cheek gently, so gently that it felt like the passing of a mild breeze, and then her fingers touched his lips and lingered there, caressing them.

'You're worried about me?'

She nodded.

'There's nothing to worry about.'

She tossed her hair at the first page of the newspaper again.

'That was probably some crackpot,' Carella said.

She lifted her face, and her eyes met his fully, wide and brown, still moist from the tears.

'I'll be careful,' he said. 'Do you love me?'

She nodded, and then ducked her head.

'What's the matter?'

She shrugged and smiled, an embarrassed, shy smile.

'You missed me?'

She nodded again.

'I missed you, too.'

She lifted her head again, and there was something else in her eyes this time, a challenge to him to read her eyes correctly this time, because she had truly missed him but he had not uncovered the subtlety of her meaning as yet. He studied her eyes, and then he knew what she was saying, and he said only, 'Oh.'

She knew that he knew then, and she cocked one eyebrow

saucily and slowly gave one exaggerated nod of her head, repeating his 'oh,' soundlessly rounding her lips.

'You're just a fleshpot,' he said jokingly.

She nodded.

'You only love me because I have a clean, strong, young body.'

She nodded.

'Will you marry me?'

She nodded.

'I've only asked you about a dozen times so far.'

She shrugged and nodded, enjoying herself immensely.

'When?'

She pointed at him.

'All right, I'll set the date. I'm getting my vacation in August. I'll marry you then, okay?'

She sat perfectly still, staring at him.

'I mean it.'

She seemed ready to cry again. He took her in his arms and said, 'I mean it, Teddy. Teddy, darling, I mean it. Don't be silly about this, Teddy, because I honestly, truly mean it. I love you, and I want to marry you, and I've wanted to marry you for a long, long time now, and if I have to keep asking you, I'll go nuts. I love you just the way you are, I wouldn't change any of you, darling, so don't get silly, please don't get silly again. It . . . it doesn't matter to me, Teddy. Little Teddy, little Theodora, it doesn't matter to me, can you understand that? You're *more* than any other woman, so much more, so please marry me.'

She looked up at him, wishing she could speak because she could not trust her eyes now, wondering why someone as beautiful as Steve Carella, as wonderful as Steve Carella, as brave and as strong and as marvellous as Steve Carella would want to marry a girl like her, a girl who could never say, 'I love you, darling. I adore you.' But he had asked her again, and now, close in the circle of his arms, now she could believe that it didn't really matter to him, that to him she was as whole as any woman, 'more than any other woman', he had said.

'Okay?' he asked. 'Will you let me make you honest?'

She nodded. The nod was a very small one.

'You mean it this time?'

She did not nod again. She lifted her mouth, and she put her answer into her lips, and his arms tightened around her, and she knew that he understood her. She broke away from him, and he said, 'Hey!' but she trotted away from his reach and went to the kitchen.

When she brought back the champagne, he said, 'I'll be damned!'

She sighed, agreeing that he undoubtedly would be damned, and he slapped her playfully on the fanny.

She handed him the bottle, did a deep curtsy, which was ludicrous in the prisoner pyjamas, and then sat on the floor cross-legged while he struggled with the cork.

The champagne exploded with an enormous pop, and though she did not hear the sound, she saw the cork leave the neck of the bottle and ricochet off the ceiling, and she saw the bubbly white fluid overspilling the lip and running over his hands.

She began to clap, and then she got to her feet and went for glasses, and he poured first a little of the wine into his, saying, 'That's the way it's done, you know. It's supposed to take off the skim and the bugs and everything,' and then filling her glass, and then going back to pour his to the brim.

'To us,' he toasted.

She opened her arms slowly, wider and wider and wider.

'A long, long, happy love,' he supplied.

She nodded happily.

'And our marriage in August.' They clinked glasses, and then sipped at the wine, and she opened her eyes wide in pleasure and cocked her head appreciatively.

'Are you happy?' he asked.

Yes, her eyes said, yes, yes.

'Did you mean what you said before?'

She raised one brow inquisitively.

'About ... missing me?'

Yes, yes, yes, yes, her eyes said.

'You're beautiful.'

She curtsied again.

'Everything about you. I love you, Teddy. Jesus, how I love you.'

She put down the wine glass and then took his hand. She kissed the palm of the hand, and the back, and then she led him into the bedroom, and she unbuttoned his shirt and pulled it out of his trousers, her hands moving gently. He lay down on the bed, and she turned off the light and then, unselfconsciously, unembarrassedly, she took off the pyjamas and went to him.

And while they made gentle love in a small room in a big apartment house, a man named David Foster walked towards his own apartment, an apartment he shared with his mother.

And while their love grew fierce and then gentle again, a man named David Foster thought about his partner Mike Reardon, and so immersed in his thoughts was he that he did not hear the footsteps behind him, and when he finally did hear them, it was too late.

He started to turn, but a ·45 automatic spat orange flame into the night, once, twice, again, again, and David Foster clutched at his chest, and the red blood burst through his brown fingers, and then he hit the concrete – dead.

CHAPTER SEVEN

There is not much you can say to a man's mother when the man is dead. There is not much you can say at all.

Carella sat in the doilied easy chair and looked across at Mrs Foster. The early afternoon sunlight seeped through the drawn blinds in the small, neat living-room, narrow razor-edge bands of brilliance against the cool dimness. The heat in the streets was still insufferable, and he was thankful for the cool living-room, but his topic was death, and he would have preferred the heat.

Mrs Foster was a small, dried-up woman. Her face was wrinkled and seamed, as brown as David's had been. She sat hunched in the chair, a small withered woman with a withered face and withered hands, and he thought: *A strong wind would blow her away, poor woman*, and he watched the grief that lay quietly contained behind the expressionless withered face.

'David was a good boy,' she said. Her voice was hollow, a narrow sepulchral voice. He had come to talk of death, and now he could smell death on this woman, could hear death in the creak of her voice, and he thought it strange that David Foster, her son, who was alive and strong and young several hours ago was now dead – and his mother, who had probably longed for the peaceful sleep of death many a time, was alive and talking to Carella.

'Always a good boy. You raise 'em in a neighbourhood like this one,' Mrs Foster said, 'and you fear for how they'll turn out. My husband was a good worker, but he died young, and it wasn't always easy to see that David wasn't needing. But he was a good boy, always. He would come home and tell me what the other boys were doing, the stealing and all the things they were doing, and I knew he was all right.'

'Yes, Mrs Foster,' Carella said.

'And they all liked him around here, too,' Mrs Foster went on, shaking her head. 'All the boys he grew up with, and all the old folks, too. The people around here, Mr Carella, they don't take much to cops. But they liked my David because he grew up among them, and he was a part of them, and I guess they were sort of proud of him, the way I was proud.'

'We were all proud of him, Mrs Foster,' Carella said.

'He was a good cop, wasn't he?'

'Yes, he was a fine cop.'

'Then why would anyone want to kill him?' Mrs Foster asked. 'Oh, I knew his job was a dangerous one, yes, but this is different, this is senseless. He wasn't even on duty. He was coming home. Who would want to shoot my boy, Mr Carella. Who would want to shoot my boy?'

'That's what I wanted to talk to you about, Mrs Foster. I hope you don't mind if I ask a few questions.'

'If it'll help you find the man who killed David, I'll answer questions all day for you.'

'Did he ever talk about his work?'

'Yes, he did. He always told me what happened around the precinct, what you were working on. He told me about his partner being killed, and he told me he was leafing through pictures in his mind, just waiting until he hit the right one.'

'Did he say anything else about the pictures? Did he say he suspected anyone?'

'No.'

'Mrs Foster, what about his friends?'

'Everyone was his friend.'

'Did he have an address book or anything in which their names might be listed?'

'I don't think he had an address book, but there's a pad near the telephone he always used.'

'May I have that before I leave?'

'Certainly.'

'Did he have a sweetheart?'

'No, not anyone steady. He went out with a lot of different girls.'

'Did he keep a diary?'

'No.'

'Does he have a photograph collection?'

'Yes, he liked music a lot. He was always playing his records whenever he—'

'No, not phonograph. Photograph.'

'Oh. No. He carried a few pictures in his wallet, but that's all.'

'Did he ever tell you where he went on his free time?'

'Oh, lots of different places. He liked the theatre a lot. The stage, I mean. He went often.'

'These boyhood friends of his. Did he pal around with them much?'

'No, I don't think so.'

'Did he drink?'

'Not heavily.'

'I mean, would you know whether or not he frequented any of the bars in the neighbourhood? Social drinking, of course.'

'I don't know.'

'Had he received any threatening letters or notes that you know of?'

'He never mentioned any.'

'Ever behave peculiarly on the telephone?'

'Peculiarly? What do you mean?'

'Well, as if he were trying to hide something from you. Or as if he were worried . . . anything like that. I'm thinking of threatening calls, Mrs Foster.'

'No, I don't ever remember him acting strange on the phone.'

'I see. Well . . .' Carella consulted his notes. 'I guess that's about it. I want to get going, Mrs Foster, because there's a lot of work to do. If you could get me that telephone pad . . .'

'Yes, of course.' She rose, and he watched her slight body

as she moved out of the cool living-room into one of the bedrooms. When she returned, she handed him the pad and said, 'Keep it as long as you like.'

'Thank you. Mrs Foster, please know that we all share your sorrow,' he said lamely.

'Find my boy's killer,' Mrs Foster said. She extended one of her withered hands and took his hand in a strong, firm grip, and he marvelled at the strength of the grip, and at the strength in her eyes and on her face. Only when he was in the hallway, with the door locked behind him, did he hear the gentle sobs that came from within the apartment.

He went downstairs and out to the car. When he reached the car, he took off his jacket, wiped his face, and then sat behind the wheel to study his worksheet:

STATEMENT OF EYEWITNESSES: None.

MOTIVE: Revenge? Con? Tie-in with Mike? Check Ballistics report.

NUMBER OF MURDERERS: Two? One Mike, one David. Or tie-in? B.R. again.

WEAPONS: ·45 automatic.

ROUTE OF MURDERER: ?

DIARIES, JOURNALS, LETTERS, ADDRESSES, TELEPHONE NUMBERS, PHOTOGRAPHS: Check with David's mthr.

ASSOCIATES, RELATIVES, SWEETHEARTS, ENEMIES, ETC.: Ditto.

PLACES FREQUENTED, HANG-OUTS: Ditto.

HABITS: Ditto.

TRACES AND CLUES FOUND ON THE SCENE: Heelprint in dog faeces. At Lab now. Four shells. Two bullets. Ditto.

FINGERPRINTS FOUND: None.

Carella scratched his head, sighed against the heat, and then headed back for the precinct house to see if the new Ballistics report had come in yet.

The widow of Michael Reardon was a full-breasted woman in her late thirties. She had dark hair and green eyes, and an Irish nose spattered with a clichéful of freckles. She had a face for merry-go-rounds and roller-coaster rides, a face that could split in laughter and girlish glee when water was splashed on her at the seashore. She was a girl who could get drunk sniffing the vermouth cork before it was passed over a martini. She was a girl who went to church on Sundays, a girl who'd belonged to the Newman Club when she was younger, a girl who was a virgin two days after Mike had taken her for his bride. She had good legs, very white, and a good body, and her name was May.

She was dressed in black on the hot afternoon of 25 July, and her feet were planted firmly on the floor before her, and her hands were folded in her lap, and there was no laughter on the face made for roller-coaster rides.

'I haven't told the children yet,' she said to Bush. 'The children don't know. How can I tell them? What can I say?'

'It's a rough thing,' Bush said in his quiet voice. His scalp felt sticky and moist. He needed a haircut, and his wild red hair was shrieking against the heat.

'Yes,' May said. 'Can I get you a beer or something? It's very hot. Mike used to take a beer when he got home. No matter what time it was, he always took a beer. He was a very well-ordered person. I mean, he did things carefully and on schedule. I think he wouldn't have been able to sleep if he didn't have that glass of beer when he got home.'

'Did he ever stop in the neighbourhood bars?'

'No. He always drank here, in the house. And never whisky. Only one or two glasses of beer.'

Mike Reardon, Bush thought. *He used to be a cop and a friend. Now he's a victim and a corpse, and I ask questions about him.*

'We were supposed to get an air-conditioning unit,' May said. 'At least, we talked about it. This apartment gets awfully hot. That's because we're so close to the building next door.'

56

'Yes,' Bush said. 'Mrs Reardon, did Mike have any enemies that you know of? I mean, people he knew outside his line of duty?'

'No, I don't think so. Mike was a very easy-going sort. Well, you worked with him. You know.'

'Can you tell me what happened the night he was killed? Before he left the house?'

'I was sleeping when he left. Whenever he had the twelve-to-eight tour, we argued about whether we should try to get any sleep before he went in.'

'Argued?'

'Well, you know, we discussed it. Mike preferred staying up, but I have two children, and I'm beat when it hits ten o'clock. So he usually compromised on those nights, and we both got to bed early – at about nine, I suppose.'

'Were you asleep when he left?'

'Yes. But I woke up just before he went out.'

'Did he say anything to you? Anything that might indicate he was worried about an ambush? Had he received a threat or anything?'

'No.' May Reardon glanced at her watch. 'I have to be leaving soon, Detective Bush. I have an appointment at the funeral parlour. I wanted to ask you about that. I know you're doing tests on ... on the body and all ... but the family ... Well, the family is kind of old-fashioned and we want to ... we want to make arrangements. Do you have any idea when ... when you'll be finished with him?'

'Soon, Mrs Reardon. We don't want to miss any bets. A careful autopsy may put us closer to finding his killer.'

'Yes, I know. I didn't want you to think ... it's just the family. They ask questions. They don't understand. They don't know what it means to have him gone, to wake up in the morning and not ... not have him here.' She bit her lip and turned her face from Bush. 'Forgive me. Mike wouldn't ... wouldn't like this. Mike wouldn't want me to ...' She shook her head and swallowed heavily. Bush watched her, feeling sudden empathy for this woman who was Wife, feeling sudden compassion for all women everywhere who had ever had their men torn from them by violence. His thoughts wandered to Alice, and he wondered idly how she would feel if he stopped a bullet, and then he put the thought out of his mind. It wasn't good to think things like that. Not these days. Not after two in a row. Jesus, was it possible there was a nut loose? Somebody who'd marked the whole goddamn precinct as his special target?

Yes, it was possible.

It was very damn possible, and so it wasn't good to think about things like Alice's reaction to his own death. You thought about things like that, and they consumed your mind, and then when you needed a clear mind which could react quickly to possible danger, you didn't have it. And that's when you were up the creek without a paddle.

What had Mike Reardon been thinking of when he'd been gunned down?

What had been in the mind of David Foster when the four slugs ripped into his body?

Of course, it was possible the two deaths were unrelated. Possible, but not very probable. The m.o. was remarkably similar, and once the Ballistics report came through they'd know for sure whether they were dealing with one man or two.

Bush's money was on the one-man possibility.

'If there's anything else you want to ask me,' May said. She had pulled herself together now, and she faced him squarely, her face white, her eyes large.

'If you'll just collect any address books, photographs, telephone numbers, newspaper clippings he may have saved, anything that may give us a lead on to his friends or even his relatives, I'd be much obliged.'

'Yes, I can do that,' May said.

'And you can't remember anything unusual that may have some bearing on this, is that right?'

'No, I can't. Detective Bush, what am I going to tell the kids? I sent them off to a movie. I told them their daddy was out on a plant. But how long can I keep it from them? How do you tell a pair of kids that their father is dead? Oh God, what am I going to do?'

Bush remained silent. In a little while, May Reardon went for the stuff he wanted.

At 3.42 p.m. on 25 July, the Ballistics report reached Carella's desk. The shells and bullets found at the scene of Mike Reardon's death had been put beneath the comparison microscope together with the shells and bullets used in the killing of David Foster.

The Ballistics report stated that the same weapon had been used in both murders.

CHAPTER EIGHT

On the night that David Foster was killed, a careless mongrel searching for food in garbage cans, had paused long enough to sully the sidewalk of the city. The dog had been careless, to be sure, and a human being had been just as careless, and there was a portion of a heelprint for the Lab boys to work over, solely because of this combined record of carelessness. The Lab boys turned to with something akin to distaste.

The heelprint was instantly photographed, not because the boys liked to play with cameras, but simply because they knew accidents frequently occurred in the making of a cast. The heelprint was placed on a black-stained cardboard scale, marked off in inches. The camera, supported above the print by a reversible tripod, the lens parallel to the print to avoid any false perspectives, clicked merrily away. Satisfied that the heelprint was now preserved for posterity – photographically, at least – the Lab boys turned to the less antiseptic task of making the cast.

One of the boys filled a rubber cup with half a pint of water. Then he spread plaster of Paris over the water, taking care not to stir it, allowing it to sink to the bottom of its own volition. He kept adding plaster of Paris until the water couldn't absorb any more of it, until he'd dumped about ten ounces of it into the cup. Then he brought the cup to one of the other boys who was preparing the print to take the mixture.

Because the print was in a soft material, it was sprayed first with shellac and then with a thin coat of oil. The plaster of Paris mixture was stirred and then carefully applied to the prepared print. It was applied with a spoon in small portions. When the print was covered to a thickness of about one-third of an inch, the boys spread pieces of twine and sticks on to the plaster to reinforce it, taking care that the debris did not touch the bottom of the print and destroy its details. They then applied another coat of plaster to the print, and allowed the cast to harden. From time to time, they touched the plaster, feeling for warmth, knowing that warmth meant the cast was hardening.

Since there was only one print, and since it was not even a full print, and since it was impossible to get a Walking Picture from this single print, and since the formula

$$H \frac{r}{l} \text{ BS } \frac{ra \; rv \; raa}{la \; lv \; laa} \cdot \frac{ll \; lb}{rl \; rb} \; X,$$

a formula designed to give the complete picture of a man's walk in terms of step length, breadth of step, length of left foot, right foot, greatest width of left foot, right foot, wear on heel and sole – since the formula could not be applied to a single print, the Lab boys did all they could with what they had.

And they decided, after careful study, that the heel was badly worn on the outside edge, a peculiarity which told them the man belonging to that heel undoubtedly walked with a somewhat duck-like waddle. They also decided that the heel was not the original heel of the shoe, that it was a rubber heel which had been put on during a repair job, and that the third nail from the shank side of the heel, on the left, had been bent when applying the new heel.

And – quite coincidentally *if* the heelprint happened to have been left by the murderer – the heel bore the clearly stamped trade name 'O'Sullivan', and everyone knows that O'Sullivan is America's Number One Heel.

The joke was an old one. The Lab boys hardly laughed at all.

The newspapers were not laughing very much, either.

The newspapers were taking this business of cop-killing quite seriously. Two morning tabloids, showing remarkable versatility in headlining the same incident, respectively reported the death of David Foster with the words SECOND COP SLAIN and KILLER SLAYS 2ND COP.

The afternoon tabloid, a newspaper hard-pressed to keep up with the circulation of the morning sheets, boldly announced KILLER ROAMS STREETS. And then, because this particular newspaper was vying for circulation, and because this particular newspaper made it a point to 'expose' anything which happened to be in the public's eye at the moment – anything from Daniel Boone to long winter underwear, anything which gave them a free circulation ride on the then-popular bandwagon – their front page carried a red banner that day, and the red banner shouted 'The Police Jungle – What Goes On In Our Precincts' and then in smaller white type against the red, 'See Murray Schneider, p. 4.'

And anyone who had the guts to wade through the first three pages of cheesecake and chest-thumping liberalism, discovered on page four that Murray Schneider blamed the deaths of Mike Reardon and David Foster upon 'the graft-loaded corruptness of our filth-ridden Gestapo'.

In the graft-loaded Squad Room of the corrupt 87th Precinct, two detectives named Steve Carella and Hank Bush stood behind a filth-ridden desk and pored over several cards their equally corrupt fellow officers had dug from the Convictions file.

'Try this for size,' Bush said.

'I'm listening,' Carella said.

'Some punk gets pinched by Mike and Dave, right?'

'Right.'

'The judge throws the book at him, and he gets room and board from the State for the next five or ten years. Okay?'

'Okay.'

'Then he gets out. He's had a lot of time to mull this over, a lot of time to build up his original peeve into a big hate. The one thing in his mind is to get Mike and Dave. So he goes out for them. He gets Mike first, and then he tries to get

Dave quick, before this hate of his cools down. Wham, he gets Dave, too.'

'It reads good,' Carella said.

'That's why I don't buy this Flannagan punk.'

'Why not?'

'Take a look at the card. Burglary, possession of burglary tools, a rape away back in '47. Mike and Dave got him on the last burglary pinch. This was the first time he got convicted, and he drew ten, just got out last month on parole after doing five years.'

'So.'

'So I don't figure a guy with a big hate is going to be good enough to cut ten years to five. Besides, Flannagan never carried a gun all the while he was working. He was a gent.'

'Guns are easy to come by.'

'Sure. But I don't figure him for our man.'

'I'd like to check him out, anyway,' Carella said.

'Okay, but I want to check this other guy out first. Ordiz. Luis 'Dizzy' Ordiz. Take a look at the card.'

Carella pulled the conviction card closer. The card was a 4 × 6 white rectangle, divided into printed rectangles of various sizes and shapes.

'A hophead,' Carella said.

'Yeah. Figure the hate a hophead can build in four years' time.'

'He went the distance?'

'Got out the beginning of the month,' Bush said. 'Cold turkey all that time. This don't build brotherly love for the cops who made the nab.'

'No, it doesn't.'

'Figure this, too. Take a look at his record. He was picked up in '51 on a dis cond charge. This was before he got on the junk, allegedly. But he was carrying a ·45. The gun had a busted hammer, but it was still a ·45. Go back to '49. Again, dis cond, fighting in a bar. Had a ·45 on him, no busted

	NAME OF PRISONER	
Precinct	(Surname)	(First Name and Init.)

87th	ORDIZ	LUIS "DIZZY"

Date & Time of Arrest **Address of Prisoner**

May 2, 1952 7:00 PM 635 6th St. South

Sex	Color	Date of Birth Mo. Day Year	Place of Birth	Alien ~~Citizen~~
M	Whte	8 12 1912	San Juan, Puerto Rico	

Social Condition **Read and Write** **Occupation** **Employed**
Married (Single) Yes (No) Dishwasher Yes (No)

Charge	Specific Offense	Date-Time Occurrence
Violation PL 1751 Subdiv. 1	Poss. of nar- cotics with intent to sell.	5/2/52 7:00 PM

Pct. Complaint No. **Place of Occurrence** **Precinct**
33A-411
D.B. Complaint No. 635 6th St.
DD 179-52 South 87th

Name of Complainant **Address of Complainant**

Arresting Officer(s) (Name-s) Michael Reardon &
David Foster
(Rank) Det. 3rd & **(Command)**
Det. 2nd Gr. Det. Bureau

(Pickup) Complaint **Authority** Warrant F.O.A.

Action of Court

Sentenced four years at state
penitentiary, Ossining, New York

Date	Judge	Court
7/6/52	Fields	

hammer this time. He got off lucky that time. Suspended sentence.'

'Seems to favour ·45s.'

'Like the guy who killed Mike and Dave. What do you say?'

'I say we take a look. Where is he?'

Bush shrugged. 'Your guess is as good as mine.'

Danny Gimp was a man who'd had polio when he was a child. He was lucky in that it had not truly crippled him. He had come out of the disease with only a slight limp, and a nickname which would last him the rest of his life. His real surname was Nelson, but very few people knew that, and he was referred to in the neighbourhood as Danny Gimp. Even his letters came addressed that way.

Danny was fifty-four years old, but it was impossible to judge his age from his face or his body. He was very small, small all over, his bones, his features, his eyes, his stature. He moved with the loose-hipped walk of an adolescent, and his voice was high and reedy, and his face bore hardly any wrinkles or other telltale signs of age.

Danny Gimp was a stool pigeon.

He was a very valuable man, and the men of the 87th Precinct called him in regularly, and Danny was always ready to comply – whenever he could. It was a rare occasion when Danny could not supply the piece of information the bulls were looking for. On these occasions, there were other stoolies to talk to. Somewhere, somebody had the goods. It was simply a question of finding the right man at the right time.

Danny could usually be found in the third booth on the right-hand side of a bar named Andy's Pub. He was not an alcoholic, nor did he even drink to excess. He simply used the bar as a sort of office. It was cheaper than paying rent someplace Downtown, and it had the added attraction of a phone booth, which he used regularly. The bar, too, was a good place to listen – and listening was one half of Danny's business. The other half was talking.

He sat opposite Carella and Bush, and first he listened. Then he talked.

'Dizzy Ordiz,' he said. 'Yeah, yeah.'

'You know where he is?'

'What'd he do?'

'We don't know.'

'Last I heard, he was on the state.'

'He got out at the beginning of the month.'

'Parole?'

'No.'

'Ordiz, Ordiz. Oh, yeah. He's a junkie.'

'That's right.'

'Should be easy to locate. What'd he do?'

'Maybe nothing,' Bush said. 'Maybe a hell of a lot.'

'Oh, you thinking of these cop kills?' Danny asked.

Bush shrugged.

'Not Ordiz. You're barkin' up the wrong tree.'

'What makes you say so?'

Danny sipped at his beer, and then glanced up at the rotating fan. 'You'd never know there was a fan going in this dump, would you? Jesus, this heat don't break soon, I'm headin' for Canada. I got a friend up there. Quebec. You ever been to Quebec?'

'No,' Bush said.

'Nice there. Cool.'

'What about Ordiz?'

'Take him with me, he wants to come,' Danny said, and then he began laughing at his own joke.

'He's cute today,' Carella said.

'I'm cute all the time,' Danny said. 'I got more dames lined up outside my room than you can count on an abacus. I'm the cutest.'

'We didn't know you was pimping,' Bush said.

'I ain't. This is all for love.'

'How much love you got for Ordiz?'

'Don't know him from a hole in the wall. Don't care to, either. Hopheads make me puke.'

'Okay, then where is he?'

'I don't know yet. Give me some time.'

'How much time?'

'Hour, two hours. Junkies are easy to trace. Talk to a few pushers, zing, you're in. He got out the beginning of the month, huh? That means he's back on it strong by now. This should be a cinch.'

'He may have kicked it,' Carella said. 'It may not be such a cinch.'

'They never kick it,' Danny said. 'Don't pay attention to fairy tales. He was probably gettin' the stuff sneaked in even up the river. I'll find him. But if you think he knocked off your buddies, you're wrong.'

'Why?'

'I seen this jerk around. He's a nowhere. A real *trombenik*, if you dig foreign. He don't know enough to come in out of an atom bomb attack. He got one big thing in his life. Horse. That's Ordiz. He lives for the White God. Only thing on his mind.'

'Reardon and Foster sent him away,' Carella said.

'So what? You think a junkie bears a grudge? All part of the game. He ain't got time for grudges. He only got time for meetin' his pusher and makin' the buy. This guy Ordiz, he was always half-blind on the stuff. He couldn't see straight enough to shoot off his own big toe. So he's gonna cool two cops? Don't be ridic.'

'We'd like to see him, anyway,' Bush said.

'Sure. Do I tell you how to run Headquarters? Am I the commissioner? But this guy is from Squaresville, fellas, I'm telling you. He wouldn't know a ·45 from a cement mixer.'

'He's owned a few in his life,' Carella said.

'Playing with them, playing with them. If one of them things ever went off within a hundred yards of him, he'd have diarrhoea for a week. Take it from me, he don't care about nothin' but heroin. Listen, they don't call him Dizzy for nothing. He's dizzy. He's got butterflies up here. He chases them away with H.'

'I don't trust junkies,' Bush said.

'Neither do I,' Danny answered. 'But this guy ain't a killer, take it from me. He don't even know how to kill time.'

'Do us a favour,' Carella said.

'Sure.'

'Find him for us. You know our number.'

'Sure. I'll buzz you in an hour or so. This is gonna be a cinch. Hopheads are a cinch.'

CHAPTER NINE

The heat on that 26th July reached a high of 95.6°F at twelve noon. At the precinct house, two fans circulated the soggy air that crawled past the open windows and the grilles behind them. Everything in the Detective Squad Room seemed to wilt under the steady, malignant pressure of the heat. Only the file cabinets and the desks stood at strict attention. Reports, file cards, carbon paper, envelopes, memos, all of these were damp and sticky to the touch, clinging to wherever they were dropped, clinging with a moist limpidity.

The men in the Squad Room worked in their shirt sleeves. Their shirts were stained with perspiration, large dark amoeba blots which nibbled at the cloth, spreading from beneath the armpits, spreading from the hollow of the spinal column. The fans did not help the heat at all. The fans circulated the suffocating breath of the city, and the men sucked in the breath and typed up their reports in triplicate, and checked their worksheets, and dreamt of summers in the White Mountains, or summers in Atlantic City with the ocean slapping their faces. They called complainants, and they called suspects, and their hands sweated on the black plastic of the phone, and they could feel Heat like a living thing which invaded their bodies and seared them with a million white-hot daggers.

Lieutenant Byrnes was as hot as any man in the Squad Room. His office was just to the left of the slatted dividing railing, and it had a large corner window, but the window was wide open and not a breath of a breeze came through it. The reporter sitting opposite him looked cool. The reporter's name was Savage, and the reporter was wearing a blue seersucker suit and a dark blue Panama, and the reporter was smoking a cigarette and casually puffing the smoke up at the

69

ceiling where the heat held it in a solid blue-grey mass.

'There's nothing more I can tell you,' Byrnes said. The reporter annoyed him immensely. He did not for a moment believe that any man on this earth had been born with a name like 'Savage'. He further did not believe that any man on this earth, on this day, could actually be as cool as Savage pretended he was.

'Nothing more, Lieutenant?' Savage asked, his voice very soft. He was a handsome man with close-cropped blond hair and a straight, almost-feminine nose. His eyes were grey, cool. Cool.

'Nothing,' the Lieutenant said. 'What the hell did you expect? If we knew who did it, we'd have him in here, don't you think?'

'I should imagine so,' Savage said. 'Suspects?'

'We're working on it.'

'Suspects?' Savage repeated.

'A few. The suspects are our business. You splash them on your front page, and they'll head for Europe.'

'Think a kid did it?'

'What do you mean, a kid?'

'A teenager.'

'Anybody could've done it,' Byrnes said. 'For all I know, *you* did it.'

Savage smiled, exposing bright white teeth. 'Lots of teen-age gangs in this precinct, aren't there?'

'We've got the gangs under control. This precinct isn't the garden spot of the city, Savage, but we like to feel we're doing the best possible here. Now I realize your newspaper may take offence at that, but we really try, Savage, we honestly try to do our little jobs.'

'Do I detect sarcasm in your voice, Lieutenant?' Savage asked.

'Sarcasm is a weapon of the intellectual, Savage. Everybody, especially your newspaper, knows that cops are just stupid, plodding beasts of burden.'

'My paper never said that, Lieutenant.'

'No?' Byrnes shrugged. 'Well, you can use it in tomorrow's edition.'

'We're trying to help,' Savage said. 'We don't like cops getting killed any more than you do.' Savage paused. 'What about the teenage gang idea?'

'We haven't even considered it. This isn't the way those gangs operate. Why the hell do you guys try to pin everything that happens in this city on the teenagers? My son is a teenager, and he doesn't go around killing cops.'

'That's encouraging,' Savage said.

'The gang phenomenon is a peculiar one to understand,' Byrnes said. 'I'm not saying we've got it licked, but we do have it under control. If we've stopped the street rumbles, and the knifings and shootings, then the gangs have become nothing more than social clubs. As long as they stay that way, I'm happy.'

'Your outlook is a strangely optimistic one,' Savage said coolly. 'My newspaper doesn't happen to believe the street rumbles have stopped. My newspaper is of the opinion that the death of these two cops may be traced directly to these "social clubs".'

'Yeah?'

'Yeah.'

'So what the hell do you want me to do about it? Round up every kid in the city and shake him down? So your goddamn newspaper can sell another million copies?'

'No. But we're going ahead with our own investigation. And if we crack this, it won't make the 87th Precinct look too good.'

'It won't make Homicide North look too good, either. And it won't make the Police Commissioner look good. It'll make everybody in the department look like amateurs as contrasted with the super-sleuths of your newspaper.'

'Yes, it might,' Savage agreed.

'I have a few words of advice for you, Savage.'

'Yes?'

'The kids around here don't like questions asked. You're not dealing with Snob Hill teenagers who tie on a doozy by drinking a few cans of beer. You're dealing with kids whose code is entirely different from yours or mine. Don't get yourself killed.'

'I won't,' Savage said, smiling resplendently.

'And one other thing.'

'Yes?'

'Don't foul up my precinct. I got enough headaches without you and your half-assed reporters stirring up more trouble.'

'What's more important to you, Lieutenant?' Savage asked. 'My not fouling up your precinct – or my not getting killed?'

Byrnes smiled and then began filling his pipe. 'They both amount to about the same thing,' he said.

The call from Danny Gimp came in fifty minutes. The desk Sergeant took the call, and then plugged it in to Carella's line.

'87th Detective Squad,' he said. 'Carella here.'

'Danny Gimp.'

'Hello, Danny, what've you got?'

'I found Ordiz.'

'Where?'

'This a favour, or business?' Danny asked.

'Business,' Carella said tersely. 'Where do I meet you?'

'You know Jenny's?'

'You kidding?'

'I'm serious.'

'If Ordiz is a junkie, what's he doing on Whore Street?'

'He's blind in some broad's pad. You're lucky you get a few mumbles out of him.'

'Whose pad?'

'That's what we meet for, Steve. No?'

'Call me "Steve" face-to-face, and you'll lose some teeth, pal,' Carella said.

72

'Okay, *Detective* Carella. You want this dope, I'll be in Jenny's in five minutes. Bring some loot.'

'Is Ordiz heeled?'

'He may be.'

'I'll see you,' Carella said.

'La Vía de Putas' was a street which ran North and South for a total of three blocks. The Indians probably had their name for it, and the teepees that lined the path in those rich days of beaver pelts and painted beads most likely did a thriving business even then. As the Indians retreated to their happy hunting grounds and the well-worn paths turned to paved roads, the teepees gave way to apartment buildings, and the practitioners of the world's oldest profession claimed the plush-lined cubby holes as their own. There was a time when the street was called 'Piazza Putana' by the Italian immigrants, and 'The Hussy Hole' by the Irish immigrants. With the Puerto Rican influx, the street had changed its language – but not its sole source of income. The Puerto Ricans referred to it as 'La Vía de Putas'. The cops called it 'Whore Street'. In any language, you paid your money, and you took your choice.

The gals who ran the sex emporiums called themselves Mama-this or Mama-that. Mama Theresa's was the best-known joint on the Street. Mama Carmen's was the filthiest. Mama Luz's had been raided by the cops sixteen times because of some of the things that went on behind its crumbling brick façade. The cops were not above visiting any of the various Mamas on social calls, too. The business calls included occasional raids and occasional rake-offs. The raids were interesting sometimes, but they were usually conducted by members of the Vice Squad who were unfamiliar with the working arrangements some of the 87th Precinct cops had going with the madams. Nothing can screw up a good deal like an ignorant cop.

Carella, perhaps, was an ignorant cop. Or an honest one, depending how you looked at it. He met Danny Gimp at

Jenny's, which was a small café on the corner of Whore Street, a café which allegedly served old-world absinthe, complete with wormwood and water to mix the stuff in. No old-world absinthe drinker had ever been fooled by Jenny's stuff, but the café still served as a sort of no-man's-land between the respectable workaday world of the proletariat, and the sinful shaded halls of the brothels. A man could hang his hat in Jenny's, and a man could have a drink there, and a man could pretend he was on a fraternity outing there, and with the third drink, he was ready to rationalize what he was about to do. Jenny's was something necessary to the operation of the Street. Jenny's, to stretch a point, served the same purpose as the shower stall does in a honeymoon suite.

On 26 July, with the heat baking the black paint that covered the lower half of Jenny's front window – a window which had been smashed in some dozen times since the establishment was founded – Carella and Danny were not interested in the Crossing-the-Social-Barrier aspects of Jenny's bistro. They were interested in a man named Luis 'Dizzy' Ordiz, who may or may not have pumped a total of six bullets into a total of two cops. Bush was out checking on the burglar named Flannagan. Carella had come down in a squad car driven by a young rookie named Kling. The squad car was parked outside now, with Kling leaning against the fender, his head erect, sweltering even in his summer blues. Tufts of blond hair stuck out of his lightweight hat. He was hot. He was hot as hell.

Inside, Carella was hot, too. 'Where is he?' he asked Danny.

Danny rolled the ball of his thumb against the ball of his forefinger. 'I haven't had a square meal in days,' he said.

Carella took a ten spot from his wallet and fed it to Danny.

'He's at Mama Luz's,' Danny said. 'He's with a broad they call La Flamenca. She ain't so hot.'

'What's he doing there?'

'He copped from a pusher a couple of hours back. Three

decks of H. He stumbled over to Mama Luz with amorous intentions, but the H won the battle. Mama Luz tells me he's been dozing for the past sixty.'

'And La Flamenca?'

'She's with him, probably cleaned out his wallet by this time. She's a big red-headed job with two gold teeth in the front of her mouth, damn near blind you with them teeth of hers. She's got mean hips, a big job, real big. Don't get rough with her, less she swallow you up in one gobble.'

'Is he heeled?' Carella asked.

'Mama Luz don't know. She don't think so.'

'Doesn't the red-head know?'

'I didn't ask the red-head,' Danny said. 'I don't deal with the hired help.'

'Then how come you know about her hips?' Carella asked.

'Your ten spot don't buy my sex life,' Danny said, smiling.

'Okay,' Carella said, 'thanks.'

He left Danny at the table and went over to where Kling was leaning on the fender.

'Hot,' Kling said.

'You want a beer, go ahead,' Carella told him.

'No, I just want to go home.'

'Everybody wants to go home,' Carella said. 'Home is where you pack your rod.'

'I never understand detectives,' Kling said.

'Come on, we have a visit to make,' Carella said.

'Where?'

'Up the street. Mama Luz. Just point the car; it knows the way.'

Kling took off his hat and ran one hand through his blond hair. 'Phew,' he said, and then he put on his hat and climbed in behind the wheel. 'Who are we looking for?'

'Man named Dizzy Ordiz.'

'Never heard of him.'

'He never heard of you, either,' Carella said.

'Yeah,' Kling said dryly, 'well, I'd appreciate it if you introduced us.'

'I will,' Carella said, and he smiled as Kling set the car in motion.

Mama Luz was standing in the doorway when they pulled up. The kids on the sidewalk wore big grins, expecting a raid. Mama Luz smiled and said, 'Hello, Detective Carella. Hot, no?'

'Hot,' Carella agreed, wondering why in hell everybody and his brother commented about the weather. It was certainly obvious to anyone but a half-wit that this was a very hot day, that this was a suffocatingly hot day, that this was probably hotter than a day in Manila, or even if you thought Calcutta hotter, this was still a lotta hotter heat than that.

Mama Luz was wearing a silk kimono. Mama Luz was a big fat woman with a mass of black hair pulled into a bun at the back of her head. Mama Luz used to be a well-known prostitute, allegedly one of the best in the city, but now she was a madam and never indulged, except for friends. She was scrupulously clean, and always smelled of lilacs. Her complexion was as white as any complexion can be, more white because it rarely saw the sun. Her features were patrician, her smile was angelic. If you didn't know she ran one of the wildest brothels on the Street, you might have thought she was somebody's mother.

She wasn't.

'You come on a social call?' she asked Carella, winking.

'If I can't have you, Mama Luz,' Carella said, 'I don't want anybody.'

Kling blinked, and then wiped the sweatband of his hat.

'For you, *toro*,' Mama Luz said, winking again, 'Mama Luz does anything. For you, Mama Luz is a young girl again.'

'You've always been a young girl,' Carella said, and he slapped her on the backside, and then said, 'Where's Ordiz?'

'With *la roja*,' Mama Luz said. 'She has picked his eyes out by now.' She shrugged. 'These new girls, all they are interested in is money. In the old days . . .' Mama Luz cocked her head wistfully. 'In the old days, *toro*, there was sometimes love, do you know? What has happened to love nowadays, eh?'

'It's all locked up in that fat heart of yours,' Carella said. 'Does Ordiz have a gun?'

'Do I shake down my guests?' Mama Luz said. 'I don't think he has a gun, Stevie. You will not shoot up the works, will you? This has been a quiet day.'

'No, I will not shoot up the works,' Carella said. 'Show me where he is.'

Mama Luz nodded. As Kling passed her, she looked down at his fly, and then laughed uproariously when he blushed. She followed the two cops in, and then passed them and said, 'This way. Upstairs.'

The stairs shook beneath her. She turned her head over her shoulder, winked at Carella, and said, 'I trust you behind me, Stevie.'

'*Gracias*,' Carella said.

'Don't look up my dress.'

'It's a temptation, I'll admit,' Carella said, and behind him he heard Kling choke back a cross between a sob and a gasp.

Mama Luz stopped on the first landing. 'The door at the end of the hall. No blood, Stevie, please. With this one, you do not need blood. He is half-dead already.'

'Okay,' Carella said. 'Get downstairs, Mama Luz.'

'And later, when the work is done,' Mama Luz said suggestively, and she bumped one fleshy hip against Carella, almost knocking him off his feet. She went past Kling, laughing, her laughter trailing up the stairwell.

Carella sighed and looked at Kling. 'What're you gonna do, kid,' he said, 'I'm in love.'

'I never understand detectives,' Kling said.

They went down the hallway. Kling drew his service revolver when he saw Carella's was already in his hand.

'She said no shooting,' he reminded Carella.

'So far, she only runs a whore house,' Carella said. 'Not the Police Department.'

'Sure,' Kling said.

Carella rapped on the door with the butt of his ·38.

'*Quién es?*' a girl's voice asked.

'Police,' Carella said. 'Open up.'

'*Momento*,' the voice said.

'She's getting dressed,' Kling advised Carella.

In a few moments, the door opened. The girl standing there was a big red-head. She was not smiling, so Carella did not have the opportunity to examine the gold teeth in the front of her mouth.

'What you want?' she asked.

'Clear out,' Carella said. 'We want to talk to the man in there.'

'Sure,' she said. She threw Carella a look intended to convey an attitude of virginity offended, and then she swivelled past him and slithered down the hallway. Kling watched her. When he turned back to the door, Carella was already in the room.

There was a bed in the room, and a night-table, and a metal wash-basin. The shade was drawn. The room smelled badly. A man lay on the bed in his trousers. His shoes and socks were off. His chest was bare. His eyes were closed, and his mouth was open. A fly buzzed around his nose.

'Open the window,' Carella said to Kling. 'Jesus, this place stinks.'

The man on the bed stirred. He lifted his head and looked at Carella.

'Who are you?' he said.

'Your name Ordiz?' Carella asked.

'Yeah. You a cop?'

'Yes.'

'What did I do wrong now?'

Kling opened the window. From the streets below came the sound of children's voices.

'Where were you Sunday night?'

'What time?'

'Close to midnight.'

'I don't remember.'

'You better, Ordiz. You better start remembering damn fast. You shoot up just now?'

'I don't know what you mean.'

'You're an H-man, Ordiz, and we know it, and we know you copped three decks a little while back. Are you stoned now, or can you read me?'

'I hear you,' Ordiz said.

He passed a hand over his eyes. He owned a thin face with a hatchet nose and thick, rubbery lips. He needed a shave badly.

'Okay, talk.'

'Friday night, you said?'

'I said Sunday.'

'Sunday. Oh yeah. I was at a poker game.'

'Where?'

'South 4th. What's the matter, you don't believe me?'

'You got witnesses?'

'Five guys in the game. You can check with any one of them.'

'Give me their names.'

'Sure. Louie DeScala, and his brother, John. Kid named Pete Diaz. Another kid they call Pepe. I don't know his last name.'

'That's four,' Carella said.

'I was the fifth.'

'Where do these guys live?'

Ordiz reeled off a string of addresses.

'Okay, what about Monday night?'

'I was home.'

'Anybody with you?'

'My landlady.'

'What?'

'My landlady was with me. What's the matter, don't you hear good?'

'Shut up, Dizzy. What's her name?'

'Olga Pazio.'

'Address?'

Ordiz gave it to him. 'What am I supposed to done?' he asked.

'Nothing. You got a gun?'

'No. Listen, I been clean since I got out.'

'What about those three decks?'

'I don't know where you got that garbage. Somebody's fooling you, cop.'

'Sure. Get dressed, Dizzy.'

'What for? I paid for the use of this pad.'

'Okay, you used it already. Get dressed.'

'Hey, listen, what for? I tell you I've been clean since I got out. What the hell, cop?'

'I want you at the precinct while I check these names. You mind?'

'They'll tell you I was with them, don't worry. And that junk about the three decks, Jesus, I don't know where you got that from. Hell, I ain't been near the stuff for years now.'

'That's plain to see,' Carella said. 'Those scabs on your arm are from beri-beri or something, I guess.'

'Huh?' Ordiz asked.

'Get dressed.'

Carella checked with the men Ordiz had named. Each of them was willing to swear that he'd been at the poker game from ten-thirty on the night of 23 July, to 4 a.m. on the morning of 24 July. Ordiz's landlady reluctantly admitted she had spent the night of the 24th and the morning of the 25th in Ordiz's room. Ordiz had solid alibis for the times someone had spent killing Reardon and Foster.

When Bush came back with his report on Flannagan, the boys were right back where they'd started.

'He's got an alibi as long as the Texas Panhandle,' Bush said.

Carella sighed, and then took Kling down for a beer before heading over to see Teddy.

Bush cursed the heat, and then went home to his wife.

CHAPTER TEN

From where Savage sat at the end of the bar, he could plainly see the scripted lettering on the back of the boy's brightly coloured jacket. The boy had caught his eye the moment Savage entered the bar. He'd been sitting in a booth with a dark-haired girl, and they'd both been drinking beer. Savage had seen the purple and gold jacket and then sat at the bar and ordered a gin and tonic. From time to time, he'd glanced over at the couple. The boy was thin and pale, a shock of black hair crowning his head. The collar of the jacket was turned up, and Savage could not see the lettering across the back at first because the boy sat with his back tight against the padded cushioning of the booth.

The girl finished her beer and left, but the boy did not vacate the booth. He turned slightly, and that was when Savage saw the lettering, and that was when the insistent idea at the back of his mind began to take full shape and form.

The lettering on the jacket read: The Grovers.

The name had undoubtedly been taken from the name of the park that hemmed in the 87th Precinct, but it was a name that rang a bell in Savage's head, and it didn't take long for that bell to begin echoing and re-echoing. The Grovers had been responsible for a good many of the street rumbles in the area, including an almost titanic struggle in one section of the park, a struggle featuring knives, broken bottles, guns, and sawed-off stickball bats. The Grovers had made their peace with the cops, or so the story went, but the persistent idea that one of the gangs was responsible for the deaths of Reardon and Foster would not leave Savage's mind.

And here was a Grover.

Here was a boy to talk to.

Savage finished his gin and tonic, left his stool, and walked over to where the boy was sitting alone in the booth.

'Hi,' he said.

The boy did not move his head. He raised only his eyes. He said nothing.

'Mind if I sit down?' Savage asked.

'Beat it, mister,' the boy said.

Savage reached into his jacket pocket. The boy watched him silently. He took out a package of cigarettes, offered one to the boy and, facing the silent refusal, hung one on his own lip.

'My name's Savage,' he said.

'Who cares?' the boy answered.

'I'd like to talk to you.'

'Yeah? What about?'

'The Grovers.'

'Mister, you don't live around here, do you?'

'No.'

'Then, Dad, go home.'

'I told you. I want to talk.'

'I don't. I'm waitin' for a deb. Take off while you still got legs.'

'I'm not scared of you, kid, so knock off the rough talk.'

The boy appraised Savage coolly.

'What's your name?' Savage asked.

'Guess, Blondie.'

'You want a beer?'

'You buying?'

'Sure,' Savage said.

'Then make it a rum-coke.'

Savage turned towards the bar. 'Rum-coke,' he called, 'and another gin and tonic.'

'You drink gin, huh?' the boy said.

'Yes. What's your name, son?'

'Rafael,' the boy said, still studying Savage closely. 'The guys call me Rip.'

'Rip. That's a good name.'

'Good as any. What's the matter, you don't like it?'

'I like it,' Savage said.

'You a nab?'

'A what?'

'A cop.'

'No.'

'What then?'

'I'm a reporter.'

'Yeah?'

'Yes.'

'So whattya want from me?'

'I only want to talk.'

'What about?'

'Your gang.'

'What gang?' Rip said. 'I don't belong to no gang.'

The waiter brought the drinks. Rip tasted his and said, 'That bartender's a crook. He cuts the juice here. This tastes like cream soda.'

'Here's luck,' Savage said.

'You're gonna need it,' Rip replied.

'About the Grovers . . .'

'The Grovers are a club.'

'Not a gang?'

'Whatta we need a gang for? We're a club, that's all.'

'Who's president?' Savage asked.

'That's for me to know and you to find out,' Rip answered.

'What's the matter? You ashamed of the club?'

'Hell, no.'

'Don't you want to see it publicized in a newspaper? There isn't another club in the neighbourhood that ever got a newspaper's full treatment.'

'We don't need no treatment. We got a big rep as it is. Ain't nobody in this city who ain't heard of The Grovers. Who you tryin' to snow, mister?'

'Nobody. I just thought you'd like some public relations work.'

'What the hell's that?'

'A favourable Press.'

'You mean . . .' Rip furrowed his brow. 'What do you mean?'

'An article telling about your club.'

'We don't need no articles. You better cut out, Dad.'

'Rip, I'm trying to be your friend.'

'I got plenty friends in The Grovers.'

'How many?'

'There must be at least . . .' Rip stopped short. 'You're a wise bastard, ain't you?'

'You don't have to tell me anything you don't want to, Rip. Why do the boys call you "Rip"?'

'We all got nicknames. That's mine.'

'But why?'

'Because I can handle a blade good.'

'Did you ever have to?'

'Handle one? You kidding? In this neighbourhood, you don't carry a knife or a piece, you're dead. Dead, man.'

'What's a piece, Rip?'

'A gun.' Rip opened his eyes wide. 'You don't know what a piece is? Man, you ain't been.'

'Do The Grovers have many pieces?'

'Enough.'

'What kind?'

'All kinds. What do you want? We got it.'

'·45s?'

'Why do you ask?'

'Nice gun, a ·45.'

'Yeah, it's big,' Rip said.

'Do you ever use these pieces?'

'You got to use them. Man, you think these diddlebops are for fun? You got to use whatever you can get your hands on. Otherwise, you wind up with a tag on your toe.' Rip drank a little more of the rum. 'This neighbourhood ain't a cream puff, Dad. You got to watch yourself all the time. That's why it helps to belong to The Grovers. They see this jacket comin' down the street, they got respect. They know if they mess with me, they got *all* The Grovers to mess with.'

'The police, you mean?'

'Naw, who wants Law trouble? We steer away from them. Unless they bother us.'

'Any cops bother you lately?'

'We got a thing on with the cops. They don't bother us, we don't bother them. Man, there ain't been a rumble in months. Things are very quiet.'

'You like it that way?'

'Sure, why not? Who wants his skull busted? The Grovers want peace. We never punk out, but we never go lookin' for trouble, either. Only time we get involved is when we're challenged, or when a stud from another club tries to make it with one of our debs. We don't go for that kind of crap.'

'So you've had no trouble with the police lately?'

'Few little skirmishes. Nothing to speak of.'

'What kind of skirmishes?'

'Agh, one of the guys was on mootah. So he got a little high, you know. So he busted a store window, for kicks, you know? So one of the cops put the arm on him. He got a suspended sentence.'

'*Who* put the arm on him?'

'Why you want to know?'

'I'm just curious.'

'One of the bulls, I don't remember who.'

'A detective?'

'I said a bull, didn't I?'

'How'd the rest of The Grovers feel about this?'

'How do you mean?'

'About this detective pulling in one of your boys?'

'Agh, the kid was a Junior, didn't know his ass from his elbow. Nobody shoulda given him a reefer to begin with. You don't handle a reefer right ... well, you know, the guy was just a kid.'

'And you felt no resentment for the cop who'd pulled him in?'

'Huh?'

'You had nothing against the cop who pulled him in?'

Rip's eyes grew suddenly wary. 'What're you drivin' at, mister?'

'Nothing, really.'

'What'd you say your name was?'

'Savage.'

'Why you askin' about how we feel about cops?'

'No reason.'

'Then why you askin'?'

'I was just curious.'

'Yeah,' Rip said flatly. 'Well, I got to go now. I guess that deb ain't comin' back.'

'Listen, stick around a while,' Savage said. 'I'd like to talk some more.'

'Yeah?'

'Yes, I would.'

'That's tough, pal,' Rip said. 'I wouldn't.' He got out of the booth. 'Thanks for the drink. I see you around.'

'Sure,' Savage said.

He watched the boy's shuffling walk as he moved out of the bar. The door closed behind him, and he was gone.

Savage studied his drink. There *had* been trouble between The Grovers and a cop – a detective, in fact. So his theory was not quite as far-fetched as the good lieutenant tried to make it. He sipped at his drink, thinking, and when he'd finished it, he ordered another. He walked out of the bar about ten minutes later, passing two neatly dressed men on his way out.

The two men were Steve Carella and a patrolman in street clothes – a patrolman named Bert Kling.

CHAPTER ELEVEN

Bush was limp when he reached the apartment.

He hated difficult cases, but only because he felt curiously inadequate to cope with them. He had not been joking when he'd told Carella he felt detectives weren't particularly brilliant men. He thoroughly believed this, and whenever a difficult case popped up, his faith in his own theory was reaffirmed. Legwork and stubbornness, that was all it amounted to.

So far, the legwork they'd done had brought them no closer to the killer than they originally were. The stubbornness? Well, that was another thing again. They would keep at it, of course. Until the break came. When would the break come? Today? Tomorrow? Never?

The hell with the case, he thought. I'm home. A man is entitled to the luxury of leaving his goddamn job at the office. A man is entitled to a few peaceful hours with his wife.

He pushed his key into the lock, twisted it, and then threw the door open.

'Hank?' Alice called.

'Yes.' Her voice sounded cool. Alice always sounded cool. Alice was a remarkable woman.

'Do you want a drink?'

'Yes. Where are you?'

'In the bedroom. Come on in, there's a nice breeze here.'

'A breeze? You're kidding.'

'No, seriously.'

He took off his jacket and threw it over the back of a chair. He was pulling off his shirt as he went into the bedroom. Bush never wore undershirts. He did not believe in the theory of sweat absorption. An undershirt, he held, was simply an additional piece of wearing apparel, and in this weather the idea was to get as close to the nude as possible.

He ripped off his shirt with almost savage intensity. He had a broad chest matted with curling red hair that matched the thatch on his head. The knife scar ran its crooked path down his right arm.

Alice lay in a chaise near the open window. She wore a white blouse and a straight black skirt. She was barefoot, and her legs were propped up on the window-sill, and the black skirt rustled mildly with the faint breeze that came through the window. She had drawn her blonde hair back into a pony tail. He went to her, and she lifted her face for his kiss, and he noticed the thin film of perspiration on her upper lip.

'Where's that drink?' he asked.

'I'll mix it,' she said. She swung her feet off the window-sill, and the skirt pulled back for an instant, her thigh winking at him. He watched her silently, wondering what it was about this woman that was so exciting, wondering if all married men felt this way about their wives even after ten years of marriage.

'Get that gleam out of your eyes,' she said, reading his face.

'Why?'

'It's too damn hot.'

'I know a fellow who claims the best way . . .'

'I know about that fellow.'

'Is in a locked room on the hottest day of the year with the windows closed under four blankets.'

'Gin and tonic?'

'Good.'

'I heard that vodka and tonic is better.'

'We'll have to get some.'

'Busy day at the mine?'

'Yes. You?'

'Sat around and worried about you,' Alice said.

'I see all those grey hairs sprouting.'

'He belittles my concern,' Alice said to the air. 'Did you find that killer yet?'

'No.'

'Do you want a lime in this?'

'If you like.'

'Means going into the kitchen. Be a doll and drink it this way.'

'I'm a doll,' Bush said.

She handed him the drink. Bush sat on the edge of the bed. He sipped at the drink, and then leaned forward, the glass dangling at the ends of his long muscular arms.

'Tired?'

'Pooped.'

'You don't look very tired.'

'I'm so pooped, I'm peeped.'

'You always say that,' Alice said. 'I wish you wouldn't always say that. There are things you always say.'

'Like what?'

'Well, like that, for one.'

'Name another.'

'When we're driving in the car and there are fixed traffic signals. Whenever you begin hitting the lights right, you say "We're in with the boys".'

'So what's wrong with that?'

'Nothing, the first hundred times.'

'Oh, hell.'

'Well, it's true.'

'All right, all right. I'm not peeped. I'm not even pooped.'

'I'm hot,' Alice said.

'So am I.'

She began unbuttoning her blouse, and even before he looked up, she said, 'Don't get ideas.'

She took off the blouse and draped it over the back of the chaise. She owned large breasts, and they were crowded into a filmy white brassière. The front slope of the cups was covered with a sheer nylon inset, and he could see the insistent pucker of her nipples. It reminded him of pictures he had seen in *National Geographic* at the dentist's office, the time he'd had that periodontal work done. The girls on Bali.

Nobody had breasts like the girls on Bali. Except maybe Alice.

'What'd you do all day?' he asked.

'Nothing much.'

'Were you in?'

'Most of the time.'

'So what'd you do?'

'Sat around, mostly.'

'Mmmm.' He could not take his eyes from the brassière. 'Did you miss me?'

'I always miss you,' she said flatly.

'I missed you.'

'Drink your drink.'

'No, really.'

'Well, good,' she said, and she smiled fleetingly. He studied the smile. It was gone almost instantly, and he had the peculiar feeling that it had been nothing more than a duty smile.

'Why don't you get some sleep?' she asked.

'Not yet,' he said, watching her.

'Hank, if you think . . .'

'What?'

'Nothing.'

'I've got to go in again later,' he said.

'They're really pushing on this one, aren't they?'

'Lots of pressure,' he said. 'I think the Old Man is scared he's next.'

'I'll bet it's all over,' Alice said. 'I don't think there'll be another killing.'

'You can never tell,' Bush said.

'Do you want something to eat before you turn in?' she asked.

'I'm not turning in yet.'

Alice sighed. 'You can't escape this damn heat,' she said. 'No matter what you do, it's always with you.' Her hand went to the button at the side of her skirt. She undid it, and

91

then pulled down the zipper. The skirt slid to her feet, and she stepped out of it. She was wearing white nylon panties frilled with a gossamer web of puffed nylon at each leg. She walked to the window, and he watched her. Her legs were long and clean.

'Come here,' he said.

'No. I don't want to, Hank.'

'All right,' he said.

'Do you think it'll cool off tonight?'

'I doubt it.' He watched her closely. He had the distinct impression that she was undressing for him, and yet she'd said ... He tweaked his nose, puzzled.

She turned from the window. Her skin was very white against the white of her underwear. Her breasts bulged over the edges of the inadequate bra. 'You need a haircut,' she said.

'I'll try to get one tomorrow. We haven't had a minute.'

'Oh, goddamn this heat, anyway,' she said, and she reached behind her to unclasp the bra. He watched her breasts spill free, watched as she tossed the bra across the room. She walked to mix herself another drink, and he could not take his eyes from her. *What's she trying to do?* he wondered. *What the hell is she trying to do to me?*

He rose swiftly, walking to where she stood. He put his arms around her, and his hands cupped her breasts.

'Don't,' she said.

'Baby ...'

'Don't.' Her voice was firm, a cold edge to it.

'Why not?'

'Because I say so.'

'Well, then why the hell are your parading around like—'

'Take your hands off me, Hank. Let me go.'

'Aw, baby ...'

She broke away from him. 'Get some sleep,' she said. 'You're tired.' There was something strange in her eyes, an almost malicious gleam.

'Can't—'

'No.'

'For Christ's sake, Alice . . .'

'No!'

'All right.'

She smiled quickly. 'All right,' she repeated.

'Well . . .' Bush paused. 'I'd . . . I'd better get to bed.'

'Yes. You'd better.'

'What I can't understand is why—'

'You won't even need a sheet in this weather,' Alice interrupted.

'No, I guess not.'

He went to the bed and took off his shoes and socks. He didn't want to undress because he didn't want to give her the satisfaction, now that he'd been denied, of knowing how she'd affected him. He took off his trousers and quickly got into the bed, pulling the sheet to his throat.

Alice watched him, smiling. 'I'm reading *Anapurna*,' she said.

'So?'

'I just happened to think of it.'

Bush rolled over on to his side.

'I'm still hot,' Alice said. 'I think I'll take a shower. And then maybe I'll catch an air-conditioned movie. You don't mind, do you?'

'No,' Bush mumbled.

She walked to the side of the bed and stood there for a moment, looking down at him. 'Yes, I think I'll take a shower.' Her hands went to her hips. Slowly, she rolled the panties down over the flatness of her stomach, past the hard jut of her crotch, over the whiteness of her thighs. The panties dropped to the floor, and she stepped out of them and stood by the bed looking down at Bush, smiling.

He did not move. He kept his eyes on the floor, but he could see her feet and her legs, but he did not move.

93

'Sleep tight, darling,' she whispered, and then she went into the bathroom.

He heard the shower when it began running. He lay on the soggy sheet and listened to the steady machine-gunning of the water. Then, over the sound of the shower, came the sound of the telephone, splitting the silence of the room.

He sat up and reached for the instrument.

'Hello?'

'Bush?'

'Yes?'

'This is Havilland. You better get down here right away.'

'What's the matter?' Bush asked.

'You know that young rookie Kling?'

'Yeah?'

'He was just shot in a bar on Culver.'

CHAPTER TWELVE

The Squad Room of the 87th resembled nothing so much as the locker room of the Boys' Club when Bush arrived. There must have been at least two dozen teenagers crammed in behind the dividing rail and the desks beyond it. Add to this a dozen or so detectives who were firing questions, the answers to which were coming in two languages, and the bedlam was equivalent to the hush of a hydrogen bomb explosion.

The boys were all wearing brilliantly contrasting purple and gold jackets, and the words 'The Grovers' decorated the back of each jacket. Bush looked for Carella in the crowded room, spotted him, and walked over towards him quickly. Havilland, a tough cop with a cherubic face, shouted at one of the boys, 'Don't give me any guff, you little punk, or I'll break your goddamn arm.'

'You try it, dick,' the kid answered, and Havilland cuffed him across the mouth. The boy staggered back, slamming into Bush as he went by. Bush shrugged his shoulders, and the boy flew back into Havilland's arms, as if he'd been brushed aside by a rhinoceros.

Carella was talking to two boys when Bush approached him.

'Who fired the gun?' he asked.

The boys shrugged.

'We'll throw you all in jail as accessories,' Carella promised.

'What the hell happened?' Bush wanted to know.

'I was having a beer with Kling. Nice, peaceful off-duty beer. I left him there, and ten minutes later, when he's leaving the joint, he gets jumped by these punks. One of them put a slug in him.'

'How is he?'

'He's at the hospital. The slug was a ·22, went through his right shoulder. We figure a zip gun.'

'You think this ties with the other kills?'

'I doubt it. The m.o.'s way off.'

'Then why?'

'How the hell do I know? Looks like the whole city figures it's open season on cops.' Carella turned back to the boys. 'Were you with the gang when the cop was jumped?'

The boys would not answer.

'Okay, fellas,' Carella said, 'play it smart. See what that gets you. See how long The Grovers are gonna last under a rap like this one.'

'We din' shoot no cop,' one of the boys said.

'No? What happened, he shoot himself?'

'You ting we crazy?' the other boy said. 'Shoot a bull?'

'This was a patrolman,' Carella said, 'not a detective.'

'He wass wear a suit,' the first boy said.

'Cops wear suits off-duty,' Bush said. 'Now how about it?'

'Nobody shoot a cop,' the first boy said.

'No, except somebody did.'

Lieutenant Byrnes came out of his office and shouted, 'All right, knock it off! KNOCK IT OFF!'

The room fell immediately silent.

'Who's your talk man?' Byrnes asked.

'I am,' a tall boy answered.

'What's your name?'

'Do-Do.'

'What's your full name?'

'Salvador Jesus Santez.'

'All right, come here, Salvador.'

'The guys call me Do-Do.'

'Okay, come here.'

Santez walked over to where Byrnes was standing. He walked with a shuffle which was considered both hip and cool. The boys in the room visibly relaxed. This was their talk man, and Do-Do was a real gone stud. Do-Do would know how to handle this jive.

'What happened?' Byrnes asked.

'Little skirmish, that's all,' Santez said.

'Why?'

'Jus' like that. We got the word passed down, so we joined the fray.'

'What word?'

'You know, like a scout was out.'

'No, I don't know. What the hell are you talking about?'

'Look, Dad . . .' Santez started.

'You call me "Dad" again,' Byrnes warned, 'and I'll beat you black and blue.'

'Well, gee, Da—' Santez stopped dead. 'What you want to know?'

'I want to know why you jumped a cop.'

'What cop? What're you talkin' about?'

'Look, Santez, don't play this too goddamn cute. You jumped one of our patrolmen as he came out of a bar. You beat him up, and one of your boys put a bullet in his shoulder. Now what the hell's the story?'

Santez considered Byrnes's question gravely.

'Well?'

'He's a cop?'

'What the hell did you think he was?'

'He was wearing a light blue summer suit!' Santez said, his eyes opening wide.

'What the hell's that got to do with it? Why'd you jump him? Why'd you shoot him?'

A mumbling was starting behind Santez. Byrnes heard the mumble and shouted, 'Shut up! You've got your talk man, let *him* talk!'

Santez was still silent.

'What about it, Santez?'

'A mistake,' Santez said.

'That's for damn sure.'

'I mean, we didn't know he was a cop.'

'Why'd you jump him?'

'A mistake, I tell you.'

'Start from the beginning.'

'Okay,' Santez said. 'We been giving you trouble lately?'

'No.'

'Okay. We been minding our own business, right? You never hear from The Grovers, except when we protectin' our own, right? The last rumble you get is over there in The Silver Culvers' territory when they pick on one of our Juniors. Am I right?'

'Go ahead, Santez.'

'Okay. Early today, there's a guy snooping around. He grabs one of our Seniors in a bar, and he starts pumpin' him.'

'Which Senior?'

'I forget,' Santez said.

'Who was the guy?'

'Said he was from a newspaper.'

'What?'

'Yeah. Said his name was Savage, you know him?'

'I know him,' Byrnes said tightly.

'Okay, so he starts askin' like how many pieces we got, and whether we got ·45s, and whether we don't like the Law, things like that. This Senior, he's real hip. He tips right off this guy is trying to mix in The Grovers with the two bulls got knocked off around here. So he's on a newspaper, and we got a rep to protect. We don't want Law trouble. If this jerk goes back to his paper and starts printing lies about how we're mixed in, that ain't good for our rep.'

'So what'd you do, Santez?' Byrnes asked wearily, thinking of Savage, and thinking of how he'd like to wring the reporter's neck.

'So this Senior comes back, and we planned to scare off the reporter before he goes printing any crap. We went back to the bar and waited for him. When he comes out, we jumped

98

him. Only he pulled a gun, so one of the boys plugged him in self defence.'

'Who?'

'Who knows?' Santez said. 'One of the boys burned him.'

'Thinking he was Savage.'

'Sure. How the hell we supposed to know he's a cop instead? He had on a light blue suit, and he had blond hair, like this reporter creep. So we burned him. It was a mistake.'

'You keep saying that, Santez, but I don't think you know just how big a mistake it was. Who fired that shot?'

Santez shrugged.

'Who was the Senior Savage talked to?'

Santez shrugged.

'Is he here?'

Santez had stopped talking, it seemed.

'You know we've got a list of every damn member in your gang, don't you, Santez?'

'Sure.'

'Okay. Havilland, get the list. I want a roll call. Whoever's not here, pick him up.'

'Hey, wait a minute,' Santez said. 'I told you it was all a mistake. You going to get somebody in trouble just 'cause we mistake a cop?'

'Listen to me, Santez, and listen hard. Your gang hasn't been in any trouble recently, and that's fine with us. Call it a truce, call it whatever you want to. But don't ever think, and I mean *ever*, Santez, that you or your boys can shoot anybody in this goddamn precinct and get away with it. You're a bunch of hoods as far as I'm concerned, Santez. You're a bunch of hoods with fancy jackets, and a seventeen-year-old hood is no less dangerous than a fifty-year-old hood. The only reason we haven't been bearing down on you is because you've been behaving yourself. All right, today you stopped behaving yourself. You shot a man in my precinct territory – and that means you're in trouble. That means you're in big trouble.'

Santez blinked.

'Put them all downstairs and call the roll there,' Byrnes said. 'Then get whoever we missed.'

'All right, let's go,' Havilland said. He began herding the boys out of the room.

Miscolo, one of the patrolmen from Clerical, pushed his way through the crowd and walked over to the lieutenant.

'Lieutenant, fella outside wants to see you,' he said.

'Who?'

'Guy named Savage. Claims he's a reporter. Wants to know what the rumble was about this aft—'

'Kick him down the steps,' Byrnes said, and he went back into his office.

CHAPTER THIRTEEN

Homicide, if it doesn't happen too close to home, is a fairly interesting thing.

You can really get involved in the investigation of a homicide case because it is the rare occurrence in the everyday life of a precinct. It is the most exotic crime because it deals with the theft of something universal – a man's life.

Unfortunately, there are other less interesting and more mundane matters to deal with in a precinct, too. And in a precinct like the 87th, these mundane matters can consume a lot of time. There are the rapes, and the muggings, and the rollings, and the knifings, and the various types of disorderly conducts, and the breakings and entries, and the burglaries, and the car thefts, and the street rumbles, and the cats caught in sewers, and oh, like that. Many of these choice items of crime are promptly turned over to special squads within the department, but the initial squeal none the less goes to the precinct in which the crime is being committed, and these squeals can keep a man hopping.

It's not so easy to hop when the temperature is high.

For cops, shocking as the notion may sound at first, are human beings. They sweat like you and me, and they don't like to work when it's hot. Some of them don't like to work even when it's cool. None of them like to draw Line-up, especially when it's hot.

Steve Carella and Hank Bush drew Line-up on Thursday, 27 July.

They were especially displeased about it because Line-up is held only from Mondays to Thursdays, and if they had missed it this Thursday, chances were they would not pull the duty unit the following week and perhaps – just perhaps – the heat would have broken by then.

The morning started the way most mornings were starting that week. There was a deceptive coolness at first, a coolness which – despite the prognostications of television's various weather men and weather women – seemed to promise a delightful day ahead. The delusions and flights of fancy fled almost instantly. It was apparent within a half-hour of being awake that this was going to be another scorcher, that you would meet people who asked, 'Hot enough for you?' or who blandly and informatively remarked, 'It's not the heat; it's the humidity.'

Whatever it was, it was hot.

It was hot where Carella lived in the suburb of Riverhead, and it was hot in the heart of the city – on High Street, where Headquarters and the line-up awaited.

Since Bush lived in another suburb – Calm's Point, west and a little south of Riverhead – they chose to meet at Headquarters at eight forty-five, fifteen minutes before the line-up began. Carella was there on the dot.

At eight-fifty, Bush strolled up. That is to say, he more or less crawled on to the pavement and slouched over to where Carella was standing and puffing on a cigarette.

'Now I know what Hell is like,' he said.

'Wait until the sun really starts shining,' Carella said.

'You cheerful guys are always good for an early-morning laugh,' Bush answered. 'Let me have a cigarette, will you?'

Carella glanced at his watch. 'Time we were up there.'

'Let it wait. We've got a few minutes yet.' He took the cigarette Carella offered, lit it, and blew out a stream of smoke. 'Any new corpses today?'

'None yet.'

'Pity. I'm getting so I miss my morning coffee and corpse.'

'The city,' Carella said.

'What?'

'Look at it. What a goddamn monster.'

'A hairy bastard,' Bush agreed.

'But I love her.'

'Yeah,' Bush said noncommittally.

'It's too hot to work today. This is a day for the beach.'

'The beaches'll be jammed. You're lucky you've got a nice line-up to attend.'

'Sure, I know. Who wants a cool, sandy beach with the breakers rolling in and—'

'You Chinese?'

'Huh?'

'You know your torture pretty good.'

'Let's go upstairs.'

They flipped their cigarettes away and entered the Headquarters building. The building had once boasted clean red brick and architecture which was modern. The brick was now covered with the soot of five decades, and the architecture was as modern as a chastity belt.

They walked into the first-floor marbled entryway, past the dick Squad Room, past the Lab, past the various records rooms. Down a shaded hallway, a frosted glass door announced 'Commissioner of Police'.

'I'll bet *he's* at the beach,' Carella said.

'He's in there hiding behind his desk,' Bush said. 'He's afraid the 87th maniac is going to get him next.'

'Maybe he's not at the beach,' Carella amended. 'I understand this building has a swimming-pool in the basement.'

'Two of them,' Bush said. He rang for the elevator. They waited in hot, suffering silence for several moments. The elevator doors slid open. The patrolman inside was sweating.

'Step into the iron coffin,' he said.

Carella grinned. Bush winced. Together they got into the car.

'Line-up?' the patrolman asked.

'No, the swimming-pool,' Bush cracked.

'Jokes I can't take in this heat,' the patrolman said.

'Then don't supply straight lines,' Bush said.

'Abbott and Costello I've got with me,' the patrolman said,

and then he lapsed into silence. The elevator crawled up the intestinal tract of the building. It creaked. It whined. Its walls were moist with the beaded exhalations of its occupants.

'Nine,' the patrolman said.

The doors slid open. Carella and Bush stepped into a sunlit corridor. Simultaneously, they reached for the leather cases to which their shields were pinned. Again simultaneously, they pinned the tin to their collars and then walked towards the desk behind which another patrolman was seated.

The patrolman eyed the tin, nodded, and they passed the desk and walked into a large room which served many purposes at Headquarters. The room was built with the physical proportions of a gymnasium, and did indeed have two basketball hoops, one at each end of the room. The windows were wide and tall, covered with steel mesh. The room was used for indoor sport, lectures, swearing in of rookies, occasional meetings of the Police Benevolent Association or the Police Honour Legion and, of course, the line-ups.

For the purpose of these Monday-to-Thursday parades of felony offenders, a permanent stage had been set up at the far end of the room, beneath the balcony there, and beyond the basketball hoop. The stage was brilliantly lighted. Behind the stage was a white wall, and upon the wall in black numerals was the graduated height scale against which the prisoners stood.

In the front of the stage, and stretching back towards the entrance doorways for about ten rows, was an array of folding-chairs, most of which were occupied by detectives from all over the city when Bush and Carella entered. The blinds at the windows had already been drawn, and a look at the raised dais and speaking stand behind the chairs showed that the Chief of Detectives was already in position and the strawberry festival would start in a few moments. To the left of the stage, the felony offenders huddled in a group, lightly guarded by several patrolmen and several detectives, the men who had made the arrests. Every felony offender who'd been picked up in the city the day before would be paraded across the stage this morning.

The purpose of the line-up, you see – despite popular misconception about the identification of suspects by victims, a practice which was more helpful in theory than in actual usage – was simply to acquaint as many detectives as possible with the men who were doing evil in their city. The ideal set-up would have been to have each detective in each precinct at each scheduled line-up, but other pressing matters made this impossible. So two men were chosen each day from each precinct, on the theory that if you can't acquaint all of the people all of the time, you can at least acquaint some of them some of the time.

'All right,' the Chief of Detectives said into his microphone, 'let's start.'

Carella and Bush took seats in the fifth row as the first two offenders walked on to the stage. It was the practice to show the offenders as they'd been picked up, in pairs, in a trio, a quartet, whatever. This simply for the purpose of establishing an m.o. If the crook works in a pair once, he will generally work in a pair again.

The police stenographer poised his pen above his pad. The Chief of Detectives intoned, 'Diamondback, One,' calling off the area of the city in which the arrest had been made, and the number of the case from that area that day. 'Diamondback, One. Anselmo, Joseph, 17 and Di Palermo, Frederick, 16. Forced the door of an apartment on Cambridge and Gribble. Occupant screamed for help, bringing patrolman to scene. No statement. How about it, Joe?'

Joseph Anselmo was a tall, thin boy with dark black hair and dark brown eyes. The eyes seemed darker than they were because they were set against a pale, white face. The whiteness was attributable to one emotion, and one emotion alone. Joseph Anselmo was scared.

'How about it, Joe?' the Chief of Detectives asked again.

'What do you want to know?' Anselmo said.

'Did you force the door to that apartment?'

'Yes.'

'Why?'

'I don't know.'

'Well, you forced a door, you must have had a reason for doing it. Did you know somebody was in the apartment?'

'No.'

'Did you force it alone?'

Anselmo did not answer.

'How about it, Freddie? Were you with Joe when you broke that lock?'

Frederick Di Palermo was blond and blue-eyed. He was shorter than Anselmo, and he looked cleaner. He shared two things in common with his friend. First, he had been picked up on a felony offence. Second, he was scared.

'I was with him,' Di Palermo said.

'How'd you force the door?'

'We hit the lock.'

'What with?'

'A hammer.'

'Weren't you afraid it would make a noise?'

'We only give it a quick rap,' Di Palermo said. 'We didn't know somebody was home.'

'What'd you expect to get in that apartment?' the Chief of Detectives asked.

'I don't know,' Di Palermo said.

'Now, look,' the Chief of Detectives said patiently, 'you both broke into an apartment. Now we know that, and you just admitted it, so you must have had a reason for going in there. What do you say?'

'The girls told us,' Anselmo said.

'What girls?'

'Oh, some chicks,' Di Palermo answered.

'What'd they tell you?'

'To bust the door.'

'Why?'

'Like that,' Anselmo said.

'Like what?'

'Like for kicks.'

'Only for kicks?'

'I don't know why we busted the door,' Anselmo said, and he glanced quickly at Di Palermo.

'To take something out of the apartment?' the Chief asked.

'Maybe a . . .' Di Palermo shrugged.

'Maybe what?'

'A couple of bucks. You know, like that.'

'You were planning a burglary then, is that right?'

'Yeah, I guess.'

'What'd you do when you discovered the apartment was occupied?'

'The lady screamed,' Anselmo said.

'So we run,' Di Palermo said.

'Next case,' the Chief of Detectives said.

The boys shuffled off the stage to where their arresting officer was waiting for them. Actually, they had said a hell of a lot more than they should have. They'd have been within their rights if they'd insisted on not saying a word at the line-up. Not knowing this, not even knowing that their position was fortified because they'd made no statement when they'd been collared, they had answered the Chief of Detectives with remarkable naïveté. A good lawyer, with a simple charge of unlawfully entering under circumstances or in a manner not amounting to a burglary, would have had his clients plead guilty to a misdemeanour. The Chief of Detectives, however, had asked the boys if they were planning to commit a burglary, and the boys had answered in the affirmative. And the Penal Law, Section 402, defines Burglary in first degree thus:

A person who, with intent to commit some crime therein, breaks and enters, in the night time, the dwelling-house of another, in which there is at the time a human being:

1. Being armed with a dangerous weapon; or
2. Arming himself therein with such a weapon; or
3. Being assisted by a confederate actually present; or . . .

Well, no matter. The boys had very carelessly tied the knot of a felony about their youthful necks, perhaps not realizing that burglary in the first degree is punishable by imprisonment in a state prison for an indeterminate term, the minimum of which shall not be less than ten years and the maximum of which shall not be more than thirty years.

Apparently 'the girls' had told them wrong.

'Diamondback, Two,' the Chief of Detectives said. 'Pritchett, Virginia, 34. Struck her quote husband unquote about the neck and head with a hatchet at 3 a.m. in the morning. No statement.'

Virginia Pritchett had walked on to the stage while the Chief of Detectives was talking. She was a small woman, barely clearing the five-foot-one-inch marker. She was thin, narrow-boned, with red hair of the fine, spider-webby type. She wore no lipstick. She wore no smile. Her eyes were dead.

'Virginia?' the Chief of Detectives said.

She raised her head. She kept her hands close to her waist, one fist folded over the other. Her eyes did not come to life. They were grey, and she stared into the glaring lights unblinkingly.

'Virginia?'

'Yes, sir?' Her voice was very soft, barely audible. Carella leaned forward to catch what she was saying.

'Have you ever been in trouble before, Virginia?' the Chief of Detectives asked.

'No, sir.'

'What happened, Virginia?'

The girl shrugged, as if she too could not comprehend

what had happened. The shrug was a small one, a gesture that would have been similar to passing a hand over the eyes.

'What happened, Virginia?'

The girl raised herself up to her full height, partly to speak into the permanently fixed microphone which dangled several inches before her face on a solid steel pipe, partly because there were eyes on her and because she apparently realized her shoulders were slumped. The room was deathly still. There was not a breeze in the city. Beyond the glaring lights, the detectives sat.

'We argued,' she said, sighing.

'Do you want to tell us about it?'

'We argued from the morning, from when we first got up. The heat. It's . . . it was very hot in the apartment. Right from the morning. You . . . you lose your temper quickly in the heat.'

'Go on.'

'He started with the orange juice. He said the orange juice wasn't cold enough. I told him I'd had it in the ice-box all night, it wasn't my fault it wasn't cold. Diamondback isn't ritzy, sir. We don't have refrigerators in Diamondback, and with this heat, the ice melts very fast. Well, he started complaining about the orange juice.'

'Were you married to this man?'

'No, sir.'

'How long have you been living together?'

'Seven years, sir.'

'Go on.'

'He said he was going down for breakfast, and I said he shouldn't go down because it was silly to spend money when you didn't have to. He stayed, but he complained about the orange juice all the while he ate. It went on like that all day.'

'About the orange juice, you mean?'

'No, other things. I don't remember what. He was watching the ball game on TV, and drinking beer, and he'd pick on little things all day long. He was sitting in his undershorts because of the heat. I had hardly anything on myself.'

'Go on.'

'We had supper late, just cold cuts. He was picking on me all that time. He didn't want to sleep in the bedroom that night, he wanted to sleep on the kitchen floor. I told him it was silly, even though the bedroom is very hot. He hit me.'

'What do you mean, he hit you?'

'He hit me about the face. He closed one eye for me. I told him not to touch me again, or I would push him out the window. He laughed. He put a blanket on the kitchen floor, near the window, and he turned on the radio, and I went into the bedroom to sleep.'

'Yes, go ahead, Virginia.'

'I couldn't sleep because it was so hot. And he had the radio up loud. I went into the kitchen to tell him to please put the radio a little lower, and he said to go back to bed. I went into the bathroom, and I washed my face, and that was when I spied the hatchet.'

'Where was the hatchet?'

'He keeps tools on a shelf in the bathroom, wrenches and a hammer, and the hatchet was with them. I thought I would go out and tell him to put the radio lower again, because it was very hot and the radio was very loud, and I wanted to try to get some sleep. But I didn't want him to hit me again, so I took the hatchet, to protect myself with, in case he tried to get rough again.'

'Then what did you do?'

'I went out into the kitchen with the hatchet in my hands. He had got up off the floor and was sitting in the chair near the window, listening to the radio. His back was to me.'

'Yes.'

'I walked over to him and he didn't turn around, and I didn't say anything to him.'

'What did you do?'

'I struck him with the hatchet.'

'Where?'

'On his head and on his neck.'

'How many times?'

'I don't remember exactly. I just kept hitting him.'

'Then what?'

'He fell off the chair, and I dropped the hatchet, and I went next door to Mr Alanos, he's our neighbour, and I told him I had hit my husband with a hatchet, and he didn't believe me. He came into the apartment, and then he called the police, and an officer came.'

'Your husband was taken to the hospital, did you know that?'

'Yes.'

'Do you know the disposition of his case?'

Her voice was very low. 'I heard he died,' she said. She lowered her head and did not look out past the lights again. Her fists were still folded at her waist. Her eyes were still dead.

'Next case,' the Chief of Detectives said.

'She *murdered* him,' Bush whispered, his voice curiously loaded with awe. Carella nodded.

'Majesta, One,' the Chief of Detectives said. 'Bronckin, David, 27. Had a lamp outage report at 10.24 p.m. last night, corner of Weaver and 69th North. Electric company notified at once, and then another lamp outage two blocks south reported, and then gunfire reported. Patrolman picked up Bronckin on Dicsen and 69th North. Bronckin was intoxicated, was going down the street shooting out lamp-post fixtures. What about it, Dave?'

'I'm only Dave to my friends,' Bronckin said.

'What about it?'

'What do you want from me? I got high, I shot out a few lights. I'll pay for the goddamn lights.'

'What were you doing with the gun?'

'You *know* what I was doing. I was shooting at the lamp-posts.'

'Did you start out with that idea? Shooting at the lamp-posts?'

'Yeah. Listen, I don't have to say anything to you. I want a lawyer.'

'You'll have plenty opportunity for a lawyer.'

'Well, I ain't answering any questions until I get one.'

'Who's asking questions? We're trying to find out what possessed you to do a damn fool thing like shooting at light fixtures.'

'I was high. What the hell, you never been high?'

'I don't go shooting at lamp-posts when I'm high,' the Chief said.

'Well, I do. That's what makes horse races.'

'About the gun.'

'Yeah, I knew we'd get down to the gun sooner or later.'

'Is it yours?'

'Sure, it's mine.'

'Where'd you get it?'

'My brother sent it home to me.'

'Where's your brother?'

'In Korea.'

'Have you got a permit for the gun?'

'It was a gift.'

'I don't give a damn if you *made* it! Have you got a permit?'

'No.'

'Then what gave you the idea you could go around carrying it?'

'I just got the idea. Lots of people carry guns. What the hell are you picking on me for? All I shot was a few lights. Why don't you go after the bastards who are shooting people?'

'How do we know you're not one of them, Bronckin?'

'Maybe I am. Maybe I'm Jack the Ripper.'

'Maybe not. But maybe you were carrying that ·45 and

112

planning a little worse mischief than shooting out a few lights.'

'Sure. I was gonna shoot the Mayor.'

'A ·45,' Carella whispered to Bush.

'Yeah,' Bush said. He was already out of his chair and walking back to the Chief of Detectives.

'All right, smart guy,' the Chief of Detectives said. 'You violated the Sullivan Law, do you know what that means?'

'No, what does it mean, smart guy?'

'You'll find out,' the Chief said. 'Next case.'

At his elbow, Bush said, 'Chief, we'd like to question that man further.'

'Go ahead,' the Chief said. 'Hillside, One. Matheson, Peter, 45 . . .'

CHAPTER FOURTEEN

David Bronckin did not appreciate the idea of being detained from his visit to the Criminal Courts Building, whereto he was being led for arraignment when Carella and Bush intercepted him.

He was a tall man, at least six-three, and he had a very loud voice and a very pugnacious attitude, and he didn't like Carella's first request at all.

'Lift your foot,' Carella said.

'What?'

The men were seated in the Detective Squad Room at Headquarters, a room quite similar to the room of the same name back at the 87th. A small fan atop one of the filing cabinets did its best to whip up the air, but the room valiantly upheld its attitude of sleazy limpidity.

'Lift your foot,' Carella repeated.

'What for?'

'Because I say so,' Carella answered tightly.

Bronckin looked at him for a moment and then said, 'You take off that badge and I'll . . .'

'I'm not taking it off,' Carella said. 'Lift your foot.'

Bronckin mumbled something and then raised his right foot, Carella held his ankle and Bush looked at the heel.

'Cat's Paw,' Bush said.

'You got any other shoes?' Carella asked.

'Sure, I got other shoes.'

'Home?'

'Yeah. What's up?'

'How long have you owned that ·45?'

'Couple of months now.'

'Where were you Sunday night?'

'Listen, I want a lawyer.'

114

'Never mind the lawyer,' Bush said. 'Answer the question.'

'What was the question?'

'Where were you Sunday night?'

'What time Sunday night?'

'About eleven-forty or so.'

'I think I was at a movie.'

'Which movie?'

'The Strand. Yeah, I was at a movie.'

'Did you have the ·45 with you?'

'I don't remember.'

'Yes or no.'

'I don't remember. If you want a yes or no, it'll have to be no. I'm no dope.'

'What picture did you see?'

'An old one.'

'Name it.'

'*The Creature from the Black Lagoon.*'

'What was it about?'

'A monster that comes up from the water.'

'What was the co-feature?'

'I don't remember.'

'Think.'

'Something with John Garfield.'

'What?'

'A prize-fight picture.'

'What was the title?'

'I don't remember. He's a bum, and then he gets to be champ, and then he takes a dive.'

'*Body and Soul*?'

'Yeah, that was it.'

'Call the Strand, Hank,' Carella said.

'Hey, what're you gonna do that for?' Bronckin asked.

'To check and see if those movies were playing Sunday night.'

'They were playing, all right.'

'We're also going to check that ·45 with Ballistics, Bronckin.'

'What for?'

'To see how it matches up against some slugs we've got. You can save us a lot of time.'

'How?'

'What were you doing Monday night?'

'Monday, Monday? Jesus, who remembers?'

Bush had located the number in the directory, and was dialling.

'Listen,' Bronckin said, 'you don't have to call them. Those were the pictures, all right.'

'What were you doing Monday night?'

'I ... I went to a movie.'

'Another movie? Two nights in a row?'

'Yeah. The movies are air-conditioned. It's better than hanging around and suffocating, ain't it?'

'What'd you see?'

'Some more old ones.'

'You like old movies, don't you?'

'I don't care about the picture. I was only tryin' to beat the heat. The places showing old movies are cheaper.'

'What were the pictures?'

'*Seven Brides for Seven Brothers* and *Violent Saturday*.'

'You remember those all right, do you?'

'Sure, it was more recent.'

'Why'd you say you couldn't remember what you did Monday night?'

'I said that?'

'Yes.'

'Well, I had to think.'

'What movie house was this?'

'On Monday night, you mean?'

'Yeah.'

'One of the RKOs. The one on North 80th.'

Bush put the receiver back into its cradle. 'Checks out,

Steve,' he said. '*Creature from the Black Lagoon* and *Body and Soul*. Like he said.' Bush didn't mention that he'd also taken down a time-table for the theatre, or that he knew exactly what times each picture started and ended. He nodded briefly at Carella, passing on the information.

'What time did you go in?'

'Sunday or Monday?'

'Sunday.'

'About eight-thirty.'

'Exactly eight-thirty?'

'Who remembers exactly? It was getting hot, so I went into the Strand.'

'What makes you think it was eight-thirty?'

'I don't know. It was about that time.'

'What time did you leave?'

'About – musta been about a quarter to twelve.'

'Where'd you go then?'

'For some coffee and.'

'Where?'

'The White Tower.'

'How long did you stay?'

'Half-hour, I guess.'

'What'd you eat?'

'I told you. Coffee and.'

'Coffee and *what*?'

'Jesus, a jelly doughnut,' Bronckin said.

'This took you a half-hour?'

'I had a cigarette while I was there.'

'Meet anybody you know there?'

'No.'

'At the movie?'

'No.'

'And you didn't have the gun with you, that right?'

'I don't think I did.'

'Do you usually carry it around?'

'Sometimes.'

'You ever been in trouble with the Law?'

'Yeah.'

'Spell it.'

'I served two at Sing Sing.'

'What for?'

'Assault with a deadly weapon.'

'What was the weapon?'

Bronckin hesitated.

'I'm listening,' Carella said.

'A ·45.'

'This one?'

'No.'

'Which?'

'Another one I had.'

'Have you still got it?'

Again, Bronckin hesitated.

'Have you still got it?' Carella repeated.

'Yes.'

'How come? Didn't the police—'

'I ditched the gun. They never found it. A friend of mine picked it up for me.'

'Did you use the business end?'

'No. The butt.'

'On who?'

'What difference does it make?'

'I want to know. Who?'

'A . . . a lady.'

'A woman?'

'Yes.'

'How old?'

'Forty. Fifty.'

'Which?'

'Fifty.'

'You're a nice guy.'

'Yeah,' Bronckin said.

'Who collared you? Which precinct?'

'Ninety-second, I think.'

'Was it?'

'Yes.'

'Who were the cops?'

'I don't know.'

'The ones who made the arrest, I mean.'

'There was only one.'

'A dick?'

'No.'

'When was this?' Bush asked.

'Fifty-two.'

'Where's that other ·45?'

'Back at my room.'

'Where?'

'831 Haven.'

Carella jotted down the address.

'What else have you got there?'

'You guys going to help me?'

'What help do you need?'

'Well, I keep a few guns.'

'How many?'

'Six,' Bronckin said.

'What?'

'Yeah.'

'Name them.'

'The two ·45s. Then there's a Luger, and a Mauser, and I even got a Tokarev.'

'What else?'

'Oh, just a ·22.'

'All in your room?'

'Yeah, it's quite a collection.'

'Your shoes there, too?'

'Yeah. What's with my shoes?'

'No permits for any of these guns, huh?'

'No. Slipped my mind.'

'I'll bet. Hank, call the Ninety-second. Find out who

119

collared Bronckin in '52. I think Foster started at our house, but Reardon may have been a transfer.'

'Oh,' Bronckin said suddenly.

'What?'

'That's what this is all about, huh? Those two cops.'

'Yes.'

'You're way off,' Bronckin said.

'Maybe. What time you get out of that RKO?'

'About the same. Eleven-thirty, twelve.'

'The other one check, Hank?'

'Yep.'

'Better call the RKO on North 80th and check this one, too. You can go now, Bronckin. Your escort's in the hall.'

'Hey,' Bronckin said, 'how about a break? I helped you, didn't I? How about a break?'

Carella blew his nose.

None of the shoes in Bronckin's apartment owned heels even faintly resembling the heel-print cast the Lab boys had.

Ballistics reported that neither of the ·45s in Bronckin's possession could have fired any of the fatal bullets.

The 92nd Precinct reported that neither Michael Reardon nor David Foster had ever worked there.

There was only one thing the investigators could bank on. The heat.

CHAPTER FIFTEEN

At seven twenty-six that Thursday night, the city looked skyward.

The city had heard a sound, and it paused to identify the sound. The sound was the roll of distant thunder.

And it seemed, simultaneously, as if a sudden breeze sprang up from the north and washed the blistering face of the city. The ominous rolling in the sky grew closer, and now there were lightning flashes, erratic, jagged streaks that knifed the sky.

The people of the city turned their faces upward and waited.

It seemed the rain would never come. The lightning was wild in its fury, lashing the tall buildings, arcing over the horizon. The thunder answered the spitting anger of the lightning, booming its own furious epithets.

And then, suddenly, the sky split open and the rain poured down. Huge drops, and they pelted the sidewalks and the gutters and the streets; and the asphalt and concrete sizzled when the first drops fell; and the citizens of the city smiled and watched the rain, watched the huge drops – God, how big the drops were! – splattering against the ground. And the smiles broadened, and people slapped each other on the back, and it looked as if everything was going to be all right again.

Until the rain stopped.

It stopped as suddenly as it had begun. It had burst from the sky like water that had broken through a dam. It rained for four minutes and thirty-six seconds. And then, as though someone had suddenly plugged the broken wall of the dam, it stopped.

The lightning still flashed across the sky, and the thunder still growled in response, but there was no rain.

The cool relief the rain had brought lasted no more than ten minutes. At the end of that time, the streets were baking again, and the citizens were swearing and mumbling and sweating.

Nobody likes practical jokes.

Even when God is playing them.

She stood by the window when the rain stopped.

She swore mentally, and she reminded herself that she would have to teach Steve sign language, so that he'd know when she was swearing. He had promised to come tonight, and the promise filled her now, and she wondered what she should wear for him.

'Nothing' was probably the best answer. She was pleased with her joke. She must remember it. To tell to him when he came.

The street was suddenly very sad. The rain had brought gaiety, but now the rain was gone, and there was only the solemn grey of the street, as solemn as death.

Death.

Two dead, two men he worked with and knew well, why couldn't he have been a street-cleaner or a flag-pole sitter or something, why a policeman, why a cop?

She turned to look at the clock, wondering what time it was, wondering how long it would be before he came, how long it would be before she spotted the slow, back-and-forth twisting of the knob, before she rushed to the door to open it for him. The clock was no comfort. It would be hours yet. If he came, of course. If nothing else happened, something to keep him at the station house, another killing, another ...

No, I mustn't think of that.

It's not fair to Steve to think that.

If I think of harm coming to him ...

Nothing will happen to him ... no. Steve is strong, Steve is a good cop, Steve can take care of himself. But Reardon was a good cop, and Foster, and they're dead now, how good can a cop be when he's shot in the back with a ·45? How good is any cop against a killer in ambush?

No, don't think these things.

The murders are over now. There will be no more. Foster was the end. It's done. Done.

Steve, hurry.

She sat facing the door, knowing it would be hours yet, but waiting for the knob to turn, waiting for the knob to tell her he was there.

The man rose.

He was in his undershorts. They were gaily patterned, and they fitted him snugly, and he walked from the bed to the dresser with a curiously ducklike motion. He was a tall man, excellently built. He examined his profile in the mirror over the dresser, looked at the clock, sighed heavily, and then went back to the bed.

There was time yet.

He lay and looked at the ceiling, and then he suddenly desired a cigarette. He rose and walked to the dresser again, walking with the strange ducklike waddle which was uncomplimentary to a man of his physique. He lit the cigarette and then went back to the bed, where he lay puffing and thinking.

He was thinking about the cop he would kill later that night.

Lieutenant Byrnes stopped in to chat with Captain Frick, commanding officer of the precinct, before he checked out that night.

'How's it going?' Frick asked.

Byrnes shrugged. 'Looks like we've got the only cool thing in this city.'

'Huh?'

'This case.'

'Oh. Yeah,' Frick said. Frick was tired. He wasn't as young as he used to be, and all this hullabaloo made him tired. If cops got knocked off, those were the breaks. Here today, gone tomorrow. You can't live for ever, and you can't take it with you. Find the perpetrator, sure, but don't push a man too hard. You can't push a man too hard in this heat, especially when he's not as young as he used to be, and tired.

To tell the truth, Frick was a tired man even when he was twenty, and Byrnes knew it. He didn't particularly care for the captain, but he was a conscientious cop, and a conscientious cop checked with the precinct commander every now and then, even if he felt the commander was an egghead.

'You're really working the boys, aren't you?' Frick asked.

'Yes,' Byrnes said, thinking that should have been obvious even to an egghead.

'I figure this for some screwball,' Frick said. 'Got himself a peeve, figured he'd go out and shoot somebody.'

'Why cops?' Byrnes asked.

'Why not? How can you figure what a screwball will do? Probably knocked off Reardon by accident, not even knowing he was a cop. Then saw all the publicity the thing got in the papers, figured it was a good idea, and purposely gunned for another cop.'

'How'd he know Foster *was* a cop? Foster was in street clothes, same as Reardon.'

'Maybe he's a screwball who's had run-ins with the law before, how do I know? One thing's for sure, though. He's a screwball.'

'Or a mighty shrewd guy,' Byrnes said.

'How do you figure that? What brains does it take to pull a trigger?'

'It doesn't take any brains,' Byrnes said. 'Unless you get away with it.'

'He won't,' Frick answered. He sighed expansively. He was

124

tired. He was getting old. Even his hair was white. Old men shouldn't have to solve mysteries in hot weather.

'Hot, ain't it?' Frick said.

'Yes indeed,' Byrnes replied.

'You heading for home now?'

'Yes.'

'Good for you. I'll be taking off in a little while, too. Some of the boys are out on an attempted suicide, though. Want to find out how it turns out. Some dame on the roof, supposed to be ready to jump.' Frick shook his head. 'Screwballs, huh?'

'Yeah,' Byrnes said.

'Sent my wife and kids away to the mountains,' Frick said. 'Damn glad I did. This heat ain't fit for man nor beast.'

'No, it's not,' Byrnes agreed.

The phone on Frick's desk rang. Frick picked it up.

'Captain Frick,' he said. 'What? Oh. Okay, fine. Right.' He replaced the receiver. 'Not a suicide at all,' he said to Byrnes. 'The dame was just drying her hair, had it sort of hanging over the edge of the roof. Screwball, huh?'

'Yes. Well, I'm taking off.'

'Better keep your gun handy. Might get you next.'

'Who?' Byrnes asked, heading for the door.

'Him.'

'Huh?'

'The screwball.'

Roger Havilland was a bull.

Even the other bulls called him a bull. A real bull. He was a 'bull' as differentiated from a 'bull' which was a detective. Havilland was built like a bull, and he ate like a bull, and he screwed like a bull, and he even snorted like a bull. There were no two ways about it. He was a real bull.

He was also not a very nice guy.

There was a time when Havilland was a nice guy, but everyone had forgotten that time, including Havilland. There was a time when Havilland could talk to a prisoner for hours

125

on end without once having to use his hands. There was a time when Havilland did not bellow every other syllable to leave his mouth. Havilland had once been a gentle cop.

But Havilland had once had a most unfortunate thing happen to him. Havilland had tried to break up a street fight one night, being on his way home at the time and being, at the time, that sort of conscientious cop who recognized his duty twenty-four hours a day. The street fight had not been a very big one, as street fights go. As a matter of fact, it was a friendly sort of argument, more or less, with hardly a zip gun in sight.

Havilland stepped in and very politely attempted to bust it up. He drew his revolver and fired a few shots over the heads of the brawlers and somehow or other one of the brawlers hit Havilland on the right wrist with a piece of lead pipe. The gun left Havilland's hand, and then the unfortunate thing happened.

The brawlers, content until then to be bashing in their own heads, suddenly decided a cop's head would be more fun to play upon. They turned on the disarmed Havilland, dragged him into an alley, and went to work on him with remarkable dispatch.

The boy with the lead pipe broke Havilland's arm in four places.

The compound fracture was a very painful thing to bear, more painful in that the damned thing would not set properly and the doctors were forced to rebreak the bones and set them all over again.

For a while there, Havilland doubted if he'd be able to keep his job on the force. Since he'd only recently made Detective 3rd Grade, the prospect was not a particularly pleasant one to him. But the arm healed, as arms will, and he came out of it just about as whole as he went into it – except that his mental attitude had changed somewhat.

There is an old adage which goes something like this: 'One guy can screw it up for the whole company.'

Well, the fellow with the lead pipe certainly screwed it up for the whole company, if not the whole city. Havilland became a bull, a real bull. He had learned his lesson. He would never be cornholed again.

In Havilland's book, there was only one way to beat down a prisoner's resistance. You forgot the word 'down', and you concentrated on beating in the opposite direction: 'up'.

Not many prisoners liked Havilland.

Not many *cops* liked him, either.

It is even doubtful whether or not Havilland liked himself.

'Heat,' he said to Carella, 'is all in the mind.'

'My mind is sweating the same as the rest of me,' Carella said.

'If I told you right this minute that you were sitting on a cake of ice in the middle of the Arctic Ocean, you'd begin to feel cool.'

'I don't feel any cooler,' Carella said.

'That's because you're a jackass,' Havilland said, shouting. Havilland always shouted. When Havilland whispered, he shouted. 'You don't want to feel cool. You want to feel hot. It makes you think you're working.'

'I am working.'

'I'm going home,' Havilland shouted abruptly.

Carella glanced at his watch. It was ten seventeen.

'What's the matter?' Havilland shouted.

'Nothing.'

'It's a quarter after ten, that's what you're looking sour about?' Havilland bellowed.

'I'm not looking sour.'

'Well, I don't care how you look,' Havilland roared. 'I'm going home.'

'So go home. I'm waiting for my relief.'

'I don't like the way you said that,' Havilland answered.

'Why not?'

'It implied that *I* am *not* waiting for my relief.'

Carella shrugged and blithely said, 'Let your conscience be your guide, brother.'

'Do you know how many hours I've been on this job?'

'How many?'

'Thirty-six,' Havilland said. 'I'm so sleepy I could crawl into a sewer and not wake up until Christmastime.'

'You'll pollute our water supply,' Carella said.

'Up yours!' Havilland shouted. He signed out and was leaving when Carella said, 'Hey!'

'What?'

'Don't get killed out there.'

'Up yours,' Havilland said again, and then he left.

The man dressed quietly and rapidly. He put on black trousers and a clean white shirt, and a gold-and-black striped tie. He put on dark blue socks, and then he reached for his shoes. His shoes carried O'Sullivan heels.

He put on the black jacket to his suit, and then he went to the dresser and opened the top drawer. The ·45 lay on his handkerchiefs, lethal and blue-black. He pushed a fresh clip into the gun, and then put the gun into his jacket pocket.

He walked to the door in a ducklike waddle, opened it, took a last look around the apartment, flicked out the lights, and went into the night.

Steve Carella was relieved at eleven thirty-three by a detective named Hal Willis. He filled Willis in on anything that was urgent, left him to catch and then walked downstairs.

'Going to see the girlfriend, Steve?' the desk sergeant asked.

'Yep,' Carella answered.

'Wish I was as young as you,' the sergeant said.

'Ah come on,' Carella replied. 'You can't be more than seventy.'

The sergeant chuckled. 'Not a day over,' he answered.

'Good night,' Carella said.

'Night.'

Carella walked out of the building and headed for his car, which was parked two blocks away in a 'No Parking' zone.

Hank Bush left the precinct at eleven fifty-two when his relief showed up.

'I thought you'd never get here,' he said.

'I thought so, too.'

'What happened?'

'It's too hot to run.'

Bush grimaced, went to the phone, and dialled his home number. He waited several moments. The phone kept ringing on the other end.

'Hello?'

'Alice?'

'Yes.' She paused. 'Hank?'

'I'm on my way, honey. Why don't you make some iced coffee?'

'All right, I will.'

'Is it very hot there?'

'Yes. Maybe you should pick up some ice-cream.'

'All right.'

'No, never mind. No. Just come home. The iced coffee will do.'

'Okay. I'll see you later.'

'Yes, darling.'

Bush hung up. He turned to his relief. 'I hope you don't get relieved 'til nine, you bastard,' he said.

'The heat's gone to his head,' the detective said to the air.

Bush snorted, signed out, and left the building.

The man with the ·45 waited in the shadows.

His hand sweated on the walnut stock of the ·45 in his jacket pocket. Wearing black, he knew he blended with the void of the alley mouth, but he was none the less nervous and a little frightened. Still, this had to be done.

He heard footsteps approaching. Long, firm strides. A man in a hurry. He stared up the street. Yes.

Yes, this was his man.

His hand tightened on the ·45.

The cop was closer now. The man in black stepped out of the alleyway abruptly. The cop stopped in his tracks. They were almost the same height. A street lamp on the corner cast their shadows on to the pavement.

'Have you got a light, Mac?'

The cop was staring at the man in black. Then, suddenly, the cop was reaching for his back pocket. The man in black saw what was happening, and he brought up the ·45 quickly, wrenching it free from his pocket. Both men fired simultaneously.

He felt the cop's bullet rip into his shoulder, but the ·45 was bucking now, again and again, and he saw the cop clutch at his chest and fall to the pavement. The Detective's Special lay several feet from the cop's body now.

He backed away from the cop, ready to run.

'You son of a bitch,' the cop said.

He whirled. The cop was on his feet, rushing for him. He brought up the ·45 again, but he was too late. The cop had him, his thick arms churning. He fought, pulling free, and the cop clutched at his head, and he felt hair wrench loose, and then the cop's fingers clawed at his face, ripping, gouging.

He fired again. The cop doubled over and then fell to the pavement, his face colliding with the harsh concrete.

His shoulder was bleeding badly. He cursed the cop, and he stood over him, and his blood dripped on to the lifeless shoulders, and he held the ·45 out at arm's length and squeezed the trigger again. The cop's head gave a sidewards lurch and then was still.

The man in black ran off down the street.

The cop on the sidewalk was Hank Bush.

CHAPTER SIXTEEN

Sam Grossman was a police lieutenant. He was also a lab technician. He was tall and angular, a man who'd have looked more at home on a craggy New England farm than in the sterile orderliness of the Police Laboratory which stretched almost half the length of the first floor at Headquarters.

Grossman wore glasses, and his eyes were a guileless blue behind them. There was a gentility to his manner, a quiet warmth reminiscent of a long-lost era, even though his speech bore the clipped stamp of a man who is used to dealing with cold scientific fact.

'Hank was a smart cop,' he said to Carella.

Carella nodded. It was Hank who'd said that it didn't take much brain power to be a detective.

'The way I figure it,' Grossman went on, 'Hank thought he was a goner. The autopsy disclosed four wounds altogether, three in the chest, one at the back of the head. We can safely assume, I think, that the head shot was the last one fired, a *coup de grâce.*'

'Go ahead,' Carella said.

'Figure he'd been shot two or three times already, and possibly knew he'd be a dead pigeon before this was over. Whatever the case, he knew we could use more information on the bastard doing the shooting.'

'The hair, you mean?' Carella asked.

'Yes. We found clumps of hair on the sidewalk. All the hairs had living roots, so we'd have known they were pulled away by force even if we hadn't found some in the palms and fingers of Hank's hands. But he was thinking overtime. He also tore a goodly chunk of meat from the ambusher's face. That told us a few things, too.'

131

'And what else?'

'Blood. Hank shot this guy, Steve. Well, undoubtedly you know that already.'

'Yes. What does it all add up to?'

'A lot,' Grossman said. He picked up a report from his desk. 'This is what we know for sure, from what we were able to piece together, from what Hank gave us.'

Grossman cleared his throat and began reading.

'The killer is a male, white, adult, not over say fifty years of age. He is a mechanic, possibly highly skilled and highly paid. He is dark complexioned, his skin is oily, he has a heavy beard which he tries to disguise with talc. His hair is dark brown and he is approximately six feet tall. Within the past two days, he took a haircut and a singe. He is fast, possibly indicating a man who is not overweight. Judging from the hair, he should weigh about 180. He is wounded, most likely above the waist, and not superficially.'

'Break it down for me,' Carella said, somewhat amazed – as he always was – by what the Lab boys could do with a rag, a bone, and a hank of hair.

'Okay,' Grossman said. 'Male. In this day and age, this sometimes poses a problem, especially if we've got only hair from the head. Luckily, Hank solved that one for us. The *head* hairs of either a male or a female will have an average diameter of less than 0.08 mm. Okay, having only a batch of head hairs to go on, we've got to resort to other measurements to determine whether or not the hair came from a male or a female. Length of the hair used to be a good gauge. If the length was more than 8 cm., we could assume the hair came from a woman. But the goddamn women nowadays are wearing their hair as short as, if not shorter than, the men. So we could have been fooled on this one, if Hank hadn't scratched this guy's face.'

'What's the scratch have to do with it?'

'It gave us a skin sample, to begin with. That's how we

knew the man was white, dark complexioned, and oily. But it also gave us a beard hair.'

'How do you know it was a beard hair?'

'Simple,' Grossman said. 'Under the microscope, it showed up in cross-section as being triangular, with concave sides. Only beard hairs are shaped that way. The diameter, too, was greater than 0.1 mm. Simple. A beard hair. Had to be a man.'

'How do you know he was a mechanic?'

'The head hairs were covered with metal dust.'

'You said possibly a highly skilled and highly paid one. Why?'

'The head hairs were saturated with a hair preparation. We broke it down and checked it against our sample sheets. It's very expensive stuff. Five bucks the bottle when sold singly. Ten bucks when sold in a set with the after-shave talc. This customer was wearing both the hair gook *and* the talc. What mechanic can afford ten bucks for such luxuries – unless he's highly paid? If he's highly paid, chances are he's highly skilled.'

'How do you know he's not over fifty?' Carella asked.

'Again, by the diameter of the hair and also the pigmentation. Here, take a look at this chart.' He extended a sheet to Carella.

Age	Diameter
12 days	0·024 mm.
6 months	0·037 mm.
18 months	0·038 mm.
15 years	0·053 mm.
Adults	0.07 mm.

'Fellow's head hair had a diameter of 0·071,' Grossman said.

'That only shows he's an adult.'

'Sure. But if we get a hair with a living root, and there are hardly any pigment grains in the cortex, we can be pretty sure the hair comes from an old person. This guy had plenty of pigment grains. Also, even though we rarely make any age guesses on such single evidence, an older person's hair has a tendency to become finer. This guy's hair is coarse and thick.'

Carella sighed.

'Am I going too fast for you?'

'No,' Carella said. 'How about the singe and the haircut?'

'The singe was simple. The hairs were curled, slightly swelled, and greyish in colour. Not naturally grey, you understand.'

'The haircut?'

'If the guy had had a haircut just before he did the shooting, the head hairs would have shown clean-cut edges. After forty-eight hours, the cut begins to grow round. We can pretty well determine just when a guy's had his last haircut.'

'You said he was six feet tall.'

'Well, Ballistics helped us on that one.'

'Spell it,' Carella said.

'We had the blood to work with. Did I mention the guy has type O blood?'

'You guys . . .' Carella started.

'Aw come on, Steve, that was simple.'

'Yeah.'

'Yeah,' Grossman said. 'Look, Steve, the blood serum of one person has the ability to agglutinate . . .' He paused. 'That means clump, or bring together the red blood cells of certain other people. There are four blood groups: Group O, Group A, Group B, Group AB. Okay?'

'Okay,' Carella said.

'We take the sample of blood, and we mix a little of it with samples from the four groups. Oh, hell, here's another chart for you to look at.' He handed it to Carella.

1. Group O – no agglutination in either serum.
2. Group A – agglutination in serum B only.
3. Group B – agglutination in serum A only.
4. Group AB – agglutination in both serums.

'This guy's blood – and he left a nice trail of it when he was running away, in addition to several spots on the back of Hank's shirt – would not agglutinate, or clump, in any of the samples. Hence, type O. Another indication that he's white, incidentally. A and O are most common in white people. 45 per cent of all white people are in the O group.'

'How do you figure he's six feet tall. You still haven't told me.'

'Well, as I said, this is where Ballistics came in. In addition to what we had, of course. The blood spots on Hank's shirt weren't of much value in determining from what height they had fallen since the cotton absorbed them when they hit. But the blood stains on the pavement told us several things.'

'What'd they tell you?'

'First that he was going pretty fast. You see, the faster a man is walking, the narrower and longer will be the blood drops and the teeth on those drops. They look something like a small gear, if you can picture that, Steve.'

'I can.'

'Okay. These were narrow and also sprinkled in many small drops, which told us that he was moving fast and also that the drops were falling from a height of somewhere around two yards or so.'

'So?'

'So, if he was moving fast, he wasn't hit in the legs or the stomach. A man doesn't move very fast under those conditions. If the drops came from a height of approximately two yards, chances are the man was hit high above the waist. Ballistics pried Hank's slug out of the brick wall of the building, and from the angle – assuming Hank only had time to shoot from a draw – they figured the man was struck somewhere around the shoulder. This indicates a tall man, I mean when you put the blood drops and the slug together.'

'How do you know he wasn't wounded superficially?'

'All the blood, man. He left a long trail.'

'You said he weighs about 180. How . . .'

'The hair was healthy hair. The guy was going fast. The speed tells us he wasn't overweight. A healthy man of six feet should weigh about 180, no?'

'You've given me a lot, Sam,' Carella said. 'Thanks.'

'Don't mention it. I'm glad I'm not the guy who has to check on doctors' gunshot wound reports, or absentee mechanics. Not to mention this hair lotion and talc. It's called "Skylark", by the way.'

'Well, thanks, anyway.'

'Don't thank me,' Grossman said.

'Huh?'

'Thank Hank.'

CHAPTER SEVENTEEN

The teletype alarm went out to fourteen states.
   It read:

XXXXX APPREHEND SUSPICION OF MURDER XXX UNIDEN-
TIFIED MALE WHITE CAUCASIAN ADULT BELOW FIFTY
XXXXX POSSIBLE HEIGHT SIX FEET OR OVER XXX POSSI-
BLE WEIGHT ONE HUNDRED EIGHTY XXX DARK HAIR
SWARTHY COMPLEXION HEAVY BEARD XXXX USES HAIR
PREPARATION AND TALC TRADE NAME 'SKYLARK' XXXX
SHOES MAY POSSIBLY CARRY HEELS WITH 'O'SULLIVAN'
TRADE NAME XXXX MAN ASSUMED TO BE SKILLED
MECHANIC MAY POSSIBLY SEEK SUCH WORK XXXXX
GUNWOUND ABOVE WAIST POSSIBLE SHOULDER HIGH
MAN MAY SEEK DOCTOR XXXX THIS MAN IS DANGEROUS
AND ARMED WITH COLT ·45 AUTOMATIC XX

'Those are a lot of "possiblys",' Havilland said.
   'Too damn many,' Carella agreed. 'But at least it's a place
to start.
   It was not so easy to start.
   They could, of course, have started by calling all the
doctors in the city, on the assumption that one or more of
them had failed to report a gunshot wound, as specified by
law. However, there were quite a few doctors in the city. To
be exact, there were:

   4,283 doctors in Calm's Point
   1,975 doctors in Riverhead
   8,728 doctors in Isola (including the Diamondback and
   Hillside sectors)
   2,614 doctors in Majesta

and 264 doctors in Bethtown
for a grand total of
COUNT 'EM!
17,864 DOCTORS 17,864

Those are a lot of medical men. Assuming each call would take approximately five minutes, a little multiplication told the cops it would take them approximately 89,320 minutes to call each doctor in the classified directory. Of course, there were 22,000 policemen on the force. If each cop took on the job of calling four doctors, every call could have been made before twenty minutes had expired. Unfortunately, many of the other cops had other tidbits of crime to occupy themselves with. So, faced with the overwhelming number of healers, the detectives decided to wait instead for one of them to call with a gunshot-wound report. Since the bullet had exited the killer's body, the wound was in all likelihood a clean one, anyway, and perhaps the killer would *never* seek the aid of a doctor. In which case the waiting would all be in vain.

If there were 17,864 doctors in the city, it was virtually impossible to tally the number of mechanics plying their trade there. So this line of approach was also abandoned.

There remained the hair lotion and talc with the innocent-sounding name 'Skylark'.

A quick check showed that both masculine beauty aids were sold over the counter of almost every drug store in the city. They were as common as – if higher-priced than – aspirin tablets.

Good for a cold.

If you don't like them . . .

The police turned, instead, to their own files in the Bureau of Identification, and to the voluminous files in the Federal Bureau of Investigation.

And the search was on for a male, white Caucasian, under fifty years in age, dark-haired, dark-complexioned, six feet tall, weighing 180 pounds, addicted to the use of a Colt ·45 automatic.

The needle may have been in the city.

But the entire United States was the haystack.

'Lady to see you, Steve,' Miscolo said.

'What about?'

'Said she wanted to talk to the people investigating the cop killer.' Miscolo wiped his brow. There was a big fan in the Clerical office, and he hated leaving it. Not that he didn't enjoy talking to the DD men. It was simply that Miscolo was a heavy sweater, and he didn't like the armpits of his uniform shirts ruined by unnecessary talk.

'Okay, send her in,' Carella said.

Miscolo vanished, and then reappeared with a small birdlike woman whose head jerked in short arcs as she surveyed first the dividing railing and then the file cabinets and then the desks and the grilled windows and then the detectives on phones everywhere in the Squad Room, most of them in various stages of sartorial inelegance.

'This is Detective Carella,' Miscolo said. 'He's one of the detectives on the investigation.' Miscolo sighed heavily and then fled back to the big fan in the small Clerical office.

'Won't you come in, ma'am?' Carella said.

'*Miss*,' the woman corrected. Carella was in his shirt sleeves, and she noticed this with obvious distaste, and then glanced sharply around the room again and said, 'Don't you have a private office?'

'I'm afraid not,' Carella said.

'I don't want them to hear me.'

'Who?' Carella asked.

'Them,' she said. 'Could we go to a desk somewhere in the corner?'

'Certainly,' Carella said. 'What did you say your name was, Miss?'

'Oreatha Bailey,' the woman said. She was at least fifty-five or so, Carella surmised, with the sharp-featured face of a stereotyped witch. He led her through the gate in the railing and to an unoccupied desk in the far right corner of the room, a corner which, unfortunately, did not receive any ventilation from the windows.

When they were seated, Carella asked, 'What can I do for you, Miss Bailey?'

'You don't have a bug in this corner, do you?'

'A ... bug?'

'One of them dictaphone things.'

'No.'

'What did you say your name was?'

'Detective Carella.'

'And you speak English?'

Carella suppressed a smile. 'Yes, I ... I picked up the language from the natives.'

'I'd have preferred an American policeman,' Miss Bailey said in all seriousness.

'Well, I sometimes pass for one,' Carella answered, amused.

'Very well.'

There was a long pause. Carella waited.

Miss Bailey showed no signs of continuing the conversation.

'Miss ... ?'

'Shh!' she said sharply.

Carella waited.

After several moments, the woman said, 'I know who killed those policemen.'

Carella leaned forward, interested. The best leads sometimes came from the most unexpected sources. 'Who?' he asked.

'Never you mind,' she answered.

Carella waited.

'They are going to kill a lot more policemen,' Miss Bailey said. 'That's their plan.'

'Whose plan?'

'If they can do away with law enforcement, the rest will be easy,' Miss Bailey said. 'That's their plan. First the police, then the National Guard, and then the regular Army.'

Carella looked at Miss Bailey suspiciously.

'They've been sending messages to me,' Miss Bailey said. 'They think I'm one of them, I don't know why. They come out of the walls and give me messages.'

'Who comes out of the walls?' Carella asked.

'The cockroach-men. That's why I asked if there was a bug in this corner.'

'Oh, the . . . cockroach-men.'

'Yes.'

'I see.'

'Do I look like a cockroach?' she asked.

'No,' Carella said. 'Not particularly.'

'Then why have they mistaken me for one of them? They look like cockroaches, you know.'

'Yes, I know.'

'They talk by radio-nuclear-thermics. I think they must be from another planet, don't you?'

'Possibly,' Carella said.

'It's remarkable that I can understand them. Perhaps they've overcome my mind; do you think that's possible?'

'Anything's possible,' Carella agreed.

'They told me about Reardon the night before they killed him. They said they would start with him because he was the Commissar of Sector Three. They used a thermo-disintegrator on him, you know that, don't you?' Miss Bailey paused, and then nodded. '·45 calibre.'

'Yes,' Carella said.

'Foster was the Black Prince of Argaddon. They had to get him. That's what they told me. The signals they put out are remarkably clear, considering the fact that they're in an alien tongue. I do wish you were an American, Mr Carella. There are so many aliens around these days, that one hardly knows who to trust.'

'Yes,' Carella said. He could feel the sweat blotting the back of his shirt. 'Yes.'

'They killed Bush because he wasn't a bush, he was a tree in disguise. They hate all plant life.'

'I see.'

'Especially trees. They need the carbon dioxide, you see, and plants consume it. Especially trees. Trees consume a great deal of carbon dioxide.'

'Certainly.'

'Will you stop them, now that you know?' Miss Bailey asked.

'We'll do everything in our power,' Carella said.

'The best way to stop them . . .' Miss Bailey paused and rose, clutching her purse to her narrow bosom. 'Well, I don't want to tell you how to run your business.'

'We appreciate your help,' Carella said. He began walking her to the railing. Miss Bailey stopped.

'Would you like to know the best way to stop these cockroach-men? Guns are no good against them, you know. Because of the thermal heat.'

'I didn't know that,' Carella said. They were standing just inside the railing. He opened the gate for her, and she stepped through.

'There's only one way to stop them,' she said.

'What's that?' Carella asked.

Miss Bailey pursed her mouth. 'Step on them!' she said, and she turned on her heel and walked past Clerical, and then down the steps to the first floor.

Bert Kling seemed to be in high spirits that night.

When Carella and Havilland came into the hospital room, he was sitting up in bed, and aside from the bulky bandage over his right shoulder, you'd never know anything was wrong with him. He beamed a broad smile, and then sat up to talk to the two visiting detectives.

He chewed on the candy they'd brought him, and he said

this hospital duty was real jazzy, and that they should get a look at some of the nurses in their tight white uniforms.

He seemed to bear no grudge whatever against the boy who'd shot him. Those breaks were all part of the game, he supposed. He kept chewing candy, and joking, and talking until it was almost time for the cops to leave.

Just before they left, he told a joke about a man who had three testicles.

Bert Kling seemed to be in high spirits that night.

CHAPTER EIGHTEEN

The three funerals followed upon each other's heels with remarkable rapidity. The heat did not help the classical ceremonies of death. The mourners followed the caskets and sweated. An evil, leering sun grinned its blistering grin, and freshly turned soil – which should have been cool and moist – accepted the caskets with dry, dusty indifference.

The beaches that week were jammed to capacity. In Calm's Point at Mott's Island, the scorekeeper recorded a record-breaking crowd of two million, four hundred and seventy thousand surf seekers. The police had problems. The police had traffic problems because everyone who owned any sort of a jalopy had put it on the road. The police had fire-hydrant problems, because kids all over the city were turning on the johnny pumps, covering the spout with a flattened coffee can, and romping beneath the improvised shower. The police had burglary problems, because people were sleeping with their windows open; people were leaving parked cars unlocked, windows wide; shopkeepers were stepping across the street for a moment to catch a quick Pepsi Cola. The police had 'floater' problems, because the scorched and heat-weary citizens sometimes sought relief in the polluted currents of the rivers that bound Isola – and some of them drowned, and some of them turned up with bloated bodies and bulging eyes.

On Walker Island, in the River Dix, the police had prisoner problems because the cons there decided the heat was too much for them to bear, and they banged their tin cups on the sweating bars of their hot cells, and the cops listened to the clamour and rushed for riot guns.

The police had all sorts of problems.

*

Carella wished she were not wearing black.

He knew this was absurd. When a woman's husband is dead, the woman wears black.

But Hank and he had talked a lot in the quiet hours of the midnight tour, and Hank had many times described Alice in the black night-gowns she wore to bed. And try as he might, Carella could not disassociate the separate concepts of black: black as a sheer and frothy raiment of seduction; black as the ashy garment of mourning.

Alice Bush sat across from him in the living-room of the Calm's Point apartment. The windows were wide open, and he could see the tall Gothic structures of the Calm's Point College Campus etched against the merciless, glaring blue of the sky. He had worked with Bush for many years, but this was the first time he'd been inside his apartment, and the association of Alice Bush in black cast a feeling of guilt over his memories of Hank.

The apartment was not at all what he would have expected for a man like Hank. Hank was big, rough-hewn. The apartment was somehow frilly, a woman's apartment. He could not believe that Hank had been comfortable in these rooms. His eyes had scanned the furniture, small-scaled stuff, stuff in which Hank could never have spread his legs. The curtains at the windows were ruffled chintz. The walls of the living-room were a sickeningly pale lemon shade. The end tables were heavy with curlicues and inlaid patterns. The corners of the room contained knick-knack shelves, and the shelves were loaded with fragile glass figurines of dogs and cats and gnomes and one of Little Bo Peep holding a delicately blown, slender, glass shepherd's crook.

The room, the apartment, seemed to Carella to be the intricately cluttered design for a comedy of manners. Hank must have been as out of place here as a plumber at a literary tea.

Not so Mrs Bush.

Mrs Bush lounged on a heavily padded chartreuse love

seat, her long legs tucked under her, her feet bare. Mrs Bush belonged in this room. This room had been designed for Mrs Bush, designed for femininity, and the Male Animal be damned.

She wore black silk. She was uncommonly big-busted, incredibly narrow-waisted. Her hip bones were wide, flesh-padded, a woman whose body had been designed for the bearing of children – but somehow she didn't seem the type. He could not visualize her squeezing life from her loins. He could only visualize her as Hank had described her – in the role of a seductress. The black silk dress strengthened the concept. The frou-frou room left no doubt. This was a stage set for Alice Bush.

The dress was not low-cut. It didn't have to be.

Nor was it particularly tight, and it didn't have to be that, either.

It was not expensive, but it fitted her figure well. He had no doubt that anything she wore would fit her figure well. He had no doubt that even a potato sack would look remarkably interesting on the woman who had been Hank's wife.

'What do I do now?' Alice asked. 'Make up beds at the precinct? That's the usual routine for a cop's widow, isn't it?'

'Did Hank leave any insurance?' Carella asked.

'Nothing to speak of. Insurance doesn't come easily to cops, does it? Besides . . . Steve, he was a young man. Who thinks of things like this? Who thinks these things are going to happen?' She looked at him wide-eyed. Her eyes were very brown, her hair was very blonde, her complexion was fair and unmarred. She was a beautiful woman, and he did not like considering her such. He wanted her to be dowdy and forlorn. He did not want her looking fresh and lovely. Goddammit, what was there about this room that suffocated a man? He felt like the last male alive, surrounded by bare-breasted beauties on a tropical island surrounded by man-eating sharks. There was no place to run to. The island was called Amazonia or something, and the island was female to the core, and he was the last man alive.

The room and Alice Bush.

The femaleness reached out to envelop him in a cloying, clinging embrace.

'Change your mind, Steve,' Alice said. 'Have a drink.'

'All right, I will,' he answered.

She rose, displaying a long white segment of thigh as she got to her feet, displaying an almost indecent oblivion to the way she handled her body. She had lived with it for a long time, he supposed. She no longer marvelled at its allure. She accepted it, and lived with it, and others could marvel. A thigh was a thigh, what the hell! What was so special about the thigh of Alice Bush?

'Scotch?'

'All right.'

'How does it feel, something like this?' she asked. She was standing at the bar across from him. She stood with the loose-hipped stance of a fashion model, incongruous because he always pictured fashion models as willowy and thin and flat-chested. Alice Bush was none of these.

'Something like what?'

'Investigating the death of a colleague and friend.'

'Weird,' Carella said.

'I'll bet.'

'You're taking it very well,' Carella said.

'I have to,' Alice answered briefly.

'Why?'

'Because I'll fall all to pieces if I don't. He's in the ground, Steve. It's not going to help for me to wail and moan all over the place.'

'I suppose not.'

'We've got to go on living, don't we? We can't simply give up because someone we love is gone, can we?'

'No,' Carella agreed.

She walked to him and handed him the drink. Their

fingers touched for an instant. He looked up at her. Her face was completely guileless. The contact, he was sure, had been accidental.

She walked to the window and looked out towards the college. 'It's lonely here without him,' she said.

'It's lonely at the house without him, too,' Carella said, surprised. He had not realized, before this, how really attached he had become to Hank.

'I was thinking of taking a trip,' Alice said, 'getting away from things that remind me of him.'

'Things like what?' Carella asked.

'Oh, I don't know,' Alice said. 'Like . . . last night I saw his hair brush on the dresser, and there was some of that wild red hair of his caught in the bristles, and all at once it reminded me of him, of the wildness of him. He was a wild person, Steve.' She paused. 'Wild.'

The word was female somehow. He was reminded again of the word portrait Hank had drawn, of the real portrait before him, standing by the window, of the femaleness everywhere around him on this island. He could not blame her, he knew that. She was only being herself, being Alice Bush, being Woman. She was only a pawn of fate, a girl who automatically embodied womanhood, a girl who . . . hell!

'How far have you come along on it?' she asked. She whirled from the window, went back to the love seat and collapsed into it. The movement was not a gracious one. It was feline, however. She sprawled in the love seat like a big jungle cat, and then she tucked her legs under her again, and he would not have been surprised if she'd begun purring in that moment.

He told her what they thought they knew about the suspected killer. Alice nodded.

'Quite a bit to go on,' she said.

'Not really.'

'I mean, if he should seek a doctor's aid.'

'He hasn't yet. Chances are he won't. He probably dressed the wound himself.'

'Badly shot?'

'Apparently. But clean.'

'Hank should have killed him,' she said. Surprisingly, there was no viciousness attached to the words. The words themselves bore all the lethal potential of a coiled rattler, but the delivery made them harmless.

'Yes,' Carella agreed. 'He should have.'

'But he didn't.'

'No.'

'What's your next step?' she asked.

'Oh, I don't know. Homicide North is up a tree on those killings, and I guess we are, too. I've got a few ideas kicking around, though.'

'A lead?' she asked.

'No. Just ideas.'

'What kind of ideas?'

'They'd bore you.'

'My husband's been killed,' Alice said coldly. 'I assure you I will not be bored by anything that may lead to finding his killer.'

'Well, I'd prefer not to air my ideas until I know what I'm talking about.'

Alice smiled. 'That's different. You haven't touched your drink.'

He raised the glass to his lips. The drink was very strong.

'Wow!' he said. 'You don't spare the alcohol, do you?'

'Hank liked his strong,' she said. 'He liked everything strong.'

And again, like an interwoven thread of personality, a personality dictated by the demands of a body that could look nothing but blatantly inviting, Alice Bush had inadvertently lit another fuse. He had the feeling that she would suddenly explode into a thousand flying fragments of breast

149

and hip and thigh, splashed over the landscape like a Dali painting.

'I'd better be getting along,' he said. 'The City doesn't pay me for sipping drinks all morning.'

'Stay a while,' she said. 'I have a few ideas myself.'

He glanced up quickly, almost suspecting an edge of *double entendre* in her voice. He was mistaken. She had turned away from him and was looking out the window again, her face in profile, her body in profile.

'Let me hear them,' he said.

'A cop hater,' she replied.

'Maybe.'

'It has to be. Who else would senselessly take three lives? It has to be a cop hater, Steve. Doesn't Homicide North think so?'

'I haven't talked to them in the past few days. That's what they thought in the beginning, I know.'

'What do they think now?'

'That's hard to say.'

'What do *you* think now?'

'Maybe a cop hater. Reardon and Foster, yes, a cop hater. But Hank . . . I don't know.'

'I'm not sure I follow you.'

'Well, Reardon and Foster were partners, so we could assume that possibly some jerk was carrying a grudge against them. They worked together . . . maybe they rubbed some idiot the wrong way.'

'Yes?'

'But Hank *never* worked with them. Oh, well maybe not never. Maybe once or twice on a plant or something. He never made an important arrest with either of them along, though. Our records show that.'

'Who says it has to be someone with a personal grudge, Steve? This may simply be some goddamned lunatic.' She seemed to be getting angry. He didn't know why she was getting angry because she'd certainly been calm enough up to this point. But her breath was coming heavier now, and her breasts heaved disconcertingly. 'Just some crazy, rotten, twisted fool who's taken it into his mind to knock off every cop in the 87th Precinct. Does that sound so far-fetched?'

'No, not at all. As a matter of fact, we've checked all the mental institutions in the area for people who were recently released who might possibly have had a history of...' He shook his head. 'You know, we figured perhaps a paranoiac, somebody who'd go berserk at the sight of a uniform. Except these men weren't in uniform.'

'No, they weren't. What'd you get?'

'We thought we had one lead. Not anyone with a history of dislike for policemen, but a young man who had a lot of officer trouble in the Army. He was recently released from Bramlook as cured, but that doesn't mean a goddamned thing. We checked with the psychiatrists there, and they felt his illness would never break out in an act of violence, no less a prolonged rampage of violence.'

'And you let it drop?'

'No, we looked the kid up. Harmless. Alibis a mile long.'

'Who else have you checked?'

'We've got feelers out to all our underworld contacts. We thought this might be a gang thing, where some hood has an alleged grievance against something we've done to hamper him, and so he's trying to show us we're not so high and mighty. He hires a torpedo and begins methodically putting us in our places. But there's been no rumble so far, and underworld revenge is not something you can keep very quiet.'

'What else?'

'I've been wading through F.B.I. photos all morning. Jesus, you'd never realize how many men there are who fit the possible description we have.' He sipped at the Scotch. He was beginning to feel a little more comfortable with Alice. Maybe she wasn't so female, after all. Or maybe her femaleness simply enveloped you after a while, causing you to lose all perspective. Whatever it was, the room wasn't as oppressive now.

'Turn up anything? From the photos?'

'Not yet. Half of them are in jail, and the rest are scattered all over the country. You see, the hell of this thing is ... well ...'

'What?'

'How'd the killer know that these men were cops? They were all in plainclothes. Unless he'd had contact with them before, how could he know?'

'Yes, I see what you mean.'

'Maybe he sat in a parked car across from the house and watched everyone who went in and out. If he did that for a while, he'd get to know who worked there and who didn't.'

'He could have done that,' Alice said thoughtfully. 'Yes, he could have.' She crossed her legs unconsciously. Carella looked away.

'Several things against that theory, though,' Carella said. 'That's what makes this case such a bitch.' The word had sneaked out, and he glanced up apprehensively. Alice Bush seemed not to mind the profanity. She had probably heard enough of it from Hank. Her legs were still crossed. They were very good legs. Her skirt had fallen into a funny position. He looked away again.

'You see, if somebody had been watching the house, we'd have noticed him. That is, if he'd been watching it long enough to know who worked there and who was visiting ... that would take time. We'd surely have spotted him.'

'Not if he were hidden.'

'There are no buildings opposite the house. Only the park.'

'He could have been somewhere in the park ... with binoculars, maybe.'

'Sure. But how could he tell the detectives from the patrolmen, then?'

'What?'

'He killed three detectives. Maybe it was chance. I don't

think so. All right, how the hell could he tell the patrolmen from the detectives?'

'Very simply,' Alice said. 'Assuming he was watching, he'd see the men when they arrived, and he'd see them after muster when they went out to their beats. They'd be in uniform then. I'm talking about the patrolmen.'

'Yes, I suppose.' He took a deep swallow of the drink. Alice moved on the love seat.

'I'm hot,' she said.

He did not look at her. He knew that his eyes would have been drawn downward if he did, and he did not want to see what Alice was unconsciously, obliviously showing.

'I don't suppose this heat has helped the investigation any,' she said.

'This heat hasn't helped *anything* any.'

'I'm changing to shorts and a halter as soon as you get out of here.'

'There's a hint if ever I heard one,' Carella said.

'No, I didn't mean . . . oh hell, Steve, I'd change to them now if I thought you were going to stay longer. I just thought you were leaving soon. I mean . . .' She made a vague motion with one hand. 'Oh, nuts.'

'I *am* leaving, Alice. Lots of photos to look through back there.' He rose. 'Thanks for the drink.' He started for the door, not looking back when she got up, not wanting to look at her legs again.

She took his hand at the door. Her grip was firm and warm. Her hand was fleshy. She squeezed his hand.

'Good luck, Steve. If there's anything I can do to help . . .'

'We'll let you know. Thanks again.'

He left the apartment and walked down to the street. It was very hot in the street.

Curiously, he felt like going to bed with somebody.

Anybody.

CHAPTER NINETEEN

'Now here's what I call a real handsome one,' Hal Willis said. Hal Willis was the only really small detective Carella had ever known. He passed the minimum height requirement of five-eight, of course, but just barely. And contrasted against the imposing bulk of the other bulls in the division, he looked more like a soft-shoe dancer than a tough cop. That he was a tough cop, there was no doubt. His bones were slight, and his face was thin, and he looked as if he would have trouble swatting a fly, but anyone who'd ever tangled with Hal Willis did not want the dubious pleasure again. Hal Willis was a Judo expert.

Hal Willis could shake your hand and break your backbone in one and the same motion. Were you not careful with Hal Willis, you might find yourself enwrapped in the excruciating pain of a Thumb Grip. Were you even less careful, you might discover yourself hurtling through space in the fury of either a Rugby or a Far-Eastern Capsize. Ankle Throws, Flying Mares, Back Wheels, all were as much a part of Hal Willis's personality as the sparkling brown eyes in his face.

Those eyes were amusedly turned now towards the FBI photo which he shoved across the desk towards Carella.

The photo was of a man who was indeed a 'real handsome one'. His nose had been fractured in at least four places. A scar ran down the length of his left cheek. Scar tissue hooded his eyes. He owned cauliflower ears and hardly any teeth. His name, of course, was 'Pretty-Boy Krajak'.

'A doll,' Carella said. 'Why'd they sent him to us?'

'Dark hair, six feet two, weighing one-eighty-five. How'd you like to run across him some dark and lonely night?'

'I wouldn't. Is he in the city?'

'He's in LA,' Willis said.

'Then we'll leave him to Joe Friday,' Carella cracked.

'Have another Chesterfield,' Willis countered. 'The only living cigarette with 60,000 filter dragnets.'

Carella laughed. The phone rang. Willis picked it up.

'87th Squad,' he said. 'Detective Willis.'

Carella looked up.

'What?' Willis said. 'Give me the address.' He scribbled something hastily on his pad. 'Hold him there, we'll be right over.' He hung up, opened the desk drawer and removed his holster and service revolver.

'What is it?' Carella asked.

'Doctor on 35th North. Has a man in his office with a bullet wound in his left shoulder.'

A squad car was parked in front of the brownstone on 35th North when Carella and Willis arrived.

'The rookies beat us here,' Willis said.

'So long as they've got him,' Carella answered, and he made it sound like a prayer. A sign on the door read, 'DOCTOR IS IN, RING BELL AND PLEASE BE SEATED.'

'Where?' Willis asked. 'On the doorstep?'

They rang the bell, opened the door, and entered the office. The office was situated off the small courtyard on the street level of the brownstone. A patrolman was seated on the long leather couch, reading a copy of *Esquire*. He closed the magazine when the detectives entered and said, 'Patrolman Curtis, sir.'

'Where's the doctor?' Carella asked.

'Inside, sir. Country is asking him some questions.'

'Who's Country?'

'My partner, sir.'

'Come on,' Willis said. He and Carella went into the doctor's office. Country, a tall gangling boy with a shock of black hair snapped to attention when they entered.

'Good-bye, Country,' Willis said dryly. The patrolman eased himself towards the door and left the office.

'Dr Russell?' Willis asked.

'Yes,' Dr Russell replied. He was a man of about fifty, with a head of hair that was silvery white, giving the lie to his age. He stood as straight as a telephone pole, broad-shouldered, immaculate in his white office tunic. He was a handsome man, and he gave an impression of great competence. For all Carella knew, he may have been a butcher, but he'd have trusted this man to cut out his heart.

'Where is he?'

'Gone,' Dr Russell said.

'How . . .'

'I called as soon as I saw the wound. I excused myself, went out to my private office, and placed the call. When I came back, he was gone.'

'Shit,' Willis said. 'Want to tell us from the beginning, doctor?'

'Certainly. He came in . . . oh, not more than twenty minutes ago. The office was empty, unusual for this time of day, but I rather imagine people with minor ailments are curing them at the seashore.' He smiled briefly. 'He said he'd shot himself while cleaning his hunting rifle. I took him into the Examination Room – that's *this* room, gentlemen – and asked him to take off his shirt. He did.'

'What happened then?'

'I examined the wound. I asked him when he had had the accident. He said it had occurred only this morning. I knew instantly that he was lying. The wound I was examining was not a fresh one. It was already highly infected. That was when I remembered the newspaper stories.'

'About the cop killer?'

'Yes. I recalled having read something about the man having a pistol wound above the waist. That was when I excused myself to call you.'

'Was this definitely a gunshot wound?'

'Without a doubt. It had been dressed, but very badly. I didn't examine it very closely, you understand, because I rushed off to make the call. But it seemed to me that iodine had been used as a disinfectant.'

'Iodine?'

'Yes.'

'But it was infected none the less?'

'Oh, definitely. That man is going to have to find another doctor, sooner or later.'

'What did he look like?'

'Well, where should I begin?'

'How old?'

'Thirty-five or thereabouts.'

'Height?'

'A little over six feet, I should say.'

'Weight?'

'About one-ninety.'

'Black hair?' Willis asked.

'Yes.'

'Colour of eyes?'

'Brown.'

'Any scars, birthmarks, other identifying characteristics?'

'His face was very badly scratched.'

'Did he touch anything in the office?'

'No. Wait, yes.'

'What?'

'I had him sit up on the table here. When I began probing the wound, he winced and gripped the stirrups here at the foot of the table.'

'This may be a break, Hal,' Carella said.

'Jesus it sounds like one. What was he wearing, Dr Russell?'

'Black.'

'Black suit?'

'Yes.'

'What colour shirt?'

'White. It was stained over the wound.'

'Tie?'

'A striped tie. Gold and black.'

'Tie clasp?'

'Yes. Some sort of design on it.'

'What kind?'

'A bugle? Something like that.'

'Trumpet, hunting horn, horn of plenty?'

'I don't know. I couldn't really identify it. It only stuck in my mind because it was an unusual clasp. I noticed it when he was undressing.'

'What colour shoes?'

'Black.'

'Clean-shaven?'

'Yes. That is, you meant was he wearing a beard?'

'Yes.'

'Well then, yes, he was clean-shaven. But he needed a shave.'

'Uh-huh. Wearing any rings?'

'None that I noticed.'

'Undershirt?'

'No undershirt.'

'Can't say I blame him in this heat. Mind if I make a call, Doc?'

'Please help yourself. Do you think he's the man?'

'I hope so,' Willis said. 'God, I hope so.'

When a man is nervous, he perspires – even if the temperature is not hovering somewhere in the nineties.

There are sweat pores on the fingertips, and the stuff they secrete contains 98·5 per cent water and 0·5 to 1·5 per cent solid material. This solid material breaks down to about one-third of inorganic matter – mainly salt – and two thirds of organic substances like urea, albumin and formic, butyric and acetic acids. Dust, dirt, grease cling to the secretion from a man's fingertips.

The perspiration, mixed with whatever happens to be clinging to it at the moment, leaves a filmy impression on whatever the man happens to touch.

The suspected killer happened to touch the smooth chromium surfaces of the stirrups in Dr Russell's office.

The tech crew dusted the latent fingerprints with one of the commercial black powders. The excess powder was allowed to fall on a sheet of paper. The prints were lightly brushed with an ostrich feather. They were then photographed.

There were two good thumbprints, one for each hand where the suspect had pressed down on the top surfaces of the stirrups. There were good second-joint prints for each hand where the suspect had gripped the undersides of the stirrups.

The prints were sent to the Bureau of Identification. A thorough search was made of the files. The search proved fruitless, and the prints were sent to the Federal Bureau of Investigation while the detectives sat back to wait.

In the meantime, a police artist went to see Dr Russell. Listening to Dr Russell's description, he began drawing a picture of the suspect. He made changes as Dr Russell suggested them – 'No, the nose is a little too long; yes, that's better. Try to give a little curl to his lip there, yes, yes, that's it' – and he finally came up with a drawing which tallied with Dr Russell's recollection of the man he had examined. The picture was sent to each metropolitan daily and to each television station in the area, together with a verbal description of the wanted man.

All this while, the detectives waited for the FBI report. They were still waiting the next day.

Willis looked at the drawing on the first page of one of the morning tabloids.

The headline screamed: HAVE YOU SEEN THIS MAN?

'He's not bad-looking,' Willis said.

'Pretty-Boy Krajak,' Carella said.

'No, I'm serious.'

'He may be handsome, but he's a son of a bitch,' Carella said. 'I hope his arm falls off.'

'It very well might,' Willis said dryly.

'Where the hell's that FBI report?' Carella asked edgily. He had been answering calls all morning, calls from citizens who reported having seen the killer. Each call had to be checked out, of course, but thus far the man had been seen all over the city at simultaneous times. 'I thought those G-men were supposed to be fast.'

'They are,' Willis said.

'I'm going to check with the Lieutenant.'

'Go ahead,' Willis said.

Carella went to the Lieutenant's door. He knocked and Byrnes called, 'Come.' Carella went into the office. Byrnes was on the phone. He signalled for Carella to stand by. He nodded then and said, 'But Harriet, I can't see anything wrong with that.'

He listened patiently.

'Yes, but . . .'

Carella walked to the window and stared out at the park.

'No, I can't see any reason for . . .'

Marriage, Carella thought. And then he thought of Teddy. *It'll be different with us.*

'Harriet, let him go,' Byrnes said. 'He's a good boy, and he won't get into any trouble. Look, take my word for it. For God's sake, it's only an amusement park.'

Byrnes sighed patiently.

'All right, then.' He listened. 'I'm not sure yet, honey. We're waiting for an FBI report. If I'll be home, I'll call you. No, nothing special. It's too damn hot to eat, anyway. Yes, dear, 'bye.'

He hung up. Carella came from the window.

'Women,' Byrnes said, not disagreeably. 'My son wants to go out to Jollyland tonight with some of the boys. She doesn't think he should. Can't see why he wants to go there in the middle of the week. She says she's read newspaper stories about boys getting into fights with other boys at these places. For Pete's sake, it's just an amusement park. The kid is seventeen.'

Carella nodded.

'If you're going to watch them every minute, they'll feel like prisoners. Okay, what are the odds on a fight starting at a place like that? Larry knows enough to avoid trouble. He's a good kid. You met him, didn't you, Steve?'

'Yes,' Carella said. 'He seemed very level-headed.'

'Sure, that's what I told Harriet. Ah, what the hell! These women never cut the umbilical cord. We get raised by one woman, and then when we're ripe, we get turned over to another woman.'

Carella smiled. 'It's a conspiracy,' he said.

'Sometimes I think so,' Byrnes said. 'But what would we do without them, huh?' He shook his head sadly, a man trapped in the labial folds of a society structure.

'Anything from the Feds yet?' Carella asked.

'No, not yet. Jesus, I'm praying for a break.'

'Mmmm.'

'We deserve a break, don't we?' Byrnes asked. 'We've worked this one right into the ground. We deserve a break.'

There was a knock on the door.

'Come,' Byrnes said.

Willis entered the room with an envelope. 'This just arrived, sir,' he said.

'FBI?'

'Yes.'

Byrnes took the envelope. Hastily, he tore open the flap and pulled out the folded letter.

'Hell!' he erupted. 'Hell and damnation!'

'Bad?'

'They've got nothing on him!' Byrnes shouted. 'Goddamnit! Goddamnit to hell!'

'Not even Service prints?'

'Nothing. The son of a bitch was probably 4-F!'

'We know *everything* about this guy,' Willis said vehemently, beginning to pace the office. 'We know what he looks like, we know his height, his weight, his bloodtype, when he got his last haircut, the size of his rectal aperture!' He slammed his fist into the opposite hand. 'The only thing we don't know is who the hell he is! Who is he, damnit, who is he?'

Neither Carella nor Byrnes answered.

That night, a boy named Miguel Aretta was taken to Juvenile House. The police had picked him up as one of the boys who'd been missing from the roundup of The Grovers. It did not take the police long to discover that Miguel was the boy who'd zip-gunned Bert Kling.

Miguel had been carrying a zip-gun on the night that Kling got it. When a Senior Grover named Rafael 'Rip' Desanga had reported to the boys that a smart guy had been around asking questions, Miguel went with them to teach the smart guy a lesson.

As it turned out, the smart guy – or the person they assumed to be the smart guy – had pulled a gun outside the bar. Miguel had taken his own piece from his pocket and burned him.

Bert Kling, of course, had not been the smart guy. He turned out to be, of all things, a cop. So Miguel Aretta was now in Juvenile House, and the people there were trying to understand what made him tick so that they could present his case fairly when it came up in Children's Court.

Miguel Aretta was fifteen years old. It could be assumed that he just didn't know any better.

The *real* smart guy – a reporter named Cliff Savage – was thirty-seven years old, and he should have known better.

He didn't.

CHAPTER TWENTY

Savage was waiting for Carella when he left the precinct at 4 p.m. the next day.

He was wearing a brown Dupioni silk suit, a gold tie, and a brown straw with a pale yellow band. 'Hello,' he said, shoving himself off the side of the building.

'What can I do for you?' Carella asked.

'You're a detective, aren't you?'

'If you've got a complaint,' Carella said, 'take it to the desk sergeant. I'm on my way home.'

'My name's Savage.'

'Oh,' Carella said. He regarded the reporter sourly.

'You in the fraternity, too?' Savage asked.

'Which one?'

'The fraternity against Savage. Eeta Piecea Cliff.'

'I'm Phi Beta Kappa myself,' Carella said.

'Really?'

'No.' He began walking towards his car. Savage fell in step with him.

'Are you sore at me, too, is what I meant,' Savage said.

'You stuck your nose in the wrong place,' Carella answered. 'Because you did, a cop is in the hospital and a kid is in Juvenile House, awaiting trial. What do you want me to do, give you a medal?'

'If a kid shoots somebody, he deserves whatever he gets.'

'Maybe he wouldn't've shot anybody if you'd kept your nose out of it.'

'I'm a reporter. My job is getting facts.'

'The lieutenant told me he'd already discussed the possibility of teenagers being responsible for the deaths. He said he told you he considered the possibility extremely remote. But you went ahead and put your fat thumb in the pie, anyway. You realize Kling could have been killed?'

'He wasn't. Do you realize *I* could have been killed?' Savage said.

Carella made no comment.

'If you people cooperated more with the Press . . .'

Carella stopped walking. 'Listen,' he said, 'what are you doing in this neighbourhood? Looking for more trouble? If any of The Grovers recognize you, we're going to have another rhubarb. Why don't you go back to your newspaper office and write a column on garbage collection?'

'Your humour does—'

'I'm not trying to be funny,' Carella said, 'nor do I particularly feel like discussing anything with you. I just came off duty. I'm going home to shower and then I have a date with my fiancée. I'm theoretically on duty twenty-four hours a day, every day of the week, but fortunately that duty does not include extending courtesy to every stray cub reporter in town.'

'Cub?' Savage was truly offended. 'Now, listen—'

'What the hell do you want from me?' Carella asked.

'I want to discuss the killings.'

'I don't.'

'Why not?'

'Jesus, you're a real leech, aren't you?'

'I'm a reporter, and a damned good one. Why don't you want to talk about the killings?'

'I'm perfectly willing to discuss them with anyone who knows what I'm talking about.'

'I'm a good listener,' Savage said.

'Sure. You turned a fine ear towards Rip Desanga.'

'Okay, I made a mistake, I'm willing to admit that. I thought it was the kids, and it wasn't. We know now it was an adult. What else do we know about him? Do we know why he did it?'

'Are you going to follow me all the way home?'

'I'd prefer buying you a drink,' Savage said. He looked at Carella expectantly. Carella weighed the offer.

'All right,' he said.

Savage extended his hand. 'My friends call me Cliff. I didn't get your name.'

'Steve Carella.'

They shook. 'Pleased to know you. Let's get that drink.'

The bar was air-conditioned, a welcome sanctuary from the stifling heat outdoors. They ordered their drinks and then sat opposite each other at the booth alongside the left-hand wall.

'All I want to know,' Savage said, 'is what you think.'

'Do you mean me personally, or the department?'

'You, of course. I can't expect you to speak for the department.'

'Is this for publication?' Carella asked.

'Hell, no. I'm just trying to jell my own ideas on it. Once this thing is broken, there'll be a lot of feature coverage. To do a good job, I want to be acquainted with every facet of the investigation.'

'It'd be a little difficult for a layman to understand every facet of police investigation,' Carella said.

'Of course, of course. But you can at least tell me what you think.'

'Sure. Provided it's not for publication.'

'Scout's honour,' Savage said.

'The department doesn't like individual cops trying to glorify—'

'Not a word of this will get into print,' Savage said. 'Believe me.'

'What do you want to know?'

'We've got the means, we've got the opportunity,' Savage said. 'What's the motive?'

'Every cop in the city would like the answer to that one,' Carella said.

'A nut maybe.'

165

'Maybe.'

'You don't think so?'

'No. Some of us do. I don't.'

'Why not?'

'Just like that.'

'Do you have a reason?'

'No, just a feeling. When you've been working on a case for any length of time, you begin to get feelings about it. I just don't happen to believe a maniac's involved here.'

'What *do* you believe?'

'Well, I have a few ideas.'

'Like what?'

'I'd rather not say right now.'

'Oh, come on, Steve.'

'Look, police work is like any other kind of work – except we happen to deal with crime. If you run an import-export business, you play certain hunches and others you don't. It's the same with us. If you have a hunch, you don't go around making a million-dollar deal on it until you've checked it.'

'Then you do have a hunch you want to check?'

'Not even a hunch, really. Just an idea.'

'What kind of an idea?'

'About motive.'

'What about motive?'

Carella smiled. 'You're a pretty tenacious guy, aren't you?'

'I'm a good reporter. I already told you that.'

'All right, look at it this way. These men were cops. Three of them killed in a row. What's the automatic conclusion?'

'Somebody doesn't like cops.'

'Right. A cop hater.'

'So?'

'Take off their uniforms. What have you got then?'

'They weren't wearing uniforms. None of them were uniform cops.'

'I know. I was speaking figuratively. I meant, make them

ordinary citizens. Not cops. What do you have then? Certainly not a cop hater.'

'But they *were* cops.'

'They were men first. Cops only coincidentally and secondarily.'

'You feel, then, that the fact that they were cops had nothing to do with the reason they were killed.'

'Maybe. That's what I want to dig into a little deeper.'

'I'm not sure I understand you.'

'It's this,' Carella said. 'We knew these men well, we worked with them every day. Cops. We knew them as cops. We didn't know them as *men*. They may have been killed because they were men, and not because they were cops.'

'Interesting,' Savage said.

'It means digging into their lives on a more personal level. It won't be fun because murder has a strange way of dragging skeletons out of the neatest closets.'

'You mean, for example . . .' Savage paused. 'Well, let's say Reardon was playing around with another dame, or Foster was a horse player, or Bush was taking money from a racketeer, something like that.'

'To stretch the point, yes.'

'And somehow, their separate activities were perhaps tied together to one person who wanted them all dead for various reasons. Is that what you're saying?'

'That's a little complicated,' Carella said. 'I'm not sure the deaths are connected in such a complicated way.'

'But we do know the same person killed all three cops.'

'Yes, we're fairly certain of that.'

'Then the deaths are connected.'

'Yes, of course. But perhaps . . .' Carella shrugged. 'It's difficult to discuss this with you because I'm not sure I know what I'm talking about. I only have this idea, that's all. This idea that motive may go deeper than the shields these men wore.'

'I see.' Savage sighed. 'Well, you can console yourself with the knowledge that every cop in the city probably has his own ideas on how to solve this one.'

Carella nodded, not exactly understanding Savage, but not willing to get into a lengthier discussion. He glanced at his watch.

'I've got to go soon,' he said. 'I've got a date.'

'Your girlfriend?'

'Yes.'

'What's her name?'

'Teddy. Well, Theodora really.'

'Theodora what?'

'Franklin.'

'Nice,' Savage said. 'Is this a serious thing?'

'As serious as they come.'

'These ideas of yours,' Savage said. 'About motive. Have you discussed them with your superiors?'

'Hell, no. You don't discuss every little pang of inspiration you get. You look into it, and then if you turn up anything that looks remotely promising, well, then you air the idea.'

'I see. Have you discussed it with Teddy?'

'Teddy? Why, no, not yet.'

'Think she'll go for it?'

Carella smiled uneasily. 'She thinks I can do no wrong.'

'Sounds like a wonderful girl.'

'The best. And I'd better get to her before I lose her.'

'Certainly,' Savage said understandingly. Carella glanced at his watch again. 'Where does she live?'

'Riverhead,' Carella said.

'Theodora Franklin of Riverhead,' Savage said.

'Yes.'

'Well, I've appreciated listening to your ideas.'

Carella rose. 'None of that was for print, remember,' he said.

'Of course not,' Savage assured him.

'Thanks for the drink,' Carella said.

They shook hands. Savage stayed in the booth and ordered

168

another Tom Collins. Carella went home to shower and shave for his date with Teddy.

She was dressed resplendently when she opened the door. She stood back, waiting for him to survey her splendour. She was wearing a white linen suit, white straw pumps, a red-stoned pin on the collar of the suit, bright scarlet oval earrings picking up the scream of the pin.

'Shucks,' he said, 'I was hoping I'd catch you in your slip.'

She made a motion to unbutton her jacket, smiling.

'We have reservations,' he said.

Where? her face asked.

'Ah Lum Fong,' he replied.

She nodded exuberantly.

'Where's your lipstick?' he asked.

She grinned and went to him, and he took her in his arms and kissed her, and then she clung to him as if he were leaving for Siberia in the next ten minutes.

'Come on,' he said, 'put on your face.'

She went into the other room, applied her lipstick, and emerged carrying a small red purse.

'They carry those on the Street,' he said. 'It's a badge of the profession,' and she slapped him on the fanny as they left the apartment.

The Chinese restaurant boasted excellent food and an exotic decor. To Carella, the food alone would not have been enough. When he ate in a Chinese restaurant, he wanted it to look and feel Chinese. He did not appreciate an expanded, upholstered version of a Culver Avenue diner.

They ordered fried wonton soup, and lobster rolls, and barbecued spare ribs and Hon Shu Gai and Steak Kew and sweet and pungent pork. The wonton soup was crisp with Chinese vegetables; luscious snow peas, and water chestnuts, and mushrooms, and roots he could not have named if he'd tried. The wontons were brown and crisp, the soup itself had a rich tangy taste. They talked very little while they ate. They dug into the lobster rolls, and then they attacked the spare ribs, succulently brown.

'Do you know that Lamb thing?' he asked. 'A Dissertation on . . .'

She nodded, and then went back to the spare ribs.

The chicken in the Hon Shu Gai was snappingly crisp. They polished off the dish. They barely had room for the Steak Kew, but they did their best with it, and when Charlie – their waiter – came to collect their dishes, he looked at them reproachfully because they had left over some of the delicious cubes of beef.

He cut a king pineapple for them in the kitchen, cut it so that the outside shell could be lifted off in one piece, exposing the ripe yellow meat beneath the prickly exterior, the fruit sliced and ready to be lifted off in long slender pieces. They drank their tea, savouring the aroma and the warmth, their stomachs full, their minds and their bodies relaxed.

'How's August nineteenth sound to you?'

Teddy shrugged.

'It's a Saturday. Would you like to get married on a Saturday?'

Yes, her eyes said.

Charlie brought them their fortune cookies and replenished the tea-pot.

Carella broke open his cookie. Then, before he read the message on the narrow slip of paper, he said, 'Do you know the one about the man who opened one of these in a Chinese restaurant?'

Teddy shook her head.

'It said, "Don't eat the soup. Signed a friend."'

Teddy laughed and then gestured to his fortune slip. Carella read it aloud to her:

'You are the luckiest man alive. You are about to marry Theodora Franklin.'

She said 'Oh!' in soundless exasperation, and then took the

slip from him. The slender script read: 'You are good with figures.'

'Your figure,' he said.

Teddy smiled and broke open her cookie. Her face clouded momentarily.

'What is it?' he asked.

She shook her head.

'Let me see it.'

She tried to keep the fortune slip from him, but he got it out of her hand and read it.

'Leo will roar – sleep no more.'

Carella stared at the printed slip. 'That's a hell of a thing to put in a cookie,' he said. 'What does it mean?' He thought for a moment. 'Oh, Leo. Leo the Lion. July 22nd to August something, isn't it?'

Teddy nodded.

'Well, the meaning here is perfectly clear then. Once we're married, you're going to have a hell of a time sleeping.'

He grinned, and the worry left her eyes. She smiled, nodded, and then reached across the table for his hand.

The broken cookie rested alongside their hands, and beside that the curled fortune slip.

Leo will roar – sleep no more.

CHAPTER TWENTY-ONE

The man's name was not Leo.

The man's name was Peter.

His last name was Byrnes.

He was roaring.

'What the hell kind of crap is this, Carella?'

'What?'

'Today's issue of this ... this goddamn rag!' he shouted, pointing to the afternoon tabloid on his desk. '4 August!'

Leo, Carella thought. 'What ... what do you mean, Lieutenant?'

'What do I mean?' Byrnes shouted. 'WHAT DO I MEAN! Who the hell gave you the authority to reel off this crap to that idiot Savage?'

'What?'

'There are cops walking beats in Bethtown because they spouted off nonsense like—'

'Savage? Let me see that...' Carella started.

Byrnes flipped open the newspaper angrily. 'Cop Defies Department!' he shouted. 'That's the headline. COP DEFIES DEPARTMENT! What's the matter, Carella, aren't you happy here?'

'Let me see—'

'And under that "MAY KNOW MURDERER", DETECTIVE SAYS.'

'May know—'

'Did you tell this to Savage?'

'That I may know who the murderer is? Of course not. Jesus, Pete—'

'Don't call me Pete! Here, read the goddamn story.'

Carella took the newspaper. For some strange reason, his hands were trembling.

Sure enough, the story was on page four, and it was headlined:

'But this—'
'Read it,' Byrnes said.
Carella read it.

The bar was cool and dim.

We sat opposite each other, Detective Stephen Carella and I. He toyed with his drink, and we talked of many things, but mostly we talked of murder.

'I've got an idea I know who killed those three cops,' Carella said. 'It's not the kind of idea you can take to your superiors, though. They wouldn't understand.'

And so came the first ray of hope in the mystery which has baffled the master minds of Homicide North and tied the hands of stubborn, opinionated Detective-Lieutenant Peter Byrnes of the 87th Precinct.

'I can't tell you very much more about it right now,' Carella said, 'because I'm still digging. But this cop-hater theory is all wrong. It's something in the personal lives of these three men, of that I'm sure. It needs work, but we'll crack it.'

So spoke Detective Carella yesterday afternoon in a bar in the heart of the Murder Belt. He is a shy, withdrawn man, a man who – in his own words – is 'not seeking glory'.

'Police work is like any other kind of work,' he told me, 'except that we deal in crime. When you've got a hunch, you dig into it. If it pans out, then you bring it to your superiors, and maybe they'll listen, and maybe they won't.'

Thus far, he has confided his 'hunch' only to his fiancée, a lovely young lady named Theodora Franklin, a girl from Riverhead. Miss Franklin feels that Carella can 'do no wrong', and is certain he will crack the case despite the inadequate fumblings of the department to date.

'There are skeletons in the closets,' Carella said. 'And those skeletons point to our man. We've got to dig deeper. It's just a matter of time now.'

We sat in the cool dimness of the bar, and I felt the quiet strength emanating from this man who has the courage to go ahead with his investigation in spite of the cop-hater theory which pervades the dusty minds of the men working around him.

This man will find the murderer, I thought.

This man will relieve the city of its constant fear, its dread of an unknown killer roaming the streets with a wanton ·45 automatic in his blood-stained fist. This man ...

'Jesus!' Carella said.

'Yeah,' Byrnes answered. 'Now what about it?'

'I never said these things. I mean, not this way. And he said it wasn't for print!' Carella suddenly exploded. 'Where's the phone? I'm going to sue this son of a bitch for libel! He can't get away with—'

'Calm down,' Byrnes said.

'Why'd he drag Teddy into this? Does he want to make her a sitting duck for that stupid bastard with the ·45? Is he out of his mind?'

'Calm down,' Byrnes repeated.

'Calm down? I never said I knew who the murderer was! I never—'

'What did you say?'

'I only said I had an idea that I wanted to work on.'

'And what's the idea?'

'That maybe this guy wasn't after cops at all. Maybe he was just after men. And maybe not even that. Maybe he was just after *one* man.'

'Which one?'

'How the hell do I know? Why'd he mention Teddy? Jesus, what's the matter with this guy?'

'Nothing that a head doctor couldn't cure,' Byrnes said.

'Listen, I want to go up to see Teddy. God knows—'

'What time is it?' Byrnes asked.

Carella looked at the wall clock. 'Six-fifteen.'

'Wait until six-thirty. Havilland will be back from supper by then.'

'If I ever meet this guy Savage again,' Carella promised, 'I'm going to rip him in half.'

'Or at least give him a speeding ticket,' Byrnes commented.

The man in the black suit stood outside the apartment door, listening. A copy of the afternoon newspaper stuck up from the right-hand pocket of his jacket. His left shoulder throbbed with pain, and the weight of the ·45 automatic tugged at the other pocket of his jacket, so that – favouring the wound, bearing the weight of the gun – he leaned slightly to his left while he listened.

There was no sound from within the apartment.

He had read the name very carefully in the newspaper, Theodora Franklin, and then he had checked the Riverhead directory and come up with the address. He wanted to talk to this girl. He wanted to find out how much Carella knew. He had to find out.

She's very quiet in there, he thought. *What's she doing?*

Cautiously, he tried the door knob. He wriggled it slowly from side to side. The door was locked.

He heard footsteps. He tried to back away from the door too late. He reached for the gun in his pocket. The door was opening, wide, wider.

The girl stood there, surprised. She was a pretty girl, small, dark-haired, wide brown eyes. She wore a white chenille robe. The robe was damp in spots. He assumed she had just come from the shower. Her eyes went to his face, and then to the gun in his hand. Her mouth opened, but no sound came from it. She tried to slam the door, but he rammed his foot into the wedge and then shoved it back.

She moved away from him, deeper into the room. He closed the door and locked it.

'Miss Franklin?' he asked.

She nodded, terrified. She had seen the drawing on the front pages of all the newspapers, had seen it broadcast on all the television programmes. There was no mistake, this was the man Steve was looking for.

'Let's have a little talk, shall we?' he asked.

His voice was a nice voice, smooth, almost suave. He was a good-looking man, why had he killed those cops? Why would a man like this . . . ?

'Did you hear me?' he asked.

She nodded. She could read his lips, could understand everything he said, but . . .

'What does your boyfriend know?' he asked.

He held the ·45 loosely, as if he were accustomed to its lethal power now, as if he considered it a toy more than a dangerous weapon.

'What's the matter, you scared?'

She touched her hands to her lips, pulled them away in a gesture of futility.

'What?'

She repeated the gesture.

'Come on,' he said, 'talk, for Christ's sake? You're not that scared!'

Again, she repeated the gesture, shook her head this time. He watched her curiously.

'I'll be damned,' he said at last. 'A dummy!' He began laughing. The laugh filled the apartment, reverberating from the walls. 'A dummy! If that don't take the cake! A dummy!' His laughter died. He studied her carefully. 'You're not trying to pull something, are you?'

She shook her head vigorously. Her hands went to the

opening of the robe, clutching the chenille to her more tightly.

'Now this has definite advantages, doesn't it?' he said, grinning. 'You can't scream, you can't use the phone, you can't do a damned thing, can you?'

Teddy swallowed, watching him.

'What does Carella know?' he asked.

She shook her head.

'The paper said he's got a lead. Does he know about me? Does he have any idea who I am?'

Again, she shook her head.

'I don't believe you.'

She nodded, trying to convince him that Steve knew nothing. What paper was he referring to? What did he mean? She spread her hands wide, indicating innocence, hoping he would understand.

He reached into his jacket pocket and tossed the newspaper to her.

'Page four,' he said. 'Read it. I've got to sit down. This goddamn shoulder . . .'

He sat, the gun levelled at her. She opened the paper and read the story, shaking her head as she read.

'Well?' he asked.

She kept shaking her head. *No, this is not true. No, Steve would never say things like these. Steve would . . .*

'What'd he tell you?' the man asked.

Her eyes opened wide with pleading. *Nothing, he told me nothing.*

'The newspaper says—'

She hurled the paper to the floor.

'Lies, huh?'

Yes, she nodded.

His eyes narrowed. 'Newspapers don't lie,' he said.

They do, they do!

'When's he coming here?'

She stood motionless, controlling her face, not wanting her face to betray anything to the man with the gun.

'Is he coming?'

She shook her head.

'You're lying. It's all over your face. He's coming here, isn't he?'

She bolted for the door. He caught her arm and flung her back across the room. The robe pulled back over her legs when she fell to the floor. She pulled it together quickly and stared up at him.

'Don't try that again,' he said.

Her breath came heavily now. She sensed a coiled spring within this man, a spring which would unleash itself at the door the moment Steve opened it. But he'd said he would not be there until midnight. He had told her that, and there were a lot of hours between now and midnight. In that time . . .

'You just get out of the shower?' he asked.

She nodded.

'Those are good legs,' he said, and she felt his eyes on her. 'Dames,' he said philosophically. 'What've you got on under that robe?'

Her eyes widened.

He began laughing. 'Just what I thought. Smart. Good way to beat the heat. When's Carella coming?'

She did not answer.

'Seven, eight, nine? Is he on duty today?' He watched her. 'Nothing from you, huh? What's he got, the four to midnight? Sure, otherwise he'd probably be with you right this minute. Well, we might as well make ourselves comfortable, we got a long wait. Anything to drink in this place?'

Teddy nodded.

'What've you got? Gin? Rye? Bourbon?' He watched her. 'Gin? You got tonic? No, huh? Club soda? Okay, mix me a Collins. Hey, where you going?'

Teddy gestured to the kitchen.

'I'll come with you,' he said. He followed her into the kitchen. She opened the refrigerator and took out an opened bottle of club soda.

'Haven't you got a fresh one?' he asked. Her back was to him, and so she could not read his lips. He seized her shoulder and swung her around. His hand did not leave her shoulder.

'I asked you if you had a fresh bottle,' he said.

She nodded and bent, taking an unopened bottle from the lowest shelf of the refrigerator. She took lemons from the fruit drawer, and then went to the cupboard for the bottle of gin.

'Dames,' he said again.

She poured a double shot of gin into a tall glass. She spooned sugar into the glass, and then she went to one of the drawers.

'Hey!'

'Don't get ideas with that. Just slice the lemon.'

He saw the knife in her hand.

She sliced the lemon and squeezed both halves into the glass. She poured club soda until the glass was three-quarters full, and then she went back to the refrigerator for the ice cubes. When the drink was finished, she handed it to him.

'Make one for yourself,' he said.

She shook her head.

'I said make one for yourself! I don't like to drink alone.'

Patiently, wearily, she made herself a drink.

'Come on. Back in the living-room.'

They went into the living-room, and he sat in an easy chair, wincing as he adjusted himself so that his shoulder was comfortable.

'When the knock comes on that door,' he said, 'you just sit tight, understand? Go unlock it now.'

She went to the door and unlocked it. And now, knowing that the door was open, knowing that Steve would enter and be faced with a blazing ·45, she felt fear crawl into her head like a nest of spiders.

'What are you thinking?' he asked.

She shrugged. She walked back into the room and sat opposite him, facing the door.

'This is a good drink,' he said. 'Come on, drink.'

She sipped at the Collins, her mind working ahead to the moment of Steve's arrival.

'I'm going to kill him, you know,' he said.

She watched him, her eyes wide.

'Won't make any difference now, anyway, will it? One cop more or less. Make it look a little better, don't you think?'

She was puzzled, and the puzzlement showed on her face.

'It's the best way,' he explained. 'If he knows something, well, it won't do to have him around. And if he doesn't know anything, it'll round out the picture.' He struggled in the chair. 'Jesus, I've got to get this shoulder fixed. How'd you like that lousy doctor? That was something, wasn't it? I thought they were supposed to be healers.'

He talks the way anyone does, she thought. *Except that he talks so casually of death. He is going to kill Steve.*

'We were figuring on Mexico, anyway. Going to leave this afternoon, until your boyfriend came up with his bright idea. We'll take off in the morning, though. Soon as I take care of this.' He paused. 'Do you suppose I can get a good doctor in Mexico? Jesus, the things a guy will do, huh?' He watched her face carefully. 'You ever been in love?'

She studied him, puzzled, confused. He did not seem like a killer. She nodded.

'Who with? This cop?'

She nodded again.

'Well, that's a shame.' He seemed sincerely sorry. 'It's a damn shame, honey, but what hasta be hasta be. There's no other way, you can see that, can't you? I mean, there was no other way right from the start, from the minute I started this thing. And when you start something, you've got to see it through right to the finish. It's a matter of survival now, you realize that? Jesus, the things a guy will do. Well, you know.' He paused. 'You'd kill for him, wouldn't you?'

She hesitated.

'To keep him, you'd kill for him, wouldn't you?' he repeated.

She nodded.

'So? So there.' He smiled. 'I'm not a professional, you know. I'm a mechanic. That's my line. I'm a damn good mechanic, too. Think I'll be able to get work in Mexico?'

Teddy shrugged.

'Sure, they must have cars down there. They've got cars everywhere. Then, later, when things have cooled down, we'll come back to the States. Hell, things should cool down sooner or later. But what I'm trying to tell you, I'm not a professional killer, so don't get that idea. I'm just a regular guy.'

Her eyes did not believe him.

'No, huh? Well, I'm telling you. Sometimes, there's no other way out. If you see something's hopeless, and somebody explains to you where there's some hope, okay, you take it. I never harmed nobody until I killed those cops. You think I wanted to kill them? Survival, that's all. Some things, you've got to do. Agh, what the hell do you understand? You're just a dummy.'

She sat silent, watching him.

'A woman gets under your skin. Some women are like that. Listen, I've been around. I've been around plenty. I had me more dames than you could count. But this one – different. Different right from the beginning. She just got under my skin. Right under it. When it gets you like that, you can't eat, you can't sleep, nothing. You just think about her all day long. And what can you do when you realize you can't really have her unless . . . well . . . unless you . . . hell, didn't she ask him for a divorce? Is it my fault he was a

181

stubborn son of a bitch? Well, he's still stubborn – only now he's dead.'

Teddy's eyes moved from his face. They covered the door behind him, and then dropped to the doorknob.

'And he took two of his pals with him.' He stared into his glass. 'Those are the breaks. He should've listened to reason. A woman like her . . . Jesus, you'd do anything for a woman like her. Anything! Just being in the same room with her, you want to . . .'

Teddy watched the knob with fascination. She rose suddenly. She brought back her glass and then threw it at him. It grazed his forehead, the liquid splashing out of the glass and cascading over his shoulder. He leaped to his feet, his face twisted in fury, the ·45 pointed at her.

'You stupid bitch!' he bellowed. 'Why the hell did you do that?'

CHAPTER TWENTY-TWO

Carella left the precinct at six-thirty on the button. Havilland had not yet come back from supper, but he could wait no longer. He did not want to leave Teddy alone in that apartment, not after the fool stunt Savage had pulled.

He drove to Riverhead quickly. He ignored traffic lights and full stop signs. He ignored everything. There was an all-consuming thought in his mind, and that thought included a man with a ·45 and a girl with no tongue.

When he reached her apartment building, he glanced up at her window. The shades were not drawn. The apartment looked very quiet. He breathed a little more easily, and then entered the building. He climbed the steps, his heart pounding. He knew he shouldn't be alarmed but he could not shake the persistent feeling that Savage's column had invited danger for Teddy.

He stopped outside her door. He could hear the persistent drone of what sounded like the radio going inside. He reached for the knob. In his usual manner, he twisted it slowly from side to side, waiting for her footsteps, knowing she would come to the door the moment she saw his signal.

He heard the sound of a chair scraping back and then someone shouted, 'You stupid bitch! Why the hell did you do that?'

His brain came alive. He reached for his ·38 and snapped the door open with his other hand.

The man turned.

'You . . . !' he shouted, and the ·45 bucked in his hand.

Carella fired low, dropping to the floor the instant he entered the room. His first two shots took the man in the thigh. The man fell face forward, the ·45 pitching out of his fist. Carella kicked back the hammer on the ·38, waiting.

'You bastard,' the man on the floor said. 'You bastard.'

Carella got to his feet. He picked up the ·45 and stuck it into his back pocket.

'Get up,' he said. 'You all right, Teddy?'

Teddy nodded. She was breathing heavily, watching the man on the floor.

'Thanks for the warning,' Carella said. He turned to the man again. 'Get up!'

'I can't, you bastard. Why'd you shoot me? For Christ's sake, why'd you shoot me?'

'Why'd you shoot three cops?'

The man went silent.

'What's your name?' Carella asked.

'Mercer. Paul Mercer.'

'Don't you like cops?'

'I love them.'

'What's the story then?'

'I suppose you're going to check my gun with what you've already got.'

'Damn right,' Carella said. 'You haven't got a chance, Mercer.'

'She put me up to it,' Mercer said, a scowl on his dark face. 'She's the real murderer. All I done was pull the trigger. She said we had to kill him, said it was the only way. We threw the others in just to make it look good, just to make it look as if a cop hater was loose. But it was her idea. Why should I take the rap alone?'

'Whose idea?' Carella asked.

'Alice's,' Mercer said. 'You see . . . we wanted to make it look like a cop hater. We wanted—'

'It was,' Carella said.

When they brought Alice Bush in, she was dressed in grey, a quiet grey. She sat in the Squad Room, crossing her legs.

'Do you have a cigarette, Steve?' she asked.

Carella gave her one. He did not light it for her. She sat

with the cigarette dangling from her lips until it was apparent she would have to light it herself. Unruffled, she struck a match.

'What about it?' Carella asked.

'What about it?' she repeated, shrugging. 'It's all over, isn't it?'

'You must have really hated him. You must have hated him like poison.'

'You're directing,' Alice said. 'I'm only the star.'

'Don't get glib, Alice!' Carella said angrily. 'I've never hit a woman in my life, but I swear to God—'

'Relax,' she told him. 'It's all over. You'll get your gold star, and then you'll—'

'Alice . . .'

'What the hell do you want me to do? Break down and cry? I hated him, all right? I hated his big, pawing hands and I hated his stupid red hair, and I hated everything about him, all right?'

'Mercer said you'd asked for a divorce. Is that true?'

'No, I didn't ask for a divorce. Hank would've never agreed to one.'

'Why didn't you give him a chance?'

'What for? Did he ever give me a chance? Cooped up in that goddamn apartment, waiting for him to come off some burglary or some knifing or some mugging? What kind of life is that for a woman?'

'You knew he was a cop when you married him.'

Alice didn't answer.

'You could've asked for a divorce, Alice. You could've tried.'

'I didn't want to, damn it. *I wanted him dead.*'

'Well, you've got him dead. Him and two others. You must be tickled now.'

Alice smiled suddenly. 'I'm not too worried, Steve.'

'No?'

'There have to be *some* men on the jury.' She paused. 'Men like me.'

There were, in fact, eight men on the jury.

The jury brought in a verdict in six minutes flat.

Mercer was sobbing as the jury foreman read off the verdict and the judge gave sentence. Alice listened to the judge with calm indifference, her shoulders thrown back, her head erect.

The jury had found them both guilty of murder in the first degree, and the judge sentenced them to death in the electric chair.

On 19 August, Stephen Carella and Theodora Franklin listened to their own sentence.

'Do either of you know of any reason why you both should not be legally joined in marriage, or if there be any present who can show any just cause why these parties should not be legally joined together, let him now speak or hereafter hold his peace.'

Lieutenant Byrnes held his peace. Detective Hal Willis said nothing. The small gathering of friends and relatives watched, dewy-eyed.

The city clerk turned to Carella.

'Do you, Stephen Louis Carella, take this woman as your lawfully wedded wife to live together in the state of matrimony? Will you love, honour and keep her as a faithful man is bound to do, in health, sickness, prosperity and adversity, and forsaking all others keep you alone unto her as long as you both shall live?'

'Yes,' Carella said. 'Yes, I will. I do. Yes.'

'Do you, Theodora Franklin, take this man as your lawfully wedded husband to live together in the state of matrimony? Will you love, honour, and cherish him as a faithful woman is bound to do, in health, sickness, prosperity and adversity, and forsaking all others keep you alone unto him as long as you both shall live?'

Teddy nodded. There were tears in her eyes, but she could not keep the ecstatic smile off her face.

'For as you both have consented in wedlock and have acknowledged it before this company, I do by virtue of the authority vested in me by the laws of this state now pronounce you husband and wife. And may God bless your union.'

Carella took her in his arms and kissed her. The clerk smiled. Lieutenant Byrnes cleared his throat. Willis looked up at the ceiling. The clerk kissed Teddy when Carella released her. Byrnes kissed her. Willis kissed her. All the male relatives and friends came up to kiss her.

Carella smiled idiotically.

'You hurry back,' Byrnes said to him.

'Hurry back? I'm going on my honeymoon, Pete!'

'Well, hurry, anyway. How are we going to run that precinct without you? You're the only cop in the city who has the courage to buck the decisions of stubborn, opinionated Detective-Lieutenant Byrnes of the—'

'Oh, go to hell,' Carella said, smiling.

Willis shook his hand. 'Good luck, Steve. She's a wonderful gal.'

'Thank you, Hal.'

Teddy came to him. He put his arm around her.

'Well,' he said, 'let's go.'

They went out of the room together.

Byrnes stared after them wistfully.

'He's a good cop,' he said.

'Yeah,' Willis answered.

'Come on,' Byrnes said, 'let's go see what's brewing back at the house.'

They went down into the street together.

'Want to get a paper,' Byrnes said. He stopped at a newstand and picked up a copy of Savage's tabloid. The trial news had been crowded right off the front pages. There was more important news.

The headlines simply read:

HEAT WAVE BREAKS!

HAPPY DAY!

THE MUGGER

Ed McBAIN

This is for Angela and Len

INTRODUCTION

Away back in the dim distant past, a magazine called *Manhunt* published a story about a former private eye named Matt Cordell, whose gun licence had been revoked after he'd pistol-whipped his wife's lover. Cordell was a drunk living on the Bowery and reluctantly solving cases for old friends who kept popping up to plague his blotto existence. I always thought of him as a defrocked shamus. The pseudonymous editor of *Manhunt* was someone named 'John McCloud' (I know his real name but will not reveal it under threat of extreme torture) who fancied the Matt Cordell stories and bought some half-dozen of them. One of the stories was called 'Now Die In It', a wordplay twist on the expression, 'You made your bed, now lie in it.' McCloud – in the trade the banter was, 'He wandered lonely as McCloud' – ran the story in 1953. The byline on it was Evan Hunter.

You will be wondering by now what all of this has to do with *The Mugger*. Well, by the time I sat down to write the second book in the 87th Precinct series, I knew that I wanted to accomplish several things.

First, *Cop Hater* had used a classic smoke-screen plot as an introduction to the series, with cops the victims of a killer who seemed out to get cops – a way of bringing my full (at the time) complement of cops onstage as both investigators and potential victims. Having set up the characters who would be around, more or less, in every book, I now wanted to experiment with my theory that the squadroom itself could function as a 'hero', with different cops taking the spotlight in each book. Carella, who'd figured largely in the first novel, would be absent this time around – off on his honeymoon, in fact. A patrolman who'd put in a brief appearance in *Cop Hater* would become involved in a case which he would solve, thereby earning him a promotion and a leap into the squadroom as a rookie detective. To accomplish this, I needed a very strong plot. In fact, in order to elevate the status of the patrolman and keep alive the detectives already introduced in *Cop Hater*, I needed two strong plots. (Please stay with me; I'm getting there.)

Second, the plot involving the detectives would derive from the title: *The Mugger*. (To this day, I will often start a novel with only a title, winging it from there.) The plot involving the patrolman would focus on a murder – it had to be a serious crime in order to earn him his promotion – and it seemed to me that a perfectly serviceable and unusually strong murder plot had been used by me earlier in a story titled (you guessed it) 'Now Die In It'.

At the time, I didn't know if there were any laws about cannibalism, but it seemed to me that many writers before me had expanded short stories into novels or one-act plays into full theatre pieces, and anyway I was a firm believer in wasting not, wanting not. Besides, my patrolman (who was Bert Kling, of course) was a far cry from Matt Cordell, who – in the hardboiled private eye tradition of the day – would as soon sock a woman as kiss her. It seemed to me that a new character would give added dimension to a plot I'd already used once. Seeing the same things through Kling's eyes would make it all seem fresh and different.

As the book turned out, and I didn't know this when I began writing it, the two plots merged – or seemed to merge. I can't tell you more about either just now or I'd spoil both for you. Let me say only that for me the combination seemed to work as a unified whole. I hope it still does. And I hope that Matt Cordell, lying in a gutter someplace with a bottle of cheap wine, will forgive me the petty theft.

'He who steals my purse' – but, after all, I didn't steal his name.

Ed McBain

The city in these pages is imaginary. The people, the places are all fictitious. Only the police routine is based on established investigatory technique.

CHAPTER ONE

The city could be nothing but a woman, and that's good because your business is women.

You know her tossed head in the auburn crowns of moulting autumn foliage, Riverhead, and the park. You know the ripe curve of her breast where the River Dix moulds it with a flashing bolt of blue silk. Her navel winks at you from the harbour in Bethtown, and you have been intimate with the twin loins of Calm's Point and Majesta. She is a woman, and she is your woman, and in the fall she wears a perfume of mingled wood smoke and carbon dioxide, a musky, musty smell bred of her streets and of her machines and of her people.

You have known her fresh from sleep, clean and uncluttered. You have seen her naked streets, have heard the sullen murmur of the wind in the concrete canyons of Isola, have watched her come awake, alive, alive.

You have seen her dressed for work, and you have seen her dressed for play, and you have seen her sleek and smooth as a jungle panther at night, her coat glistening with the pin-point jewels of reflected harbour light. You have known her sultry, and petulant, and loving and hating, and defiant, and meek, and cruel and unjust, and sweet, and poignant. You know all of her moods and all of her ways.

She is big and sprawling and dirty sometimes, and sometimes she shrieks in pain, and sometimes she moans in ecstasy.

But she could be nothing but a woman, and that good because your business is women.

You are a mugger.

Katherine Ellio sat in a hard, wooden chair in the Detective

1

Squad Room of the 87th Precinct. The early-afternoon sunlight, burnished by autumn, tarnished as a Spanish coin, filtered through the long grilled windows, shadowing her face with a meshed-square pattern.

Her face would not have been a pretty one under any circumstances. The nose was too long, and the eyes were a washed-out brown, arched with brows that needed plucking. The lips were thin and bloodless, and the chin was sharply pointed. It was not pretty at all now, because someone had discoloured her right eye and raised a swollen welt along her jaw line.

'He came up so very suddenly,' she said. 'I really don't know whether he'd been following me all along or whether he stepped out of an alley. It's hard to say.'

Detective 3rd Grade Roger Havilland looked down at the woman from his six-foot-four height advantage. Havilland owned the body of a wrestler and the face of a Botticelli cherub. He spoke in a loud, heavy voice, not because Miss Ellio was hard of hearing, but simply because Havilland liked to shout.

'Did you hear footsteps?' he shouted.

'I don't remember.'

'Miss Ellio, try to remember.'

'I am trying.'

'All right, was the street dark?'

'Yes.'

Hal Willis looked at the woman, and then at Havilland. Willis was a small detective, barely topping the five-foot-eight minimum height requirement. His deceptive height and bone structure, however, gave no clue to the lethal effectiveness with which he pursued his chosen profession. His sparkling, smiling brown eyes added to the misconception of a happy gnome. Even when he was angry, Willis smiled. He was, at the moment, not angry. He was, to be absolutely truthful, simply bored. He had heard this story, or variations of it, many times before. Twelve times, to be exact.

'Miss Ellio,' he said, 'when did this man hit you?'

'After he took my purse.'

'Not before?'

'No.'

'How many times did he hit you?'

'Twice.'

'Did he say anything to you?'

'Yes, he . . .' Miss Ellio's face contorted with the pain of remembrance. 'He said he was only hitting me as a warning. So that I wouldn't scream for help when he left.'

'What do you think, Rog?' Willis asked. Havilland sighed, and then half shrugged, half nodded.

Willis, in pensive agreement, was silent for a moment. Then he asked, 'Did he give you his name, Miss Ellio?'

'Yes,' Miss Ellio said. Tears welled up into her inexpressive eyes. 'I know this sounds silly. I know you don't believe me. But it's true. I didn't make this up. I – I never had a black eye in my life.'

Havilland sighed. Willis was suddenly sympathetic. 'Now, now, Miss Ellio,' he said, 'we believe every word you've told us. You're not the first person who's come to us with this story, you see. We're trying to relate the facts of your experience to the facts we already have.' He fished into the breast pocket of his jacket and handed Miss Ellio a handkerchief. 'Here now, dry your eyes.'

'Thank you,' Miss Ellio sobbed. Havilland, bewildered and mystified, blinked at his chivalrous colleague. Willis smiled in his most pleasant A. & P. clerk manner. Miss Ellio, responding immediately, sniffed, dried her eyes, and began to feel as if she were buying a half pound of onions rather than being interrogated on the activities of a mugger.

'Now then,' Willis said kindly, 'when did he give you his name?'

'After he hit me.'

'What did he say?'

'Well, he – he did something first.'

'And what was that?'

'He – I know this sounds silly.'

Willis smiled reassuringly, radiantly. Miss Ellio lifted her face and smiled back girlishly, and Havilland wondered if perhaps they weren't falling in love.

'Nothing a mugger does sounds silly,' Willis said. 'Tell us.'

'He hit me,' Miss Ellio said, 'and he warned me, and then he ... he bowed from the waist.' She looked up as if expecting shock and surprise to register on the faces of the detectives. She met level, implacable gazes. 'He bowed from the waist,' she repeated, as if disappointed with the mild response.

'Yes?' Willis prompted.

'And then he said, "Clifford thanks you, madam." '

'Well, that figures,' Willis said.

'Mmm,' Havilland answered non-committally.

'Clifford thanks you,' Miss Ellio repeated. 'And then he was gone.'

'Did you get any kind of a look at him?' Havilland asked.

'Yes, I did.'

'What did he look like?'

'Well . . .' Miss Ellio paused, thinking. 'He looked just like anybody else.'

Havilland and Willis exchanged patient glances. 'Could you be a little more definite?' Willis asked, smiling. 'Was he blond? Dark-haired? Redheaded?'

'He was wearing a hat.'

'What colour were his eyes?'

'He was wearing sunglasses.'

'The bright night lights blind him,' Havilland said sarcastically. 'Either that, or he's come up with a rare eye disease.'

'Maybe,' Willis said. 'Was he clean-shaven? Bearded? Moustached?'

'Yes,' Miss Ellio said.

'Which one?' Havilland asked.

'The man who attacked me,' she said.

'I meant which one of the thr—'

'Oh, Clean-shaven.'

'Long nose or short nose?'

'Well . . . I guess a medium nose.'

'Thin lips or fat lips?'

'Medium, I guess.'

'Was he short or tall?'

'He was medium height,' Miss Ellio said.

'Fat or thin?'

'Medium,' she said again.

Willis, somehow, was no longer smiling. Miss Ellio regarded his face, and her own smile disintegrated.

'Well, he was,' she said defiantly. 'I can't help it if he didn't have a big strawberry mark on his cheek or a mole on his nose or anything. Listen, I didn't ask for him to be an average person. I didn't ask for him to steal my purse, either. There was a lot of money in that bag.'

'Well,' Havilland shouted, 'we'll do what we can to apprehend him. We have your name and address, Miss Ellio, and if anything comes up we'll notify you. Do you think you'd be able to make a positive identification if you saw the man again?'

'Definitely,' Miss Ellio said. 'He took a lot of money from me. There was a lot of money in that purse.'

Willis bit. 'How much, exactly, was in the purse?' he asked.

'Nine dollars and seventy-two cents,' Miss Ellio answered.

'Plus a fortune in rare gems,' Havilland added in one of his choicer attempts at wit.

'What?' Miss Ellio said.

'We'll call you,' Havilland answered, and he took her elbow and escorted her to the slatted railing that divided the Squad Room from the corridor. When he got back to the desk, Willis was doodling on a sheet of paper.

'Nude broads again?' Havilland asked.

'What?'

'You're a sex fiend.'

5

'I know. But I'm big enough to admit it. What do you make of Miss Ellio?'

'I think she invented the story.'

'Come on, Rog.'

'I think she's been reading in the newspapers about the mugger named Clifford. I think she's an old maid who lives in a two-room apartment. I think she looks under the bed every night and finds nothing but the chamber pot. I think she tripped over the chamber pot last night, bruised herself, and decided to make a bid for a little excitement.' Havilland caught his breath. 'I also think you and her would make a good couple. Why don't you ask her to marry you?'

'You're very comical on Tuesdays,' Willis said. 'You don't believe she was mugged?'

'The sunglasses part was a stroke of real genius! Jesus, the lengths people will go to when they're lying.'

'He *may* have been wearing sunglasses,' Willis said.

'Sure. And Bermuda shorts, too. Like I said, he's suddenly contracted pink eye.' Havilland snorted. ' "Clifford thanks you, madam." Straight out of the papers. There ain't a citizen of this city who hasn't heard about Cliff the Mugger and his punch in the mouth and his bow from the waist.'

'I think she was telling the truth,' Willis said.

'Then you type up the report,' Havilland answered. 'Just between you and me, Cliff's beginning to give me a big pain in the ass.'

Willis stared at Havilland.

'What's the matter?' Havilland shouted.

'When's the last time you typed up a report?'

'Who wants to know?'

'I do,' Willis said.

'When did you become police commissioner?'

'I don't like the way you goof off,' Willis answered. He wheeled over the typing cart, opened the desk drawer, and took out three sheets of the DD report form.

6

'Everybody else is goofing off, ain't they?' Havilland asked. 'What's Carella doing, if not goofing off?'

'He's on his honeymoon, for Christ's sake,' Willis said.

'So? What kind of an excuse is that? I say this Ellio broad is a nut. I say this doesn't call for a report. I say if you feel like typing one up, go ahead.'

'Do you feel strong enough to take another look at the Lousy File?'

'Under what?' Havilland mocked. 'Muggers named Clifford who wears sunglasses and Bermuda shorts?'

'We may have missed something,' Willis said. 'Of course, the cabinet's at least four feet away. I don't want you to strain yourself.'

'I been through the file and back again,' Havilland said. 'Every time this Clifford character hits another broad. There's nothing, nothing. And what this Ellio broad gave us ain't gonna add one bit to the picture.'

'It might,' Willis said.

'No,' Havilland said, shaking his head. 'And you know why? Because that mugging didn't take place in the street, like she said it did.'

'No? Then where did it take place?'

'In her head, pal,' Havilland said. 'All in Miss Ellio's head.'

CHAPTER TWO

The shoulder didn't hurt at all now.

It was funny. You figure you get shot in the shoulder, it's going to hurt for a long time. But it didn't. Not at all.

As a matter of fact, if Bert Kling had had his way, he'd be back on the job, and that job was working as a patrolman out of the 87th Precinct. But Captain Frick was the boss of the uniformed cops at the house, and Captain Frick had said, 'Now you take another week, Bert. I don't care whether the hospital let you go or not. You take another week.'

And so Bert Kling was taking another week, and not enjoying it very much. 'Another week' had started with Monday, and this was Tuesday, and it seemed like a nice brisk autumn day outside and Kling had always liked autumn, but he was bored silly with it now.

The hospital duty hadn't been bad in the beginning. The other cops had come up to see him, and even some of the detectives had dropped around, and he'd been something of a precinct celebrity, getting shot up like that. But after a while, he had ceased to be a novelty, and the visits had been less frequent, and he had leaned back against the fat hospital mattress and begun his adjustment to the boredom of convalescence.

His favourite indoor sport had become the crossing off of days on the calendar. He had also ogled the nurses, but the joy of such diversion had evaporated when he had realized his activities – so long as he was a patient, at any rate – could never rise higher than the spectator level. So he had crossed off the days, one by one, and he had looked forward to returning to the job, yearned for it with almost ferocious intensity.

And then Frick had said, 'Take another week, Bert.'

He'd wanted to say, 'Now look, Captain, I don't need any more rest. I'm as strong as an ox. Believe me, I can handle *two* beats.'

But knowing Frick, and knowing he was a thickheaded old jerk, Kling had kept his peace. He was still keeping his peace. He was very tired of keeping his peace. It was almost better getting shot.

Now that was a curious attitude, he realized, wanting to get back to the job which had been responsible for the bullet in his right shoulder. Not that he'd been shot doing his job, actually. He'd been shot off duty, coming out of a bar, and he wouldn't have been shot if he hadn't been mistaken for someone else.

The shot had been intended for a reporter named Savage, a reporter who'd done some snooping around, a reporter who'd asked too many leading questions of a teenage gang member who'd later summoned all his pals and colleagues to the task of taking care of Savage.

It happened to be Kling's misfortune that he'd been coming out of the same bar in which Savage had earlier interrogated the kid. It was also his misfortune that he was blond, because Savage, inconsiderately, was blond, too. The kids had jumped Kling, anxious to mete out justice, and Kling had pulled his service revolver from his back pocket.

And that's how heroes are made.

Kling shrugged.

Even when he shrugged, the shoulder didn't hurt. So why should he be sitting here in a stupid furnished room when he could be out walking a beat?

He rose and walked to the window, looking down toward the street. The girls were having trouble keeping their skirts tucked against the strong wind. Kling watched.

He liked girls. He liked all girls. Walking his beat, he would watch the girls. He always felt pleased when he did. He was twenty-four years old, and a veteran of the Korean fracas, and he could remember the women he'd seen there,

9

but he never once connected those women with the pleasure he felt in watching the girls in America.

He had seen women crouched in the mud, their cheeks gaunt, their eyes glowing with the reflected light of napalm infernos, wide with terror at the swishing roar of the jet bombers. He had seen underfed bodies hung with baggy quilted garments. He had seen women nursing babies, breasts exposed. The breasts should have been ripe and full with nourishment. They had been, instead, puckered and dried – withered fruits clinging to starved vines.

He had seen young women and old women clawing in the rubble for food, and he could still remember the muted, begging faces and the hollow eyes.

And now, he watched the girls. He watched the strong legs, and the firm breasts, and the well-rounded buttocks, and he felt good. Maybe he was crazy, but there was something exhilarating about strong white teeth and sun-tanned faces and sun-bleached hair. Somehow, they made *him* feel strong, too, and maybe he was crazy, and never once did he make any connexion with what he had seen in Korea.

The knock on the door startled him. He whirled from the window and called, 'Who is it?'

'Me,' the voice answered. 'Peter.'

'Who?' he asked.

'Peter. Peter Bell.'

Who's Peter Bell? he wondered. He shrugged and went to the dresser. He opened the top drawer and took his ·38 from where it lay alongside a box holding his tie clasps. With the gun dangling at his side, he walked to the door and opened it a crack. A man can get shot only once before he realizes you don't open doors too wide, even when the man outside has already given his name.

'Bert?' a voice said. 'This is Peter Bell. Open the door.'

'I don't think I know you,' Kling said cautiously, peering into the darkened hallway, half expecting a volley of shots to splinter the door's wood.

'You don't *know* me? Hey, kid, this is Peter. Hey, don't you remember me? When we were kids? Up in Riverhead? This is me. Peter Bell.'

Kling opened the door a little wider. The man standing in the hallway was no older than twenty-seven. He was tall and muscularly built. He wore a brown leather jacket and yachting cap. In the dimness, Kling could not make out his features clearly, but there was something familiar in the face and he began to feel a little foolish holding a gun. He swung the door open.

'Come in,' he said.

Peter Bell walked into the room. He saw the gun almost instantly, and his eyes went wide. 'Hey!' he said. 'Hey, Jesus, Bert, what's the matter?'

Holding the gun loosely, finally recognizing the man who stood before him in the centre of the room, Kling felt immensely ridiculous. He smiled sheepishly. 'I was cleaning it,' he said.

'You recognize me now?' Bell asked, and Kling had the distinct impression that his lie had not been accepted.

'Yes,' he said. 'How are you, Peter?'

'Oh, soso, can't kick.' He extended his hand, and Kling took it, studying his face more carefully in the light of the room. Bell would have been a good-looking man were it not for the prominence and structure of his nose. In fact, if there was any one part of the face Kling did not recognize, it was the massive, craggy structure that protruded incongruously between sensitive brown eyes. Peter Bell, he remembered now, had been an extremely handsome youth, and he imagined the nose had been one of those things which, during adolescence, simply grow on you. The last time he'd seen Bell had been fifteen years ago, when Bell had moved to another section of Riverhead. The nose, then, had been acquired sometime during that span of years. He realized abruptly that he was staring at the protuberance, and his

11

discomfort increased when Bell said, 'Some schnoz, huh? Eeek, what a beak? Is it a nose or a hose?'

Kling chose that point in the conversation to return his revolver to the open dresser drawer.

'I guess you're wondering what I want,' Bell said.

Kling was, in truth, wondering just that. He turned from the dresser and said, 'Well, no. Old friends often . . .' He stopped, unable to complete the lie. He did not consider Peter Bell a friend. He had not laid eyes on him for fifteen years, and even when they'd been boys together, they'd never been particularly close.

'I read in the papers where you got shot,' Bell said. 'I'm a big reader. I buy six newspapers every day. How do you like that? Bet you didn't even know there was six papers in this city. I read them all, cover to cover. Never miss anything.'

Kling smiled, not knowing what to say.

'Yes, sir,' Bell went on, 'and it certainly came as a shock to me and Molly when we read you got shot. I ran into your mother on Forrest Avenue a little while after that. She said her and your dad were very upset about it, but that's to be expected.'

'Well, it was only a shoulder wound,' Kling said.

'Only a scratch, huh?' Bell said, grinning. 'Well, I got to hand it to you, kid.'

'You said Forrest Avenue. Have you moved back to the old neighbourhood?'

'Huh? Oh, no, no. I'm a hackie now. Got my own cab, medallion and everything. I usually operate in Isola, but I had a Riverhead call, and that's how I happened to be on Forrest Avenue, and that's how I happened to spot your mom. Yeah, sure.'

Kling looked at Bell again, realizing the 'yachting cap' was simply his working headgear.

'I read in the papers where the hero cop got discharged from the hospital,' Bell said. 'Gave your address and everything. You don't live with the folks no more, huh?'

'No,' Kling said. 'When I got back from Korea . . .'

'I missed that one,' Bell said. 'Punctured eardrum, how's that for a laugh? I think the real reason they rejected me was because of the schnoz.' He touched his nose. 'So the papers said where your commanding officer ordered you to take another week's rest.' Bell smiled. His teeth were very white and very even. There was an enviable cleft in his chin. *It's too bad about the nose*, Kling thought. 'How does it feel being a celebrity? Next thing you know, you'll be on that television show, answering questions about Shakespeare.'

'Well . . .' Kling said weakly. He was beginning to wish that Peter Bell would go away. He had not asked for the intrusion, and he was finding it tiresome.

'Yep,' Bell said, 'I certainly got to hand it to you, kid,' and then a heavy silence fell over the room.

Kling bore the silence as long as he was able. 'Would you like a drink . . . or anything?' he asked.

'Never touch it,' Bell said.

The silence returned.

Bell touched his nose again. 'The reason I'm here,' he said at last.

'Yes?' Kling prompted.

'Tell you the truth, I'm a little embarrassed, but Molly figured –' Bell stopped. 'I'm married now, you know.'

'I didn't know.'

'Yeah, Molly. Wonderful woman. Got two kids, another on the way.'

'That's nice,' Kling said, his feeling of awkwardness increasing.

'Well, I might as well get right down to it, huh? Molly's got a sister, nice kid. Her name is Jeannie. She's seventeen. She's been living with us ever since Molly's mom died – two years now, it must be. Yeah.' Bell stopped.

'I see,' Kling said, wondering what Bell's marital life had to do with him.

'The kid's pretty. Look, I might as well level with you, she's

13

a knockout. Matter of fact, she looks just the way Molly looked when she was that age, and Molly's no slouch – even now, pregnant and all.'

'I don't understand, Peter.'

'Well, the kid's been running around.'

'Running around?'

'Well, that's what Molly thinks, anyway.' Bell seemed suddenly uncomfortable. 'You know, she doesn't see her dating any of the local kids or anything, and she knows the kid goes out, so she's afraid she's in with the wrong crowd, do you know what I mean? It wouldn't be so bad if Jeannie wasn't such a pretty kid, but she is. I mean, look, Bert. I'll level with you. She's my sister-in-law and all that, but she's got it all over a lot of older dames you see around. Believe me, she's a knockout.'

'Okay,' Kling said.

'So Jeannie won't tell us anything. We talk to her until we're blue in the face, and we don't get a peep out of her. Molly got the idea of getting a private detective to follow her, see where she goes, that kind of thing. Bert, on the money I make, I can't afford a private dick. Besides, I don't really think the kid is doing anything wrong.'

'You want *me* to follow her?' Kling asked, suddenly getting the picture.

'No, no, nothing like that. Jesus, would I come ask a favour like that after fifteen years? No, Bert, no.'

'What then?'

'I want you to talk to her. That way, Molly'll be happy. Look, Bert, when a woman is carrying, she gets goofy ideas. Pickles and ice cream, you know? Okay, so this is the same thing. She's got this nutty idea that Jeannie is a juvenile delinquent or something.'

'*Me* talk to her?' Kling was flabbergasted. 'I don't even know her. What good would it do for me to –'

'You're a cop. Molly respects law and order. If I bring a cop around, she'll be happy.'

'Hell, I'm practically still a rookie.'

'Sure, but that don't matter. Molly'll see the uniform and be happy. Besides, you really might help Jeannie. Who knows? I mean if she *is* involved with some young toughs.'

'No, I couldn't Peter. I'm sorry, but –'

'You got a whole week ahead of you,' Bell said, 'nothing to do. Look, Bert, I read the papers. Would I ask you to give up any spare time if I knew you were pounding a beat during the day? Bert, give me credit.'

'That's not it, Peter. I wouldn't know what to say to the girl. I just – I don't think so.'

'Please, Bert. As a personal favour to me. For old time's sake, what do you say?'

'No,' Kling answered.

'There's a chance, too, she *is* in with some crumbs. What then? Ain't a cop supposed to prevent crime, nip it in the bud? You're a big disappointment to me, Bert.'

'I'm sorry.'

'Okay, okay, no hard feelings,' Bell said. He rose, seemingly ready to go. 'If you should change your mind, though, I'll leave my address with you.' He took his wallet out of his pocket and fished for a scrap of paper.

'There's no sense . . .'

'Just in case you should change your mind,' Bell said. 'Here, now.' He took a pencil stub from the pocket of the leather jacket and began scribbling on the paper scrap. 'It's on De Witt Street, the big house in the middle of the block. You can't miss it. If you should change your mind, come around tomorrow night. I'll keep Jeannie home until nine o'clock. Okay?'

'I don't think I'll change my mind,' Kling said.

'If you should,' Bell answered. 'I'd appreciate it, Bert. That's tomorrow night. Wednesday. Okay? Here's the address.' He handed Bert the paper. 'I put the telephone number down, too, in case you should get lost. You better put it in your wallet.'

15

Kling took the paper, and then, because Bell was watching him so closely, he put it into his wallet.

'I hope you come,' Bell said. He walked to the door. 'Thanks for listening to me, anyway. It was good seeing you again, Bert.'

'Yes,' Kling said.

'So long now.' Bell closed the door behind him. The room was suddenly very quiet.

Kling went to the window. He saw Bell when he emerged from the building. He watched as Bell climbed into a green-and-yellow taxicab and then gunned away from the kerb. The cab had been parked alongside a fire hydrant.

CHAPTER THREE

They write songs about Saturday night.

The songs all promote the idea that Saturday is a particularly lonely night. The myth has become a part of American culture, and everybody is familiar with it. Stop anybody, six to sixty, and ask, 'What's the loneliest night of the week?' and the answer you'll get is 'Saturday'.

Well, Tuesday's not such a prize, either.

Tuesday hasn't had the benefit of press agentry and promotion, and nobody's written a song about Tuesday. But to a lot of people the Saturday nights and the Tuesday nights are one and the same. You can't estimate degrees of loneliness. Who is more lonely, a man on a desert island on a Saturday night, or a woman carrying a torch in the biggest, noisiest night club on a Tuesday night? Loneliness doesn't respect the calendar. Saturday, Tuesday, Friday, Thursday – they're all the same, and they're all grey.

On Tuesday night, 12 September, a black Mercury sedan was parked on one of the city's loneliest streets, and the two men sitting on the front seat were doing one of the world's loneliest jobs.

In Los Angeles, they call this job 'stakeout'. In the city for which these two men worked, the job was known as 'a plant'.

A plant requires a certain immunity to sleepfulness, a definite immunity to loneliness, and a good deal of patience.

Of the two men sitting in the Mercury sedan, Detective 2nd Grade Meyer was the more patient. He was, in fact, the most patient cop in the 87th Precinct, if not the entire city. Meyer had a father who considered himself a very humorous man. His father's name was Max. When Meyer was born, Max named him Meyer. This was considered convulsively comic, a kid named Meyer Meyer. You have to be very patient if you're born a Jew to begin with. You have to be supernaturally patient if your hilarious old man tags you with a handle like Meyer Meyer. He was patient. But a lifelong devotion to patience often provides a strain and, as the saying goes, something's got to give. Meyer Meyer was as bald as a cue ball, even though he was only thirty-seven years old.

Detective 3rd Grade Temple was falling asleep. Meyer could always tell when Temple was ready to cork off. Temple was a giant of a man, and big men needed more sleep, Meyer supposed.

'Hey!' he said.

Temple's shaggy brows shot up on to his forehead. 'What's the matter?'

'Nothing. What do you think of a mugger who calls himself Clifford?'

'I think he should be shot,' Temple said. He turned and faced the penetrating stare of Meyer's mild blue eyes.

'I think so, too,' Meyer said, smiling. 'You awake?'

'I'm awake.' Temple scratched his crotch. 'I've had this damn itch for the past three days. Drives me nuts. You can't scratch it in public, either.'

'Jungle Rot,' Meyer said.

'Something like that. Jesus, it's ruining me.' He paused. 'My wife won't come near me. She's afraid she'll catch it.'

'Maybe she *gave* it to you,' Meyer suggested.

Temple yawned. 'I never thought of that. Maybe she did.' He scratched himself again.

'If I were a mugger,' Meyer said, figuring the only way to keep Temple awake was to talk to him, 'I wouldn't pick a name like Clifford.'

'Clifford sounds like a pansy,' Temple agreed.

'Steve is a good name for a mugger,' Meyer said.

'Don't let Carella hear you say that.'

'But Clifford. I don't know. You think it's his real name?'

'It could be. Why bother giving it, if it's not his real name?'

'That's a point,' Meyer said.

'I got him tabbed as a psycho, anyway,' Temple said. 'Who else would take a deep bow and then thank his victim? He's a screwball.'

'Do you know the one about the headline?' Meyer, a man who was fond of a good joke, asked.

'No. What's that?'

'The headline they put on the newspaper when this maniac escaped from an insane asylum, ran for three miles, and then raped a neighbourhood girl?'

'No,' Temple said. 'What was the headline?'

Meyer spelled it out grandly with his hands.

'NUTS!

BOLTS AND SCREWS!'

'You and your jokes,' Temple said. 'Sometimes I think you enjoy these damn plants.'

'Sure, I love them.'

'Well, psycho or not, he's knocked over thirteen so far. Did Willis tell you about the dame who came in this afternoon?'

Mayer glanced at his watch. '*Yesterday* afternoon,' he corrected. 'Yes, he told me. Maybe thirteen'll be Cliff's unlucky number, huh?'

'Yeah, maybe. I don't like muggers, you know? They give me a pain.' He scratched himself. 'I like gentleman thieves.'

'Like what?'

'Like murderers even. Murderers, it seems to me, have more class than muggers.'

'Give Cliff time,' Meyer said. 'He's still warming up.'

Both men fell silent. Meyer seemed to be getting something straight in his mind. At last, he said, 'I've been following this case in the papers. One of the other precincts. Thirty-third, I think.'

'Yeah, what about it?'

'Some guy's going around stealing cats.'

'Yeah?' Temple asked. 'You mean cats?'

'Yeah,' Meyer said, watching Temple closely. 'You know,

house pets. So far, they've had eighteen squeals on it in the past week. Something, huh?'

'I'll say,' Temple said.

'I've been following it,' Meyer said. 'I'll let you know how it turns out.' He kept watching Temple, a twinkle in his blue eyes. Meyer was a very patient man. If he'd told Temple about the kidnapped cats, he'd done so for a very good reason. He was still watching Temple when he saw him sit suddenly erect.

'What?' he said.

'Shhh!' Temple said.

They listened together. From far off down the darkened street, they could hear the steady clatter of a woman's high-heeled shoes on the pavement. The city was silent around them, like an immense cathedral closed for the night. Only the hollow, piercing chatter of the wooden heels broke the stillness. They sat in silence, waiting, watching.

The girl went past the car, not turning her head to look at it. She walked quickly, her head thigh. She was in her early thirties, a tall girl with long blonde hair. She swept past the car, and the sound of her heels faded, and still the men were silent, listening.

The even cadence of a second pair of heels came to them. Not the light, empty chatter a woman's feet make. This was heavy conversation. These were the footsteps of a man.

'Clifford?' Temple asked.

'Maybe.'

They waited. The footsteps came closer. They watched the man approaching in the rear-view mirror. Then, simultaneously, both Temple and Meyer stepped out of the car from opposite sides.

The man stopped, fright darting into his eyes.

'What —' he said. 'What is this? A holdup?'

Meyer cut around behind the car and came up alongside of the man. Temple was already blocking his path.

'Your name Clifford?' Temple asked.

'Wah?'

'Clifford.'

'No,' the man said, shaking his head violently. 'You got the wrong party. Look, I –'

'Police,' Temple said tersely, and he flashed the tin.

'P – p – police? What'd I do?'

'Where're you going?' Meyer asked.

'Home. I just come from a movie.'

'Little late to be getting out of a movie, isn't it?'

'Wah? Oh, yeah, we stopped in a bar.'

'Where do you live?'

'Right down the street.' The man pointed, perplexed, frightened.

'What's your name?'

'Frankie's my name.' He paused. 'Ask anybody.'

'Frankie what?'

'Oroglio. With a *g*.'

'What were you doing following that girl?' Meyer shot.

'Wah? Girl? Hey, whatta you nuts or something?'

'You were following a girl?' Temple said. 'Why?'

'Me?' Oroglio pointed both hands at his chest. 'Me? Hey, listen, you made a mistake, fellers. I mean it. You got the wrong guy.'

'A blonde just walked down this street,' Temple said, 'and you came along behind her. If you weren't following –'

'A blonde? Oh, Jesus,' Oroglio said.

'Yes, a blonde,' Temple said, his voice rising. 'Now how about it, mister?'

'In a blue coat?' Oroglio asked. 'Like in a little blue coat? Is that who you mean?'

'That's who we mean,' Temple said.

'Oh, Jesus,' Oroglio said.

'HOW ABOUT IT?' Temple shouted.

'That's my wife!'

'What?'

'My wife, my wife, Conchetta.' Oroglio was wagging his

21

head wildly now. 'My wife, Conchetta. She ain't no blonde. She bleaches it.'

'Look, mister.'

'I swear. We went to the show together, and then we stopped for a few beers. We had a fight in the bar. So she walked out alone. She always does that. She's nuts.'

'Yeah?' Meyer said.

'I swear on my Aunt Christina's hair. She blows up, and she takes off, and I give her four, five minutes. Then I follow her. That's all there is to it. Jesus, I wouldn't follow no blonde.'

Temple looked at Meyer.

'I'll take you up to the house,' Oroglio said, plunging on. 'I'll introduce you. She's my wife! Listen, what do you want? She's my wife!'

'I'll bet she is,' Meyer said resignedly. Patiently, he turned to Temple. 'Go back to the car, George,' he said. 'I'll check this out.'

Oroglio sighed. 'Gee, this is kind of funny, you know that?' he said, relieved. 'I mean being accused of following my own wife. It's kind of funny.'

'It could've been funnier,' Meyer said.

'Yeah? How?'

'She could've been somebody else's wife.'

He stood in the shadows of the alley, wearing the night like a cloak. He could hear his own shallow breathing and beyond that the vast murmur of the city, the murmur of a big-bellied woman in sleep. There were lights in some of the apartments, solitary sentinels piercing the blackness with unblinking yellow. It was dark where he stood, though, and the darkness was a friend to him, and they stood shoulder to shoulder. Only his eyes glowed in the darkness, watching, waiting.

He saw the woman long before she crossed the street.

She was wearing flats, rubber-soled and rubber-heeled, and she made no sound, but he saw her instantly and he tensed himself against the sooty brick wall of the building, waiting, studying her, watching the careless way in which she carried her purse.

She looked athletic, this one.

A beer barrel with squat legs. He liked them better when they looked feminine. This one didn't wear high heels, and there was a springy bounce to her walk; she was probably one of these walkers, one of these girls who do six miles before breakfast. She was closer now, still with that bounce in her step as if she were on a pogo stick. She was grinning, too, grinning like a big baboon picking lice; maybe she was coming home from bingo, or maybe a poker session; maybe she'd just made a big killing, and maybe this big bouncing baby's bag was just crammed full of juicy bills.

He reached out.

His arm circled her neck, and he pulled her to him before she could scream, yanking her into the blackened mouth of the alley. He swung her around then, releasing her neck, catching her sweater up in one big hand, holding it bunched in his fist, slamming her against the brick wall of the building.

'Quiet,' he said. His voice was very low. He looked at her face. She had hard green eyes, and the eyes were narrow now, watching him. She had a thick nose and leathery skin.

'What do you want from me?' she asked. Her voice was gruff.

'Your purse,' he answered. 'Quick.'

'Why are you wearing sunglasses?'

'Give me your purse!'

He reached for it, and she swung it away from him. His hand tightened on the sweater. He pulled her off the wall for an instant, and then slammed her back against the bricks again. 'The purse!'

'No!'

He bunched his left fist and hurled it at her mouth. The woman's head rocked back. She shook it, dazed.

'Listen,' he said, 'listen to me. I don't want to hurt you, you hear? That was just a warning. Now give me the purse, and don't make a peep after I'm gone, you hear? Not a peep!'

The woman slowly wiped the back of her hand across her mouth. She looked at the blood in the darkness, and then she hissed, 'Don't touch me again, you punk!'

He brought back his fist. She kicked him suddenly, and he bent over in pain. She struck out at his face, her fleshy fists bunched, hitting him over and over again.

'You stupid –' he started, and then he caught her hands and shoved her back against the wall. He hit her twice, feeling his bunched knuckles smashing into her stupid, ugly face. She fell back against the wall, moaned, and then collapsed to the concrete at his feet.

He stood over her, breathing heavily. He looked over his shoulder, staring off down the street, lifting the sunglasses for a better view. There was no one in sight. Hastily, he bent down and retrieved the purse from where it had fallen.

The woman did not move.

He looked at her again, wondering. Dammit, why had she been so stupid? He hadn't wanted this to happen. He bent down again, and he put his head on her bosom. Her breast was hard, like a man's pectorals, but she was breathing. He rose, satisfied, and a small smile flitted across his face.

He stood over her, and he bowed, the hand with the purse crossing his waist gallantly, and he said, 'Clifford thanks you, madam.'

And then he ran into the night.

24

CHAPTER FOUR

The bulls of the 87th Squad, no matter what else they agreed upon, generally disagreed upon the comparative worth of the various stool pigeons they employed from time to time. For as the old maid remarked upon kissing the cow, 'It's all a matter of taste,' and one cop's pigeon might very well be another cop's poison.

It was generally conceded that Danny Gimp was the most trustworthy of the lot, but even Danny's staunchest supporters realized that some of their colleagues got better results from some of the other birds. That all of them relied heavily upon information garnered from underworld contacts was an undisputed fact; it was simply a question of whom you preferred to use.

Hal Willis favoured a man named Fats Donner.

In fact, with Donner's solicited and recompensed aid, he had cracked many a tough nut straight down the middle. And there was no question but that Clifford, the mugger with the courtly bow, was beginning to be a tough nut.

There was only one drawback to using Donner, and that was his penchant for Turkish baths. Willis was a thin man. He did not enjoy losing three or four pounds whenever he asked Donner a question.

Donner, on the other hand, was not only fat; he was Fats. And Fats, for the benefit of the uninitiated, is 'fat' in the plural. He was obese. He was immense. He was mountainous.

He sat with a towel draped across his crotch, the thick layers of flesh quivering everywhere on his body as he sucked in the steam that surrounded him and Willis. His body was a pale, sickly white, and Willis suspected he was a junkie, but he'd be damned if he'd pull in a good pigeon on a holding rap.

Donner sat, a great white Buddha, sucking in steam. Willis watched him, sweating.

'Clifford, huh?' Donner asked. His voice was a deep, sepulchral rattle, as if Death were his silent partner.

'Clifford,' Willis said. He could feel the perspiration seeping up into his close-cropped hair, could feel it trickling down the back of his neck, over his narrow shoulders, across his naked backbone. He was hot. His mouth was dry. He watched Donner languishing like a huge, contented vegetable and he cursed all fat men, and he said, 'Clifford. You must have read about him. It's in all the papers.'

'I don't dig papers, man,' Donner said. 'Only the funnies.'

'Okay, he's a mugger. He slams his victims before he takes off, and then he bows from the waist and says, "Clifford thanks you, madam."'

'Only chicks this guy taps?'

'So far,' Willis said.

'I don't make him, dad,' Donner said, shaking his head, sprinkling sweat on to the tiled walls around him. 'Clifford. The name's from nowhere. Hit me again.'

'He wears sunglasses. Last two times out, anyway.'

'Cheaters? He flies by night, this cat?'

'Yes?'

'Clifford, chicks, cheaters. All *C*'s. A cokie?'

'We don't know.'

'*C*, you dig me?' Donner said. 'Clifford, chicks . . .'

'I caught it the first time around,' Willis answered.

Donner shrugged. It seemed to be getting hotter in the steam room. The steam billowed up from hidden instruments of the devil, smothering the room with a thick blanket of soggy, heat-laden mist. Willis sighed heavily.

'Clifford,' Donner said again. 'This his square handle?'

'I don't know.'

'I mean, dad, I grip with a few muggers, but none with a

Clifford tag. If this is just a party stunt to gas the chicks, that's another thing again. Still, Clifford. This he picked from hunger.'

'He's knocked over fourteen women,' Willis said. 'He's not so hungry any more.'

'Rape?'

'No.'

'No eyes for the chicks, the Clifford cat, huh? He's a faggot?'

'We don't know.'

'Big hauls?'

'Fifty-four bucks was tops. Mostly peanuts.'

'Small time,' Donner said.

'Do you know any *big-time* muggers?'

'The ones who work the Hill don't go for chewing-gum loot. I've known plenty big muggers in my day.' Donner lay back on the marble seat, readjusting the towel across his middle. Willis wiped sweat from his face with a sweaty hand.

'Listen, don't you ever conduct business outside?' Willis asked.

'What do you mean, outside?'

'Where there's air.'

'Oh. Sure, I do. This summer I was out a lot. Man, it was a great summer, wasn't it?'

Willis thought of the record-breaking temperatures that had crippled the back of the city. 'Yeah, great,' he said. 'So what about this, Fats? Have you got anything for me?'

'No rumble, if that's what you mean. He's either new, or he keeps still.'

'Many new faces in town?'

'Always new faces, dad,' Donner said. 'None I peg for muggers, though. Tell the truth, I don't know many hit-and-run boys. This is for the wet-pants nowadays. You figure Clifford for a kid?'

'Not from what the victims have told us about him.'

'Old man?'

'Twenties.'

'Tough age,' Donner said. 'Not quite a boy, yet not quite a man.'

'He hits like a man,' Willis said. 'He sent the one last night to the hospital.'

'I tell you,' Donner said, 'let me go on the earie. I listen a little here and there, and I buzz you. Dig?'

'When?' Willis asked.

'Soon.'

'How soon is soon?'

'How high is up?' Donner asked. He rubbed his nose with his forefinger. 'You looking for a lead or a pinch?'

'A lead would suit me fine,' Willis said.

'Gone. So let me sniff a little. What's today?'

'Wednesday,' Willis said.

'Wednesday,' Donner repeated, and then for some reason, he added, 'Wednesday's a good day. I'll try to get back to you sometime tonight.'

'If you'll call, I'll wait for it. Otherwise, I go home at four.'

'I'll call,' Donner promised.

'Okay,' Willis said. He rose, tightened the towel about his waist and started out.

'Hey, ain't you forgetting something?' Donner called.

Willis turned. 'All I came in with was the towel,' he said.

'Yeah, but I come here every day, man,' Donner said. 'This can cost a man, you know.'

'We'll talk cost when you deliver,' Willis said. 'All I got so far is a lot of hot air.'

Bert Kling wondered what he was doing here.

He came down the steps from the elevated structure, and he recognized landmarks instantly. This had not been his old neighbourhood, but he had listed this area among his teenage stamping grounds and he was surprised now to find a faint nostalgia creeping into his chest.

If he looked off down the Avenue, he could see the wide

sweep of the train tracks where the El screeched sparkingly around Cannon Road, heading north. He could see, too, the flickering lights of a Ferris wheel against the deepening sky – the carnival, every September and every April, rain or shine, setting up business in the empty lot across from the housing project. He had gone to the carnival often when he was a kid, and he knew this section of Riverhead as well as he knew his own old neighbourhood. Both were curious mixtures of Italians, Jews, Irish, and Negroes. Somebody had set a pot to melting in Riverhead, and somebody else had forgotten to turn off the gas.

There had never been a racial or religious riot in this section of the city, and Kling doubted if there ever would be one. He could remember back to 1935 and the race riots in Diamondback, and the way the people in Riverhead had wondered if the riots would spread there, too. It was certainly a curiously paradoxical thing; for while white men and black men were slitting each other's throats in Diamondback, white men and black men in Riverhead prayed together that the disease would not spread to their community.

He was only a little boy at the time, but he could still remember his father's words: 'If you help spread any of this filth, you won't be able to sit for a week, Bert. I'll fix you so you'll be lucky if you even can *walk*!'

The disease had not spread.

He walked up the Avenue now, drinking in the familiar landmarks. The *latticini*, and the kosher butcher shop, and the paint store, and the big A. & P., and the bakeshop, and Sam's candy store there on the corner. God, how many ice-cream sundaes had he eaten in Sam's? He was tempted to stop in and say Hello, but he saw a stranger behind the counter, a short, bald-headed man, not Sam at all, and he realized with painful clarity that a lot of things had changed since he was a carefree adolescent.

The thought was sobering as well as painful, and he wondered for the fiftieth time why he had come back to

29

Riverhead, why he was walking toward De Witt Street and the home of Peter Bell. To talk to a young girl? What could he say to a seventeen-year-old kid? Keep your legs crossed, honey?

He shrugged his wide shoulders. He was a tall man, and he was wearing his dark blue suit tonight, and his blond hair seemed blonder against the dark fabric. When he reached De Witt, he turned south and then reached into his wallet for the address Peter had given him. Up the street, he could see the yellow brick and the cyclone fence of the junior high school. The street was lined with private houses, mostly wooden structures, here and there a brick dwelling tossed in to break the monotony. Old trees grew close to the kerbs on either side of the street, arching over the street to embrace in a blazing, autumn-leaved cathedral. There was something very quiet and very peaceful about De Witt Street. He saw the bushels of leaves piled near the gutter, saw a man standing with a rake in one hand, the other hand on his hip, solemnly watching the small, smoky fire of leaves burning at his feet. The smell was a good one. He sucked it deep into his lungs. This was a lot different from the crowded, bulging streets the 87th Precinct presided over. This was a lot different from crowded tenements and soot-stained buildings reaching grimy concrete fingers to the sky. The trees here were of the same species found in Grover's Park, which hemmed in the 87th on the south. But you could be sure no assassins lurked behind their stout trunks. That was the difference.

In the deepening dusk, with the street lamps going on suddenly, Bert Kling walked and listened to the sound of his footsteps and – quite curiously – he was glad he had come.

He found Bell's house: the big one in the middle of the block, just as he'd promised. It was a tall, two-family, clapboard-and-brick structure, the clapboard white. A rutted concrete driveway sloped upward toward a white garage at the back of the house. A flight of steps led to the front door.

Kling checked the address again, and then climbed the steps and pressed the bell button set in the doorjamb. He waited a second, and the door buzzed, and he heard the small click as he twisted the knob and shoved it inward. He was in a small foyer, and he saw another door open instantly, and then Peter Bell stepped into the foyer, grinning.

'Bert you came! Jesus, I don't know how to thank you.'

Kling nodded and smiled. Bell took his hand.

'Come in, come in.' His voice dropped to a whisper. 'Jeannie's still here. I'll introduce you as a cop friend of mine, and then Molly and me'll take off, okay?'

'Okay,' Kling said. Bell led him to the open doorway. There were still cooking smells in the house, savoury smells that heightened Kling's feeling of nostalgia. The house was warm and secure, welcome after the slight nip there had been in the air outside.

Bell closed the door and called, 'Molly!'

The house, Kling saw immediately, was constructed like a railroad flat, one room following the other, so that you had to walk through every room in the house if you wanted to get to the end room. The front door opened into the living-room, a small room furnished with a three-piece sofa-and-easy-chair set that had undoubtedly been advertised as a 'Living Room Suite' by one of the cheaper furniture stores. There was a mirror on the wall over the sofa. A badly framed landscape hung over one of the easy chairs. The inevitable television set stood in one corner of the room, and a window under which was a radiator, occupied the other corner.

'Sit down, Bert,' Bell said. 'Molly!' he called again.

'Coming,' a voice called from the other end of the house, an end he suspected was the kitchen.

'She's doing the dishes,' Bell explained. 'She'll be right in. Sit down, Bert.' Kling sat in one of the easy chairs. Bell hovered over him, being the gracious host. 'Can I get you something? A glass of beer? Cigar? Anything?'

'The last time I had a glass of beer,' Kling said, 'I got shot right afterwards.'

'Well, ain't nobody going to shoot you here. Come on, have a glass. We've got some cold in the Frigidaire.'

'No, thanks anyway,' Kling said politely.

Molly Bell came into the room, drying her hands on a dish towel.

'You must be Bert,' she said. 'Peter's told me all about you.' She gave her right hand a final wipe and then crossed to where Kling had stood up, and extended her hand. Kling took it, and she squeezed it warmly. In describing her, Bell had said, 'Molly's no slouch – even now, pregnant and all.' Kling hated to disagree, but he honestly found very little that was attractive in Molly Bell. She might at one time have been a knockout, but them days were gone forever. Even discounting the additional waist-high bulge of the expectant mother, Kling saw only a washed-out blonde with faded blue eyes. The eyes were very tired, and wrinkles radiated from their edges. Her hair had no lustre; it hung from her head disconsolately. Her smile did not help, because it happened to be a radiant smile which served only as a contrast for the otherwise drab face. He was a little shocked, partly because of Bell's advance publicity, partly because he realized the girl couldn't have been much older than twenty-four or twenty-five.

'How do you do, Mrs Bell?' he said.

'Oh, call me Molly. Please.' There was something very warm about Molly, and he found himself liking her immensely, and somewhat disliking Bell for giving a build-up which couldn't fail to be disappointing. He wondered, too, if Jeannie was the 'knock-out' Bell had described. He had his doubts now.

'I'll get you a beer, Bert,' Bell said.

'No, really, I –'

'Come on, come on,' Bell said, overriding him and starting out toward the kitchen.

32

When he was gone, Molly said, 'I'm so glad you could come, Bert. I think your talking to her will do a lot of good.'

'Well, I'll try,' Kling said. 'Where is she?'

'In her room.' Molly gestured with her head toward the other end of the house. 'With the door locked.' She shook her head. 'That's what I mean. She behaves so strangely. I was seventeen once, Bert, and I didn't behave that way. She's a girl with troubles.'

Kling nodded noncommittally.

Molly sat, her hands folded in her lap, her feet close together. 'I was a fun-loving girl when I was seventeen,' Molly said, somewhat wistfully. 'You can ask Peter. But Jeannie . . . I don't know. She's a girl with secrets. Secrets, Bert.' She shook her head again. 'I try to be a sister and a mother both to her, but she won't tell me a thing. There's a wall between us, something that was never there before, and I can't understand it. Sometimes I think – I think she hates me. Now why should she hate me? I've never done a thing to her, not a thing.' Molly paused, sighing heavily.

'Well,' Kling said diplomatically, 'you know how kids are.'

'Yes, I do,' Molly said. 'It hasn't been so long ago that I've forgotten. I'm only twenty-four, Bert. I know I look a lot older than that, but taking care of two kids can knock you out – and now another one coming, it isn't easy. And trying to handle Jeannie, too. It takes a lot out of a woman. But I was seventeen, too, and not so long ago, and I can remember. Jeannie isn't acting right. Something's troubling her, Bert. I read so much about teenagers belonging to gangs and what not. I'm afraid. I think she may be in with a bad crowd, kids who are making her do bad things. That's what's troubling her, I think. I don't know. Maybe you can find out.'

'Well, I'll certainly try.'

'I'd appreciate it. I asked Peter to get a private detective, but he said we couldn't afford it. He's right, of course. God knows, I can barely make ends meet with what he brings home.' She sighed again. 'But the big thing is Jeannie. If I can just find out what's *wrong* with her, what's made her the way she is now. She didn't used to be like this, Bert. It's only . . . I don't know . . . about a year ago now, I suppose. She suddenly became a young lady, and just as suddenly she – she's slipped away from me.'

Bell came back into the room, carrying a bottle of beer and a glass.

'Did you want one, honey?' he asked Molly.

'No, I've got to be careful.' She turned to Kling. 'The doctor says I'm putting on too much weight.'

Bell poured the beer for Kling. He handed him the glass and said, 'There's more in the bottle. I'll leave it here on the end table for you.'

'Thank you,' Kling said. He lifted his glass. 'Well, here's to the new baby.'

'Thank you,' Molly said, smiling.

'Seems every time I turn around, Molly's pregnant again,' Bell said. 'It's fantastic.'

'Oh, Peter,' Molly said, still smiling.

'All I have to do is take a deep breath, and Molly's pregnant. She brought in a specimen of me to the hospital. The doctors told her I had enough there to fertilize the entire female population of China. How do you like that?'

'Well,' Kling said, a little embarrassed.

'Oh, he's such a *man*,' Molly said sarcastically. 'It's me who has to carry them around, though.'

'Did she tell you a little more about Jeannie?'

'Yes,' Kling said.

'I'll get her for you in a few minutes.' He looked at his watch. 'I got to be taking the cab out soon, and I'll drop Molly off at a movie. Then you and Jeannie can talk alone – until our sitter gets here, anyway.'

'You drive a lot at night?' Kling asked, making conversation.

'Three, four times a week. Depends on how good I do during the day. It's my own cab, and I'm my own boss.'

34

'I see,' Kling said. He sipped at the beer. It was not as cold as Bell had advertised it. He began to doubt seriously *any* of Bell's advance promotion, and he looked forward to meeting Jeannie with vague scepticism.

'I'll get her,' Bell said.

Kling nodded. Molly tensed where she sat on the edge of the sofa. Bell left the room and walked through the apartment. Kling heard him knocking on the closed door, and then heard his voice saying 'Jeannie? Jeannie?'

There was a muffled answer which Kling could not decipher; then Bell said, 'There's a friend of mine I'd like you to meet. Nice young feller. Come on out, won't you?'

There was another muffled answer, and then Kling heard a lock being unsnapped and a door opening and a young girl's voice asking, 'Who is he?'

'Friend of mine,' Bell said. 'Come on, Jeannie.'

Kling heard footsteps coming through the apartment. He busied himself with the glass of beer. When he lifted his head, Bell was standing in the doorway to the room, the girl beside him – and Kling no longer doubted his veracity.

The girl was a little taller than Molly. She wore her blonde hair clipped close to her head, and it was the blondest hair Kling had ever seen in his life. It was almost yellow, like ripe corn, and he knew instantly that she had never touched it. The hair was as natural as her face, and her face was a perfect oval with a slightly tilted nose and wide, clear blue eyes. Her brows were black, as if fate hadn't been able to make up its mind, and they arched over the blue eyes, suspended between them and the yellow hair, strikingly beautiful. Her lips were full, and she wore a pale orange lipstick, and her mouth was not smiling.

She wore a straight black skirt and a blue sweater, the sleeves shoved up to her elbows. She was a slender girl, but a slender girl with the remarkable combination of good hips and firm, full breasts that crowded her sweater. Her legs were good, too. Her thighs were full, and her calves were beautifully curved, and even the loafers she wore could not hide the natural splendour of her legs.

She was a woman, and a beautiful woman.

Peter Bell hadn't lied. His sister-in-law was a knockout.

'Jeannie, this is Bert Kling. Bert, I'd like you to meet my sister-in-law, Jeannie Paige.'

Kling got to his feet. 'How do you do?' he said.

'Hi,' Jeannie answered. She did not move from where she stood alongside Bell.

'Bert's a cop,' Bell said. 'Maybe you read about him. He got shot in a bar downtown.'

'*Outside* the bar,' Kling corrected.

'Sure, well,' Bell said. 'Honey, your sister and I have to go now, and Bert only just got here, so I thought you wouldn't mind talking to him a while – until the sitter gets here, huh?'

'Where are you going?' Jeannie asked.

'I got to hack a while, and Molly's taking in a movie.'

'Oh,' Jeannie said, looking at Kling suspiciously.

'So okay?' Bell asked.

'Sure,' Jeannie replied.

'I'll take off this apron and comb my hair,' Molly said. Kling watched her as she rose. He could see the resemblance between her and Jeannie now, and he could now believe that Molly, too, had been a damned attractive woman once. But marriage and motherhood, and work and worry, had taken a great deal out of her. She was no match now for her younger sister, if she had ever been. She went out of the living-room and into a room Kling supposed was the bathroom.

'It's a nice night,' Kling said awkwardly.

'Is it?' Jeannie asked.

'Yes.'

'Molly! Hurry up!' Bell called.

'Coming,' she answered from the bathroom.

'Very mild. For autumn, I mean,' Kling said. Jeannie made no comment.

In a few minutes, Molly came out of the bathroom, her

hair combed, fresh lipstick on her mouth. She put on her coat and said, 'If you go out, don't come home too late, Jeannie.'

'Don't worry,' Jeannie answered.

'Well, good night. It was nice meeting you, Bert. Call us, won't you?'

'Yes, I will.'

Bell paused with his hand on the doorknob. 'I'm leaving her in your hands, Bert,' he said. 'Good night.' He and Molly went out of the room, closing the door behind them. Kling heard the outside door slam shut. The room was dead silent. Outside, he heard a car starting. He assumed it was Bell's cab.

'Whose idea was this?' Jeannie asked.

'I don't understand,' Kling said.

'Your coming here. Hers?'

'No. Peter's an old friend of mine.'

'Yeah?'

'Yes.'

'How old are you?' Jeannie asked.

'Twenty-four,' Kling said.

'Is she trying to fix us up or something?'

'What?'

'Molly. Is she trying to finagle something?'

'I don't know what you mean.'

Jeannie stared at him levelly. Her eyes were very blue. He watched her face, suddenly overwhelmed by her beauty. 'You're not as dumb as you sound, are you?' she asked.

'I'm not trying to sound dumb,' Kling said.

'I'm asking you whether or not Molly has plans for you and me.'

Kling smiled. 'No, I don't think she has.'

'I wouldn't put it past her,' Jeannie said.

'I take it you don't like your sister very much.'

Jeannie seemed suddenly alert. 'She's okay,' she answered.

'But?'

'No buts. My sister is fine.'

'Then why do you resent her?'

'Because I know Peter wouldn't go hollering cop, so this must be her idea.'

'I'm here as a friend, not as a cop.'

'Yeah, I'll bet,' Jeannie said. 'You'd better drink your beer. I'm leaving as soon as that sitter arrives.'

'Got a date?' Kling asked casually.

'Who wants to know?'

'I do.'

'It's none of your business.'

'That puts me in my place, I guess.'

'It should,' Jeannie said.

'You seem a lot older than seventeen.'

For a moment, Jeannie bit her lip. 'I *am* a lot older than seventeen,' she answered then. 'A whole lot older, Mr Kling.'

'Bert,' he corrected. 'What's the matter, Jeannie? You haven't smiled once since I met you.'

'Nothing's the matter.'

'Trouble at school?'

'No.'

'Boyfriend?'

She hesitated. 'No.'

'Ah-ha,' Kling said. 'When you're seventeen, it's usually a boyfriend.'

'I haven't got a boyfriend.'

'No. What then? Crush on someone who doesn't care?'

'Stop it!' Jeannie said harshly. 'This is none of your business. You've no right to pry!'

'I'm sorry,' Kling said. 'I was trying to help. You're not in any kind of trouble, are you?'

'No.'

'I meant with the law.'

'No. And if I was, I certainly wouldn't tell it to a cop.'

'I'm a friend, remember?'

'Sure, friend.'

'You're a very pretty girl, Jeannie.'

'So I've been told.'

'A pretty girl can find herself in with the wrong crowd. A pretty girl –'

'– is like a melody,' Jeannie concluded. 'I'm *not* in with the wrong crowd. I'm fine. I'm a healthy, normal teenager. Leave me alone.'

'Do you date much?'

'Enough.'

'Anyone steady?'

'No.'

'Anyone in mind for a steady?'

'Do *you* date much?' Jeannie countered.

'Not much.'

'Anyone steady?'

'No,' Kling answered, smiling.

'Anyone in mind for a steady?'

'No.'

'Why not? I should think a hero cop would be in wild demand.'

'I'm shy,' Kling said.

'I'll just bet you are. We haven't known each other ten minutes, and we're discussing my love life. What'll you ask next? My brassière size?' Kling's eyes dropped inadvertently to the sweater. 'I'll save you the trouble,' Jeannie snapped. 'It's a thirty-eight, C-cup.'

'I figured as much,' Kling answered.

'That's right, I keep forgetting you're a cop. Cops are very observant, aren't they? Are you the force's prize detective?'

'I'm a patrolman,' Kling said levelly.

'Smart fellow like you, only a patrolman?'

'What the hell's eating you?' Kling asked suddenly, his voice rising.

'Nothing. What's eating you?'

'I never met a kid like you. You've got a decent home, you've got looks any other girl would chop off her right arm for, and you sound –'

39

'I'm the belle of Riverhead, didn't you know? I've got boys crying for –'

'– and you sound as if you're sixty years old living in a tenement flat! What the hell's eating you, girl?'

'Nothing. I simply don't like the idea of a cop coming around to ask me questions.'

'Your people felt you needed help,' Kling said wearily. 'I don't know why. Seems to me you could step into a cage of tigers and come out unscratched. You're about as soft as an uncut diamond.'

'Thanks.'

Kling rose. 'Take care of your beauty, kid,' he said. 'You may not have it when you're thirty-five.' He started for the door.

'Bert,' she called.

He turned. She was staring at the floor. 'I'm sorry,' she said. 'I'm not usually a bitch.'

'What is it?' he asked.

'Nothing, really. I have to work it out for myself, that's all.' She smiled tremulously. 'Everything'll be all right.'

'Okay,' he said. 'Don't let it kill you. Everybody's got troubles. Especially at seventeen.'

'I know,' she said, still smiling.

'Listen, can I buy you an ice-cream or something? Take your mind off your troubles.'

'No, thanks,' she said. She looked at her watch. 'I have an appointment.'

'Oh. Well, okay. Have fun, Jeannie.' He looked at her closely. 'You're a beautiful girl. You should be enjoying yourself.'

'I know,' she answered.

'If you should need anything – if you should feel I can help – you can call me at the 87th Precinct.' He smiled. 'That's where I work.'

'All right. Thanks.'

'Want to walk down with me?'

'No, I have to wait for the sitter.'

Kling snapped his fingers. 'Sure.' He paused. 'If you'd like me to wait with you . . .'

'I'd rather you didn't. Thanks, anyway.'

'Okay,' Kling said. He looked at her once more. Her face was troubled, very troubled. He knew there was more to say, but he didn't know how to say it. 'Take care of yourself,' he managed.

'I will. Thanks.'

'Sure,' Kling said. He opened the door and stepped into the foyer. Behind him, Jeannie Paige locked the door.

CHAPTER FIVE

Willis did not like working overtime. There are very few people who enjoy working overtime, unless they are paid for it. Willis was a detective 3rd Grade and his salary was $5,230 a year. He was not paid by the hour, nor was he paid by the number of crimes he solved yearly. His salary was $5,230, and that was what he got no matter how many hours he put in.

He was somewhat miffed, therefore, when Fats Donner failed to call him that Wednesday night. He had hung around the Squad Room, answering the phone every time it rang, and generally making a nuisance of himself with the bulls who had come in on relief. He had listened for a while to Meyer, who was telling Temple about some case the 33rd had, where some guy was going around stealing cats. The story had not interested him, and he had continually glanced at the big clock on the wall, waiting. He left the house at nine, convinced that Donner would not call that night.

When he reported for work at seven-forty-five the next morning, the desk sergeant handed him a note which told him Donner had called at eleven-fifteen the night before. Donner had asked that Willis call him back as soon as possible. A number was listed on the sheet of paper. Willis walked past the desk and to the right, where a rectangular sign and a pointing hand showed the way to the DETECTIVE DIVISION. He climbed the metal steps, turned where the grilled window threw a pale greyish morning light on a five-by-five-square interruption of the steps, and then proceeded up another sixteen steps to the second floor.

He turned his back to the doors at the end of the corridor, the doors marked LOCKERS. He walked past the benches and the MEN'S LAVATORY, and the CLERICAL office, and then through the slatted rail divider and into the Detective Squad

Room. He signed in, said good morning to Havilland and Simpson, who were having coffee at one of the desks, and then went to his own desk and slid the phone toward him. It was a grey, dull morning, and the hanging light globes cast a dust-covered luminescence over the room. He dialled the number and waited, looking over toward Byrnes' office. The lieutenant's door was wide open, which meant the lieutenant had not yet arrived. Byrnes generally closed his door as soon as he was in his office.

'Got a hot lead, Hal?' Havilland called.

'Yeah,' Willis said. A voice on the other end of his phone said, 'Hello?' The voice was sleepy, but he recognized it as Donner's.

'Fats, this is Willis. You called me last night?'

'What?' Donner said.

'Detective Willis, 87th Squad,' Willis said.

'Oh. Hi. Man, what time is it?'

'About eight.'

'Don't you cats never sleep?'

'What've you got for me?'

'You make a stud going by Skippy Randolph?'

'Not off the bat. Who is he?'

'He's recently from Chi, but I'm pretty sure he's got a record here, too. He's been mugging.'

'You sure?'

'Straight goods. You want to meet him?'

'Maybe.'

'There's gonna be a little cube rolling tonight. Randolph'll be there. You can rub elbows.'

'Where?'

'I'll take you,' Donner said. He paused. 'Steam baths cost, you know.'

'Let me check him out first,' Willis said. 'He may not be worth meeting. You sure he'll be at this crap game?'

'Posilutely, dad.'

'I'll call you back later. Can I reach you at this number?'

'Until eleven. I'll be at the baths after that.'

Willis looked at the name he'd written on his pad. 'Skippy Randolph. His own moniker?'

'The Randolph is. I'm not so sure about the Skippy.'

'But you're sure he's mugging?'

'Absotively,' Donner said.

'Okay. I'll call you back.' Willis replaced the receiver, thought for a moment, and then dialled the Bureau of Criminal Identification. Miscolo, one of the patrolmen from Clerical came into the office and said, 'Hey, Hal, you want some coffee?'

'Yes,' Willis said, and then he told the IB what he wanted.

The Bureau of Criminal Identification was located at Headquarters, downtown on High Street. It was open twenty-four hours a day, and its sole reason for existence was the collection and compilation and cataloguing of any and all information descriptive of criminals. The IB maintained a Fingerprint File, a Criminal Index File, a Wanted File, a Degenerate File, a Parolee File, a Released Prisoner File, a Known Gamblers, Known Rapists, Known Muggers, Known Any-and-All Kinds of Criminal Files. Its Modus Operandi File contained more than 80,000 photographs of known criminals. And since all persons charged with and convicted of a crime are photographed and fingerprinted as specified by law, the file was continually growing and continually being brought up to date. Since the IB received and classified some 206,000 sets of prints yearly, and since it answered requests for some 250,000 criminal records from departments all over the country, Willis' request was a fairly simple one to answer, and they delivered their package to him within the hour. The first photostated item Willis dug out of the envelope was Randolph's fingerprint card.

Willis looked at this rapidly. The fingerprints were worthless to him at this stage of the game. He reached into

POLICE DEPARTMENT

No. 571-210 | Sex Male | Color White | Classification 4 S 1 R III 9 / S 1 U III 10

Name Sanford Richard Randolph

| 1. Right Thumb | 2. Right Index Finger | 3. Right Middle Finger | 4. Right Ring Finger | 5. Right Little Finger |
| 6. Left Thumb | 7. Left Index Finger | 8. Left Middle Finger | 9. Left Ring Finger | 10. Left Little Finger |

45

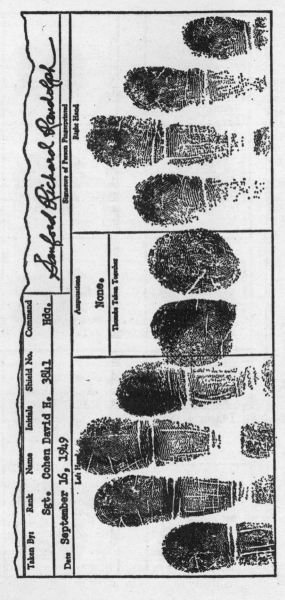

Taken By:	Rank	Name	Initials	Shield No.	Command
	Sgt.	Cohen David H.		3841	Hdq.

Date September 16, 1949

Sanford Richard Randolph

Signature of Person Fingerprinted

Right Hand

Amputations

None.

Thumbs Taken Together

Left Hand

IDENTIFICATION BUREAU

Name **Sanford Richard Randolph**

Identification Jacket Number **M381904**

Alias **"Skippy" "Skip" "Skipper" "Scuppers"**
Randolph Color **White**

Residence **29 Hunter Lane, Calm's Point**

Date of Birth **January 12, 1918** Age **31**

Birthplace **Chicago, Illinois**

Height **5' 10"** Weight **163** Hair **Brown** Eyes **Blue**

Comp. **Fair** Occupation **Truck driver**

Scars and Tattoos **Knife scar on left temple, half inch**
in length. Tattoo on right biceps, "Mother"
in heart. Tattoo on right forearm, Anchor.
Tattoo on left forearm, Marine Corps Shield and
"Semper Fidelis." Bullet-wound scar, left leg.

Arrested By: **Det. 2nd/Gr. Peter Di Labbio**

Detective Division Number **37-1046-1949**

Date of Arrest **9/15/49** Place **South 74 Street, Isola**

Charge **Assault with intent to commit a felony**

Brief Details of Crime **Randolph attacked a 53-year-old**
man, beat him, and then demanded his wallet.
Det. Di Labbio, cruising in area, apprehended
him as he held victim against wall of building.

Previous Record **None**

Indicted **Criminal Courts, September 16, 1949**

Final Charge **Assault in second degree,**
Penal Law 242

Disposition **One year's imprisonment in workhouse**
at Baily's Island.

the envelope and pulled out the next item, a photostated copy of the back of Randolph's fingerprint card.

Willis looked through the other items in the envelope. There was a card stating that Randolph had been released from Baily's after eight months of good behaviour on 2 May 1950. He had notified his parole officer that he wished to return to Chicago, the city in which he was born, the city he should have returned to as soon as he'd been discharged from the Marine Corps. Permission had been granted, and he'd left the city for Chicago on 5 June 1950. There was a written report from the Chicago parole office to which Randolph's records had been transferred. Apparently, he had in no way violated his parole.

Willis thumbed through the material and came up with a transcript of Randolph's Marine Corps record. He had enlisted on 8 December, the day after Pearl Harbour. He was twenty-three years old at the time, almost twenty-four. He had risen to the rank of corporal, had taken part in the landings at Iwo Jima and Okinawa and had personally been responsible for the untimely demise of fifty-four Japanese soldiers. On 17 June 1945 he was wounded in the leg during a Sixth Marine Division attack against the town of Mezado. He had been sent back for hospitalization on Pearl, and after convalescence he was sent to San Francisco, where he was honourably discharged.

And four years later, he mugged a fifty-three-year-old man and tried to take his wallet.

And now, according to Donner, he was back in the city – and mugging again.

Willis looked at his watch, and then dialled Donner's number.

'Hello?' Donner asked.

'This crap game tonight,' Willis said. 'Set it up.'

The crap game in question was of the floating variety, and on this particular Thursday night it was being held in a warehouse close to the River Highway. Willis, in keeping with the festive spirit of the occasion, wore a sports shirt patterned with horses' heads and a sports jacket. When he met Donner, he almost didn't recognize him. Somehow, the flabby quivering pile of white flesh that sucked in steam at the Turkish baths managed to acquire stature and even eminence when it was dumped into a dark blue suit. Donner still looked immense, but immense now like a legendary giant, magnificent, almost regal in his bearing. He shook hands with Willis, during which ceremony a ten-dollar bill passed from one palm to another, and then they headed for the warehouse, the crap game, and Skippy Randolph.

A skinny man at the side-door recognized Donner, but took pause until Donner introduced Hal Willis as 'Willy Harris, an old chum'. He passed them into the warehouse then, the first floor of which was dark except for a light bulb hanging in one corner of the room. The crapshooters were huddled under that bulb. The rest of the room was crowded with what seemed to be mostly refrigerators and ranges.

'There's a fix in with the watchman and the cop on the beat,' Donner explained. 'Won't anybody bother us here.' They walked across the room, their heels sounding noisily on the concrete floor. 'Randolph is the one in the green jacket,' Donner said. 'You want me to introduce you, or will you make it alone?'

'Alone is better,' Willis said. 'If this gets fouled, I don't want it going back to you. You're valuable.'

'The harm's already done,' Donner said. 'I passed you through the door, didn't I?'

'Sure, but I *could* be a smart cop who even had you fooled.'

'Gone,' Donner said. And then – in a whisper, so that his heartfelt compliment would not sound like apple-polishing – he added, 'You *are* a smart cop.'

If Willis heard him, he gave no sign of it. They walked over to where the blanket was spread beneath the light bulb. Donner crowded into the circle of betters, and Willis moved into the circle opposite him, standing alongside Randolph. A short man with a turtle-neck sweater was rolling.

'What's his point?' Willis asked Randolph.

Randolph looked down at Willis. He was a tall man with brown hair and blue eyes. The knife scar on his temple gave his otherwise pleasant face a menacing look. 'Six,' he said.

'He hot?'

'Luke,' Randolph replied.

The man in the turtle-neck sweater picked up the cubes and rolled again.

'Come on six,' someone across the circle said.

'Stop praying,' another man warned. Willis counted heads. Including himself and Donner, there were seven men in the game. The dice rolled to a stop.

'Six,' the man in the turtle-neck sweater said. He picked up most of the bills on the blanket, leaving twenty-five dollars. He retrieved the dice then and said, 'Bet twenty-five.'

'You're covered,' a big man with a gravelly voice said. He dropped two tens and a five on to the blanket. The man in the turtle-neck rolled.

'Come seven,' he said.

Willis watched. The dice bounced, then stopped moving.

'Little Joe,' the turtle-neck said.

'Two-to-one no four,' Willis said. He held out a ten-spot.

A man across the circle said, 'Got you,' and handed him a five. Turtle Neck rolled again.

'That's a crazy bet,' Randolph whispered to Willis.

'You said he was luke.'

'He's getting warmer every time he rolls. Watch him.'

Turtle Neck rolled a six, and then a five. The man across the circle said to Willis, 'Take another five on that?'

'It's a bet,' Willis said. He palmed a ten, and the man covered it with a five. Turtle Neck rolled. He got his four on the next throw. Willis handed the thirty dollars to the man across the circle. Turtle Neck left the fifty on the blanket.

'I'll take half of it,' Gravel said.

'I've got the other half,' Willis said.

They dropped their money, covering Turtle Neck's.

'You're nuts,' Randolph said.

'I came here to bet,' Willis answered. 'When I want to knit argyles, I'll stay home.'

Turtle Neck rolled a seven on his first throw.

'Son of a bitch!' Gravel said.

'Leave the hundred,' Turtle Neck replied, smiling.

'You're covered,' Willis told him. From across the circle, Donner eyed Willis dubiously. Gravel's eyebrows went up on to his forehead.

'We've got a sport with us,' Turtle Neck said.

'Is this a sewing circle or a crap game?' Willis asked. 'Shoot.'

Turtle Neck rolled an eight.

'Six-to-five no eight,' Willis said. The men in the circle were silent. 'All right, eight-to-five.' Six-to-five was the proper bet.

'Bet,' Gravel said, handing Willis a fiver.

'Roll,' Willis said.

Turtle Neck rolled.

'Box cars,' Randolph said. He looked at Willis for a moment. 'I've got another eight bucks says no eight,' he said.

'Same bet?' Gravel asked.

'Same.'

'You're on.' He handed Randolph his five.

'I thought this guy was getting hot,' Willis said, smiling at Randolph.

'What gets hot, gets cool,' Randolph replied.

Turtle Neck rolled his eight. Gravel collected from Willis and Randolph. A hook-nosed man across the circle sighed.

'Bet the two hundred,' Turtle Neck said.

'This is getting kind of steep, ain't it?' Hook Nose asked.

'If it's too steep for you, go home to bed,' Randolph answered.

'Who's taking the two hundred?' Turtle Neck asked.

'I'll take fifty of it,' Hook Nose said, sighing.

'That leaves a C and a half,' Turtle Neck said. 'Am I covered?'

'Here's a century,' Willis said. He dropped a bill on to the blankets.

'I'll take the last fifty,' Randolph said, throwing his money down with Willis'. 'Roll, hot-shot.'

'These are big-timers,' a round-faced man standing on Willis' right said. 'Big gamblers.'

Turtle Neck rolled. The cubes bounced across the blanket. One die stopped, showing a deuce. The second die clicked against it and abruptly stopped with a five face up.

'Seven,' Turtle Neck said, smiling.

'He's hot,' Round Face said.

'Too damn hot,' Hook Nose mumbled.

'Bet,' Gravel put in.

'Bet the four hundred.'

'Come on,' Hook Nose said. 'You trying to drive us home?'

Willis looked across the circle. Hook Nose was carrying a gun, its outline plainly etched against his jacket. And, if he was not mistaken, both Turtle Neck and Gravel were heeled, too.

'I'll take two bills of it,' Willis said.

'Anybody covering the other two?' Turtle Neck asked.

'You got to cool off sometime,' Randolph said. 'You got a bet.' He dropped two hundred on to the blanket.

'Roll 'em,' Willis said. 'Shake 'em first.'

'Papa's shoes got holes, dice,' Turtle Neck said, and he rolled an eleven.

'Man, I'm hot tonight. Bet it all,' he said. 'Am I covered?'

'Slow down a little, cousin,' Willis said suddenly.

'I'm betting the eight,' Turtle Neck answered.

'Let's see the ivories,' Willis said.

'What!'

'I said let me see the cubes. They act talented.'

'The talent's in the fist, friend,' Turtle Neck said. 'You covering me or not?'

'Not until I see the dice.'

'Then you ain't covering me,' Turtle Neck answered dryly. 'Who's betting?'

'Show him the dice,' Randolph said. Willis watched him. The ex-Marine had lost two bills on that last roll. Willis had intimated that the dice were crooked, and now Randolph wanted to see for himself.

'These dice are straight,' Turtle Neck said.

Gravel stared at Willis peculiarly. 'They're Honest Johns, stranger,' he put in. 'We run a square game.'

'They act drunk,' Willis said. 'Prove it to me.'

'You don't like the game, you can cut out,' Hook Nose said.

'I've dropped half a G since I walked in,' Willis snapped. 'I practically own those dice. Do I get a look or don't I?'

'You bring this guy in, Fats?' Gravel asked.

'Yeah,' Donner said. He was beginning to sweat.

'Where'd you dig him up?'

'We met in a bar,' Willis said, automatically clearing Donner. 'I told him I was looking for action. I didn't expect educated dice.'

'We told you the dice are square,' Gravel said.

'Then give me a look.'

'You can study them when they're passed to you,' Turtle Neck said. 'It's still my roll.'

'Nobody rolls till I see them dice,' Willis snapped.

'For a small man, you talk a big game,' Gravel said.

'Try me,' Willis said softly.

Gravel looked him over, apparently trying to determine whether or not Willis was heeled. Deciding that he wasn't, he said, 'Get out of here, your scrawny punk. I'd snap you in two.'

'Try me, you big tub of crap!' Willis shouted.

Gravel stared hotly at Willis for an instant, and then made the same mistake countless men before him had made. There was, you see, no way of telling from Willis' appearance what his training had been. There was no way of knowing that he was expert in the ways of judo, or that he could practically break your back by snapping his fingers. Gravel simply assumed he was a scrawny punk, and he rushed across the circle, ready to squash Willis like a bug.

53

He was, to indulge in complete understatement, somewhat surprised by what happened to him next.

Willis didn't watch Gravel's face or Gravel's hands. He watched his feet, timing himself to rush forward when Gravel's right foot was in a forward position. He did that suddenly, and then dropped to his right knee and grabbed Gravel's left ankle.

'Hey, what the hell –' Gravel started, but that was all he ever said. Willis pulled the ankle toward him and upward off the ground. In the same instant, he shoved out at Gravel's gut with the heel of his right hand. Gravel, seeing his opponent drop to his knees, feeling the fingers tight around his ankle, feeling the sharp thrust at his mid-section, didn't know he was experiencing an Ankle Throw. He only knew that he was suddenly falling backward, and then he felt the wind rush out of him as his back collided with the concrete floor. He shook his head, bellowed, and jumped to his feet.

Willis was standing opposite him, grinning.

'Okay, smart guy,' Gravel said. 'Okay, you smart little bastard,' and he rushed forward again.

Willis didn't move a muscle. He stood balanced evenly, smiling, waiting, and then he struck suddenly.

He grabbed Gravel's left arm at the elbow bend, cupping it with his right hand. Without hesitation, he snapped Gravel's left arm upward and forced his left hand into Gravel's armpit. His hand was opened flat, but the fingers were not spread. They lay close together, the thumb tucked under them, out of the way. Willis wheeled to the right, swinging Gravel's arm over his left shoulder and forcing it downwards by pressing on the elbow grip.

He bent forward suddenly, and Gravel's feet left the ground, and then Willis gave a sharp jerk and Gravel found himself spinning upward in a Shoulder Overthrow, the concrete coming up to meet him.

Considerately, and because he didn't want to break Gravel's arm, Willis released his grip on the elbow before

Gravel smashed into the concrete. Gravel shook his head, dazed. He tried to get up, and then he sat down again, still shaking his head. Across the circle, Hook Nose's hand snaked toward the opening of his jacket.

'Hold it right there!' a voice said.

Willis turned. Randolph was holding a ·45 in his fist, covering the others. 'Thanks,' Willis said.

'Scoop up that eight hundred,' Randolph answered. 'I don't like crooked games.'

'Hey, that's my dough!' Turtle Neck shouted.

'It used to be ours,' Randolph replied.

Willis picked up the money and put it in his pocket. 'Come on,' Randolph said. They started for the side door, Randolph backing away from the circle, still holding the ·45. The skinny man who'd passed Willis in looked confused, but he didn't say anything. Most men don't when a ·45 is in the picture. Willis and Randolph ran down the street. Randolph pocketed the gun, and hailed a cab on the corner.

'You like a cup of coffee?' Randolph asked.

'Sure,' Willis said.

Randolph extended his hand. 'My name's Skippy Randolph.'

Willis took it. 'Mine's Willy Harris.'

'Where'd you learn judo?' Randolph asked.

'In the Marines,' Willis said.

'It figured. I was in the corps, too.'

'No kidding?' Willis said, feigning surprise.

'Sixth Division,' Randolph said proudly.

'I was in the Third,' Willis said.

'Iwo?'

'Yes,' Willis said.

'I was in Iwo and Okinawa both. My company was attached with the Fifth when we hit Iwo.'

'That was a goddamn mess,' Willis said.

'You said it. Still, I had some good times with the corps. Caught a slug at Okinawa, though.'

'I was lucky,' Willis said. He looked around for wood to knock, and then rapped his knuckles on his head.

'You think we're far enough away from those creeps?' Randolph asked.

'I think so.'

'Any place here,' Randolph told the cabbie. The driver pulled up to the curb, and Randolph tipped him. They stood on the sidewalk, and Randolph looked up the street. 'There's a coffee-pot,' he said, pointing.

Willis took the eight hundred dollars from his pocket. 'Half of this is yours,' he said. He handed Randolph the bills.

'I figured them dice were a little too peppy,' Randolph said, taking the money.

'Yeah,' Willis said dryly. They opened the door to the coffee-pot and walked to a table in the corner. They ordered coffee and French crullers. When the order came, they sat quietly for a while.

'Good coffee,' Randolph said.

'Yeah,' Willis agreed.

'You a native in this burg?'

'Yeah. You?'

'Chicago, originally,' Randolph said. 'I drifted here when I was discharged. Stuck around for four years.'

'When were you discharged?'

'Forty-five,' Randolph said. 'Went back to Chicago in fifty.'

'What happened to forty-nine?'

'I did some time,' Randolph said, watching Willis warily.

'Haven't we all?' Willis said evenly. 'What'd they get you on?'

'I mugged an old duffer.'

'What brings you back here?' Willis asked.

'What'd they get *you* for?' Randolph asked.

'Oh, nothing,' Willis said.

'No, come on.'

'What difference does it make?'

'I'm curious,' Randolph said.

'Rape,' Willis said quickly.

'Hey,' Randolph said, raising his brows.

'It ain't like what it sounds. I was going with this dame, and she was the biggest tease alive. So one night –'

'Sure, I understand.'

'Do you?' Willis said levelly.

'Sure. You think I wanted to mug that old crumb? I just needed dough, that's all.'

'What're you doing for cash now?' Willis asked.

'I been makin' out.'

'Doing what?'

Randolph hesitated. 'I'm a truck driver.'

'Yeah?'

'Yeah.'

'Who do you work for?'

'Well, I ain't workin' at it right now.'

'What *are* you working at?'

'I got something going, brings in a little steady cash.' He paused. 'You looking for something?'

'I might be.'

'Two guys could really make out.'

'Doing what?'

'You figure it,' Randolph said.

'I don't like playing "What's My Line?",' Willis answered. 'If you've got something for me, let me hear it.'

'Mugging,' Randolph said.

'Old guys?'

'Old guys, young guys, what's the diff?'

'There ain't much dough in mugging.'

'In the right neighbourhoods, there is.'

'I don't know,' Willis said. 'I don't like the idea of knocking over old guys.' He paused. 'And dames.'

'Who said anything about dames? I steer away from them. You get all kinds of trouble with dames.'

'Yeah?' Willis said.

'Sure. Well, Jesus, don't *you* know? They get you on

57

attempted rape as well as assault. Even if you didn't lay a hand on the bitch.'

'That right?' Willis said, somewhat disappointed.

'Sure. I stay away like they're poison. Besides, most dames don't carry too much cash.'

'I see,' Willis said.

'So what do you think? You know judo and I know it, too. We could knock this city on its ass.'

'I don't know,' Willis said, convinced that Randolph was not his man now, but wanting to hear more so that he could set him up for a pinch. 'Tell me more about how you work it.'

While the two men talked in one part of the city, the girl lay face down in the bushes in another part of the city.

The bushes were at the base of a sharp incline, a miniature cliff of earth and stone. The cliff sloped down toward the bushes, and beyond the bushes was the River, and arching overhead was the long span of the bridge leading to the next state.

The girl lay in a crooked heap.

Her stockings had been torn when she rolled down the incline to the bushes, and her skirt was twisted so that the backs of her legs were exposed clear to her buttocks. The legs were good legs, youthful legs, but one was twisted at a curious angle, and there was nothing attractive about the girl's body as it lay in the bushes.

The girl's face was bleeding. The blood spread from the broken features to the stiff branches of the bushes and then to the ground, where the parched autumn earth drank it up thirstily. One arm was folded across the girl's full breasts, pressed against the sharp, cutting twigs of the bushes. The other arm dangled loosely at her side. Her hand was open.

On the ground, close to the spreading blood, several feet from the girl's open palm, a pair of sunglasses rested. One of the lenses in the glasses was shattered.

The girl had blonde hair, but the bright yellow was stained with blood where something hard and unyielding had repeatedly smashed at her skull.

The girl was not breathing. She lay face down in the bushes at the bottom of the small cliff, her blood rushing on to the ground, and she would never breathe again.

The girl's name was Jeannie Paige.

CHAPTER SIX

Lieutenant Byrnes studied the information on the printed sheet.

POLICE DEPARTMENT

Date: September 15

From: Commanding Officer, Lt. Peter Byrnes, 87th Pct.

To: Chief Medical Examiner

SUBJECT: DEATH OF Jeanne Rita Paige

Please furnish information on items checked below in connection with the death of the above named. Body was found on September 14 at foot of Hamilton Bridge, Isola.

Autopsy performed or examination made? Preliminary

By Dr. Bertram Nelson, Asst. Medical Examiner, St. Joan's Hosp.

Date: September 14 Where? County Mortuary

Cause of death: Brain concussion apparently. (Note: only cursory examination made before your request for information.)

Result of chemical analysis: Not performed as yet.

Body identified to Medical Examiner by: Mrs. Peter Bell

Address: 412 De Witt Street, Riverhead

Relationship: Sister

Body claimed by: (name and address):

If not claimed, disposition of same: Body is at mortuary. Complete autopsy is now being undertaken. Mrs. Bell has indicated she will claim body upon completion of tests. Full necropsy report will follow.

Burial Permit No.

Other information desired:

Arthur N. Burgher MD

OFFICE OF CHIEF MEDICAL EXAMINER

Translated into English, it simply meant that somebody had goofed. The body had been taken to the mortuary, and some half-assed intern there had probably very carefully studied the broken face and the shattered skull and come up with the remarkable conclusion that death had been caused by 'brain concussion apparently'. He could understand why a full report was not on his desk, but even understanding, the knowledge griped him. He could not expect people, he supposed, to go gallivanting around in the middle of the night – the body had probably been delivered to the mortuary in the wee hours – trying to discover whether or not a stomach holds poison. No, of course not. Nobody starts work until nine in the morning, and nobody works after five in the afternoon. A wonderful country. Short hours for everyone.

Except the fellow who killed this girl, of course.

He hadn't minded a little overtime, not him.

Seventeen years old, Byrnes thought. *Jesus, my son is seventeen!*

He walked to the door of his office. He was a short, solidly packed man with a head that seemed to have been blasted loose from a huge chunk of granite. He had small blue eyes which constantly darted, perpetually alert. He didn't like people getting killed. He didn't like young girls getting their heads smashed in. He opened the door.

'Hal!' he called.

Willis looked up from his desk.

'Come in here, will you?' He left the door and began pacing the office. Willis came into the room and stood quietly, his hands behind his back.

'Anything on those sunglasses yet?' Byrnes asked, still pacing.

'No, sir. There was a good thumbprint on the unbroken lens, but it's not likely we'll get a make on a single print.'

'What about your pal? The one you brought in last night?'

'Randolph. He's mad as hell because I conned him into

making a full confession to a cop. I think he suspects it won't stand up in court, though. He's screaming for a lawyer right now.'

'I'm talking about the thumbprint.'

'It doesn't match up with his, sir,' Willis said.

'Think it's the girl's?'

'No, sir, it isn't. We've already checked that.'

'Then Randolph isn't our man.'

'No, sir.'

'I didn't think he was, anyway. This girl was probably knocked over while Randolph was with you.'

'Yes, sir.'

'It's a goddamn shame,' Byrnes said, 'a goddamn shame.' He began pacing again. 'What's Homicide North doing?'

'They're on it, sir. Rounding up all sex offenders.'

'We can give them a hand with that. Check our files and put the boys to work, will you?' He paused. 'You think our mugger did this?'

'The sunglasses might indicate that, sir.'

'So Clifford's finally crossed the line, the bastard.'

'It's a possibility, sir.'

'My name is Pete,' Byrnes said. 'Why the formality?'

'Well, sir, I had an idea.'

'About this thing?'

'Yes, sir. If our mugger did it, sir.'

'*Pete!*' Byrnes roared.

'Pete, this son of a bitch is terrorizing the city. Did you see the papers this morning? A seventeen-year-old kid, her face beaten to a bloody pulp! In our precinct, Pete. Okay, it's a rotten precinct. It stinks to high heaven, and there are people who think it'll always stink. But it burns me up, Pete. Jesus, it makes me sore.'

'This precinct isn't so bad,' Byrnes said reflectively.

'Ah, Pete,' Willis said, sighing.

'All right, it smells. We're doing our best. What the hell do they expect here? Snob Hill?'

'No. But we've got to give them protection, Pete.'

'We are, aren't we? Three hundred and sixty-five days a year, every goddamn year. It's only the big things that make the papers. This goddamn mugger –'

'That's why we have to get him. Homicide North'll dicker around with this thing forever. Another body. All Homicide cops *see* is bodies. You think another one's going to get them in an uproar?'

'They do a good job,' Byrnes said.

'I know, I know,' Willis said impatiently. 'But I think my idea'll help them.'

'Okay,' Byrnes said, 'let's hear it.'

The living-room on that Friday afternoon was silent with the pallor of death. Molly Bell had done all her crying, and there were no more tears inside her, and so she sat silently, and her husband sat opposite her, and Bert Kling stood uneasily by the door, wondering why he had come.

He could clearly remember the girl Jeannie when she'd called him back as he was leaving Wednesday night. Incredible beauty, and etched beneath the beauty the clutching claws of trouble and worry. And now she was dead. And, oddly, he felt somehow responsible.

'Did she say anything to you?' Bell asked.

'Not much,' Kling replied. 'She seemed troubled about something . . . seemed . . . very cynical and bitter for a kid her age. I don't know.' He shook his head.

'I knew there was something wrong,' Molly said. Her voice was very low, barely audible. She clutched a handkerchief in her lap, but the handkerchief was dry now, and there were no more tears to wet it.

'The police think it's the mugger, honey,' Bell said gently.

'Yes,' Molly said. 'I know what they think.'

'Honey, I know you feel –'

'But what was she doing in Isola? Who took her to that

deserted spot near the Hamilton Bridge? Did she go there alone, Peter?'

'I suppose so,' Bell said.

'Why would she go there alone? Why would a seventeen-year-old girl go to a lonely spot like that?'

'I don't know, honey,' Bell said. 'Honey, please, don't get yourself all upset again. The police will find him. The police will —'

'Find *who*?' Molly said. 'The mugger? But will they find whoever took her to that spot? Peter, it's all the way down in Isola. Why would she go there from Riverhead?'

Bell shook his head again. 'I don't know, honey. I just don't know.'

'We'll find him, Molly,' Kling said. 'Both Homicide North and the detectives in my precinct will be working on this one. Don't worry.'

'And when you find him,' Molly asked, 'will that bring my sister back to life?'

Kling watched her, an old woman at twenty-four, sitting in her chair with her shoulders slumped, mourning a life, and carrying a new life within her. They were silent for a long time. Finally Kling said he had to be leaving, and Molly graciously asked if he wouldn't like a cup of coffee. He said No, and he thanked her, and then he shook hands with Bell and went outside where the brittle afternoon sunlight washed the streets of Riverhead.

The kids were piling out of the junior high school up the street, and Kling watched them as he walked, young kids with clean-scrubbed faces, rowdy boys and pretty girls, chasing each other, shouting at each other, discovering each other.

Jeannie Paige had been a kid like this not many years ago. He walked slowly.

There was a bite in the air, a bite that made him wish winter would come soon. It was a peculiar wish, because he truly loved autumn. It was strange, he supposed, because autumn was a time of dying, summer going quietly to rest, dying leaves, and dying days, and . . .

Dying girls.

He shook the thought aside. On the corner opposite the junior high, a hot-dog cart stood, and the proprietor wore a white apron, and he owned a moustache and a bright smile, and he dipped his fork into the steaming frankfurter pot, and then into the sauerkraut pot, and then he put the fork down and took the round stick from the mustard jar and spread the mustard and handed the completed masterpiece to a girl of no more than fourteen who stood near the cart. She paid for the frankfurter, and there was pure joy on her face as she bit into it, and Kling watched her and then walked on.

A dog darted into the gutter, leaping and frisking, chasing a rubber ball that had bounced from the sidewalk. A car skidded to a stop, tyres screeching, and the driver shook his head and then smiled unconsciously when he saw the happy pup.

The leaves fell toward the pavement, oranges and reds and yellows and russets and browns and pale golds, and they covered the sidewalks with crunching mounds. He listened to the rasp of the leaves underfoot as he walked, and he sucked in the brisk fall air, and he thought, *It isn't fair; she had so much living to do.*

A cold wind came up when he hit the Avenue. He started for the elevated station, and the wind rushed through the jacket he wore, touching the marrow of his bones.

The voices of the junior-high-school kids were far behind him now, up De Witt Street, drowned in the controlled shriek of the new wind.

He wondered if it would rain.

The wind howled around him, and it spoke of secret tangled places, and it spoke of death, and he was suddenly colder than he'd been before, and he wished for the comforting warmth of a coat collar, because a chill suddenly worked its way up his spine to settle at the back of his neck like a cold, dead fish.

He walked to the station and climbed the steps and, curiously, he was thinking of Jeannie Paige.

CHAPTER SEVEN

The girl's legs were crossed.

She sat opposite Willis and Byrnes in the lieutenant's office on the second floor of the 87th Precinct. They were good legs. The skirt reached to just a shade below her knees, and Willis could not help noticing they were good legs. Sleek and clean, full-calved, tapering to slender ankles, enhanced by the high-heeled black-patent pumps.

The girl was a redhead, and that was good. Red hair is obvious hair. The girl had a pretty face, with a small Irish nose and green eyes. She listened to the men in serious silence, and you could feel intelligence on her face and in her eyes. Occasionally she sucked in a deep breath, and when she did, the severe cut of her suit did nothing to hide the sloping curve of her breast.

The girl earned $5,555 a year. The girl had a ·38 in her purse.

The girl was a detective 2nd Grade, and her name was Eileen Burke, as Irish as her nose.

'You don't have to take this one if you don't want it, Miss Burke,' Byrnes said.

'It sounds interesting,' Eileen answered.

'Hal – Willis'll be following close behind all the way, you understand. But that's no guarantee he can get to you in time should anything happen.'

'I understand that, sir,' Eileen said.

'And Clifford isn't such a gentleman,' Willis said. 'He's beaten, and he's killed. Or at least we think so. It might not be such a picnic.'

'We don't think he's armed, but he used something on his last job, and it wasn't his fist. So you see, Miss Burke . . .'

'What we're trying to tell you,' Willis said, 'is that you

needn't feel any compulsion to accept this assignment. We would understand completely were you to refuse it.'

'Are you trying to talk me *into* this or *out* of it?' Eileen asked.

'We're simply asking you to make your own decision. We're sending you out as a sitting duck, and we feel –'

'I won't be such a sitting duck with a gun in my bag.'

'Still, we felt we should present the facts to you before –'

'My father was a patrolman,' Eileen said. 'Pops Burke, they called him. He had a beat in Hades Hole. In 1938, an escaped convict named Flip Danielsen took an apartment on Prime and North Thirtieth. When the police closed in, my father was with them. Danielsen had a Thompson sub-machine gun in the apartment with him, and the first round he fired caught my father in the stomach. My father died that night, and he died painfully, because stomach wounds are not easy ones.' Eileen paused. 'I think I'll take the job.'

Byrnes smiled. 'I knew you would,' he said.

'Will we be the only pair?' Eileen asked Willis.

'To start, yes. We're not sure how this'll work. I can't follow too close or Clifford'll panic. And I can't lag too far behind or I'll be worthless.'

'Do you think he'll bite?'

'We don't know. He's been hitting in the precinct and getting away with it, so chances are he won't change his m.o. – unless this killing has scared him. And from what the victims have given us, he seems to hit without any plan. He just waits for a victim and then pounces.'

'I see.'

'So we figured an attractive girl walking the streets late at night, apparently alone, might smoke him out.'

'I see.' Eileen let the compliment pass. There were about four million attractive girls in the city, and she knew she was no prettier than most. 'Has there been any sex motive?' she asked.

Willis glanced at Byrnes. 'Not that we can figure. He hasn't molested any of his victims.'

'I was only trying to figure what I should wear,' Eileen said.

'Well, no hat,' Willis said. 'That's for sure. We want him to spot that red hair a mile away.'

'All right,' Eileen said.

'Something bright, so I won't lose you – but nothing too flashy,' Willis said. 'We don't want the Vice Squad picking you up.'

Eileen smiled. 'Sweater and skirt?' she asked.

'Whatever you'll be most comfortable in.'

'I've got a white sweater,' she said. 'That should be clearly visible to both you and Clifford.'

'Yes,' Willis said.

'Heels or flats?'

'Entirely up to you. You may have to – well, he may give you a rough time. If heels will hamper you, wear flats.'

'He can hear heels better,' Eileen said.

'It's up to you.'

'I'll wear heels.'

'All right.'

'Will anyone else be in on this? I mean, will you have a walkie-talkie or anything?'

'No,' Willis said, 'it'd be too obvious. There'll be just the two of us.'

'And Clifford, we hope.'

'Yes,' Willis said.

Eileen Burke sighed. 'When do we start?'

'Tonight?' Willis asked.

'I was going to have my hair done,' Eileen said, smiling, 'but I suppose that can wait.' The smile broadened. 'It isn't every girl who can be sure at least *one* man is following her.'

'Can you meet me here?'

'What time?' Eileen asked.

'When the shift changes. Eleven-forty-five?'

'I'll be here,' she said. She uncrossed her legs and rose. 'Lieutenant,' she said, and Byrnes took her hand.

'Be careful, won't you?' Byrnes said.

'Yes, sir. Thank you.' She turned to Willis. 'I'll see you later.'

'I'll be waiting for you.'

'Goodbye now,' she said, and she left the office.

When she was gone, Willis asked, 'What do you think?'

'I think she'll be okay,' Byrnes said. 'She's got a record of fourteen subway-masher arrests.'

'Mashers aren't muggers,' Willis said.

Byrnes nodded reflectively. 'I still think she'll be okay.'

Willis smiled. 'I think so, too,' he said.

In the Squad Room outside, Detective Meyer was talking about cats.

'The tally is now up to twenty-four,' he told Temple. 'The damnedest thing the 33rd has ever come across.'

Temple scratched his crotch. 'And they got no lead yet, huh?'

'Not a single clue,' Meyer said. He watched Temple patiently. Meyer was a very patient man.

'He just goes around grabbing cats,' Temple said, shaking his head. 'What would a guy want to steal cats for?'

'That's the big question,' Meyer said. 'What's the motive? He's got the 33rd going crazy. I'll tell you something, George, I'm glad this one isn't in our laps.'

'Argh,' Temple said, 'I've had some goofy ones in my time, too.'

'Sure, but *cats*? Have you ever had cats?'

'I had cats up telephone poles when I was walking a beat,' Temple said.

'Everybody had cats up telephone poles,' Meyer said. 'But this is a man who's going around stealing cats from apartments. Now tell me, George, have you ever heard anything like that?'

'Never,' Temple said.

'I'll let you know how it works out,' Meyer promised. 'I'm really interested in this one. Tell you the truth, I don't think they'll ever crack it.'

'The 33rd is pretty good, ain't it?' Temple asked.

'There's a guy waiting outside,' Havilland shouted from his desk. 'Ain't anybody gonna see what he wants?'

'The walk'll do you good, Rog,' Meyer said.

'I just took a walk to the water cooler,' Havilland said, grinning. 'I'm bushed.'

'He's very anaemic,' Meyer said, rising. 'Poor fellow, my heart bleeds for him.' He walked to the slatted rail divider. A patrolman was standing there, looking into the Squad Room.

'Busy, huh?' he asked.

'Soso,' Meyer said indifferently. 'What've you got?'

'An autopsy report for . . .' He glanced at the envelope. 'Lieutenant Peter Byrnes.'

'I'll take it,' Meyer said.

'Sign this, will you?' the patrolman said.

'He can't write,' Havilland answered, propping his feet up on the desk. Meyer signed for the autopsy report. The patrolman left.

An autopsy report is a coldly scientific thing.

It reduces flesh and blood to medical terms, measuring in centimetres, analysing with calm aloofness. There is very little warmth and emotion in an autopsy report. There is no room for sentiment, no room for philosophizing. There is only one or more eight-and-one-half-by-eleven sheets of official-looking paper, and there are typewritten words on the sheets, and those words explain in straightforward medical English the conditions under which such and such a person met death.

The person whose death was open to medical scrutiny in the autopsy report which Meyer brought to the lieutenant was a young girl named Jeanne Rita Paige.

The words were very cold.

Death is not famous for its compassion.

The words read:

PAIGE, JEANNE RITA

Female, white, Caucasian. Apparent age, 21. Chronological age, 17. Apparent height, 64 inches. Apparent weight, 120 lb.

GROSS INSPECTION:

Head and face:

(a) face – Multiple contusions visible. Frontal area of skull reveals marked depression of the tablet of bone which measures approximately 10 cm.; commencing 3 cm. above the right orbit the depression then descends obliquely downward across the bridge of the nose and terminates in the mid-portion of the left maxilla.

There are marked haemorrhagic areas visible in the conjunctival areas of both eyes. Gross examination also reveals the presence of clotted blood within the nasal and otic orifices.

(b) head – There is an area of cerebral concussion with depression of tablet of bone which involves the left temporal region of the skull. The depression measures approximately 11 cm. and runs obliquely downward from the bregma to a point 2 cm. above the lateral to the superior aspect of left ear. There are multiple blood clots matted in the head hair.

Body:

The dorsal and ventral aspects of thorax and chest reveal multiple superficial and slight lacerations.

The right buttock reveals an area of severe abrasion.

The right lower extremity reveals a compound fracture of the distal portion of tibia and fibula with bone protruding through medial distal third of the extremity.

Examination of pelvis grossly and internally reveals following:

1. No evidence of blood in vaginal vault.

2. No evidence of attempted forced entrance or coitus.

72

3. No evidence of seminal fluid or sperm demonstrable on gross and microscopic examination of vaginal secretions.

4. Uterus is spherical in outline grossly and measures approximately 13·5 × 10 × 7·5 cm.

5. Placental tissue as well as chorionic and decidual tissue are present.

6. A foetus measuring 7 cm. long and weighing 29 gm. is present.

IMPRESSIONS:

1. Death instantaneous due to blows inflicted upon skull and face. Cerebral concussion.

2. Multiple abrasions and lacerations inflicted over body and compound fracture of lower right extremity, tibia and fibula probably incurred by descent over cliff.

3. There is no evidence of sexual assault.

4. Examination of uterine contents reveals a three-month pregnant uterus.

CHAPTER EIGHT

He could not shake the dead girl from his mind.

Back on the beat Monday morning, Kling should have felt soaring joy. He had been inactive for too long, and now he was back on the job, and the concrete and asphalt should have sung beneath his feet. There was life everywhere around him; teeming, crawling life. The precinct was alive with humanity, and in the midst of all this life, Kling walked his beat and thought of death.

The precinct started with the River Highway.

There a fringe of greenery turned red and burnt umber hugged the river, broken by an occasional tribute to World War I heroes and an occasional concrete bench. You could see the big steamers on the river, cruising slowly toward the docks farther downtown, their white smoke puffing up into the crisp fall air. An aircraft carrier lay anchored in the centre of the river, long and flat, in relief against the stark brown cliffs on the other side. The excursion boats plied their idle autumn trade. Summer was dying, and with it the shouts and joyous revelry of the sun-seekers.

And up the river, like a suspended, glistening web of silver, the Hamilton Bridge regally arched over the swirling brown waters below, touching two states with majestic fingers.

At the base of the bridge, at the foot of a small stone-and-earth cliff, a seventeen-year-old girl had died. The ground had sucked up her blood, but it was still stained a curious maroon-brown.

The big apartment buildings lining the River Highway turned blank faces to the bloodstained earth. The sun was reflected from the thousands of windows in the tall buildings, buildings which still employed doormen and elevator operators, and the windows blinked across the river with fiery-eyed blindness. The governesses wheeled their baby carriages up past the synagogue on the corner, marching their charges south toward the Stem, which pierced the heart of the precinct like a multi-coloured, multi-feathered, slender, sharp arrow. There were groceries and five-and-tens, and movie houses, and delicatessens, and butchers, and jewellers, and candy stores on the Stem. There was also a cafeteria on one of the corners, and on any day of the week, Monday to Sunday, you could spot at least twenty-five junkies in that cafeteria, waiting for the man with the White God. The Stem was slashed up its middle by a wide, iron-pipe-enclosed island, broken only by the side streets which crossed it. There were benches on each street end of the island, and men sat on those benches and smoked their pipes, and women sat with shopping bags clutched to their abundant breasts, and sometimes the governesses sat with their carriages, reading paper-backed novels.

The governesses never wandered south of the Stem.

South of the Stem was Culver Avenue.

The houses on Culver had never been really fancy. Like poor and distant relatives of the buildings lining the river, they had basked in the light of reflected glory many years ago. But the soot and the grime of the city had covered their bumpkin faces, had turned them into city people, and they stood now with hunched shoulders and dowdy clothes, wearing mournful faces. There were a lot of churches on Culver Avenue. There were also a lot of bars. Both were frequented regularly by the Irish people who still clung to their neighbourhood tenaciously – in spite of the Puerto Rican influx, in spite of the Housing Authority, which was condemning and knocking down dwellings with remarkable rapidity, leaving behind rubble-strewn open fields in which grew the city's only crop: rubbish.

The Puerto Ricans hunched in the side streets between Culver Avenue and Grover's Park. Here were the *bodegas, carnicerías, zapaterías, joyerías, cuchifritos* joints. Here was

'La Vía de Putas', 'The Street of the Whores', as old as time, as thriving and prosperous as General Motors.

Here, bludgeoned by poverty, exploited by pushers and thieves and policemen alike, forced into cramped and dirty dwellings, rescued occasionally by the busiest fire department in the entire city, treated like guinea pigs by the social workers, like aliens by the rest of the city, like potential criminals by the police, here were the Puerto Ricans.

Light-skinned and dark-skinned. Beautiful young girls with black hair and brown eyes and flashing white smiles. Slender men with the grace of dancers. A people alive with warmth and music and colour and beauty, six per cent of the city's population, crushed together in ghettos scattered across the face of the town. The ghetto in the 87th Precinct, sprinkled lightly with some Italians and some Jews, more heavily with the Irish, but predominantly Puerto Rican, ran south from the River Highway to the park, and then east and west for a total of thirty-five blocks. One-seventh of the total Puerto Rican population lived in the confines of the 87th Precinct. There were ninety thousand people in the streets Bert Kling walked.

The streets were alive with humanity.

And all he could think of was death.

He did not want to see Molly Bell, and when she came to him he was distressed.

She seemed frightened of the neighbourhood, perhaps because there was life within her, and perhaps because she felt the instinctive, savagely protective urge of the mother-to-be. He had just crossed Tommy, a Puerto Rican kid whose mother worked in one of the candy stores. The boy had thanked him, and Kling had turned to go back on the other side of the street again, and that was when he saw Molly Bell.

There was a sharp bite to the air on that 18 September, and Molly wore a topcoat which had seen better days, even though those better days had begun in a bargain basement downtown. Because of her coming child, she could not button the severely tailored coat much further than her breasts, and she presented a curiously dishevelled appearance; the limp blonde hair, the tired eyes, the frayed coat buttoned from her throat over her full breasts, and then parting in a wide V from her waist to expose her bulging belly.

'Bert!' she called, and she raised her hand in a completely feminine gesture, recapturing for a fleeting instant the beauty that must have been hers several years back, looking in that instant the way her sister, Jeannie, had looked when she was alive.

He lifted his billet in a gesture of greeting, motioned for her to wait on the other side of the street, and then crossed to meet her.

'Hello, Molly,' he said.

'I went to the station house first,' she said hurriedly. 'They told me you were on the beat.'

'Yes,' he answered.

'I wanted to see you, Bert.'

'All right,' he said. They cut down one of the side streets, and then walked with the park on their right, the trees a blazing pyre against the grey sky.

''allo, Bert,' a boy shouted, and Kling waved his billet.

'Have you heard?' Molly asked. 'About the autopsy report?'

'Yes,' he said.

'I can't believe it,' she told him.

'Well, Molly, they don't make mistakes.'

'I know, I know.' She was breathing heavily. He stared at her for a long moment.

'Listen, are you sure you should be walking around like this?'

'Yes, it's very good for me. The doctor said I should walk a lot.'

'Well, if you get tired —'

'I'll tell you. Bert, will you help?'

77

He looked at her face. There was no panic in her eyes, and the grief, too, had vanished. There was only a steadfastness of purpose shining there, a calm resolve.

'What could I possibly do?' he asked.

'You're a cop,' she said.

'Molly, the best cops in the city are working on this. Homicide North doesn't let people get away with murder. I understand one of the detectives from our precinct has been working with a policewoman for the past two days. They've –'

'None of these people knew my sister, Bert.'

'I know, but –'

'You knew her, Bert.'

'I only talked to her for a little while. I hardly –'

'Bert, these men who deal with death . . . My sister is only another corpse to them.'

'That's not true, Molly. They see a lot of it, but that doesn't stop them from doing their best on each case. Molly, I'm just a patrolman. I *can't* fool around with this, even if I wanted to.'

'Why not?'

'I'd be stepping on toes. I've got my beat. This is my beat, this is my job. My job isn't investigating a murder case. I can get into a lot of trouble for that, Molly.'

'My sister got into a lot of trouble, too,' Molly said.

'Ah, Molly,' Kling sighed, 'don't ask me, please.'

'I'm asking you.'

'I can't do anything. I'm sorry.'

'Why did you come to see her?' Molly asked.

'Because Peter asked me to. As a favour. For old time's sake.'

'I'm asking you for a favour too, Bert. Not for old time's sake. Only because my sister was killed, and my sister was just a young kid, and she deserved to live a little longer, Bert, just a little longer.'

They walked in silence for a time.

'Bert?' Molly said.

'Yes.'

'Will you please help?'

'I –'

'Your Homicide detectives think it was the mugger. Maybe it was, I don't know. But my sister was pregnant, and the mugger didn't do that. And my sister was killed at the foot of the Hamilton Bridge, and I want to know why she was there. The killer's cliff is a long way from where we live, Bert. Why was she there? Why? Why?'

'I don't know.'

'My sister had friends. I know she had. Maybe her friends know. Doesn't a young girl have to confide in someone? A young girl with a baby inside her, a secret inside her? Doesn't she tell someone?'

'Are you interested in finding the killer,' Kling asked, '– or the father of the child?'

Molly considered this gravely. 'They may be one and the same,' she said at last.

'I – I don't think that's likely, Molly.'

'But it's a possibility, isn't it? And your Homicide detectives are doing nothing about that possibility. I've met them, Bert. They've asked me questions, and their eyes are cold, and their mouths are stiff. My sister is only a body with a tag on its toe. My sister isn't flesh and blood to them. She isn't now, and she never was.'

'Molly –'

'I'm not blaming them. Their jobs . . . I know that death becomes a commodity to them, the way meat is a commodity to a butcher. But this girl is my sister!'

'Do you – do you know who her friends were?'

'I only know that she went to one club a lot. A cellar club, one of these teenage –' Molly stopped. Her eyes met Kling's hopefully. 'Will you help?'

'I'll try,' Kling said, sighing. 'Strictly on my own. After hours. I can't do anything officially, you understand that.'

'Yes, I understand.'

'What's the name of this club?'

'Club Tempo.'

'Where is it?'

'Just off Peterson, a block from the Avenue. I don't know the address. All the clubs are clustered there in the side-street, in the private houses.' She paused. 'I belonged to one when I was a kid, too.'

'I used to go to their Friday-night socials,' Kling said. 'But I don't remember one called Tempo. It must be new.'

'I don't know,' Molly said. She paused. 'Will you go?'

'Yes.'

'When?'

'I don't knock off until four. I'll ride up to Riverhead then and see if I can find the place.'

'Will you call me afterwards?'

'Yes, certainly.'

'Thank you, Bert.'

'I'm only a uniformed cop,' Kling said. 'I don't know if you've got anything to thank me for.'

'I've got a lot to thank you for,' she said. She squeezed his hand. 'I'll be waiting for your call.'

'All right,' he said. He looked down at her. The walk seemed to have tired her. 'Shall I call a cab for you?'

'No,' she said, 'I'll take the subway. Goodbye, Bert. And thank you.'

She turned and started up the street. He watched her. From the back, except for the characteristically tilted walk of the pregnant woman, you could not tell she was carrying. Her figure looked quite slim, from the back, and her legs were good.

He watched her until she was out of sight, and then he crossed the street and turned up one of the side-streets, waving to some people he knew.

CHAPTER NINE

Unlike detectives, who figure out their own work schedules, patrolmen work within the carefully calculated confines of the eight-hour-tour system. They start with five consecutive tours from 8 a.m. to 4 p.m., and then they relax for fifty-six hours. When they return to work, they do another five tours from midnight to 8 a.m. after which another fifty-six-hour swing commences. The next five tours are from 4 p.m. to midnight. Comes the fifty-six-hour break once more, and then the cycle starts from the top again.

The tour system doesn't respect Saturdays, Sundays, or holidays. If a cop's tour works out that way, he may get Christmas off. If not, he walks his beat. Or he arranges a switch with a Jewish cop who wants Rosh Hashana off. It's something like working in an aircraft factory during wartime. The only difference is that cops find it a little more difficult to get life insurance.

Bert Kling started work that Monday morning at 7.45 a.m., the beginning of the tour cycle. He was relieved on post at 3.40 p.m. He went back to the house, changed to street clothes in the locker room down the hall from the Detective Squad Room, and then went out into the late-afternoon sunshine.

Ordinarily, Kling would have walked the beat a little more in his street clothes. Kling carried a little black loose-leaf pad in his back pocket, and into that pad he jotted down information from WANTED circulars and from the bulls in the precinct. He knew, for example, that there was a shooting gallery at 3112 North Eleventh. He knew that a suspected pusher was driving a powder-blue 1953 Cadillac with the licence plate RX 42-10. He knew that a chain department store in the mid-town area had been held up the night before, and he knew who was suspected of the crime. And he knew that a few good collars would put him closer to Detective 3rd Grade, which, of course, he wanted to become.

So he ordinarily walked the precinct territory when he was off duty, a few hours each day, watching, snooping, unhampered by the shrieking blue of his uniform, constantly amazed by the number of people who didn't recognize him in street clothes.

Today he had something else to do, and so he ignored his extracurricular activities. Instead, he boarded a train and headed uptown to Riverhead.

He didn't have much trouble finding Club Tempo. He simply stopped into one of the clubs he'd known as a kid, asked where Tempo was, and was given directions.

Tempo covered the entire basement level of a three-storey brick house off Peterson Avenue on Klausner Street. You walked up a concrete driveway toward a two-car garage at the back of the house, made an abrupt left turn, and found yourself face to face with the back of the house, the entrance doorway to the club, and a painted sign pierced with an elongated quarter note on a long black shaft.

The sign read:

CLUB TEMPO

Kling tried the knob. The door was locked. From somewhere inside the club, he heard the lyric, sonnet-like words to 'Sh-Boom' blasting from a record player. He raised his fist and knocked. He kept knocking, realizing abruptly that all the *sh-booming* was drowning out his fist. He waited until the record had exhausted its serene, madrigal-like melody, and then knocked again.

'Yeah?' a voice called. It was a young voice, male.

'Open up,' Kling said.

'Who is it?'

He heard footsteps approaching the door, and then a voice close by on the other side of the door. 'Who is it?'

He didn't want to identify himself as a cop. If he were going to start asking questions, he didn't want a bunch of kids automatically on the defensive.

'Bert Kling,' he said.

'Yeah?' the voice answered. 'Who's Bert Kling?'

'I want to hire the club,' Kling answered.

'Yeah?'

'Yeah.'

'What for?'

'If you'll open the door, we can talk about it.'

'Hey, Tommy,' the voice yelled, 'some guy wants to hire the club.'

Kling heard a mumbled answer, and then the door lock clicked, and the door opened wide on a thin, blond boy of eighteen.

'Come on in,' the boy said. He was holding a stack of records in his right hand, clutched tight against his chest. He wore a green sweater and dungaree pants. A white dress shirt, collar unbuttoned, showed above the V neck of the sweater. 'My name's Hud. That's short for Hudson. Hudson Patt. Double *t*. Come on in.'

Kling stepped down into the basement room. Hud watched him.

'You're kind of old, ain't you?' Hud asked at last.

'I'm practically decrepit,' Kling replied. He looked around. Whoever had decorated the room had done a good job with it. The pipes in the ceiling had been covered with plaster-board which had been painted white. The walls were knotty pine to a man's waist, plasterboard above that. Phonograph records, shellacked and then tacked to the white walls and ceiling, gave the impression of curious two-dimensional balloons that had drifted free of their vendor's strings. There were easy chairs and a long sofa scattered about the room. A record player painted white and then covered with black notes and a G clef and a musical staff stood alongside a wide arch through which a second room was visible. There was no one but Hud and Kling in either of the two rooms. Whoever Tommy was, he seemed to have vanished into thin air.

'Like it?' Hud asked, smiling.

'It's pretty,' Kling said.

'We done it all ourselves. Bought all those records on the ceiling and walls for two cents each. They're real bombs – stuff the guy wanted to get rid of. We tried playing one of them. All we got was scratches. Sounded like London during an air-raid.'

'Which you no doubt remember clearly,' Kling said.

'Huh?' Hud asked.

'Do you belong to this club?' Kling asked back.

'Sure. Only members are allowed down during the day. In fact, non-members ain't allowed down except on Friday and Sunday nights. We have socials then.' He stared at Kling. His eyes were wide and blue. 'Dancing, you know?'

'Yes, I know,' Kling said.

'A little beer sometimes, too. Healthy. This is healthy recreation.' Hud grinned. 'Healthy recreation is what strong, red-blooded American teenagers need, am I right?'

'Absolutely.'

'That's what Dr Mortesson says.'

'Who?'

'Dr Mortesson. Writes a column in one of the papers. Every day. Healthy recreation.' Hud continued grinning. 'So what do you want to hire the club for?' he asked.

'I belong to a group of war veterans,' Kling said.

'Yeah?'

'Yeah. We're ... uh ... having a sort of a get-together, meet the wives, girlfriends, like that, you know.'

'Oh sure,' Hud said.

'So we need a place.'

'Why don't you try the American Legion hall?'

84

'Too big.'

'Oh.'

'I figured one of these cellar clubs. This is an unusually nice one.'

'Yeah,' Hud said. 'Done it all ourselves.' He walked over to the record player, seemed ready to put the records down, then turned, changing his mind. 'Listen, for what night is this?'

'A Saturday,' Kling said.

'That's good – because we have our socials on Friday and Sunday.'

'Yes, I know,' Kling said.

'How much you want to pay?'

'That depends. You're sure the landlord here won't mind our bringing girls down? Not that anything funny would be going on or anything, you understand. Half the fellows are married.'

'Oh, certainly,' Hud said, suddenly drawn into the fraternity of the adult. 'I understand completely. I never once thought otherwise.'

'But there *will* be girls.'

'That's perfectly all right.'

'You're sure?'

'Sure. We have girls here all the time. Our club is co-ed.'

'Is that right?'

'That's a fact,' Hud said. 'We got twelve girls belong to the club.'

'Girls from the neighbourhood?' Kling asked.

'Mostly. From around, you know. Here and there. None of them come from too far.'

'Anybody I might know?' Kling asked.

Hud estimated Kling's age in one hasty glance. 'I doubt it, mister,' he said, the glowing bond of fraternal adulthood shattered.

'I used to live in this neighbourhood,' Kling lied. 'Took out a lot of girls around here. Wouldn't be surprised if some of the girls in your club aren't their younger sisters.'

'Well, that's a possibility,' Hud conceded.

'What are some of their names?'

'Why do you want to know, pal?' a voice from the archway said. Kling whirled abruptly. A tall boy walked through the arch and into the room, zipping up the fly on his jeans. He was excellently built, with wide shoulders bulging the seams of his T-shirt, tapering down to a slender waist. His hair was chestnut brown, and his eyes were a deeper chocolate brown. He was extremely handsome, and he walked with arrogant knowledge of his good looks.

'Tommy?' Kling said.

'That's my name,' Tommy said. 'I didn't get yours.'

'Bert Kling.'

'Glad to know you,' Tommy said. He watched Kling carefully.

'Tommy's president of Club Tempo,' Hud put in. 'He gave me the okay to hire the place to you. Provided the price was right.'

'I was in the john,' Tommy said. 'Heard everything you said. Why're you so interested in our chicks?'

'I'm not interested,' Kling answered. 'Just curious.'

'Your curiosity, pal, should concern itself only with hiring the club. Am I right, Hud?'

'Sure,' Hud answered.

'What can you pay, pal?'

'How often did Jeannie Paige come down here, pal?' Kling said. He watched Tommy's face. The face did not change expression at all. A record slid from the stack Hud was holding, clattering to the floor.

'Who's Jeannie Paige?' Tommy said.

'A girl who was killed last Thursday night.'

'Never heard of her,' Tommy said.

'Think,' Kling told him.

'I am thinking.' Tommy paused. 'You a cop?'

'What difference does it make?'

'This is a clean club,' Tommy said. 'We never had any trouble with the cops, and we don't want none. We ain't even had any trouble with the landlord, and he's a son of a bitch from way-back.'

'Nobody's looking for trouble,' Kling said. 'I asked you how often Jeannie Paige came down here.'

'Never,' Tommy said. 'Ain't that right, Hud?'

Hud, reaching for the pieces of the broken record, looked up. 'Yeah, that's right, Tommy.'

'Suppose I am a cop?' Kling said.

'Cops have badges.'

Kling reached into his back pocket, opened his wallet, and showed the tin. Tommy glanced at the shield.

'Cop or no cop, this is still a clean club.'

'Nobody said it was dirty. Stop bulging your weight-lifter muscles and answer my questions straight. When was Jeannie Paige down here last?'

Tommy hesitated for a long time. 'Nobody here had anything to do with killing her,' he said at last.

'Then she *did* come down?'

'Yes.'

'How often.'

'Every now and then.'

'*How often?*'

'Whenever there was socials. Sometimes during the week, too. We let her in 'cause one of the girls –' Tommy stopped.

'Go ahead, finish it.'

'One of the girls knows her. Otherwise we wouldn't've let her in except on social nights. That's all I was gonna say.'

'Yeah,' Hud said, placing the broken record pieces on the player cabinet. 'I think this girl was gonna put her up for membership.'

'Was she here last Thursday night?' Kling asked.

'No,' Tommy answered quickly.

'Try it again.'

'No, she wasn't here. Thursday night is Work Night. Six kids from the club get the duty each week – different kids, you understand. Three guys and three girls. The guys do the heavy work, and the girls do the curtains, the glasses, things like that. No outsiders are allowed on Work Night. In fact, no members except the kids who are working are allowed. That's how I know Jeannie Paige wasn't here.'

'Were you here?'

'Yeah,' Tommy said.

'Who else was here?'

'What difference does it make? Jeannie wasn't here.'

'What about her girlfriend? The one she knows?'

'Yeah, she was here.'

'What's her name?'

Tommy paused. When he answered, it had nothing whatever to do with Kling's question. 'This Jeannie kid, like you got to understand her. She never even *danced* with nobody down here. A real zombie. Pretty as sin, but an iceberg. Ten below, I'm not kidding.'

'Why'd she come down then?'

'Ask me an easy one. Listen, even when she did come down, she never stayed long. She'd just sit on the sidelines and watch. There wasn't a guy in this club wouldn'ta liked to dump her in the hay, but, Jesus, what a terrifying creep she was.' Tommy paused. 'Ain't that right, Hud?'

Hud nodded. 'That's right. Dead and all, I got to say it. She was a regular icicle. A real spook. After a while, none of the guys even bothered askin' her to dance. We just let her sit.'

'She was in another world,' Tommy said. 'I thought for a while she was a dope addict or something. I mean it. You know, you read about them in the papers all the time.' He shrugged. 'But it wasn't that. She was just a Martian, that's all.' He shook his head disconsolately. 'Such a piece, too.'

'A terrifying creep,' Hud said, shaking his head.

'What's her girlfriend's name?' Kling asked again.

A glance of muted understanding passed between Tommy and Hud. Kling didn't miss it, but he bided his time.

'You get a pretty girl like Jeannie was,' Tommy said, 'and you figure, Here's something. Pal, did you ever see her? I mean, they don't make them like that any –'

'What's her girlfriend's name?' Kling repeated, a little louder this time.

'She's an older girl,' Tommy said, his voice very low.

'How old?'

'Twenty,' Tommy said.

'That almost makes her middle-aged like me,' Kling said.

'Yeah,' Hud agreed seriously.

'What's her age got to do with it?'

'Well . . .' Tommy hesitated.

'For Christ's sake, what is it?' Kling exploded.

'She's been around,' Tommy said.

'So?'

'So – so we don't want any trouble down here. This is a clean club. No, really, I'm not snowing you. So – so if once in a while we fool around with Claire –'

'Claire what?' Kling snapped.

'Claire –' Tommy stopped.

'Look,' Kling said tightly, 'let's just cut this crap, okay? A seventeen-year-old kid had her head smashed in, and I don't feel like playing around! Now what the hell is this girl's name, and say it damn fast!'

'Claire Townsend.' Tommy wet his lips. 'Look, if our mothers found out we were . . . well, you know . . . fooling around with Claire down here, well, Jesus. Look, can't we leave her out of this? What's to gain? Jesus, is there anything wrong with a little fun?'

'Nothing,' Kling said. 'Do you find murder funny? Do you find it comical, you terrifying creep?'

'No, but –'

'Where does she live?'

'Claire?'

89

'Yes.'

'Right on Peterson. What's the address, Hud?'

'Seven twenty-eight, I think,' Hud said.

'Yeah, that sounds about right. But look, Officer, leave us out of it, will you?'

'How many of you do I have to protect?' Kling said dryly.

'Well ... only Hud and me, actually,' Tommy said.

'The Bobbsey Twins.'

'Huh?'

'Nothing.' Kling started for the door. 'Stay away from big girls,' he said. 'Go lift some weights.'

'You'll leave us out of it?' Tommy called.

'I may be back,' Kling said, and then he left them standing by the record player.

CHAPTER TEN

In Riverhead – and throughout the city for that matter – but especially in Riverhead, the cave-dwellers have thrown up a myriad number of dwellings which they call middle-class apartment houses. These buildings are usually constructed of yellow brick, and they are carefully set on the street so that no wash is seen hanging on the lines, except when an inconsiderate city transit authority constructs an elevated structure that cuts through back yards.

The fronts of the buildings are usually hung with a different kind of wash. Here is where the women gather. They sit on bridge chairs and stools and they knit and they sun themselves, and they talk and their talk is the dirty wash of the apartment building. In three minutes flat, a reputation can be ruined by these Mesdames Defarge. The axe drops with remarkable abruptness, whetted by a friendly discussion of last night's mah-jong game. The head, with equally remarkable suddenness rolls into the basket, and the discussion idles on to topics like 'Should birth control be practised in the Virgin Isles?'

Autumn was a bold seductress on that late Monday afternoon, 18 September. The women lingered in front of the buildings, knowing their hungry men would soon be home for dinner, but lingering none the less, savouring the tantalizing bite of the air. When the tall, blond man stopped in front of 728 Peterson, paused to check the address over the arched doorway, and then stepped into the foyer, speculation ran rife among the women knitters. After a brief period of consultation, one of the women – a girl named Birdie – was chosen to sidle unobtrusively into the foyer and, if the opportunity were ripe, perhaps casually follow the good-looking stranger upstairs.

Birdie, so carefully unobtrusive was she, missed her golden opportunity. By the time she had wormed her way into the inner foyer, Kling was nowhere in sight.

He had checked the name 'Townsend' in the long row of brass-plated mailboxes, pushed the bell button, and then leaned on the inner door until an answering buzz released its lock mechanism. He had then climbed to the fourth floor, found Apartment 47, and pushed another button.

He was now waiting.

He pushed the button again.

The door opened suddenly. He had heard no approaching footsteps, and the sudden opening of the door surprised him. Unconsciously, he looked first to the girl's feet. She was barefoot.

'I was raised in the Ozarks,' she said, following his glance. 'We own a vacuum cleaner, a carpet sweeper, a broiler, a set of encyclopedias, and subscriptions to most of the magazines. Whatever you're selling, we've probably got it, and we're not interested in putting you through college.'

Kling smiled. 'I'm selling an automatic apple corer,' he said.

'We don't eat apples,' the girl replied.

'This one mulches the seeds, and converts them to fibre. The corer comes complete with an instruction booklet telling you how to weave fibre mats.'

The girl raised a speculative eyebrow.

'It comes in six colours,' Kling went on. 'Toast Brown, Melba Peach, Tart Red –'

'Are you on the level?' the girl asked, puzzled now.

'Proofreader Blue,' Kling continued, 'Bilious Green, and Midnight Dawn.' He paused. 'Are you interested?'

'Hell, no,' she said, somewhat shocked.

'My name is Bert Kling,' he said seriously. 'I'm a cop.'

'Now you sound like the opening to a television show.'

'May I come in?'

'Am I in trouble?' the girl asked. 'Did I leave that damn shebang in front of a fire hydrant?'

'No.'

And then, as an afterthought, 'Where's your badge?'

Kling showed her his shield.

'You're supposed to ask,' the girl said. 'Even the man from the gas company. Everybody's supposed to carry identification like that.'

'Yes, I know.'

'So come in,' she said. 'I'm Claire Townsend.'

'I know.'

'*How* do you know?'

'The boys at Club Tempo sent me here.'

Claire stared at Kling levelly. She was a tall girl. Even barefoot, she reached to Kling's shoulder. In high heels, she would give the average American male trouble. Her hair was black. Not brunette, not brownette, but black, a total black, the black of a starless, moonless night. Her eyes were a deep brown, arched with black brows. Her nose was straight, and her cheeks were high, and there wasn't a trace of make-up on her face, not a tint of lipstick on her wide mouth. She wore a white blouse, and black toreador pants, which tapered down to her naked ankles and feet. Her toenails were painted a bright red.

She kept staring at him. At last, she said, 'Why'd they send you here?'

'They said you knew Jeannie Paige.'

'Oh.' The girl seemed ready to blush. She shook her head slightly, as if to clear it of an erroneous first impression, and then said, 'Come in.'

Kling followed her into the apartment. It was furnished with good middle-class taste.

'Sit down,' she said.

'Thank you.' He sat in a low easy chair. It was difficult to sit erect, but he managed it. Claire went to the coffee table, shoved the lid off a cigarette box, took one of the cigarettes for herself, and then asked, 'Smoke?'

'No, thanks.'

'Your name was Kling, did you say?'

'Yes.'

'You're a detective?'

'No. A patrolman.'

'Oh.' Claire lighted the cigarette, shook out the match, and then studied Kling. 'What's your connexion with Jeannie?'

'I was about to ask you the same thing.'

Claire grinned. 'I asked first.'

'I know her sister. I'm doing a favour.'

'Um-huh.' Claire nodded, digesting this. She puffed on the cigarette, folded her arms across her breasts and then said, 'Well, go ahead. Ask the questions. You're the cop.'

'Why don't you sit down?'

'I've been sitting all day.'

'You work?'

'I'm a college girl,' Claire said. 'I'm studying to be a social worker.'

'Why that?'

'Why not?'

Kling smiled. 'This time, *I* asked first.'

'I want to get to people before you do,' she said.

'That sounds reasonable,' Kling said. 'Why do you belong to Club Tempo?'

Her eyes grew suddenly wary. He could almost see a sudden film pass over the pupils, masking them. She turned her head and blew out a ball of smoke. 'Why shouldn't I?' she asked.

'I can see where our conversation is going to run around in the why–why not rut,' Kling said.

'Which is a damn sight better than the why–because rut, don't you think?' There was an edge to her voice now. He wondered what had suddenly changed her earlier friendliness. He weighed her reaction for a moment, and then decided to plunge onward.

'The boys there are a little young for you, aren't they?'

'You're getting a little personal, aren't you?'

'Yes,' Kling said. 'I am.'

'Our acquaintance is a little short for personal exchanges,' Claire said icily.

'Hud can't be more than eighteen –'

'Listen –'

'And what's Tommy? Nineteen? They haven't got an ounce of brains between them. Why do you belong to Tempo?'

Claire squashed out her cigarette. 'Maybe you'd better leave, Mr Kling,' she said.

'I just got here,' he answered.

She turned. 'Let's set the record straight. So far as I know, I'm not obliged to answer any questions you ask about my personal affairs, unless I'm under suspicion for some foul crime. To bring the matter down to a fine technical point, I don't have to answer *any* questions a patrolman asks me, unless he is operating in an official capacity, which you admitted you were not. I liked Jeannie Paige, and I'm willing to cooperate. But if you're going to get snotty, this is still my home, and my home is my castle, and you can get the hell out.'

'Okay,' Kling said, embarrassed. 'I'm sorry, Miss Townsend.'

'Okay,' Claire said. A silence clung to the atmosphere. Claire looked at Kling. Kling looked back at her.

'I'm sorry, too,' Claire said finally. 'I shouldn't be so goddamn touchy.'

'No, you were perfectly right. It's none of my business what you –'

'Still, I shouldn't have –'

'No, really, it's –'

Claire burst out laughing, and Kling joined her. She sat, still chuckling, and said, 'Would you like a drink, Mr Kling?'

Kling looked at his watch. 'No, thanks,' he said.

'Too early for you?'

'Well –'

'It's never too early for cognac,' she said.

'I've never tasted cognac,' he admitted.

'You haven't?' Her eyebrows shot up on to her forehead. 'Ah, monsieur, you are meesing one of ze great treats of life. A little, *oui*? *Non*?'

'A little,' he said.

She crossed to a bar with green leatherette doors, opened them, and drew out a bottle with a warm, amber liquid showing within.

'Cognac,' she announced grandly, 'the king of brandies. You can drink it as a highball, cocktail, punch – or in coffee, tea, hot chocolate, and milk.'

'Milk?' Kling asked, astonished.

'Milk, yes indeed. But the best way to enjoy cognac is to sip it – neat.'

'You sound like an expert,' Kling said.

Again, quite suddenly, the veil passed over her eyes. 'Someone taught me to drink it,' she said flatly, and then she poured some of the liquid into two medium-sized, tulip-shaped glasses. When she turned to face Kling again, the mask had dropped from her eyes.

'Note that the glass is only half filled,' she said. 'That's so you can twirl it without spilling any of the drink.' She handed the glass to Kling. 'The twirling motion mixes the cognac vapours with the air in the glass, bringing out the bouquet. Roll the glass in your palms, Mr Kling. That warms the cognac and also brings out the aroma.'

'Do you smell this stuff or drink it?' Kling wanted to know. He rolled the glass between his big hands.

'Both,' Claire said. 'That's what makes it a good experience. Taste it. Go ahead.'

Kling took a deep swallow, and Claire opened her mouth and made an abrupt 'Stop!' signal with one outstretched hand. 'Good God,' she said, 'don't gulp it! You're committing an obscenity when you gulp cognac. Sip it, roll it around your tongue.'

'I'm sorry,' Kling apologized. He sipped the cognac, rolled it on his tongue. 'Good,' he said.

'Virile,' she said.

'Velvety,' he added.

'End of commercial.'

They sat silently, sipping the brandy. He felt very cosy and very warm and very comfortable. Claire Townsend was a pleasant person to look at, and a pleasant person to talk to. Outside the apartment, the shadowy greys of autumn dusk were washing the sky.

'About Jeannie,' he said. He did not feel like discussing death.

'Yes?'

'How well did you know her?'

'As well as anyone, I suppose. I don't think she had many friends.'

'What makes you say that?'

'You can tell. That lost-soul look. A beautiful kid, but lost. God, what I wouldn't have given for the looks she had.'

'You're not so bad,' Kling said, smiling. He sipped more brandy.

'That's the warm, amber glow of the cognac,' Claire advised him. 'I'm a beast in broad daylight.'

'I'll just bet you are,' Kling said. 'How'd you first meet her?'

'At Tempo. She came down one night. I think her boyfriend sent her. In any case, she had the name of the club and the address written on a little white card. She showed it to me, almost as if it were a ticket of admission, and then she just sat in the corner and refused dances. She looked . . . It's hard to explain. She was there, but she wasn't there. Have you seen people like that?'

'Yes,' Kling said.

'I'm like that myself sometimes,' Claire admitted. 'Maybe that's why I spotted it. Anyway, I went over and introduced myself and we started talking. We got along very well. By the end of the evening we'd exchanged telephone numbers.'

'Did she ever call you?'

'No. I only saw her at the club.'

'How long ago was this?'

'Oh, a long time now.'

'How long?'

'Let me see.' Claire sipped her cognac and thought. 'Gosh, it must be almost a year.' She nodded. 'Yes, just about.'

'I see. Go ahead.'

'Well, it wasn't hard to find out what was troubling her. The kid was in love.'

Kling leaned forward. 'How do you know?'

Claire's eyes did not leave his face. 'I've been in love, too,' she said tiredly.

'Who was her boyfriend?' Kling asked.

'I don't know.'

'Didn't she tell you?'

'No.'

'Didn't she mention his name ever? I mean, in conversation?'

'No.'

'Hell,' Kling said.

'Understand, Mr Kling, that this was a new bird taking wing. Jeannie was leaving the nest, testing her feathers.'

'I see.'

'Her first love, Mr Kling, and shining in her eyes, and glowing on her face, and putting her in this dream world of hers where everything outside it was shadowy.' Claire shook her head. 'God, I've seen them green, but Jeannie –' She stopped and shook her head again. 'She just didn't know anything, do you know? Here was this woman's body... Well, had you ever seen her?'

'Yes.'

'Then you know what I mean. This was the real item, a woman. But inside – a little girl.'

'How do you figure that?' Kling asked, thinking of the autopsy results.

'Everything about her. The way she used to dress, the way she talked, the questions she asked, even her handwriting. All a little girl's. Believe me, Mr Kling, I've never –'

'Her handwriting?'

'Yes, yes. Here, let me see if I've still got it.' She crossed the room and scooped her purse from a chair. 'I'm the laziest girl in the world. I never copy an address into my address book. I just stick it in between the pages until I've . . .' She was thumbing through a little black book. 'Ah, here it is,' she said. She handed Kling a white card. 'She wrote that for me the night we met. Jeannie Paige, and then the phone number. Now, look at the way she wrote.'

Kling looked at the card in puzzlement. 'This says "Club Tempo",' he said. '"Eighteen twelve Klausner Street."'

'What?' Claire frowned. 'Oh, yes. That's the card she came down with that night. She used the other side to give me her number. Turn it over.'

Kling did.

'See the childish scrawl? That was Jeannie Paige a year ago.'

Kling flipped the card over again. 'I'm more interested in *this* side,' he said. 'You told me you thought her boyfriend might have written this. Why do you say that?'

'I don't know. I just assumed he was the person who sent her down, that's all. It's a man's handwriting.'

'Yes,' Kling said. 'May I keep this?'

Claire nodded. 'If you like.' She paused. 'I guess I have no further use for Jeannie's phone number.'

'No,' Kling said. He put the card into his wallet. 'You said she asked you questions. What kind of questions?'

'Well, for one, she asked me how to kiss.'

'What?'

'Yes. She asked me what to do with her lips, whether she

99

should open her mouth, use her tongue. And all this delivered with that wide-eyed, baby-blue stare. It sounds incredible, I know. But, remember, she was a young bird, and she didn't know how strong her wings were.'

'She found out,' Kling said.

'Huh?'

'Jeannie Paige was pregnant when she died.'

'No!' Claire said. She put down the brandy glass. 'No, you're joking!'

'I'm serious.'

Claire was silent for several moments. Then she said, 'First time at bat, and she gets beaned. Dammit! Goddammit!'

'But you don't know who her boyfriend was?'

'No.'

'Had she continued seeing him? You said this was a year ago. I mean –'

'I know what you mean. Yes, the same one. She'd been seeing him regularly. In fact, she used the club for that.'

'He came to the club!' Kling said, sitting erect.

'No, no.' Claire was shaking her head impatiently. 'I think her sister and brother-in-law objected to her seeing this fellow. So she told them she was going down to Tempo. She'd stay there a little while, just in case anyone was checking, and then she'd leave.'

'Let me understand this,' Kling said. 'She came to the club, and then left to meet him. Is that right?'

'Yes.'

'This was standard procedure? This happened each time she came down?'

'Almost each time. Once in a while she'd stay at the club until things broke up.'

'Did she meet him in the neighbourhood?'

'No, I don't think so. I walked her down to the El once.'

'What time did she generally leave the club?'

'Between ten and ten-thirty.'

'And she walked to the El, is that right? And you assume she took a train there and went to meet him.'

'I *know* she went to meet him. The night I walked her, she told me she was going downtown to meet him.'

'Downtown where?'

'She didn't say.'

'What did he look like, this fellow?'

'She didn't say.'

'She never described him?'

'Only to say he was the handsomest man in the world. Look, who ever describes his love? Shakespeare, maybe. That's all.'

'Shakespeare and seventeen-year-olds,' Kling said. 'Seventeen-year-olds shout their love to the rooftops.'

'Yes,' Claire said gently. 'Yes.'

'But not Jeannie Paige. Dammit, why not her?'

'I don't know.' Claire thought for a moment. 'This mugger who killed her –'

'Um?'

'The police don't think he was the fellow she was seeing, do they?'

'This is the first anyone connected with the police is hearing about her love life,' Kling said.

'Oh. Well, he – he didn't sound that way. He sounded gentle. I mean, when Jeannie did talk about him, he sounded gentle.'

'But she never mentioned his name?'

'No. I'm sorry.'

Kling rose. 'I'd better be going. That *is* dinner I smell, isn't it?'

'My father'll be home soon,' Claire said. 'Mom is dead. I whip something up when I get home from school.'

'Every night?' Kling asked.

'What? I'm sorry . . .'

He didn't know whether to press it or not. She hadn't

heard him, and he could easily have shrugged his comment aside. But he chose not to.

'I said, "Every night?"'

'Every night what?'

She certainly was not making it easy for him. 'Do you prepare supper every night? Or do you occasionally get a night off?'

'Oh, I get nights off,' Claire said.

'Maybe you'd enjoy dinner out some night?'

'With you, do you mean?'

'Well, yes. Yes, that's what I had in mind.'

Claire Townsend looked at him long and hard. At last she said, 'No, I don't think so. I'm sorry. Thanks. I couldn't.'

'Well ... uh ...' Quite suddenly, Kling felt like a horse's ass. 'I ... uh ... guess I'll be going then. Thanks for the cognac. It was very nice.'

'Yes,' she said, and he remembered her discussing people who were there and yet not there, and he knew exactly what she meant because she was not there at all. She was somewhere far away, and he wished he knew where. With sudden, desperate longing, he wished he knew where she was because, curiously, he wanted to be there with her.

'Goodbye,' he said.

She smiled in answer, and closed the door behind him.

The dime in the slot brought him Peter Bell.

Bell's voice was sleepy. 'I didn't wake you, did I?' Kling asked.

'Yes, you did,' Bell said, 'but that's all right. What is it, Bert?'

'Well, is Molly there?'

'Molly? No. She went down to pick up a few things. What is it?'

'I've been – well, she asked me to check around a little.'

'Oh? Did she?'

'Yeah. I went to Club Tempo this afternoon, and I also talked with a girl named Claire Townsend. Nice girl.'

'What did you find out, Bert?'

'That Jeannie was seeing some guy regularly.'

'Who?'

'Well, that's just it. Miss Townsend didn't know. She ever mention anybody's name to you or Molly?'

'No, not that I can remember.'

'That's too bad. Might give me something to go on, you know. If we had even a first name. Something to work with.'

'No,' Bell said, 'I'm sorry but –' He stopped dead. There was a painful silence on the line, and then he said, 'Oh, my God!'

'What's the matter?'

'She did, Bert. She *did* mention someone. Oh, my God!'

'Who? When was this?'

'We were talking once. She was in a good mood, and she told me – Bert, she told me the name of the fellow she was seeing.'

'What was the name?'

'Clifford! Holy Jesus, Bert! His name is Clifford!'

CHAPTER ELEVEN

It was Roger Havilland who brought in the first real suspect in the alleged mugger murder.

The suspect was a kid named Sixto Fangez, a Puerto Rican boy who had been in the city for a little more than two years. Sixto was twenty years old, and had until recently been a member of a street gang known as 'The Tornadoes'. He was no longer active, having retired in favour of marriage to a girl named Angelita. Angelita was pregnant.

Sixto had allegedly beat up a hooker and stolen thirty-two dollars from her purse. The girl was one of the better-known prostitutes in the precinct territory and had, in fact, rolled in the hay on a good many occasions with members of the legion in blue. Some of these policemen had paid her for the privilege of her company.

In ordinary circumstances, in spite of the fact that the girl had made a positive identification of Sixto Fangez, Havilland might have been willing to forget the whole matter in consideration of a little legal tender. Assault charges had been known to slip the minds of many policemen when the right word together with the right amount of currency was exchanged.

It happened, however, that the newspapers were giving a big play to the funeral of Jeannie Paige – a funeral which had been delayed by the extensive autopsy examination performed on the body – on the morning that Sixto was brought upstairs to the Squad Room. The newspapers were also pressuring the cops to do something about the rampant mugger, and so perhaps Havilland's extreme enthusiasm could have been forgiven.

He booked a bewildered and frightened Sixto, barked 'Follow me!' over his shoulder, and then led him to a room politely marked INTERROGATION. Inside the room, Havilland locked the door and calmly lighted a cigarette. Sixto watched him. Havilland was a big man who, in his own words, 'took crap from nobody'. He had once started to break up a street fight and had in turn had his arm broken in four places. The healing process, considering the fact that the bones would not set properly the first time and had to be rebroken and reset, was a painful thing to bear. The healing process had given Havilland a lot of time to think. He thought mostly about being a good cop. He thought also about survival. He formed a philosophy.

Sixto was totally unaware of the thinking process which had led to the formation of Havilland's credo. He only knew that Havilland was the most hated and the most feared cop in the barrio. He watched him with interest, a light film of sweat beading his thin upper lip. His eyes never left Havilland's hands.

'Looks like you're in a little trouble, huh, Sixto?' Havilland said.

Sixto nodded, his eyes blinking. He wet his lips.

'Now, why'd you go and beat up on Carmen, huh?' Havilland said. He leaned against the table in the room, leisurely blowing out a stream of smoke. Sixto, thin, birdlike, wiped his bony hands on the coarse tweed of his trousers. Carmen was the prostitute he'd allegedly mugged. He knew that she had on occasion been friendly with the bulls. He did not know the extent of her relationship with Havilland. He maintained a calculating silence.

'Huh?' Havilland asked pleasantly, his voice unusually soft. 'Now why'd you go and beat up on a nice-looking little girl like Carmen?'

Sixto remained silent.

'Were you looking for some trim, huh, Sixto?'

'I am married,' Sixto said formally.

'Looking for a little gash, huh, Sixto?'

'No, I am married. I don't go to the prostitutes,' Sixto said.

'What were you doing with Carmen then?'

'She owe me money,' Sixto said. 'I wenn to collec' it.'

'You lent her money, is that right, Sixto?'

'*Sí*,' Sixto said.

'How much money?'

'Abou' forty dollars.'

'And so you went to her and tried to collect it, is that right?'

'*Sí*. Iss my money. I lenn it to her maybe three maybe four munns ago.'

'Why'd she need it. Sixto?'

'Hell, she's a junkie. Don't you know that?'

'I heard something along those lines,' Havilland said, smiling pleasantly. 'So she needed a fix and she came to you for the loot, that right, Sixto?'

'She dinn come to me. I happen to be sittin' in the bar, an' she say she wass low, so I lay the forty on her. Thass all. So now I wenn aroun' to collec' it. So she give me a hard time.'

'What kind of a hard time?'

'She say business iss bad, an' she don't get many johns comin' from downtown, an' like that. So I tell her I don't care abou' her business. All I wann is my forty dollars back. I'm a married man. I'm gonna have a baby soon. I cann fool aroun' lennin money to hookers.'

'You working, Sixto?'

'*Sí*. I work in a res'aurant downtown.'

'How come you needed this forty bucks so bad right now?'

'I tol' you. My wife's pregin. I got doctor bills, man.'

'So why'd you hit Carmen?'

'Becauss I tell her I don't have to stann aroun' bullin' with a hooker. I tell her I wann my money. So she come back and say my Angelita iss a hooker, too! Christ, man, thass my wife. Angelita! She's clean like the Virgin Mary! So I bust her in the mouth. Thass what happen.'

'And then you went through her purse, huh, Sixto?'

'Only to get my forty dollars.'

'And you got thirty-two, right?'

'*Sí*. She still owe me eight.'

Havilland nodded sympathetically, and then slid an ashtray across the table top. With small, sharp stabs, he stubbed out his cigarette. He looked up at Sixto then, a smile on his cherubic face. He sucked in a deep breath, his massive shoulders heaving.

'Now what's the real story, Sixto?' he said softly.

'Thass the real story,' Sixto said. 'Thass the way it happen.'

'What about these other girls you've been mugging?'

Sixto looked at Havilland unblinkingly. For a moment, he seemed incapable of speech. Then he said, 'What?'

'These other girls all over the city? How about it, Sixto?'

'What?' Sixto said again.

Havilland moved off the table gracefully. He took three steps to where Sixto was standing. Still smiling, he brought his fist back and rammed the knuckles into Sixto's mouth.

The blow caught Sixto completely by surprise. His eyes opened wide, and he felt himself staggering backward. Then he collided with the wall and automatically wiped the back of his hand across his mouth. A red smear stained the tan of his fingers. He blinked his eyes and looked across at Havilland.

'What for you hit me?' he asked.

'Tell me about the other girls, Sixto,' Havilland said, moving toward him again.

'*What* other girls? Jesus, what are you crazy or something? I hit a hooker to get back my –'

Havilland lashed out backhanded, then swung his open palm around to catch Sixto's other cheek. Again the hand lashed back, forward, back, forward, until Sixto's head was rocking like a tall blade of grass in a stiff breeze. He tried to cover his face, and Havilland jabbed out at his stomach. Sixto doubled over in pain.

'Ave Maria,' he said, 'why are you –'

'Shut up!' Havilland shouted. 'Tell me about the muggings, you spic son of a bitch! Tell me about that seventeen-year-old blonde you killed last week!'

'I dinn kill –'

Havilland hit him again, throwing his huge fist at Sixto's head. He caught Sixto under the eye, and the boy fell to the floor, and Havilland kicked him with the point of his shoe.

'Get up.'

'I dinn –'

Havilland kicked him again. The boy was sobbing now. He climbed to his feet, and Havilland punched him once in the stomach and then again in the face. Sixto crumpled against the wall, sobbing wildly.

'Why'd you kill her?'

Sixto couldn't answer. He kept shaking his head over and over again, sobbing. Havilland seized his jacket front and began pounding the boy's head against the wall.

'Why, you friggin spic? Why? Why? Why?'

But Sixto only kept shaking his head, and after a while his head lolled to one side, and he was unconscious.

Havilland studied him for a moment. He let out a deep sigh, went to the washbasin in the corner, and washed the blood from his hands. He lighted a cigarette then and went to the table, sitting on it and thinking. It was a damn shame, but he didn't think Sixto was the man they wanted. They still had him on the Carmen thing, of course, but they couldn't hang this mugger kill on him. It was a damn shame.

In a little while, Havilland unlocked the door and went next door to Clerical. Miscolo looked up from his typewriter.

'There's a spic next door,' Havilland said, puffing on his cigarette.

'Yeah?' Miscolo said.

Havilland nodded. 'Yeah. Fell down and hurt himself. Better get a doctor, huh?'

In another part of the city, a perhaps more orthodox method

of questioning was being undertaken by Detectives Meyer and Temple.

Meyer, personally, was grateful for the opportunity. In accordance with Lieutenant Byrnes' orders, he had been questioning known sex offenders until he was blue in the face. It was not that he particularly disliked questioning; it was simply that he disliked sex offenders.

The sunglasses found alongside the body of Jeannie Paige had borne a small 'C' in a circle over the bridge. The police had contacted several jobbers, one of whom identified the © as the trade-mark of a company known as Candrel, Inc. Byrnes had extricated Meyer and Temple from the sticky, degenerate web at the 87th, and sent them shuffling off to Majesta, where the firm's factory was located.

The office of Geoffrey Candrel was on the third floor of the factory, a soundproofed rectangle of knotty-pine walls and modern furniture. The desk seemed suspended in space. A painting on the wall behind the desk resembled an electronic computing machine with a nervous breakdown.

Candrel was a fat man in a big leather chair. He looked at the broken sunglasses on his desk, shoved at them with a pudgy forefinger as if he were prodding a snake to see if it were still alive.

'Yes,' he said. His voice was thick. It rumbled up out of his huge chest. 'Yes, we manufacture those glasses.'

'Can you tell us something about them?' Meyer asked.

'Can I tell you something about them?' Candrel smiled in a peculiarly superior manner. 'I've been making frames for *all* kinds of glasses for more than fourteen years now. And you ask me if I can tell you something about them? My friend, I can tell you whatever you want to know.'

'Well, can you tell us –'

'The trouble with most people,' Candrel went on, 'is that they think it's a simple operation to make a pair of sunglass frames – or any kind of eyeglass frames for that matter. Well, gentlemen, that's simply not true. Unless you're a sloppy workman who doesn't give a damn about the product you're putting out. Candrel gives a damn. Candrel considers the consumer.'

'Well, perhaps you can –'

'We get this sheet stock first,' Candrel said, ignoring Meyer. 'It's called zyl – that's the trade term for cellulose nitrate, optical grade. We die-stamp the fronts and temple shapes from that sheet stock.'

'Fronts?' Meyer said.

'Temples?' Temple said.

'The front is the part of the eyeglass that holds the lenses. The temples are the two gizmos you put over your ears.'

'I see,' Meyer said. 'But about these glasses –'

'After they're stamped, the fronts and temples are machined,' Candrel said, 'to put the grooves in the rims, and to knock off the square edges left by the stamping. Then the nose pads are cemented to the fronts. After that, a cutter blends the pads to the fronts in a "phrasing" operation.'

'Yes, sir, but –'

'Nor is that the end of it,' Candrel said. 'To blend the nose pads further, they are rubbed on a wet pumice wheel. Then the fronts and temples go through a roughing operation. They're put into a tumbling barrel of pumice, and the tumbling operation takes off all the rough machine marks. In the finishing operation, these same fronts and temples are put into a barrel of small wooden pegs – about an inch long by three-sixteenths of an inch wide – together with a lubricant and our own secret compound. The pegs slide over the fronts and temples, polishing them.'

'Sir, we'd like to get on with –'

'After that,' Candrel said, frowning, a man obviously not used to being interrupted, 'the fronts and temples are slotted for hinges, and then the hinges are fastened with shields, and then fronts are assembled to temples with screws. The corners are mitred, and then the ends are rounded on a pumice wheel in the Rubbing Room. After that –'

'Sir –'

'After that, the frames are washed and cleaned and sent to the Polishing Room. All of our frames are *hand-polished*, gentlemen. A lot of companies simply dip the frames into a solvent to give it a polished look. Not us. We *hand-polish* them.'

'That's admirable, Mr Candrel,' Meyer said, 'but –'

'And when we insert plain glass lenses, we use a six-base lens, a lens that has been ground and is without distortion. Our plano sunglasses are six-diopter lenses, gentlemen. And remember, *a six-base lens is optically correct.*'

'I'm sure it is,' Meyer said tiredly.

'Why, our best glasses retail for as high as twenty dollars,' Candrel said proudly.

'What about these?' Meyer asked, pointing to the glasses on Candrel's desk.

'Yes,' Candrel said. He poked at the glasses with his finger again. 'Of course, we also put out a cheaper line. We injection-mould them out of polystyrene. It's a high-speed die-casting operation done under hydraulic pressure. Semi-automatic, you understand. And, of course, we use less expensive lenses.'

'Are these glasses a part of your cheaper line?' Meyer asked.

'Ah ... yes.' Candrel seemed suddenly embarrassed.

'How much do they cost?'

'We sell them to our jobbers for thirty-five cents a pair. They probably retail anywhere from seventy-five cents to a dollar.'

'What about your distribution?' Temple asked.

'Sir?'

'Where are these glasses sold? Any particular stores?'

Candrel pushed the glasses clear to the other side of his desk, as if they had grown suddenly leprous.

'Gentlemen,' he said, 'you can buy these glasses in any five-and-ten-cent store in the city.'

CHAPTER TWELVE

At two o'clock on the morning of Thursday, 21 September, Eileen Burke walked the streets of Isola in a white sweater and a tight skirt.

She was a tired cop.

She had been walking the streets of Isola since eleven-forty-five the previous Saturday night. This was her fifth night of walking. She wore high-heeled pumps, and they had definitely not been designed for hikes. In an attempt to lure the mugger, whose basic motivation in choosing women might or might not have been sexually inspired, she had hitched up her brassière a notch or two higher so that her breasts were cramped and upturned, albeit alluring.

The allure of her mammary glands was not to be denied by anyone, least of all someone with so coldly analytical a mind as Eileen Burke possessed.

During the course of her early-morning promenades, she had been approached seven times by sailors, four times by soldiers, and twenty-two times by civilians in various styles of male attire. The approaches had ranged from polite remarks such as, 'Nice night, ain't it?' to more direct opening gambits like, 'Walking all alone, honey?' to downright unmistakable business inquiries like, 'How much, babe?'

All of these, Eileen had taken in her stride.

They had, to be truthful, broken the monotony of her otherwise lonely and silent excursions. She had never once caught sight of Willis behind her, though she knew with certainty that he was there. She wondered now if he was as bored as she, and she concluded that he was possibly not. He did, after all, have the compensating sight of a backside which she jiggled jauntily for the benefit of any unseen, observant mugger.

Where are you, Clifford? she mentally asked.

Have we scared you off? Did the sight of the twisted and bloody young kid whose head you split open turn your stomach, Clifford? Have you decided to give up this business, or are you waiting until the heat's off?

Come on, Clifford.

See the pretty wiggle? The bait is yours, Clifford. And the only hook is the ·38 in my purse.

Come on, Clifford!

From where Willis jogged doggedly along behind Eileen, he could make out only the white sweater and occasionally a sudden burst of bright red when the lights caught at her hair.

He was a tired cop.

It had been a long time since he'd walked a beat, and this was worse than walking any beat in the city. When you had a beat, you also had bars and restaurants and sometimes tailor shops or candy stores. And in those places you could pick up, respectively, a quick beer, cup of coffee, snatch of idle conversation, or warmth from a hissing radiator.

This girl Eileen liked walking. He had followed behind her for four nights now, and this was the fifth, and she hadn't once stopped walking. This was an admirable attitude, to be sure, a devotion to duty which was not to be scoffed aside.

But good Christ, man, did she have a motor?

What propelled those legs of hers? (Good legs, Willis. Admit it.)

And why so fast? Did she think Clifford was a cross-country track star? He had spoken to her about her speed after their first night of breakneck pacing. She had smiled easily, fluffed her hair like a virgin at a Freshman tea and said, 'I always walk fast.'

That, he thought now, had been the understatement of the year.

What she meant, of course, was, 'I always *run* slow.'

He did not envy Clifford. Whoever he was, wherever he

113

was, he would need a motorcycle to catch this redhead with the paperback-cover bazzoms.

Well, he thought, she's making the game worth the candle.

Wherever you are, Clifford, Miss Burke's going to give you a run for your money.

He had first heard the tapping of her heels.

The impatient beaks of woodpeckers riveting at the stout mahogany heart of his city. Fluttering taps, light-footed, strong legs and quick feet.

He had then seen the white sweater, a beacon in the distance, coming nearer and nearer, losing its two-dimensionality as it grew closer, expanding until it had the three-sidedness of a work of sculpture, then taking on reality, becoming woollen fibre covering firm high breasts.

He had seen the red hair then, long, lapped by the nervous fingers of the wind, enveloping her head like a blazing funeral pyre. He had stood in the alleyway across the street and watched her as she pranced by, cursing his station, wishing he had posted himself on the other side of the street instead. She carried a black patent-leather sling bag over her shoulder, the strap loose, the bag knocking against her left hipbone as she walked. The bag looked heavy.

He knew that looks could be deceiving, that many women carried all sorts of junk in their purses, but he smelled money in this one. She was either a whore drumming up trade or a society bitch out for a late evening stroll – it was sometimes difficult to tell them apart. Whichever she was, the purse promised money, and money was what he needed pretty badly right now.

The newspapers shrieking about Jeannie Paige. Jesus!

They had driven him clear off the streets. But how long can a murder remain hot? And doesn't a man have to eat?

He watched the redhead swing past, and then he ducked into the alleyway, quickly calculating a route which would intersect her apparent course.

He did not see Willis coming up behind the girl.

Nor did Willis see him.

There are three lamp-posts on each block, Eileen thought.

It takes approximately one and one-half minutes to cover the distance between lamp-posts. Four and a half minutes a block. That's plain arithmetic.

Nor is that exceptionally fast. If Willis thinks that's fast, he should meet my brother. My brother is the type of person who rushes through everything – breakfast, dinner . . .

Hold it now!

Something was moving up ahead.

Her mind, as if instantly sucked clean of debris by a huge vacuum cleaner, lay glistening like a hard, cut diamond. Her left hand snapped to the drawstrings on her purse, wedging into the purse and enlarging the opening. She felt the reassuring steel of the ·38, content that the butt was in a position to be grasped instantly by a cross-body swipe of her right hand.

She walked with her head erect. She did not break her stride. The figure ahead was a man, of that much she was certain. He had seen her now, and he moved toward her rapidly. He wore a dark blue suit, and he was hatless. He was a big man, topping six feet.

'Hey!' he called. 'Hey, you!' and she felt her heart lurch into her throat because she knew with rattling certainty that this was Clifford.

And suddenly, she felt quite foolish.

She had seen the markings on the sleeve of the blue suit, had seen the slender white lines on the collar. The man she'd thought to be Clifford was only a hatless sailor. The tenseness flooded from her body. A small smile touched her lips.

The sailor came closer to her, and she saw now that he was weaving unsteadily, quite unsteadily. He was, to be kind, as drunk as a lord, and his condition undoubtedly accounted for his missing white hat.

'Wal now,' he bawled, 'if'n it ain't a redhaid! C'mere, redhaid!'

He grabbed for Eileen, and she knocked his arm aside quickly and efficiently. 'Run along, sailor,' she said. 'You're in the wrong pew!'

The sailor threw back his head and guffawed boisterously. 'Th' wrong pew!' he shouted. 'Wal now, Ah'll be hung fer a hoss thief!'

Eileen, not caring at all what he was hung for so long as he kept his nose out of the serious business afoot, walked briskly past him and continued on her way.

'Hey!' he bellowed. 'Wheah y'goin'?'

She heard his hurried footsteps behind her, and then she felt his hand close on her elbow. She whirled, shaking his fingers free.

'Whutsamatter?' he asked. 'Doan'choo like sailors?'

'I like them fine,' Eileen answered. 'But I think you ought to be getting back to your ship. Now go ahead. Run along.' She stared at him levelly.

He returned her stare soberly, and then quite suddenly asked, 'Hey, you-all like t'go to bed wi' me?'

Eileen could not suppress the smile. 'No,' she said. 'Thank you very much.'

'Why not?' he asked, thrusting forward his jaw.

'I'm married,' she lied.

'Why, tha's awright,' he said. 'Ah'm married, too.'

'My husband is a cop,' she further lied.

'Cops doan scare me none. On'y the SOBSP. Ah got to worry 'bout. Hey now, how 'bout it, huh?'

'No,' Eileen said firmly. She turned to go, and he wove quickly around her, skidding to a stop in front of her.

'We can talk 'bout yo' husbin an' mah wife, how's that? Ah got th' sweetes' li'l wife in th' whole wide world.'

'Then go home to her,' Eileen said.

'Ah cain't! Dammit all, she's in Alabama!'

'Take off, sailor,' Eileen said. 'I'm serious. Take off before you get yourself in trouble.'

'No,' he said, pouting. 'Ah wanna go t'bed wi' you.'

'Oh, for Pete's sake,' she said.

'Ain't nothin' wrong wi' that, is they? Everythin' 'bout it is puffectly normal.'

'Except your timing,' Eileen said.

'Huh?'

'Nothing.' She turned and looked over her shoulder for Willis. He was nowhere in sight. He was undoubtedly resting against an alley wall, laughing his fool head off. She walked around the sailor and started up the street. The sailor fell in beside her.

'Nothin' Ah like better'n walkin',' he said. 'Ah'm goan walk mah big feet off, right here 'longside you, till you admit you're just a-dyin' to climb into bed with me. Ah'm goan walk till hell freezes over.'

'Stick with me, and you will,' Eileen muttered, and then she wondered how soon it would be until she spotted an SP. Dammit, there never was a cop around when you needed one!

Now she's picking up sailors, Willis thought.

We've got nothing better to do than humour the fleet. Why doesn't she conk the silly son of a bitch on the head and leave him to sleep it off in an alleyway?

How the hell are we going to smoke Clifford if she insists on a naval escort? Shall I go break it up? Or has she got something up her sleeve?

The terrible thing about working with women is that you can never count on them to think like men.

I should have stayed in bed.

He watched silently, and he cursed the sailor.

Where had the fool materialized from? How could he get that purse now? Of all the goddamn rotten luck, the first good thing that had come along on his first night out since the papers started that Jeannie Paige fuss, and this stupid sailor had to come along and screw it up.

Maybe he'd go away.

Maybe she'd slap him across the face and he'd go away.

Or maybe not. If she was a prostitute, she'd take the sailor with her, and that would be the end of that.

Why did the police allow the Navy to dump its filthy cargoes into the streets of the city, anyway?

He watched the wiggle of the girl's backside, and he watched the swaying, bobbing motion of the sailor, and he cursed the police, and he cursed the fleet, and he even cursed the redhead.

And then they turned the corner, and he ducked through the alley and started through the back yard, hoping to come out some two blocks ahead of the pair, hoping she'd have got rid of him by then, his fingers aching to close around the purse that swung so heavily from her left shoulder.

'What ship are you on?' Eileen asked the sailor.

'USS *Huntuh*,' the sailor said. 'You-all beginnin' t'take an intrust in me, redhaid?'

Eileen stopped. She turned to face the sailor, and there was a deadly glint in her green eyes. 'Listen to me, sailor,' she said. 'I'm a policewoman, understand? I'm working now, and you're cluttering up my job, and I don't like it.'

'A *what*?' the sailor said. He threw back his head, ready to let out with a wild guffaw, but Eileen's coldly dispassionate voice stopped him.

'I've got a ·38 Detective's Special in my purse,' she said evenly. 'In about six seconds, I'm going to take it out and shoot you in the leg. I'll leave you on the sidewalk and then put a call in to the Shore Patrol. I'm counting, sailor.'

'Hey, whut you –'

'One . . .'

'Listen, whut you gettin' all het up about? Ah'm on'y –'

'Two . . .'

'I don't even believe you got an' ol' gun in that –'

The ·38 snapped into view suddenly. The sailor's eyes went wide.

'Three,' Eileen said.

'Wal, ah'll be –'

'Four . . .'

The sailor looked at the gun once more.

'G'night, lady,' he said, and he turned on his heel and began running. Eileen watched him. She returned the gun to her purse, smiled, turned the corner, and walked into the darkened street. She had taken no more than fifteen steps when the arm circled her throat and she was pulled into the alleyway.

The sailor came down the street at such a fast clip that Willis almost burst out laughing. The flap of the sailor's jumper danced in the wind. He charged down the middle of the asphalt with a curious mixture of a sailor's roll, a drunk lopsided gait, and the lope of a three-year-old in the Kentucky Derby. His eyes were wide, and his hair flew madly as he jounced along.

He skidded to a stop when he saw Willis and then, puffing for breath, he advised, 'Man, if'n you-all see a redhaid up theah, steer clear of her, Ah'm tellin' you.'

'What's the matter?' Willis asked paternally, holding back the laugh that crowded his throat.

'Whutsamatter! Man, she got a twenty-gauge shotgun in her handbag, tha's whutsamatter. Whoo-ie, Ah'm gettin' clear the hell out o' here!'

He nodded briefly at Willis, and then blasted off again. Willis watched his jet trail, indulged himself in one short chuckle, and then looked for Eileen up ahead. She had probably turned the corner.

He grinned, changing his earlier appraisal of the sailor's intrusion. The sailor had, after all, presented a welcome diversion from this dull business of plodding along and hoping for a mugger who probably would never materialize.

She was reaching for the ·38 in her purse when the strap left her shoulder. She felt the secure weight of the purse leaving her hip-bone, and then the bag was gone. And just as she planted her feet to throw the intruder over her shoulder, he spun her around and slammed her against the wall of the building.

'I'm not playing around,' he said in a low, menacing voice, and she realized instantly that he wasn't. The collision with the wall of the building had knocked the breath out of her. She watched his face, dimly lighted in the alleyway. He was not wearing sunglasses, but she could not determine the colour of his eyes. He was wearing a hat, too, and she cursed the hat because it hid his hair.

His fist lashed out suddenly, exploding just beneath her left eye. She had heard about purple and yellow globes of light which followed a punch in the eye, but she had never experienced them until this moment. She tried to move away from the wall, momentarily blinded, but he shoved her back viciously.

'That's just a warning,' he said. 'Don't scream when I'm gone, you understand?'

'I understand,' she said levelly. *Willis, where are you?* her mind shrieked. *For God's sake, where are you?*

She had to detain this man. She had to hold him until Willis showed. Come on, Willis.

'Who are you?' she asked.

His hand went out again, and her head rocked from his strong slap.

'Shut up!' he warned. 'I'm taking off now.'

If this were Clifford, she had a chance. If this were Clifford, she would have to move in a few seconds, and she tensed herself for the move, knowing only that she had to hold the man until Willis arrived.

There!

He was going into it now.

'Clifford thanks you, madam,' he said, and his arm swept across his waist, and he went into a low bow, and Eileen clasped both hands together, raised them high over her head, and swung them at the back of his neck as if she were wielding a hammer.

The blow caught him completely by surprise. He began to pitch forward, and she brought up her knee, catching him under the jaw. His arms opened wide. He dropped the purse and staggered backward, and when he lifted his head again, Eileen was standing with a spike-heeled shoe in one hand. She didn't wait for his attack. With one foot shoeless, she hobbled forward and swung out at his head.

He backed away, missing her swing, and then he bellowed like a wounded bear, and cut loose with a roundhouse blow that caught her just below her bosom. She felt the sharp knifing pain, and then he was hitting her again, hitting her cruelly and viciously now. She dropped the shoe, and she caught at his clothes, one hand going to his face, trying to rip, trying to claw, forgetting all her police knowledge in that one desperate lunge for self-survival, using a woman's weapons – nails.

She missed his face, and she stumbled forward, catching at his jacket again, clawing at his breast pocket. He pulled away, and she felt the material tear, and then she was holding the torn shield of his pocket patch in her hands, and he hit her again, full on the jaw, and she fell back against the wall and heard Willis' running footsteps.

The mugger stooped down for the fallen purse, seizing it by the shoulder straps as Willis burst into the mouth of the alley, a gun in his fist.

Clifford came erect, swinging the bag as he stood. The bag caught Willis on the side of the head, and he staggered sideways, the gun going off in his hand. He shook his head, saw the mugger taking flight, shot without aiming, shot again, missing both times. Clifford turned the corner, and Willis took off after him, rounding the same bend.

The mugger was nowhere in sight.

He went back to where Eileen Burke sat propped against the wall of the building. Her knees were up, and her skirt was pulled back, and she sat in a very unladylike position, cradling her head. Her left eye was beginning to throb painfully. When she lifted her head, Willis winced.

'He clipped you,' he said.

'Where the hell were you?' Eileen Burke answered.

'Right behind you. I didn't realize anything was wrong until I heard a man's voice shout, "Shut up!"'

'The son of a bitch packs a wallop,' Eileen said. 'How does my eye look?'

'You're going to have a hell of a mouse,' Willis told her. 'We'll get a steak for it whenever you feel like going.' He paused. 'Was it Clifford?'

'Sure,' she said. She got to her feet, and then winced. 'Ow, I think he broke one of my ribs.'

'Are you kidding me?' Willis asked, concerned.

Eileen felt the area beneath her breasts. 'It only feels that way. Oooooh, God!'

'Did you get a look at him?'

'Too dark,' she said. She held up her hand. 'I got his pocket, though.'

'Good.' Willis looked down. 'What's all this on the sidewalk?'

'What?'

He bent. 'Cigarettes,' he said. 'Good. We may get some latents from the cellophane.' He picked the package up with his handkerchief, carefully holding the linen around it.

'He was probably carrying them in his pocket,' Eileen said. She touched the throbbing eye. 'Let's get that steak, huh?'

'Sure. Just one thing.'

'What?'

'Matches. If he was carrying cigarettes in that pocket, he

was probably carrying matches, too.' He took a pocket flash and thumbed it into life. The light spilled on to the sidewalk, travelling in a slow arc. 'Ah, there they are,' he said. He stooped to pick up the match folder, using a second handkerchief he took from his inside pocket.

'Listen, can't we get that steak?' Eileen asked.

Willis looked at the folder. 'We may be in luck,' he said.

'How so?'

'The ad on these matches. It's for a place here in the city. A place named the Three Aces. Maybe we've got a hangout for Clifford now.'

He looked at Eileen and grinned broadly. She stooped, put on her shoe.

'Come on,' he said, 'let's take care of that peeper.'

'I was beginning to think you didn't care any more,' Eileen said. She took his arm, and they started up the street together.

CHAPTER THIRTEEN

That Thursday afternoon, Kling called Claire Townsend the first chance he got.

The first chance he got was on his lunch hour. He ordered a Western sandwich and a cup of coffee, went to the phonebook, looked up Townsend at 728 Peterson in Riverhead, and came up with a listing for Ralph Townsend. He went into the booth, deposited a dime, and dialled the number. He allowed the phone to ring for a total of twelve times, and then he hung up.

There were a lot of things to keep him busy on the beat that afternoon. A woman, for no apparent reason other than that her husband had called her 'Babe', had struck out at him with a razor, opening a gash the size of a banana on the side of his face. Kling made the pinch. The razor, by the time he arrived on the scene, had gone the way of all discreet assault weapons – down the nearest sewer.

No sooner was he back on the street than a gang of kids attacked a boy as he was coming home from school. The boy had committed the unpardonable sin of making a pass at a deb who belonged to a rival street gang. Kling arrived just as the gang members were ready to stomp the kid into the pavement. He collared one of them, told him he knew the faces of all the kids who'd participated in the beating, and that if anything happened to the boy they'd jumped from here on in, he'd know just where to look. The gang member nodded solemnly, and then took off after his friends. The boy they'd jumped survived with only a few bumps on his head. This time, fists had been the order of the day.

Kling them proceeded to break up a crap game in the hallway of one of the buildings, listen to the ranting complaints of a shopkeeper who insisted that an eight-year-old boy had swiped a bolt of blue Shantung, warn one of the bar owners that his licence was kaput the next time any hustlers were observed soliciting in his joint, have a cup of coffee with one of the better-known policy runners in the neighbourhood, and then walk back to the precinct house, where he changed into street clothes.

As soon as he hit the street again, he called Claire. She picked up the instrument on the fourth ring.

'Who is it?' she said. 'And I hope to hell you apologize for getting me out of the shower. I'm wringing wet.'

'I apologize,' Kling said.

'Mr Kling?' she asked, recognizing his voice.

'Yes.'

'I was going to call you, but I didn't know where. I remembered something that might help.'

'What is it?'

'The night I walked Jeannie down to the train station she said something.'

'What?'

'She said she had a half-hour ride ahead of her. Does that help?'

'It might. Thanks a lot.' He paused. 'Listen, I've been thinking.'

'Yes.'

'About ... about this dinner setup. I thought maybe –'

'Mr Kling,' she interrupted, 'you don't want to take me to dinner.'

'I do,' he insisted.

'I'm the dullest girl in the world, believe me. I'd bore you stiff.'

'I'd like to take the chance.'

'You're only asking for trouble for yourself. Don't bother, believe me. Buy your mother a present with the money.'

'I bought my mother a present last week.'

'Buy her another one.'

'Besides, I was thinking of going Dutch.'

Claire chuckled. 'Well, now you make it sound more attractive.'

'Seriously, Claire –'

'Seriously, Mr Kling, I'd rather not. I'm a sad sack, and you wouldn't enjoy me, not one bit.'

'I enjoy you already.'

'Those were company manners.'

'Say, have you got an inferiority complex or something?'

'It's not that I have an inferiority complex, doctor,' she said, 'it's that I really *am* inferior.' Kling laughed, and she said, 'Do you remember that cartoon?'

'No, but it's wonderful. How about dinner?'

'Why?'

'I like you.'

'There are a million girls in this city.'

'More than that even.'

'Mr Kling –'

'Bert.'

'Bert, there's nothing here for you.'

'I haven't said what I want yet.'

'Whatever you want, it's not here.'

'Claire, let me gamble on it. Let me take you to dinner, and let me spend what may turn out to be the most miserable evening in my entire life. I've gambled with larger stakes involved. In the service, I even gambled with my life once in a while.'

'Were you in the service?' she asked.

'Yes.'

There seemed to be sudden interest in her voice. 'Korea?'

'Yes.'

There was a long silence on the line.

'Claire?'

'I'm here.'

'What's the matter?'

'Nothing.'

126

'Deposit five cents for the next three minutes, please,' the operator said.

'Oh, hell, just a minute,' Kling replied. He dug into his pocket and deposited a nickel. 'Claire?' he said.

'I'm costing you money already,' she told him.

'I've got money to burn,' he answered. 'How about it? I'll call for you tonight at about six-thirty.'

'No, tonight is out of the question.'

'Tomorrow night then.'

'I have a late class tomorrow. I don't get out until seven.'

'I'll meet you at the school.'

'That won't give me any time to change.'

'It'll be a come-as-you-are date, okay?'

'I usually wear flats and a dirty old sweater to school.'

'Fine!' he said enthusiastically.

'I suppose I could wear a dress and heels, though. It might shock some of the slobs in our hallowed halls, but then again it might set a precedent.'

'Seven o'clock?'

'All right,' she said.

'Good, I'll see you then.'

'Goodbye.'

''Bye.' He hung up, grinning. He was stepping out of the booth when he remembered. Instantly, he reached into his pocket for another dime. He had no change. He went to the proprietor of the candy store, who was busy doling out a couple of two-cent seltzers. By the time he got his change, five minutes had rushed by. He dialled the number rapidly.

'Hello?'

'Claire, this is me again.'

'You got me out of the shower again, you know that, don't you?'

'Gee, I'm awfully sorry, but you didn't tell me *which* school.'

'Oh.' Claire was silent. 'Nope, I didn't. It's Women's U. Do you know where that is?'

'Yes.'

'Fine. Go to Radley Hall. You'll find the office of our alleged college newspaper there. The paper is called the *Radley Clarion*, but the sign on the door says *Radley Rag*. I keep my coat in a locker there. Don't let all the predatory females frighten you.'

'I'll be there on the dot,' Kling said.

'And I, exercising a woman's prerogative, shall be there ten minutes *after* the dot.'

'I'll wait.'

'Good. Now you don't mind, do you, but I'm making a big puddle on the carpet.'

'I'm sorry. Go wash.'

'You said that as if you thought I was dirty.'

'If you'd rather talk, I've got all night.'

'I'd rather wash. Goodbye, Tenacious.'

'Goodbye, Claire.'

'You *are* tenacious, you realize that, don't you?'

Kling grinned. 'Tenacious, anyone?' he asked.

'Ouch!' Claire said. 'Goodbye,' and then she hung up.

He sat in the booth grinning foolishly for a good three minutes. A fat lady knocked on the glass panel in the door and said, 'Young man, that booth isn't a hotel.'

Kling opened the doors. 'That's funny,' he said. 'Room service just sent up a sandwich.'

The woman blinked, pulled a face, and then stuffed herself into the booth, slamming the door emphatically.

At ten o'clock that night, Kling stepped off an express train on to the Peterson Avenue station platform of the Elevated Transit System. He stood for a moment looking out over the lights of the city, warm and alive with colour against the tingling autumn air. Autumn did not want to die this year. Autumn refused to be lowered into the grave of winter. She clung tenaciously ('Tenacious, anyone?' he thought, and he grinned all over again) to the trailing robes of summer. She

128

was glad to be alive, and humanity caught some of her zest for living, mirrored it on the faces of the people in the streets.

One of the people in the streets was a man named Clifford.

Somewhere among people who rushed along grinning, there was a man with a scowl on his face.

Somewhere among the thousands who sat in movie houses, there might be a murderer watching the screen.

Somewhere where lovers walked and talked, he might be sitting alone on a bench, brooding.

Somewhere where open, smiling faces dispelled plumed, brittle vapour on to the snappish air, a man walked with his mouth closed and his teeth clenched.

Clifford.

How many Cliffords were there in a city of this size? How many Cliffords in the telephone directory? How many unlisted Cliffords?

Shuffle the deck of Cliffords, cut, and then pick a Clifford, any Clifford.

This was not a time for picking Cliffords.

This was a time for walks in the country, with the air spanking your cheeks, and the leaves crisp and crunching underfoot, and the trees screaming in a riot of splendid colour. This was a time for brier pipes and tweed overcoats and juicy red McIntosh apples. This was a time to contemplate pumpkin pie and good books and thick rugs and windows shut tight against the coming cold.

This was not a time for Clifford, and this was not a time for murder.

But murder had been done, and the Homicide cops were cold-eyed men who had never been seventeen.

Kling had once been seventeen.

He walked down the steps and directly to the change booth. The man behind the grilled window was reading a 'comic' book. Kling recognized it as one of the more hilarious attempts now on the stands, a strip dealing with a widow who had multiple sclerosis. The attendant looked up.

'Good evening,' Kling said.

The attendant eyed him suspiciously. 'Evening,' he replied.

'Mind if I ask you a few questions?'

'Depends what the questions are,' the attendant said.

'Well –'

'If you're planning a holdup, young man, forget it,' the attendant advised. 'You won't get a hell of a lot for your trouble, and the cops in this town are pretty damn good on transit stick-ups.'

'Thanks. I wasn't planning a holdup.'

'Good thing. My name's Ruth, Sam Ruth. The fellows call this "Ruth's Booth". What can I do for you?'

'Are you usually working nights?'

'Sometimes yes, sometimes no. Why?'

'I'm trying to trace a young girl who generally boarded a train from this platform.'

'Lots of young girls get on trains here.'

'This one usually came up between ten and ten-thirty. Are you on at that time?'

'When I work the afternoon shift, I come on at four, and I go off at midnight.'

'Then you're on at ten.'

'It would appear that way, yeah.'

'This girl was a blonde,' Kling said. 'A very pretty blonde.'

'There's a blonde widow works in the bakeshop downstairs. She comes up about eight each night.'

'This girl was young. Seventeen.'

'Seventeen, huh?'

'Yes.'

'Don't recall,' Ruth said.

'Think.'

'What for? I don't recall her.'

'Very pretty. If you'd seen her, you'd remember her. Well built, big blue eyes, a knockout.'

Ruth squinched up his eyes. 'Yeah,' he said.

'Huh?'

'I remember. Nice young kid. Yeah, I remember.'

'What time did she come up?'

''Bout ten-twenty-five usually. Yeah, I remember her, all right. Always went up the downtown side of the platform. Used to watch her all the way. A damn pretty girl. Only seventeen, you say? Seemed a lot older.'

'Only seventeen. Are you sure we're talking about the same girl?'

'Listen, how do I know? This blonde came up about ten-twenty-five most of the time. Reason I remember her is she once asked me to change a ten-dollar bill. We ain't allowed to change bigger than two dollars, not that many folks carry two-dollar bills, you know. Consider it hard luck. Superstition's bad, bad,' Ruth shook his head.

'Did you change it for her?' Kling asked.

'Out of my own pocket. That's how I remember her. She gave me a big smile. Nice smile, that girl. Nice everything, you ask me. Yeah, she's the one, all right. Used to go up on the downtown side, caught the ten-thirty train.' Ruth pulled a gold watch from his pocket. He nodded, replaced the watch. 'Yeah, caught the ten-thirty.'

'All the time?'

'Whenever I seen her, she caught the same train. After I cashed that bill for her, she always give me a smile. She was worth looking at, all right. Biggest damn boobies I ever seen on a woman.'

Kling glanced over his shoulder. The clock on the wall read 10.16

'If I got on that ten-thirty train,' he asked, 'where would I get off a half hour from now?'

'Say, I don't know,' Ruth said. He thought for a moment. 'Can tell you how to find out, though.'

'Yes?'

'Get on it,' Ruth said.

'Thanks.'

'Not at all. Glad to be of help.' He turned back to his

comic book, anxious to get back to the funny pages about the sick widow.

The train screeched through the heart of the city, on intimate terms with the windows of the buildings it passed. Kling sat and watched the city pass by in review outside. It was a big city, and a dirty city, but when you were born and raised in it, it became as much a part of you as your liver or your intestinal tract. He watched the city, and he watched the hands of his timepiece.

Jeannie Paige had told Claire there was a half-hour ride ahead of her. She had generally boarded a ten-thirty train, and so Kling watched the advancing hands of his watch. The train swooped underground, piercing the bowels of the city. He sat and waited. Passengers came and went. Kling's eyes did not leave his watch.

At 11.02, the train pulled into a station platform underground. The last stop had been at 10.58. It was a tossup, either way. He left the train and went up to the street.

He was in the heart of Isola.

The buildings reached up to touch the sky, tinting the night with gaudy smears of red and orange and green and yellow light. There was a men's clothing store on the corner, and a bakery shop, and a hack stand, and a dress shop, and a bus stop up the street, and a movie marquee, and a candy store, and a Chinese restaurant, and a bar, and all the stores and signs that clustered together like close relatives of the same family all over the city.

He sighed heavily.

If Jeannie had met her boyfriend here, and if her boyfriend's name was Clifford, combing the area would be like searching for a blade of hay in a mountain of needles.

He went to the subway kiosk again, boarding an uptown train this time. He travelled for one stop, figuring the half hour Jeannie had estimated could just as easily have brought her to this station.

The stores and signs he encountered on the street were much the same as those he had just seen. The trappings of a busy intersection. Hell, this stop was almost a dead ringer for the one he'd just visited.

Almost – but not quite.

Kling boarded the train again and headed for his furnished room.

There had been one landmark at the first stop which had been missing at the second stop, Kling's eyes had recorded the item on his brain and buried it in his unconscious.

Unfortunately, however, it was useless there at the moment.

CHAPTER FOURTEEN

Science, as any fool knows, is the master sleuth.

Give the Police Lab a sliver of glass and they can tell you what make car the suspect was driving, when he last had it washed, what states he'd visited, and whether or not he'd ever necked in the back seat.

Provided the breaks are with them.

When the breaks are going the wrong way, science is about as master a sleuth as the corner iceman.

The breaks in the Jeannie Paige case managed to show a total disregard for the wishes and earnest endeavours of the boys in the Police Laboratory. There had, in all truth, been a good thumb-print on one lens of the sunglasses found near the girl's body. Unfortunately, it is about as difficult to trace a single print as it is to unmask a Moslem woman. This did not faze the boys in the lab.

Sam Grossman was a lab technician and a police lieutenant.

He was tall and thin, a gentle man with gentle eyes and a quiet manner. He wore glasses, the only sign of science on a rock-hewn face that seemed to have been dispossessed from a New England farm. He worked at Headquarters in the clean, white lab that stretched across half the first-floor length of the building. He liked police work. He owned an orderly, precise mind, and there was something neat and truthful about the coupling of indisputable scientific fact to police theory.

He was an emotional man, but he had long ago ceased identifying the facts of sudden death with the people it summarily visited. He had seen too many bundles of bloody clothing, had studied the edges of too many powder burns, had analysed the liquid contents of too many poisoned stomachs. Death, to Sam Grossman, was the great equalizer. It reduced human beings to arithmetical problems. If the breaks went with the lab, two and two added up to four.

If the breaks were indifferent or downright ornery, two and two sometimes equalled five, or six, or eleven.

There had been a man at the scene of Jeannie Paige's death. The man had been equipped with a soft-pine sketchboard attached to a photographic tripod. He had also carried a small alidade, a compass, graph paper, a soft-lead pencil, indiarubber, common pins, a wooden triangle with scale, a scale, a tape measure, and a flexible steel ruler.

The man had worked quietly and efficiently. While photographers swarmed over the site, while technicians dusted for latent prints, while the position of the body was marked and while the body was transported into the waiting meat wagon, while the area was carefully scrutinized for footprints or tyre tracks – the man stood like an artist doing a picture of a farmer's barn on Cape Cod.

He said Hello to the detectives who occasionally stopped to chat with him. He seemed unmindful of the activity which erupted everywhere around him.

Quietly, efficiently, carefully, methodically, he sketched the scene of the crime. Then he packed up and went to his office, where, working from the preliminary sketch, he made a more detailed drawing. The drawing was printed up and, together with the detailed photos taken at the site, sent to the many departments interested in solving the mugger murder.

Sam Grossman's interest was definitely turned in that direction, and so a copy of the drawing reached his desk. Since colour or the lack of colour played no important part in this particular homicide, the drawing was in black and white.

Grossman studied it with the dispassionate scrutiny an art dealer gives a potentially fake van Gogh.

The girl had been found at the base of a fifteen-foot drop, one of the shelf-like levels which sloped down in a cliff to the river bed. A footpath led through evergreens and maples from an Emergency Repairs turnoff to the highest point of the cliff, some thirty feet above the River Harb.

The Repairs cutoff was plainly visible from the River Highway, which swung around in a wide arc under the Hamilton Bridge approach. The footpath, however, was screened from the highway by trees and shrubs, as were the actual sloping sides of the cliff itself.

A good set of tyre tracks had been found in a thin layer of earth caked on the River side of the Repairs cutoff. A pair of sunglasses had been found alongside the dead girl's body.

That was all.

Unfortunately, the sides of the cliff sloped upward in igneous formidability. The path wound its way over solid prehistoric rock. Neither the girl nor her murderer had left any footprints for the lab boys to play with.

Unfortunately, too, though the path was screened by bushes and trees, none of the plant life encroached upon the path's right to meander on the top of the cliff. In short, there was no fabric, leather, feathers, or tell-tale dust caught upon twigs or resting upon leaves.

It was a reasonable assumption that the girl had been driven to the spot of her death. There were no signs of any repairs having been made in the cutoff. If the auto had pulled in with a flat tyre, the jack would have left marks on the pavement, and the tools might have left grease stains or metal scrapings. There was the possibility, of course, that the car had suffered an engine failure, in which case the hood would have been lifted and the mechanism studied. But the caked earth spread in an arc that covered the corners and sides of the cutoff. Anyone standing at the front of the car to lift the hood would surely have left footprints. There were none, nor were there any signs of prints having been brushed away.

The police assumed, therefore, that the girl and her murderer had been driving west on the River Highway, had

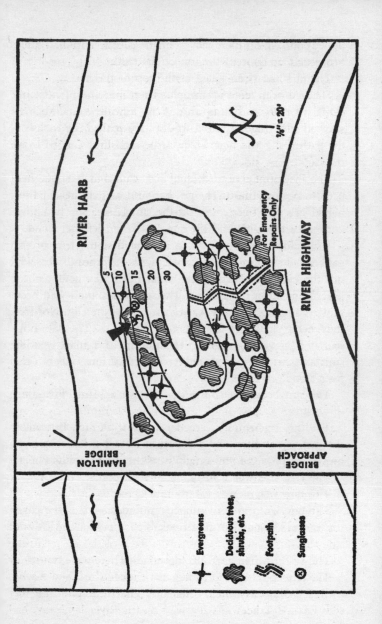

RIVER HARB

RIVER HIGHWAY

For Emergency
Repairs Only

5
10
15
20
30

⅛" = 20'

HAMILTON
BRIDGE

BRIDGE APPROACH

Evergreens

Deciduous trees,
shrubs, etc.

Footpath

Sunglasses

137

pulled into the Emergency Repairs cutoff, and had then proceeded on foot to the top of the cliff.

The girl had been killed at the top of the cliff.

She had been alive up to then. There were no bloodstains along the path leading upward. With a head wound such as she had suffered, her blood would have soaked the rocks on the path if she had been killed earlier and then carried from the car.

The instrument used to split her skull and her face had been heavy and blunt. The girl had undoubtedly reached for her killer's face, snatching off the sunglasses. She had then gone over the cliff, and the sunglasses had left her hand.

It would have been easy to assume that the lens of the glasses had shattered upon contact with the ground. This was not the case. The technicians could not find a scrap, not a sliver of glass on the ground. The sunglasses, then, had been shattered before they went over the side of the cliff. Nor had they been shattered anywhere in the area. The lab boys searched in vain for glass. The notion of a man wearing sunglasses with one ruptured lens was a curious one, but the facts stood.

The sunglasses, of course, had drawn a blank. Five-and-dime stuff.

The tyre tracks had seemed promising at first. But when the cast was studied and comparison data checked, the tyres on the car proved to be as helpful as the sunglasses had been.

The tyre size was 6.70-15.

The tyre weight was twenty-three pounds.

The tyre was made of rubber reinforced with nylon cord, the thread design featuring hook 'sipes' to block skids and side-slip.

The tyre retailed for $18.04, including Federal tax.

The tyre could be had by any man jack in the US of A who owned a Sears, Roebuck catalogue. The trade name of the tyre was 'Allstate'.

You could order one or a hundred and one by sending your dough and asking for catalogue number 95N03067K.

There were probably eighty thousand people in the city who had four of the tyres on each of their cars, not to mention a spare in the trunk.

The tyre tracks told Grossman one thing: The car that had pulled into the cutoff was a light car. The tyre size and weight eliminated any of the heavier cars on the road.

Grossman felt like a man who was all dressed up with no place to go.

Resignedly, he turned to the pocket patch Eileen Burke had ripped from the mugger's jacket.

When Roger Havilland stopped by for the test results that Friday afternoon, Grossman said the patch was composed of hundred per cent nylon and that it belonged to a suit which retailed for $32.00 in a men's clothing chain. The chain had sixty-four stores spread throughout the city. The suit came in only one colour: blue.

Havilland gravely considered the impossibility of getting any lead from a suit sold in sixty-four stores. He scratched his head in misery.

And then he said, 'Nylon? Who the hell wears nylon in the fall?'

Meyer Meyer was exuberant.

He burst into the Squad Room, and he waltzed over to where Temple was fishing in the file, and he slapped his partner on the back.

'They cracked it!' he shouted.

'What?' Temple said. 'Jesus, Meyer, you damn near cracked my back. What the hell are you talking about?'

'The cats,' Meyer said, shrewdly studying Temple.

'What cats?'

'The 33rd Precinct. This guy who was going around kidnapping cats. Jesus Christ, I tell you this is the eeriest case they've ever cracked. I was talking to Agnucci, do you know him? He's 3rd Grade down there, been working on this one all along, handled most of the squeals. Well, man, they've cracked it.' Meyer studied Temple patiently.

'So what'd it turn out to be?' Temple asked, his interest piqued.

'They got their first lead the other night,' Meyer said. 'They got a squeal from some woman who said an Angora had been swiped. Well, they came upon this guy in an alleyway, and guess what he was doing?'

'What?' Temple asked.

'Burning the cat!'

'Burning the cat? You mean, setting fire to the cat?'

'Yep,' Meyer said, nodding. 'He stopped when they showed, and he ran like hell. They saved the cat, and they also got a good description of the suspect. After that, it was duck soup.'

'When'd they get him?' Temple asked.

'This afternoon. They broke into his apartment, and it was the damnedest thing ever, I'm telling you. This guy was actually burning up the cats, burning them to this powdery ash.'

'I don't believe it,' Temple said.

'So help me. He'd kidnap the cats and burn them into ashes. He had shelves and shelves of these little jars, full of cat ashes.'

'But what in holy hell for?' Temple asked. 'Was the guy nuts?'

'Nossir,' Meyer said. 'But you can bet the boys at the 33rd were asking the same question.'

'Well, what was it?'

'They asked him, George. They asked him just that. Agnucci took him aside and said, "Listen, Mac, are you nuts or something? What's the idea burnin' up all them cats and then puttin' the ashes in jars like that?" Agnucci asked, all right.'

'Well, what'd the guy say?'

Meyer patiently said, 'Just what you'd expect him to say. He explained that he wasn't crazy, and that there was a good reason for those cat ashes in all those jars. He explained that he was making something.'

'What?' Temple asked anxiously. 'What in hell was he making?'

'Instant pussy,' Meyer said softly, and then he began chuckling.

CHAPTER FIFTEEN

The report on the package of Pall Mall cigarettes and the match folder came in later that afternoon. It simply stated that each article, as such articles are wont to be, had been fingered a good many times. The only thing the fingerprint boys got from either of them was an overlay of smeared, worthless latents.

The match folder, with its blatant advertisement for the Three Aces was turned over to the Detective Bureau, and the detectives of Homicide North and the 87th Precinct sighed heavily because the match folder meant more goddamned leg-work.

Kling dressed for his date carefully.

He didn't know exactly why, but he felt that extreme care should be exercised in the handling and feeding of Claire Townsend. He admitted to himself that he had never – well, hardly ever – been so taken with a girl, and that he would probably be devastated forever – well, for a long time – if he lost her. He had no ideas on exactly how to win her, except for this intuition which urged him to proceed with caution. She had, after all, warned him repeatedly. She had put out the KEEP OFF! sign, and then she had read the sign aloud to him, and then she had translated it into six language, but she had none the less accepted his offer.

Which proves beyond doubt, he thought, *that the girl is wildly in love with me.*

Which piece of deduction was about on a par with the high level of detective work he had done so far. His abortive attempts at getting anywhere with the Jeannie Paige murder left him feeling a little foolish. He wanted very much to be promoted to Detective 3rd Grade someday, but he entertained severe doubts now as to whether he really was detective material. It was almost two weeks since Peter Bell had come to him with his plea. It was almost two weeks since Bell had scribbled his address on a scrap of paper, a scrap still tucked in one of the pockets of Kling's wallet. A lot had happened in those nearly two weeks. And those happenings gave Kling reason for a little healthy soul-searching.

He was, at this point, just about ready to leave the case to the men who knew how to handle such things. His amateurish leg-work, his fumbling questions, had netted a big zero – or so he thought. The only important thing he'd turned up was Claire Townsend. Claire, he was certain, was important. She was important now, and he felt she would become more important as time went by.

So let's polish our goddamn shoes. You want to look like a slob?

He took his shoes from the closet, slipped them on over socks he would most certainly smear with polish and later change, and set to work with his shine kit.

He was spitting on his right shoe when the knock sounded on the door.

'Who is it?' he called.

'Police. Open up,' the voice said.

'Who?'

'Police.'

Kling rose, his trouser cuffs rolled up high, his hands smeared with black polish. 'Is this a gag?' he said to the closed door.

'Come on, Kling,' the voice said. 'You know better than that.'

Kling opened the door. Two men stood in the hallway. Both were huge, both wore tweed jackets over V-necked sweaters, both looked bored.

'Bert Kling?' one of them asked.

'Yes?' he said puzzled.

A shield flashed. 'Monoghan and Monroe,' one of them said. 'Homicide. I'm Monoghan.'

'I'm Monroe,' the other one said.

They were like Tweedledum and Tweedledee, Kling thought. He suppressed his smile. Neither of his visitors was smiling. Each looked as if he had just come from an out-of-town funeral.

'Come in, fellers,' Kling said. 'I was just dressing.'

'Thank you,' Monoghan said.

'Thank you,' Monroe echoed.

They stepped into the room. They both took off their fedoras. Monoghan cleared his throat. Kling looked at them expectantly.

'Like a drink?' he asked, wondering why they were here, feeling somehow awed and frightened by their presence.

'A short one,' Monoghan said.

'A tiny hooker,' Monroe said.

Kling went to the closet and pulled out a bottle. 'Bourbon okay?'

'When I was a patrolman,' Monoghan said, 'I couldn't afford bourbon.'

'This was a gift,' Kling said.

'I never took whisky. Anybody on the beat wanted to see me, it was cash on the line.'

'That's the only way,' Monroe said.

'This was a gift from my father. When I was in the hospital. The nurses wouldn't let me touch it there.'

'You can't blame them,' Monoghan said.

'Turn the place into an alcoholic ward,' Monroe said, unsmiling.

Kling brought them their drinks. Monoghan hesitated.

'Ain't you drinking with us?'

'I've got an important date,' he said. 'I want to keep my head.'

Monoghan looked at him with the flat look of a reptile. He

shrugged, then turned to Monroe and said, 'Here's looking at you.'

Monroe acknowledged the toast. 'Up yours,' he said unsmilingly and then tossed off the shot.

'Good bourbon,' Monoghan said.

'Excellent,' Monroe amplified.

'More?' Kling asked.

'Thanks,' Monoghan said.

'No,' Monroe said.

Kling looked at them. 'You said you were from Homicide?'

'Homicide North.'

'Monoghan and Monroe,' Monroe said. 'Ain't you heard of us? We cracked the Nelson–Nichols–Permen triangle murder.'

'Oh,' Kling said.

'Sure,' Monoghan said modestly. 'Big case.'

'One of our biggest,' Monroe said.

'Big one.'

'Yeah.'

'What are you working on now?' Kling asked, smiling.

'The Jeannie Paige murder,' Monoghan said flatly.

A dart of fear shot up into Kling's throat. 'Oh?' he said.

'Yeah,' Monoghan said.

'Yeah,' Monroe said.

Monoghan cleared his throat. 'How long you been with the force, Kling?' he asked.

'Just – just a short while.'

'That figures,' Monoghan said.

'Sure,' Monroe said.

'You like your job?'

'Yes,' Kling answered hesitantly.

'You want to keep it?'

'You want to go on being a cop?'

'Yes, of course.'

'Then keep your ass out of Homicide.'

'What?' Kling said.

145

'He means,' Monroe explained, 'keep your ass out of Homicide.'

'I – I don't know what you mean.'

'We mean keep away from stiffs. Stiffs are *our* business.'

'We like stiffs,' Monroe said.

'We're specialists, you understand? You call in a heart doctor when you got heart disease, don't you? You call in an eye, ear, nose, and throat man when you got laryngitis, don't you? Okay, when you got a stiff, you call in Homicide. That's us. Monoghan and Monroe.'

'You don't call in a wet-pants patrolman.'

'Homicide. Not a beat-walker.'

'Not a pavement-pounder.'

'Not a night-stick-twirler.'

'Not a traffic jockey.'

'Not *you!*' Monoghan said.

'Clear?' Monroe asked.

'Yes,' Kling said.

'It's gonna get a lot clearer,' Monoghan added. 'The lieutenant wants to see you.'

'What for?'

'The lieutenant is a funny guy. He thinks Homicide is the best damn department in the city. He runs Homicide, and he don't like people coming in where they ain't asked. I'll let you in on a secret. He don't even like the *detectives* from your precinct to go messing around in murder. Trouble is, he can't refuse their assistance or their cooperation, specially when your precinct manages to stack up so many goddamn homicides each year. So he suffers the dicks – but he don't have to suffer no goddamn patrolman.'

'But – but why does he want to see me? I understand now. I shouldn't have stuck my nose in, and I'm sorry I –'

'You shouldn't have stuck your nose in,' Monoghan agreed.

'You definitely shouldn't have.'

'But I didn't do any harm. I just –'

'Who knows what harm you done?' Monoghan said.

'You may have done untold harm,' Monroe said.

'Ah, hell,' Kling said, 'I've got a date.'

'Yeah,' Monoghan said. 'With the lieutenant.'

'Call your broad,' Monroe advised. 'Tell her the police are bugging you.'

Kling looked at his watch. 'I can't reach her,' he said. 'She's at school.'

'Impairing the morals of a minor,' Monoghan said, smiling.

'Better you shouldn't mention that to the lieutenant.'

'She's in *college*,' Kling said. 'Listen, will I be through by seven?'

'Maybe,' Monoghan said.

'Get your coat,' Monroe said.

'He don't need a coat. It's nice and mild.'

'It may get chilly later. This is pneumonia weather.'

Kling sighed heavily. 'All right if I wash my hands?'

'What?' Monoghan asked.

'He's polite,' Monroe said. 'He has to take a leak.'

'No, I have to wash my hands.'

'Okay, so wash them. Hurry up. The lieutenant don't like to be kept waiting.'

The building that housed Homicide North was the shabbiest, dowdiest, dirtiest, crummiest building Kling had ever seen. It was a choice spot for Homicide, Kling thought instantly. It even stinks of death. He had followed Monoghan and Monroe past the desk sergeant and then through a narrow, dimly lighted hallway lined with benches. He could hear typewriters clacking behind closed doors. An occasional open door revealed a man in shirt sleeves and shoulder holster. The entire place gave the impression of being the busy office of a numbers banker. Phones rang, people carried files from one office to another, men stopped at the water cooler – all in a dimly illuminated Dante interior.

'Sit down,' Monoghan had said.

'Cool your heels a little,' Monroe added.

'The lieutenant is dictating a memo. He'll be with you in a little while.'

Whatever the good lieutenant was dictating, Kling decided after waiting an hour, it was not a memo. It was probably volume two of his autobiography: *The Patrolman Years*. He had long ago given up the possibility of being on time for his date with Claire. It was now 6.45, and *tempus* was *fugiting* along at a merry clip. With luck, though, he might still catch her at the school, assuming she'd give him the benefit of the doubt and wait around a while. Which, considering her reluctance to make the date in the first place, was a hell of a lot to assume.

Impatiently, Kling bided his time.

At 8.20, he stopped a man in the corridor and asked if he could use a phone. The man studied him sourly and said, 'Better wait until after the lieutenant sees you. He's dictating a memo.'

'On what?' Kling cracked. 'How to dismantle a radio motor-patrol car?'

'What?' the man said. 'Oh, I get it. Pretty funny.' He left Kling and went to the water cooler. 'You want some water?'

'I haven't eaten since noon,' Kling said.

'Take a little water. Settle your stomach.'

'No bread to go with it?' Kling asked.

'What?' the man said. 'Oh, I get it. Pretty funny.'

'How much longer do you think he'll be?'

'Depends. He dictates slow.'

'How long has he been with Homicide North?'

'Five, ten years. I don't know.'

'Where'd he work before this? Dachau?'

'What?' the man said. 'Oh, I get it.'

'Pretty funny,' Kling said dryly. 'Where are Monoghan and Monroe?'

'They went home. They're hard workers, those two. Put in a big day.'

'Listen,' Kling said, 'I'm hungry. Can't you kind of goose him a little?'

'The lieutenant?' the man said. '*Me* goose the lieutenant? Jesus, that's the funniest thing you said yet.' He shook his head and walked off down the corridor, turning once to look back at Kling incredulously.

At 10.33, a detective with a ·38 tucked into his waistband came into the corridor.

'Bert Kling?' he asked.

'Yes,' Kling said wearily.

'Lieutenant Hawthorne will see you now,' he said.

'Glory hall –'

'Don't make wisecracks with the lieutenant,' the detective advised. 'He ain't eaten since suppertime.'

He led Kling to a frosted door appropriately marked LIEUTENANT HENRY HAWTHORNE, threw it open, said, 'Kling, Lieutenant,' and then ushered Kling into the room. The detective left, closing the door behind him.

Hawthorne sat behind a desk at the far end of the room. He was a small man with a bald head and bright blue eyes. The sleeves on his white shirt were rolled up past the elbows. The collar was unbuttoned, the tie knot yanked down. He wore a shoulder holster from which protruded the walnut stock of a ·45 automatic. His desk was clean and bare. Green file cabinets formed a fortress wall behind the desk and on the side of it. The blinds on the window to the left of the desk were pulled tightly closed. A wooden plaque on the desk read: LT HAWTHORNE.

'Kling?' he said. His voice was high and brassy, like a double C forced from the bell of a broken trumpet.

'Yes, sir,' Kling said.

'Sir down,' Hawthorne said, indicating the straight-backed chair alongside the desk.

'Thank you, sir,' Kling said. He walked to the chair and sat.

He was nervous, very nervous. He certainly didn't want to lose his job, and Hawthorne seemed like a tough customer. He wondered if a lieutenant in Homicide could ask the commissioner to fire a patrolman, and he decided a lieutenant in Homicide definitely could. He swallowed. He wasn't thinking of Claire any longer, nor was he thinking of food.

'So you're Mr Sherlock Holmes, eh?' Hawthorne said.

Kling didn't know what to answer. He didn't know whether to smile or cast his eyes downward. He didn't know whether to sit or go blind.

Hawthorne watched him. Emphatically, he repeated, 'So you're Mr Sherlock Holmes, eh?'

'Sir?' Kling said politely.

'Diddling around with a murder case, eh?'

'I didn't realize, sir, that –'

'Listen to me, Sherlock,' Hawthorne said, slamming his open palm on to the desk. 'We got a phone call here this afternoon.' He opened the top drawer. 'Clocked in at' – he consulted a pad – 'sixteen thirty-seven. Said you were farting around with this Jeannie Paige thing.' Hawthorne crashed the desk drawer shut. 'I've been very kind to you, Sherlock. I could have gone straight to Captain Frick at the 87th. The 87th happens to be your precinct, and Captain Frick happens to be an old and dear friend of mine, and Captain Frick doesn't take crap from runny-nosed patrolmen who happen to be walking beats. Lieutenant Byrnes of your precinct likes to stick his nose in murder cases, too, and I can't do a hell of a lot about that, except occasionally show him I don't too much appreciate his goddamn Aunt Suzianna help! But if the 87th thinks it's going to run in a patrolman on me, if the 87th thinks –'

'Sir, the precinct didn't know anything about my –'

'AND THEY STILL DON'T KNOW!' Hawthorne shouted. 'And they don't know because I was kind enough not to mention this to Captain Frick. I'm being good to you,

150

Sherlock, remember that. I'm being goddamn good and kind to you, so don't give me any crap!'

'Sir, I wasn't –'

'All right, listen to me, Sherlock. If I hear again that you're even *thinking* about Jeannie Paige, your ass is going to be in one big sling. I'm not talking about a transfer to a beat in Bethtown, either. I'm talking about OUT! You are going to be out in the street. You are going to be out and cold. And don't think I can't do it.'

'Sir, I didn't think –'

'I know the commissioner the way I know the back of my own hand. The commissioner would sell his wife if I asked him to, that's the way I know the commissioner. So don't for one second think the commissioner wouldn't toss a snot-nosed patrolman right out on his ear if I asked him to. Don't for a minute think that, Sherlock.'

'Sir –'

'And don't for a minute think I'm kidding, Sherlock, because I never kid around where it concerns murder. You're fooling with murder, do you realize that? You've been barging around asking questions, and Christ alone knows who you've scared into hiding, and Christ alone knows how much of our careful work you've fouled up! SO LAY OFF! Go walk your goddamn beat! If I get another squeal about you –'

'Sir?'

'WHAT IS IT?'

'Who called you, sir?'

'That's none of your goddamn business!' Hawthorne shouted.

'Yes, sir.'

'Get out of my office. Jesus, you make me sick. Get out of my office.'

'Yes, sir,' Kling said. He turned and went to the door.

'AND DON'T FOOL WITH MURDER!' Hawthorne shouted after him.

He called Claire at 11.10. The phone rang six times, and he was ready to hang up, afraid he'd caught her asleep, when the receiver was lifted.

'Hello?' she said. Her voice was sleepy.

'Claire?'

'Yes, who's this?'

'Did I wake you?'

'Yes.' There was a pause, and then her voice became a bit more lively. 'Bert? Is that you?'

'Yes. Claire, I'm sorry I –'

'The last time I got stood up was when I was sixteen and had a –'

'Claire, I didn't stand you up, honest. Some Homicide cops –'

'It *felt* like being stood up. I waited in the newspaper office until a quarter to eight, God knows why. Why didn't you call?'

'They wouldn't let me use the phone.' Kling paused. 'Besides, I didn't know how I could reach you.'

Claire was silent.

'Claire?'

'I'm here,' she said wearily.

'Can I see you tomorrow? We'll spend the day together. I'm off tomorrow.'

Again, there was silence.

'Claire?'

'I heard you.'

'Well?'

'Bert, why don't we call it quits, huh? Let's consider what happened tonight an ill omen, and just forget the whole thing, shall we?'

'No,' he said.

'Bert –'

'No! I'll pick you up at noon, all right?'

Silence.

'Claire?'

'All right. Yes,' she said. 'Noon.'

'I'll explain then. I . . . I got into a little trouble.'

'All right.'

'Noon?'

'Yes.'

'Claire?'

'Yes?'

'Goodnight, Claire.'

'Goodnight, Bert.'

'I'm sorry I woke you.'

'That's all right. I'd just dozed off, anyway.'

'Well . . . goodnight, Claire.'

'Goodnight, Bert.'

He wanted to say more, but he heard the click of the receiver being replaced in the cradle. He sighed, left the phone booth, and ordered a steak with mushrooms, French fried onions, two baked potatoes, a huge salad with Roquefort dressing, and a glass of milk. He finished off the meal with three more glasses of milk and a slab of chocolate cream pie.

On the way out of the restaurant, he bought a candy bar. Then he went home to sleep.

CHAPTER SIXTEEN

A common and much-believed fallacy in popular literature is the one which links romantic waiters with starry-eyed couples who are obviously in love. The waiter hovers over the table, suggesting special dishes ('Per'aps the pheasant under ground glass for ze lady, yas?'), kissing his fingers, or wringing his hands against his chest while his heart bursts with romance.

Bert Kling had been in a good many restaurants in the city, as boy and man, with a good many young ladies ranging from the plain to the beautiful. He had come to the conclusion a long while back that most waiters in most restaurants had nothing more romantic on their minds than an order of scrambled eggs with lox.

He did not for a moment believe that he and Claire looked starry-eyed with love, but they were without doubt a nice-enough-looking couple, and they were in a fashionable restaurant which overlooked the River Harb, high atop one of the city's better-known hotels. And, even discounting the absence of the starry-eyes (which he was fast coming to believe were nothing more than a Jon Whitcomb creation – ah, once a man begins to doubt . . .), he felt that any waiter with more than a stone for a heart should have recognized and aided the fumbling and primitive ritual of two young people who were trying to get to know each other.

The day, by any standards, had not been what Kling would have called a rousing success.

He had planned on a picnic in Bethtown, with its attendant ferry ride from Isola across the river. Rain had destroyed that silly notion.

He had drippingly called for Claire at twelve on the dot. The rain had given her a 'horrible headache'. Would he mind

154

f they stayed indoors for a little while, just until the Empirin took hold?

Kling did not mind.

Claire had put some good records into the record player, and then had lapsed into a heavy silence which he attributed to the throbbing headache. The rain had oozed against the window panes, streaking the city outside. The music had oozed from the record player – Bach's Brandenburg Concerto No 5 in D, Strauss's *Don Quixote*, Franck's *Psyche*.

Kling almost fell asleep.

They left the apartment at two. The rain had let up somewhat, but it had put a knife-edge on the air, and they sloshed along in a sullen, uncommunicative silence, hating the rain with common enmity, but somehow having allowed the rain to build a solid wedge between them. When Kling suggested a movie, Claire accepted the offer eagerly.

The movie was terrible.

The feature was called *Apache Undoing*, or some such damn thing, and it starred hordes of painted Hollywood extras who screeched and whooped down upon a small band of blue-clothed soldiers. The handful of soldiers fought off the wily Apaches until almost the end of the movie. By this time, the hordes flung against the small, tired band must have numbered in the tens of thousands. With five minutes to go in the film, another small handful of soldiers arrived, leaving Kling with the distinct impression that the war would go on for another two hours in a subsequent film to be titled *Son of Apache Undoing*.

The second film on the bill was about a little girl whose mother and father are getting divorced. The little girl goes with them to Reno – Dad conveniently has business there at the same time Mom must establish residence – and through an unvarying progression of mincing postures and bright-eyed, smirking little-girl facial expressions, convinces Mom and Dad to stay together eternally and live in connubial bliss with their mincing, bright-eyed, smirking little smart-assed daughter.

They left the theatre bleary-eyed. It was six o'clock.

Kling suggested a drink and dinner. Claire, probably in self-defence, agreed that a drink and dinner would be just dandy along about now.

And so they sat in the restaurant high atop one of the city's better-known hotels, and they looked through the huge windows which faced the river; and across the river there was a sign.

The sign first said: SPRY.

Then it said: SPRY *for* FRYING.

Then it said: SPRY *for* BAKING.

Then it said, again: SPRY.

'What'll you drink?' Kling asked.

'A whisky sour, I think,' Claire said.

'No cognac?'

'Later maybe.'

The waiter came over to the table. He looked as romantic as Adolf Hitler.

'Something to drink, sir?' he asked.

'A whisky sour, and a Martini.'

'Lemon peel, sir?'

'Olive,' Kling said.

'Thank you, sir. Would you care to see a menu now?'

'We'll wait until after we've had our drinks, thank you. All right, Claire?'

'Yes, fine,' she said.

They sat in silence. Kling looked through the windows.

SPRY *for* FRYING.

'Claire?'

'Yes?'

SPRY *for* BAKING.

'It's been a bust, hasn't it?'

'Please, Bert.'

'The rain . . . and that lousy movie. I didn't want it to be this way. I wanted –'

'I knew this would happen, Bert. I tried to tell you, didn't I? Didn't I try to warn you off? Didn't I tell you I was the dullest girl in the world? Why did you insist, Bert? Now you make me feel like a – like a –'

'I don't want you to feel *any* way,' he said. 'I was only going to suggest that we – we start afresh. From now. Forgetting everything that's – that's happened.'

'Oh, what's the use?' Claire said.

The waiter came with their drinks. 'Whisky sour for the lady?' he asked.

'Yes.'

He put the drinks on the table. Kling lifted the Martini glass.

'To a new beginning,' he said.

'If you want to waste a drink,' she answered, and she drank.

'About last night –' he started.

'I thought this was to be a new beginning.'

'I wanted to explain. I got picked up by two Homicide cops and taken to their lieutenant who warned me to keep away from the Jeannie Paige potato.'

'Are you going to?'

'Yes, of course.' He paused. 'I'm curious, I admit, but . . .'

'I understand.'

'Claire,' he said evenly, 'what the hell's the matter with you?'

'Nothing.'

'Where do you go when you retreat?'

'What?'

'Where do you . . . ?

'I didn't think it showed. I'm sorry.'

'It shows,' Kling said. 'Who was he?'

Claire looked up sharply. 'You're a better detective than I realized.'

157

'It doesn't take much detection,' he said. There was a sad undertone to his voice now, as if her confirmation of his suspicions had suddenly taken all the fight out of him. 'I don't mind your carrying a torch. Lots of girls –'

'It's not that,' she interrupted.

'Lots of girls do,' he continued. 'A guy drops them cold, or else it just peters out the way romances sometimes –'

'It's not that!' she said sharply, and when he looked across the table at her, her eyes were filmed with tears.

'Hey, listen, I –'

'Please, Bert, I don't want to –'

'But you said it *was* a guy. You said –'

'All right,' she answered. 'All right, Bert.' She bit down on her lip. 'All right, there was a guy. And I was crazy in love with him. I was seventeen – just like Jeannie Paige – and he was nineteen.'

Kling waited. Claire lifted her drink and drained the glass. She swallowed hard, and then sighed, and Kling watched her, waiting.

'I met him at Club Tempo. We hit it off right away – do you know how such things happen, Bert? It happened that way with us. We made a lot of plans, big plans. We were young, and we were strong, and we were in love.'

'I – I don't understand,' he said.

'He was killed in Korea.'

Across the river, the sign blared, SPRY *for* FRYING.

The table was very silent. Claire stared at the tablecloth. Kling folded his hands nervously.

'So don't ask me why I go down to Tempo and make a fool of myself with kids like Hud and Tommy. I'm looking for *him* all over again. Bert, can't you see that? I'm looking for his face, and his youth, and –'

Cruelly, Bert Kling said, 'You won't find him.'

'I –'

'You won't find him. You're a fool for trying. He's dead and buried. He's –'

'I don't want to listen to you,' Claire said. 'Take me home, please.'

'No,' he said. 'He's dead and buried, and *you're* burying yourself alive, you're making a martyr of yourself, you're wearing a widow's weeds at twenty! What the hell's the matter with you? Don't you know that people die every day? Don't you know?'

'Shut up!' she said.

'Don't you know you're killing yourself? Over a kid's puppy love – over a –'

'Shut up!' she said again, and this time her voice was on the edge of hysteria, and some of the diners around them turned at her outburst.

'Okay!' Kling said tightly. 'Okay, bury yourself! Bury your beauty, and try to hide your sparkle! Wear black every day of the week for all I give a damn! But I think you're a phony! I think you're a fourteen-carat phony!' He paused, and then said angrily, 'Let's get the hell out of this goldfish bowl!'

He started to rise, signalling for the waiter at the same time. Claire sat motionless opposite him. And then, quite suddenly, she began to cry. The tears, started slowly at first, forcing their way past clenched eyelids, trickling silently down her cheeks. And then her shoulders began to heave, and she sat as still as a stone, her hands clasped in her lap, her shoulders heaving, sobbing silently while the tears coursed down her face. He had never seen such honest misery before. He turned his face away. He did not want to watch her.

'You are ready to order, sir?' the waiter asked, sidling up to the table.

'Two more of the same,' Bert said. The waiter started off, and he caught at his arm. 'No. Change the whisky sour to a double shot of Canadian Club.'

'Yes, sir,' the waiter said, padding off.

'I don't want another drink,' Claire muttered.

'You'll have one.'

'I don't want one.' She erupted into tears again, and this time Kling watched her. She sobbed steadily for several moments, and then the tears stopped as suddenly as they had begun, leaving her face looking as clean as a city street does after a sudden summer storm.

'I'm sorry,' she said.

'Don't be.'

'I should have cried a long time ago.'

'Yes.'

The waiter brought the drinks. Kling lifted his glass. 'To a new beginning,' he said.

Claire studied him. It took her a long while to reach for the double hooker before her. Finally, her hand closed around the glass. She lifted it and touched the rim of Kling's glass. 'To a new beginning,' she said. She threw off the shot quickly.

'That's strong,' she said.

'It'll do you good.'

'Yes. I'm sorry, Bert. I shouldn't have burdened you with my troubles.'

'Offhand, can you think of anyone who'd accept them so readily?'

'No,' she said immediately. She smiled tiredly.

'That's better.'

She looked across at him as if she were seeing him for the first time. The tears had put a sparkle into her eyes. 'It – it may take time, Bert,' she said. Her voice came from a long way off.

'I've got all the time in the world,' he said. And then almost afraid she would laugh at him, he added, 'All I've been doing is killing time, Claire, waiting for you to come along.'

She seemed ready to cry again. He reached across the table and covered her hand with his.

'You're ... you're very good, Bert,' she said, her voice growing thin, the way a voice does before it collapses into tears. 'You're good, and kind, and gentle, and you're quite beautiful, do you know that? I ... I think you're very beautiful.'

'You should see me when my hair is combed,' he said, smiling, squeezing her hand.

'I'm not joking,' she said. 'You always think I'm joking, and you really shouldn't because I'm – I'm a serious girl.'

'I know.'

'So –'

He shifted his position abruptly, grimacing.

'Is something wrong?' she asked, suddenly concerned.

'No. This goddamn pistol.' He shifted again.

'Pistol?'

'Yes. In my back pocket. We have to carry them, you know. Even off duty.'

'Not really? A gun? You have a gun in your pocket?'

'Sure.'

She leaned closer to him. Her eyes were clear now, as if they had never known tears or sadness. They sparkled with interest. 'May I see it?'

'Sure.' He reached down, unbuttoned his jacket, and then pulled the gun with its leather holster from his hip pocket. He put it on the table. 'Don't touch it, or it'll go off in your face.'

'It looks menacing.'

'It *is* menacing. I'm the deadest shot in the 87th Precinct.'

'Are you really?'

'"Kling the King" they call me.'

She laughed suddenly.

'I can shoot any damn elephant in the world at a distance of three feet,' Kling expanded. Her laugh grew. He watched her laughing. She seemed unaware of the transformation.

'Do you know what I feel like doing?' he said.

'What?'

'I feel like taking this gun and shooting out that goddamned Spry sign across the river.'

'Bert,' she said, 'Bert,' and she put her other hand over his, so that three hands formed a pyramid on the table. Her face grew very serious. 'Thank you, Bert. Thank you so very, very much.'

He didn't know what to say. He felt embarrassed and stupid and happy and very big. He felt about eighty feet tall.

'What – what are you doing tomorrow?' he asked.

'Nothing. What are you doing tomorrow?'

'I'm calling Molly Bell to explain why I can't snoop around any more. And then I'm stopping by at your place, and we're going on a picnic. *If* the sun is shining.'

'The sun'll be shining, Bert.'

'I know it will,' he said.

She leaned forward suddenly and kissed him, a quick, sudden kiss that fleetingly touched his mouth and then was gone. She sat back again, seeming very unsure of herself, seeming like a frightened little girl at her first party. 'You – you must be patient,' she said.

'I will,' he promised.

The waiter suddenly appeared. The waiter was smiling. He coughed discreetly. Kling watched him in amazement.

'I thought,' the waiter said gently, 'perhaps a little candlelight at the table, sir? The lady will look even more lovely by candlelight.'

'The lady looks lovely just as she is,' Kling said.

The waiter seemed disappointed. 'But . . .'

'But the candlelight, certainly,' Kling said. 'By all means, the candlelight.'

The waiter beamed. 'Ah, yes, sir. Yes, sir. And then we will order, yes? I have some suggestions, sir, whenever you're ready.' He paused, his smile lighting his face. 'It's a beautiful night, sir, isn't it?'

'It's a wonderful night,' Claire answered.

CHAPTER SEVENTEEN

Sometimes, they crack open like litchi nuts.

You struggle with something that seems to be a Brazil nut, poking at the diamond-hard exterior, yearning to get at the meat – and suddenly it's a litchi nut with a fragile, paper-thin skin, and it bursts open under the slightest pressure of your fingers.

It happened that way with Willis and Havilland.

The Three Aces that Sunday afternoon, 24 September, had barely begun picking up business after its late opening. There were a few drinkers at the bar, but the tables were empty, and both the snooker table and the bowling pinball machine were empty of players. The bar was a run-down joint with three playing cards painted on the mirror: the ace of clubs, the ace of hearts, and the ace of spades. The fourth ace was nowhere visible. Judging from the looks of the bartender, it was probably up his sleeve, together with a fifth ace.

Willis and Havilland took stools at the end of the bar. The bartender lingered with the drinkers at the opposite end of the bar for a few minutes, then slouchingly pulled himself away from the conversation, walked to Willis and Havilland, and said, 'Yep?'

Havilland threw the match folder on to the bar. 'This yours?'

The bartender studied it at great length. The identical three aces on the mirror fronted the match folder. The name Three Aces was plastered on the cardboard in red letters a half inch high. The bartender none the less took his time.

At last, he said, 'Yep.'

'How long have you been stocking them?' Willis asked.

'Why?'

'We're police officers,' Havilland said wearily. He reached into his pocket for his shield.

'Save it,' the bartender said. 'I can smell law at sixty paces.'

'Is that how you got your nose broken?' Havilland asked, clenching his fists on the bar top.

The bartender touched his nose. 'I used to box,' he said. 'What's with the matches?'

'How long have you stocked them?'

'About three months. It was a big bargain. There's this kid in the neighbourhood, sells Christmas cards and like that. Came around saying the matches would give the joint a little class. So I tumbled. Ordered a coupla gross.' The bartender shrugged. 'Didn't do no harm, as I can see. What's the beef?'

'No beef,' Willis said. 'Routine check.'

'On what? Matchbooks?'

'Yeah,' Havilland said. 'On matchbooks. Do you sell cigarettes?'

'Only in the machine.' The bartender indicated the vending apparatus in the corner near the door.

'You stock these matches in the machine?'

'No. We keep 'em on the bar in a small box. Anybody runs out of matches, he comes up and grabs himself a book. Why? What's so important with the matches?'

'We'll ask the questions,' Havilland said.

'I'm only trying to help, officer,' the bartender said. His voice conveyed the distinct impression that he would have liked nothing better than to punch Havilland in the mouth.

'Then anyone who drinks here can walk up to the bar and help himself to the matches, that right?' Willis asked.

'Yep,' the bartender said. 'Makes it homey, don't you think?'

'Mister,' Havilland said evenly, 'you better wipe that wise-guy smirk off your voice, or something's gonna make *you* homey.'

'Cops have always scared me,' the bartender said dryly, 'ever since I was a wee babe.'

'If you're looking for a fight, pal,' Havilland said, 'you picked the right cop.'

'I'm lookin' to mind my own business,' the bartender said.

'I'd hate like hell to have a judge decide on whose word to take in a "resisting an officer" case,' Havilland persisted.

'I ain't fighting, and I ain't resisting nothing,' the bartender replied. 'So cool off. You want a beer?'

'I'll have a Scotch,' Havilland said.

'That figures,' the bartender drawled. 'How about you?' he asked Willis.

'Nothing,' Willis said.

'Come on,' the bartender egged. 'It's just like grabbing an apple from the pushcart.'

'When you're ready for that fight,' Willis said, 'you've got two of us now.'

'Whenever I fought, I got paid for it,' the bartender said. 'I don't believe in exhibition bouts.'

'Especially when you know your ass'll be spread over six counties,' Havilland said.

'Sure,' the bartender said. He poured a hooker of Scotch and then slid the glass to Havilland.

'You know most of your customers?' Willis asked.

'The steadies, sure.'

The door opened, and a woman in a faded green sweater walked into the bar, looked around, and then sat at a table near the door. The bartender glanced at her.

'She's a lush,' he said. 'She'll sit there until somebody offers to buy her a drink. I'd kick her out, but I feel Christian on Sunday.'

'It shows all over you,' Havilland said.

'What is it you guys want, anyway?' the bartender asked. 'The fight? Is that what this is all about?'

'What fight?' Willis asked.

'We had a rhubarb here week or so ago. Listen, don't snow me. What have you got up your sleeve? Disorderly conduct? You figure on yanking my licence?'

'You're doing all the talking so far,' Willis said.

The bartender sighed wearily. 'All right, what'll it cost?'

'Oh, this man lives dangerously,' Havilland said. 'Are you attempting to bribe us, you son of a bitch?'

'I was talking about the price of the new Lincoln Continental,' the bartender said. 'I asked what it'll cost.' He paused. 'A hundred, two hundred? How much?'

'Do I look like a two-hundred-dollar cop?' Havilland asked.

'I'm a two-hundred-dollar bartender,' the bartender said. 'That's the limit. The goddamn fight was over in about two seconds flat.'

'What kind of a fight?' Willis asked.

'You mean you don't know?'

'Put your money back in your sock,' Willis said. 'This isn't a shakedown. Tell us about the fight.'

The bartender seemed relieved. 'You sure you don't want a drink, Officer?' he asked.

'The fight,' Willis said.

'It was nothing,' the bartender said. 'Couple of guys got hot-headed, and wham! One took a swing at the other, the other swung back, and I came over and busted it up. That's all.'

'Who swung at who?' Willis asked.

'These two characters. What's the hell's the name of the little guy? I don't remember. The bigger guy is called Jack. He comes in here a lot.'

'Jack, huh?'

'Yeah. Nice guy, except he's a little weird. So him and this little guy were watching the rassling on TV, and I guess Jack said something the little guy didn't like – about one of the rasslers, you know? So the little guy hauls off and pops Jack. So Jack takes a swing at the little guy, and that's when I came over. Big fight, huh?'

'And you broke it up?'

'Sure. I tell you, the funny thing about this whole business was that the little guy come out of it better than Jack.' The bartender chuckled. 'He really gave him a shot, I swear. You wouldn't think a little guy could pack such a wallop.'

'I'll bet Jack was surprised,' Willis said, losing interest.

'Surprised? I'll say he was. Especially when he took a gander in the mirror. That little son of a bitch gave him a shiner like I never saw in my life.'

'Too bad for Jack,' Willis said. 'About your other customers. Have you ever heard any of them talking about –'

'Boy, that shiner was a beaut! Hell, Jack had to wear sunglasses for about a week afterward.'

The lush sitting at the table near the door coughed. Willis kept staring at the bartender.

'What did you say?' he asked.

'Jack,' the bartender said. 'Had to wear these sunglasses. To hide the shiner, you know. It was a beautiful shiner, I mean it. Like a rainbow.'

'This Jack,' Willis said. He could feel the tenseness of Havilland alongside him. 'Does he smoke?'

'Jack? Yeah, sure. He smokes.'

'What brand?'

'Brand? Jesus, you must think I'm a – Wait a minute, the red package, what's the red package?'

'Pall Mall?'

'Yep. That's his brand.'

'You're sure?'

'I think so. Listen. I didn't go around taking a picture of what he smokes. I think it's Pall Mall. Why?'

'You're sure his name is Jack?' Havilland asked. 'It isn't something else?'

'Jack,' the bartender said, nodding.

'Think. Are you sure his name is Jack?'

'I'm positive. Listen, don't I know him? For God's sake, he's been coming in here for years. Don't you think I know Jack Clifford?'

*

Jack Clifford came into the Three Aces at three-fifteen that afternoon. The woman in the green sweater still sat at the table near the door. The bartender nodded when he entered, and Willis and Havilland moved off their stools quickly and intercepted him as he walked toward the bar.

'Jack Clifford?' Willis asked.

'Yeah?'

'Police officers,' Havilland said. 'You're coming with us.'

'Hey, what for?' Clifford said. He pulled his arm away from Havilland.

'Assault and suspicion of murder,' Willis snapped. He was running his hands over Clifford's body, frisking him quickly and efficiently.

'He's clea—' he started, and Clifford broke for the door.

'Get him!' Willis shouted. Havilland was reaching for his gun. Clifford didn't look back. He kept his eyes glued to the entrance doorway, and he ran like a bat out of hell, and then he fell flat on his face.

He looked up from the floor instantly, startled. The lush still sat at the table, one leg spread out in front of her. Clifford looked at the leg which had tripped him, looked at it as if he wanted to cut it off at the hipbone. He was scrambling to his feet when Havilland reached him. He kicked out at Havilland, but Havilland was a cop with big hands, and Havilland enjoyed using those hands. He scooped Clifford off the floor and rammed his fist into Clifford's face. Clifford staggered back against the door, and then collapsed on the floor. He sat there shaking his head while Havilland put the cuffs on him.

'Did you enjoy your trip?' Havilland asked pleasantly.

'Go to hell,' Clifford said. 'If it wasn't for that old drunken bag you'd never have got me.'

'Ah, but we did,' Havilland said. 'Get up!'

Clifford got to his feet. Willis came over and took his arm. He turned to the bartender. 'Thanks,' he said.

Together, the three men started out of the bar. Havilland

stopped just inside the doorway, at the table with the lush. The woman raised her head and studied him with alcohol-soaked eyes.

Havilland smiled, bowed, and swept one gorilla-like arm across his waist.

'Havilland thanks you, madam,' he said.

He admitted he had committed a total of thirty-four muggings in the past year. Fourteen of his victims had complained to the police. His last victim had turned out to be, of all goddamn things, a policewoman.

He denied flatly that he had assaulted and murdered Jeannie Paige.

They booked, mugged, and printed him – and then they sat with him in the Interrogation Room at the 87th and tried to break down his story. There were four cops in the room with him. Willis, Havilland, Meyer, and Lieutenant Byrnes. Were it not for the presence of the lieutenant, Havilland would have been practising his favourite indoor sport. As it was, his barrage was confined to words alone.

'We're talking about the night of September fourteenth. That was a Thursday night. Now think about it a little, Clifford,' Meyer said.

'I'm thinking. I got an alibi a mile long for that night.'

'What were you doing?' Willis asked.

'I was sitting up with a sick friend.'

'Don't get smart!' Byrnes said.

'I swear to God, it's the truth. Listen, you got me on eight thousand counts of assault. What're you trying to stick me with, a murder rap?'

'Shut your goddamn mouth and answer the questions,' Havilland said, contradicting himself.

'I am answering the questions. I was with a sick friend. The guy had ptomaine poisoning or something. I was with him all night.'

'What night was this?'

'September fourteenth,' Clifford said.

'How come you remember the date?'

'I was supposed to go bowling.'

'With whom?'

'This friend of mine.'

'Which friend?'

'What's your friend's name?'

'Where were you going bowling?'

'His name is Davey,' Clifford said.

'Davey what?'

'Davey Crockett, Clifford? Come on, Clifford.'

'Davey Lowenstein. He's a Jew. You gonna hang me for that?'

'Where does he live?'

'Base Avenue.'

'Where on Base?'

'Near Seventh.'

'What's his name?'

'Davey Lowenstein. I told you already.'

'Where were you going bowling?'

'The Cosy Alleys.'

'Downtown?'

'Yes.'

'Where downtown?'

'Jesus, you're mixing me up.'

'What'd your friend eat?'

'Did he have a doctor?'

'Where'd you say he lived?'

'Who says he had ptomaine poisoning?'

'He lives on Base, I told you. Base and Seventh.'

'Check that, Meyer,' Lieutenant Byrnes said. Meyer quickly left the room.

'Did he have a doctor?'

'No.'

'Then how do you know it was ptomaine?'

'He said it felt like ptomaine.'

'How long were you with him?'

'I went by for him at eight. That was when I was supposed to pick him up. The alley we were going to is on Division.'

'He was sick in bed?'

'Yeah.'

'Who answered the door?'

'He did.'

'I thought he was sick in bed.'

'He was. He got out of bed to answer the door.'

'What time was this?'

'Eight.'

'You said eight-thirty.'

'No, it was eight. Eight, I said.'

'What happened?'

'He said he was sick, said he had ptomaine, said he couldn't go with me. To the bowling alley, I mean.'

'Then what?'

'He told me to go without him.'

'Did you?'

'No, I stayed with him all night.'

'Until when?'

'Until the next morning. All night, I stayed with him.'

'Until what time?'

'All night.'

'WHAT TIME?

'About nine in the morning. We had eggs together.'

'What happened to his ptomaine?'

'He was all right in the morning.'

'Did he sleep?'

'What?'

'Did he sleep at all that night?'

'No.'

'What'd you do?'

'We played checkers.'

'Who?

'Me and Davey.'

'What time did you stop playing checkers?'

'About four in the morning.'

'Did he go to sleep then?'

'No.'

'What did he do?'

'We began telling jokes. I was trying to take his mind off his stomach.'

'You told jokes until nine the next morning?'

'No, until eight. We started breakfast at eight.'

'What'd you eat?'

'Eggs.'

'What bowling alley did you say that was?'

'The Cosy –'

'Where's it located?'

'On Division.'

'What time did you get to Davey's house?'

'Eight o'clock.'

'Why'd you kill Jeannie Paige?'

'I didn't. Jesus, the newspapers are killing *me*! I didn't go anywhere near the Hamilton Bridge.'

'You mean that night?'

'That night, any night. I don't even know that cliff they wrote about. I thought cliffs were out west.'

'Which cliff?'

'Where the girl was found.'

'Which girl?'

'Jeannie Paige.'

'Did she scream? Is that why you killed her?'

'She didn't scream.'

'What did she do?'

'She didn't do nothing! I wasn't there! How do I know what she did?'

'But you beat up your other victims, didn't you?'

'Yes. You got me on that, okay.'

'You son of a bitch, we've got a thumbprint on the

sunglasses you dropped. We'll get you on that, so why don't you tell us about it?'

'There's nothing to tell. My friend was sick. I don't know Jeannie Paige. I don't know that cliff. Lock me up. Try me on assault. I didn't kill that girl!'

'Who did?'

'I don't know.'

'You did!'

'No.'

'Why'd you kill her?'

'I didn't kill her!'

The door opened. Meyer Meyer came into the room. 'I called this Lowenstein character,' he said.

'Yeah?'

'The story is true. Clifford was with him all that night.'

When the comparison tests were made with Clifford's thumbprints and the single print found on the sunglasses, there was no longer any doubt. The prints did not match.

Whatever else Jack Clifford had done, he had not murdered Jeannie Paige.

CHAPTER EIGHTEEN

There was only Molly Bell to call.

Once he'd done that, he could leave the Jeannie Paige thing with a clear conscience. He had tried, he had honestly tried. And his efforts had led him into the jealously guarded realm of Homicide North, where he'd damn near wound up minus a shield and a uniform.

So now he would call her, and he would explain how useless he was, and he would apologize, and that would be the end of it.

Sitting in an armchair in his furnished room, Kling pulled the telephone toward him. He reached into his back pocket for his wallet, opened it, and then began leafing through the cards and scraps of paper, looking for the address and telephone number Bell had given him so long ago. He spread the cards on the end table. Christ, the collection of junk a man can . . .

He looked at the date on a raffle ticket. The drawing had been held three months ago. There was a girl's name and telephone number on a match folder. He didn't remember the girl at all. There was an entrance card to a discount house. There was the white card Claire had given him to explain Jeannie's childish handwriting. He put the card on the table so that the reverse side showed, the side reading 'Club Tempo, 1812 Klausner Street'.

And then he found the scrap of paper Peter Bell had handed to him, and he put that face up on the table alongside the other cards, and he reached for the phone receiver, studying the number at the same time.

And suddenly he remembered what he'd seen in the street at the first subway stop. He dropped the receiver.

He put all the cards and scraps of paper back into his wallet.

Then he put on his coat.

He was waiting for a murderer.

He had taken a train uptown, and he had got off at the first stop he'd visited earlier that week, and he was in the street now, standing alongside a Police Department sign, and waiting for a murderer, the murderer of Jeannie Paige.

The night had turned cold, and there weren't many people in the street. The men's clothing store was closed, and the Chinese restaurant belched steam into the air from a vent on the side of the building. A few people straggled into the movie house.

He waited, and when the car pulled up, he put one hand on the police sign alongside him and waited for the door to open.

The man came out of the car and started walking toward the curb. He was not a bad-looking man. He had even white teeth and an enviable cleft in his chin. He was tall and muscularly built. There was only one bad feature on his face.

'Hello,' Kling said.

The man looked up, startled. His eyes fled to Kling's face and then to the sign alongside Kling.

The sign read:

HACK STAND
NO PARKING
THREE TAXICABS

Peter Bell said, 'Bert? Is that you, Bert?'

Kling stepped into the light. 'It's me, Peter,' he said.

Bell looked confused. 'Hi,' he said. 'What – what brings you down here?'

'You, Peter.'

'Well, good. Always glad to have a friend –' He stopped.

'Listen, you want a cup of coffee or something? Take the chill off?'

'No, Peter,' Kling said.

'Well ... uh ... what is it?'

'I'm taking you with me, Peter. Up to the house.'

'The house? You mean the precinct?' Bell's brows swooped down. 'What for? What's the matter with you, Bert?'

'For the murder of your sister-in-law, Jeannie Paige,' Kling said.

Bell stared at Kling and then smiled tremulously. 'You're kidding.'

'I'm not kidding, Peter.'

'Well, you ... you must be kidding! I never heard such a stupid –'

'You're a son of a bitch!' Kling said vehemently. 'I ought to beat you black and blue and then –'

'Listen, hold it. Just hold –'

'Hold, crap!' Kling shouted. 'You egotistical son of a bitch, did you think I was an absolute moron? Is that why you picked me to begin with? A rookie cop? A cop who wouldn't know his ass from his elbow? Is that why you picked me to placate Molly? Bring a cop around, show the little woman you're trying, and that would make everything all right, wouldn't it? What was it you said, Peter? "*That way, Molly'll be happy. If I bring a cop around, she'll be happy.*" Isn't that what you said, you bastard?'

'Yes, but –'

'You read six newspapers a day! You stumbled on the item about your old pal Bert Kling being discharged from the hospital and resting up, so you figured he was the perfect chump. Bring him around, get Molly off your neck, and then you'd be free to –'

'Listen, Bert, you've got this all wrong. You're –'

'I've got it all right, Peter! My coming around would have been the end of it, but something else came up, didn't it?

176

Jeannie told you she was pregnant. Jeannie told you she was carrying your child!'

'No, listen –'

'Don't "No" me, Peter! Isn't that what happened? She said she had an appointment the night I talked to her. Was the appointment with you? Did she drop her bombshell then? Did she tell you and then give you time to mull it over for the next day, give you time to work out the way you were going to kill her?'

Bell was silent for a long time. Then he said, 'I didn't see her that Wednesday night. Her appointment wasn't with me.'

'Who then?'

'A doctor.' Bell swallowed. 'I saw her on Thursday. She met me here, at the hack stand, the way she always did. Bert, this isn't what you think, believe me. I loved her, I loved her.'

'I'll just bet you did! I'll bet you adored her, Peter, I'll bet you –'

'Why does marriage go stale?' Bell said plaintively. 'Why does it have to go stale, Bert? Why couldn't Molly have stayed the way she was? Young and fresh and pretty . . . like –'

'Like Jeannie? "*She looks just the way Molly looked when she was that age.*" That's what you told me, Peter. Remember?'

'Yes! She was Molly all over again, and I watched her growing up, and I – I fell in love with her. Is that so hard to understand? Is it so goddamn difficult to understand that a man could fall in love?'

'That's not the hard part, Peter.'

'What then? What? What can you –'

'You don't kill somebody you love,' Kling said.

'She was hysterical!' Bell said. 'I met her here, and we drove, and she told me the doctor had said she was pregnant. She said she was going to tell Molly all about it! How could I let her do that?'

'So you killed her.'

'I – we parked on the River Highway. She walked ahead of me, to the top of the cliff. I – I had a monkey wrench with me. I – I carry one in the cab, in case of burglaries, in case of –'

'Peter, you didn't have to . . .'

Bell wasn't listening to Kling. Bell was reliving the night of 14 September. 'I . . . I hit her twice. She fell backwards, rolling, rolling. Then the bushes stopped her, and she lay there like a broken doll. I . . . I went back to the cab. I was ready to drive away when I remembered the newspaper stories about Clifford the mugger. I . . . I carried a cheap pair of sunglasses in the glove compartment. I . . . I took them out and broke one lens in the cab, so that it would look like the glasses were broken in a struggle and then fell over the side of the cliff. I went back up the cliff again, and she still lay there, broken and bleeding, and I threw the glasses down, and then I rode off, and I left her there.'

'Was it you who sicked Homicide North on me, Peter?'

'Yes.' Bell's voice was very low. 'I – I didn't know how much you knew. I couldn't take any chances.'

'No.' Kling paused. 'You took a chance the first night you met me, Peter.'

'What?'

'You wrote your address and phone number for me. And the handwriting is the same as the writing on a card Jeannie took to Club Tempo.'

'I knew the club from when I was a kid,' Bell said. 'I figured – as a blind, a cover-up – to throw Molly off if she got wise. Bert, I –' He stopped. 'You can't prove anything with that handwriting. So what if I –?'

'We've got all the proof we need, Peter.'

'You haven't got a damn –'

'We've got your thumbprint on the sunglasses.'

Bell was silent again. And then, as if the words were torn bleeding and raw from him, he shouted, 'I loved her!'

'And she loved you, and the poor damn kid had to keep

her first love hidden like a thief. And like a thief, Peter, you stole her life. What I said still goes. You're a son of a bitch.'

'Bert, look, she's dead now. What difference does it make? Can't we –?'

'No.'

'Bert, how can I tell this to Molly? Do you know what this'll do to her? Bert, how can I tell her? Bert, give me a break, please. How can I tell her?'

Bert Kling looked at Bell quite coldly. 'You made your bed,' he said at last. 'Come on.'

CHAPTER NINETEEN

On Monday morning, 25 September, Steve Carella burst into the Squad Room, raring to go.

'Where the hell is everybody?' he shouted. 'Where's my welcoming committee?'

'Well, well,' Havilland said, 'look who's back.'

'The hero returning from the Trojan war,' Meyer cracked.

'How was it, boy?' Temple asked.

'Wonderful,' Carella said. 'Jesus, it's wonderful in the Poconos this time of year.'

'It's wonderful *any*where,' Meyer said. 'Haven't you heard?'

'You're a bunch of lewd bastards,' Carella said. 'I knew it all along, but this confirms it.'

'You're one of us,' Meyer said. 'We are your brothers.'

'Brother!' Carella said. 'So what've you been doing for the past month? Sitting on your duffs and collecting salaries?'

'Oh,' Meyer said, 'few things been going on.'

'Tell him about the cats,' Temple prompted.

'What cats?' Carella said.

'I'll tell you later,' Meyer said patiently.

'We had a homicide,' Havilland said.

'Yeah?'

'Yeah,' Temple said. 'We also got a new Detective 3rd Grade.'

'Yeah?' Carella said. 'A transfer?'

'Nope. A promotion. Up from the ranks.'

'Who?'

'Bert Kling. You know him?'

'Sure, I do. Good for Bert. What'd he do? Rescue the commissioner's wife?'

'Oh, nothing much,' Meyer said. 'Just sat on his duff and collected his salary.'

'So how's married life?' Havilland asked.

'Wonderful.'

'These cats George was talking about,' Meyer said.

'Yeah?'

'One hell of a thing, believe me. One of the roughest cases the 33rd has ever had.'

'No kidding?' Carella said. He walked over to Havilland's desk and helped himself to the coffee container there. The room seemed very warm and very friendly, and he suddenly did not regret being back on the job.

'Damnedest thing,' Meyer said patiently. 'They had this guy, you see, who was going around kidnapping cats.'

Carella sipped at his coffee. The sunlight streamed through the meshed windows. Outside, the city was coming to life.

Another work-day was beginning.

☐ **The Empty Hours** £6.99
978-0-7528-6411-2

☐ **Like Love** £6.99
978-0-7528-6546-1

☐ **Money, Money, Money** £6.99
978-0-7528-4839-6

☐ **Fat Ollie's Book** £6.99
978-0-7528-4276-9

☐ **The Frumious Bandersnatch** £6.99
978-0-7528-5916-3

☐ **Hark** £6.99
978-0-7528-6564-5

☐ **Fiddlers** £6.99
978-0-7528-7802-7

☐ **Transgressions Volume 1** £7.99
978-0-7528-7947-5

☐ **Transgressions Volume 2** £7.99
978-0-7528-7948-2

☐ **Transgressions Volume 3** £7.99
978-0-7528-7949-9

The Pusher

Two a.m. in the bitter cold of winter: the young Hispanic man's body is found in a tenement basement. The rope around his neck suggests a clear case of suicide – until the autopsy reveals he'd overdosed on heroin.

Who set up the phony hanging? Whose fingerprints were on the syringe found at the scene? Who was making threatening phone calls, attempting to implicate Lieutenant Byrnes' teenage son? Somebody is pushing the 87th Precinct hard, and Detective Steve Carella and Lieutenant Pete Byrnes have to push back harder – before a frightening and deadly chain tightens its grip.

Like Love

A young girl jumps to her death. A salesman gets blown apart. Two semi-naked bodies are found dead on a bed with all the hallmarks of a love pact . . .

Steve Carella and Cotton Hawes thought the double suicide stank of homicide, but they just couldn't get a break. Fortunately Hawes has something else going on in his life at the moment – something like love.

The Empty House

She was young, wealthy – and dead. Strangled to death in a slum apartment. All they had to go on was her name and some cancelled cheques. As Steve Carella said, 'Those cheques are the diary of her life. We'll find the answer there.' But how was he to know that they would reveal something much stranger than murder?

On Passover the rabbi bled to death. Someone had brutally stabbed him and painted a J on the synagogue wall. Everyone knew who the killer was – it had to be Finch, the Jew-hater. Or did it...?

The snow was pure white except where Cotton Hawes stared down at the bright red pool of blood spreading away from the dead girl's body. Hawes was supposed to be on a skiing holiday, but he couldn't just stand by and watch the local cops make a mess of the case. He had to catch the ski-slope slayer before he killed again.

Lady, Lady I Did It

October on the 87th Precinct. Indian summer. Telephones ring lazily in the police squad room. Tired cops slump at their desks, measuring their hours with cups of coffee.

Then it happened. A multiple murder in a downtown bookshop. Four people are dead, and one of them is Detective Bert Kling's fiancée. The summer was over.

There's no time for tears – and Kling was the first to admit it. There are clues to find, leads to follow, people to see. And Kling was going to get the sonofabitch who murdered the only person in the world he cared for. For him, it would be a long, cold winter . . .

See Them Die

Kill me if you can – that was Pepe Miranda's challenge. Murderer, two-bit hero of the street gangs, he was holed up somewhere in the 87th Precinct, making the cops look like fools and cheered on by every neighbourhood punk.

It was not a challenge Lieutenant Pete Byrnes and the detectives in the squad room could leave alone. Not in the sticky, July heat of the city with the gangs just waiting to explode into violence . . .

The Heckler

All over town, phones were ringing. Shopkeepers and merchants were being threatened by anonymous cranks. And the threats were getting more and more serious.

When the angry victims started yelling to the local cops for help, Steve Carella and the boys of the 87th Precinct didn't know what to make of the whole thing. Were they facing a plague of harmless pranksters – or the danger of a city-wide wave of violence?

All they had to go on were the constant attention of 'the deaf man' and the knowledge that if they didn't catch their cold-blooded callers before the end of the month, the prophecies of murder and mayhem might prove all too true.

Give the Boys a Great Big Hand

The mystery man wore black, and he was a real cut-up king. Why else was he leaving blood-red severed hands all over the city? Was he an everyday maniac with a meat cleaver, or did he have a special grudge against the 87th Precinct?

Steve Carella and Cotton Hawes went along with the grudge theory, because the black-cloaked killer didn't leave any clues to go on – the grisly hands even had the fingertips sliced off. And how do you nail a murderer when you can't identity or unearth most of his victims?

That's what the boys of the 87th Precinct have to do: find a killer before he carves up any more corpseless hands.

King's Ransom

Wealthy Douglas King has received a ransom demand. But it isn't his own son who has been kidnapped, it's his chauffeur's. If he pays up, it could ruin the biggest deal he ever made in his life, and throw away his future. But is the alternative to sacrifice a child's life?

Detective Steve Carella and the rest of the 87th Precinct can only keep trying to nab the kidnappers and hope that Doug King decides to give them the payoff. But if King doesn't play ball, they'll have a cold-blooded murder on their hands . . .

'Til Death

The groom in question is Tommy Giordano – and he's about to marry Steve Carella's sister, Angela. So the wedding party suddenly becomes a deadly game of hide-and-seek for Steve and the boys of the 87th Precinct.

Tommy is 'it' and Steve has only a few hours to find a killer and prevent Tommy from being tagged out for good.

But how do you find a murderer with hundreds of wedding guests to choose from? Carella has to work fast, or someone is going to make Angela a widow on her wedding day . . .

The Con Man

A trickster taking money from an old woman for his own private charity. A cheater fleecing the businessmen of their thousands with the oldest gimmick in town. A lady-killer after the ladies' dollars with just a little bit of love . . .

The guys of the 87th Precinct thought they knew every trick in the book so why are there bodies still washing up on the shore?

The Con Man: handsome, charming – and deadly.

Alice in Jeopardy

Alice thought she had lost everything when her husband's yacht was found empty and adrift. He had slipped out to sail under the stars and is never going to come back. A year on, Alice and her two children are still struggling to come to terms with their new life – but troubles are only just beginning . . .

One sunny day, Alice's children don't come home. The police are caught up in interdepartmental battles and Alice, now very much alone in the world, believes that the only way to save her children is to find them herself. But as the questions multiply, the answers seem more elusive than ever.

All Orion/Phoenix titles are available at your local bookshop or from the following address:

> Mail Order Department
> Littlehampton Book Services
> FREEPOST BR535
> Worthing, West Sussex, BN13 3BR
> *telephone* 01903 828503, *facsimile* 01903 828802
> *e-mail* MailOrders@lbsltd.co.uk
> (Please ensure that you include full postal address details)

Payment can be made either by credit/debit card (Visa, Mastercard, Access and Switch accepted) or by sending a £ Sterling cheque or postal order made payable to *Littlehampton Book Services*.
DO NOT SEND CASH OR CURRENCY.

Please add the following to cover postage and packing

UK and BFPO:
£1.50 for the first book, and 50p for each additional book to a maximum of £3.50

Overseas and Eire:
£2.50 for the first book plus £1.00 for the second book and 50p for each additional book ordered

---

BLOCK CAPITALS PLEASE

name of cardholder ....

address of cardholder ....

....

....

postcode ....

delivery address
(if different from cardholder)

....

....

....

postcode ....

☐ I enclose my remittance for £............................

☐ please debit my Mastercard/Visa/Access/Switch (delete as appropriate)

card number ☐☐☐☐☐☐☐☐☐☐☐☐☐☐☐☐

expiry date ☐☐☐☐   Switch issue no. ☐☐

signature ....

prices and availability are subject to change without notice